THE BEQUEST

John de Falbe

THE BEQUEST

THE HARVILL PRESS

LONDON

Published by The Harvill Press 2003

2 4 6 8 10 9 7 5 3

First published in Great Britain in 2003 by
The Harvill Press
Random House, 20 Vauxhall Bridge Road,
London SW1V 2SA

Random House Australia (Pty) Limited
20 Alfred Street, Milsons Point, Sydney,
New South Wales 2061, Australia

Random House New Zealand Limited
18 Poland Road, Glenfield,
Auckland 10, New Zealand

Random House South Africa (Pty) Limited
Endulini, 5A Jubilee Road, Parktown 2193, South Africa

The Random House Group Limited Reg. No. 954009
www.randomhouse.co.uk/harvill

A CIP catalogue record for this book
is available from the British Library

ISBN 1 84343 039 8

Papers used by Random House are natural,
recyclable products made from wood grown in sustainable forests;
the manufacturing processes conform to the environmental
regulations of the country of origin

Typeset in Bodoni by Palimpsest Book Production Limited,
Polmont, Stirlingshire

Printed and bound in Great Britain
by Clays Ltd, St Ives plc

For my mother

&

in memory of my father,

C.V.W. de F.

1923–2002

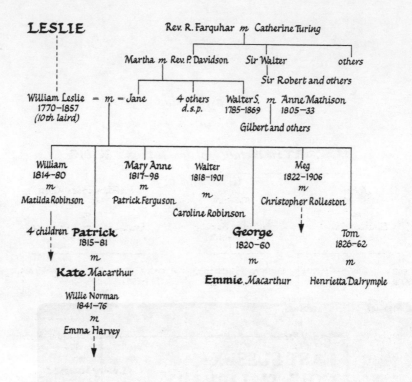

LESLIE

Rev. R. Farquhar *m* Catherine Turing

Martha *m* Rev. P. Davidson   Sir Walter   others

Sir Robert and others

William Leslie — *m* — Jane   4 others   Walter S. *m* Anne Mathison
1770–1857   d.s.p.   1785–1869   1805–33
(10th laird)

Gilbert and others

William   Mary Anne   Walter   Meg
1814–80   1817–98   1818–1901   1822–1906
m   *m*
Matilda Robinson   Patrick Ferguson   Christopher Rolleston
                            m
                   Caroline Robinson

4 children **Patrick**   **George**   Tom
            1815–81   1820–60   1826–62
            m   *m*   *m*
     Kate Macarthur   **Emmie** Macarthur   Henrietta Dalrymple

       Willie Norman
       1841–76
          m
       Emma Harvey

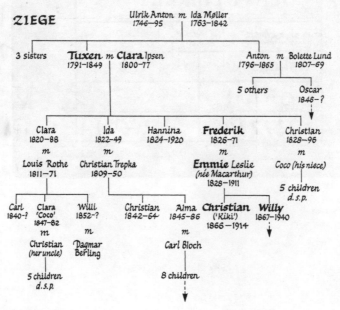

ZIEGE

Ulrik Anton *m* Ida Møller
1746–95   1763–1842

3 sisters   **Tuxen** *m* **Clara** Ipsen   Anton *m* Bolette Lund
            1791–1849   1800–77   1796–1865   1807–69

                                                  5 others   Oscar
                                                              1848–?

Clara   Ida   Hannina   **Frederik**   Christian
1820–88   1822–49   1824–1920   1826–71   1828–96
m   *m*   *m*   *m*
Louis Rothe Christian Trepka   **Emmie** Leslie   Coco (his niece)
1811–71   1809–50   (née Macarthur)
                                     1828–1911   5 children
                                                         d.s.p.

Carl   Clara   Willi   Christian   Alma   **Christian** **Willy**
1840–? 'Coco'   1852–?   1842–64   1845–86 ('Kiki')   1867–1940
       1847–82   1866–1914
       m   *m*   *m*
    Christian Dagmar   Carl Bloch
    (her uncle) Berling

    5 children   8 children
    d.s.p.

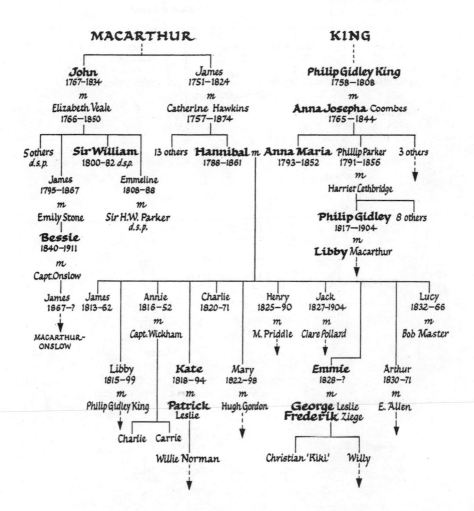

MACARTHUR   **KING**

John 1767–1834   James 1751–1824   **Philip Gidley King** 1758–1808
m   m   m
Elizabeth Veale 1766–1850   Catherine Hawkins 1757–1874   **Anna Josepha** Coombes 1765–1844

5 others   **Sir William** 1800–82 d.s.p.   13 others   **Hannibal** 1788–1861 m **Anna Maria** 1793–1852   Phillip Parker 1791–1856   3 others
d.s.p.

James 1795–1867   Emmeline 1808–88   m
m   m   Harriet Lethbridge
Emily Stone   Sir H.W. Parker
                           d.s.p.   **Philip Gidley** 1817–1904   8 others
Bessie 1840–1911   m
m   **Libby** Macarthur
Capt. Onslow

James 1867–?   James 1813–62   Annie 1816–52   Charlie 1820–71   Henry 1825–90   Jack 1827–1904   Lucy 1832–66
                               m   m   m   m
MACARTHUR-   Capt. Wickham   M. Priddle   Clare Pollard   Bob Master
ONSLOW

          Libby 1815–99   **Kate** 1818–94   Mary 1822–98   **Emmie** 1828–?   Arthur 1830–71
          m   m   m   m   m
          Philip Gidley King **Patrick** Leslie Hugh Gordon   **George** Leslie   E. Allen
                                                                   Frederik Ziege

                  Charlie   Carrie   Christian 'Kiki'   Willy

                       Willie Norman

PART ONE
Meetings

Hôtel des Quatre Nations, Genoa, March 1865

EMMELINE Leslie was perched on the edge of a mulberry-coloured sofa in the hotel foyer. Her hair was pinned into a thick black knot at the nape of her neck, suggesting that it would fall beyond her shoulders when loose. A slender nose made her seem more fragile than she was. She had alert, pale blue eyes set deep above high cheekbones. Beside her sat Sydney Raymond, her companion, whose sister, christened Australia, was married to Emmie's cousin Robert King. She might have passed for Emmie's maid, but the maid was at that moment darning some buttonholes for Sydney. In the simplicity of her grey dress, Sydney deferred to Emmie, whose bluebottle crinoline was respectable rather than grand. Desirable as London fashions were in New South Wales, they had not been suited to Emmie's life in the bush. But her taste in such matters was dependable, and she knew that only fools scorn appearances.

A trim lady entered the foyer, accompanied by a gentleman in a neat suit the colour of old vellum. She had dark hair pulled flat against her ears and she was furling a parasol which Emmie recognised at once to be the one she had noticed in the Hôtel de Russie a month ago. Even on this stretch of coast, where there were many fine parasols, this one was unusual.

The canopy was of embroidered white cotton with a lace fringe like snowflakes. The handle consisted of two slim lengths of ivory joined by a brass clasp, which the lady released so that the handle folded up on itself. The upper half was plain, while the lower half was criss-crossed with transverse spiral ribs that continued in gold onto the

distinctive green enamel grip. The parasol was crowned by a double sphere: the bottom one matched the handle; the top one was pierced to allow a silk string to pass through, with a tassel at each end suggestive of ease and frivolity.

Emmie considered the use of a parasol in mid-March to be unnecessary, but its owner was not otherwise ostentatious. Although she looked well-to-do, Emmie did not think she was a member of one of the royal families who now visited this part of the world, nor did she possess the demeanour or trappings of a lady of fashion. Despite the parasol, she seemed serious. She was in early middle age; she appeared efficient, even severe. Emmie doubted that she was married to her companion.

Her parasol folded, the lady looked about her. The gentleman, standing like a soldier at ease, did likewise. He had whiskers, and his thick brown hair bore the circular imprint of the hat he now held in his hand. He glanced at Emmie as if he thought he recognised her, and she was surprised by the gentleness of his eyes. She didn't think she had ever seen him before but she was confused because she recognised the parasol. He nodded to her politely. Then he turned and spoke to the lady, who raised her eyebrows a fraction, whereupon they sat down together on another sofa.

It dawned on Emmie that they were also waiting for Mr Ker.

It was the aged Mr Ker who had recommended the Hôtel des Quatre Nations to Emmie. She had met him in Cannes, where he had retired after a distinguished career in law following the example of the ineffably filthy Lord Brougham, who still lived in some style at the Villa Eleanor Louise. It was Mr Ker who first took Emmie to see Sir Thomas Woolfield's garden, where the mimosa brought three years before as seeds from the Royal Botanic Gardens in Sydney had made her want to cry as she remembered the garden she had planted all of seventeen years ago.

"I myself," Mr Ker confided, "am a cultivator of orchids."

"Are you, indeed?" Emmie said. "Then you may know of Allan Cunningham, the Australian explorer and botanist. He often visited us when I was a girl."

Hearing Cunningham's name from Emmie was an odd sensation for Mr Ker. She seemed so young to him, yet Cunningham had been a friend of his father's. As the editor of the *Botanical Register* and friend of Sir Joseph Banks, the elder Mr Ker had followed Cunningham's field work with avidity, both when he was sent out to gather specimens near Rio de Janeiro and then later in Australia. Some years after his arrival there he was instructed by Banks to join a surveying expedition led by Phillip Parker King. On their second trip out from Sydney, while charting inside the Great Barrier Reef in Captain Cook's path, Cunningham had honoured his friend by persuading Captain King to name a mountain after him. Mr Ker's pride in this distant peak was intense, and Emmie's reference to his father's protégé, dead these twenty-five years, moved him. It was a validation not only of Cunningham but also of his own passion for botany.

Until then, Emmie had felt that Mr Ker's friendship might be explained by his childlessness, which afforded him a natural but tacit sympathy with her own sadness. But when he told Emmie about the compliment paid to his father all those years ago, she felt a net of nostalgia wrap itself around her and she was transported to a childhood as remote to her now as Mount Ker was to the world at large.

"You mean one of the *Mermaid* voyages?"

Astonishment made Mr Ker recoil, so that he trod in Sir Thomas's parterre. He would have fallen had Emmie not steadied him.

"The *Mermaid* was commanded by my uncle! Captain King was my uncle!" she cried. "Further up the same coast he named some islands for *my* father – The Hannibal Isles!"

The next day she wrote to her cousin in Australia, Sir William Macarthur, to request some species of orchid that would be new to her ardent friend.

Mr Ker's friendship, and others similar, had been a solace for Emmie. It was now three years since she had put aside her widow's mourning, and this winter in Cannes her soul had been calmer than for many years. She could think with affection rather than anguish of Vineyard, the home near Sydney where she had grown up with her large family. Built by her father before she was born, it was lost shortly after she married George Leslie because her father was declared bankrupt. And Canning Downs, the station where she had lived with George on the Darling Downs, was now too distant from her life for the memory of it to cause excessive pain. At last she felt she could look upon the future without active dread, if not with serenity. She had no idea yet what she was going to do with herself, but the desolation ahead that had seemed set like pack ice was beginning to break apart. She could not say precisely how or when this shift had taken place, but she was conscious from her letters to Mary Anne, her sister-in-law in Scotland, and to her own sisters, that her mood was altered; and the only agents to which she could ascribe this change were quiet living and the gentle attentions of friends such as Miss Raymond and Mr Ker. But as the season drew to a close in Cannes and the railway took away the seasonal visitors, Emmie was sad. She felt once again the baleful pressure of a future without shape, like a nightmare prospect of death without burial. She knew she had to resist its influence and establish a coherent life for herself. It was time for her to live on her own initiative, and she owed it to her friends to demonstrate that she had profited from their benevolence.

When she informed Mr Ker that she was moving on to Rome, he advised her to proceed via Genoa instead of going back to Marseille to catch the steamer. He was going there himself for a few days, he said. He would like to introduce her to some Danish friends he expected to find there.

*

Viewed from a distance, the ships in the harbour at Genoa were restful and picturesque, but as Emmie approached the port itself, the stillness that she had enjoyed since San Remo began to fragment and a raucous bustle swelled around her. Close up, the ships' great flanks heaved against the wharves like cattle at market, while small boats were rowed back and forth to vessels anchored further out. Sailors could be seen clambering about decks and rigging; stevedores shouted as goods were hoisted, creaking and thumping, to land. After the pretty villages and little towns of the Riviera, the scene made Emmie's blood quicken.

Since their arrival two days ago, she and Miss Raymond had been on one brief excursion together to the Acqua Sole Garden, and another to the gloomy Duomo; then to the English pharmacist in the Piazzetta delle Vigne, for Emmie felt a cold coming on and she wished to buy some lavender water for Sydney to sprinkle on her handkerchiefs as a meagre antidote to the city's smells. She was otherwise content to sit on the broad terrace of the hotel observing the port, anticipating her rendezvous with Mr Ker and his friends.

Mr Ker now hurried from the drawing room and greeted them all in the same breath: "Mrs Leslie, what a joy! Pray forgive me for keeping you waiting! How do you do, Miss Raymond? Miss Ziege, Captain Ziege, how kind! Madame your mother wished to sit in the drawing room with your charming nieces."

With a little bow, he ushered them past a waiter into the drawing room to a group of seats near the far side of the room. Although the nearest curtain was drawn, the room was bright with the afternoon sun from other windows. An elderly lady, in voluminous black satin and a lace cap, occupied one sofa with a pretty girl in white. Another young lady, also in white, sat stiffly in a wing-backed chair. Mrs Ker was bolt upright on a hard chair, smiling. A lifetime's trussing in corsets had taught her that it was the only posture in which a scrap of comfort might be salvaged. Emmie felt the old mother's inspection, but she did not feel offended. It was what she was used to. Indeed, she felt that she could like this woman: her gaze had an edge that must be sharpened by experience, but it seemed to express curiosity rather than cynicism.

Emmie sat in an armchair beside the old lady whom Mr Ker introduced as Madame Ziege. The older girl was Alma, the younger was presented as Clara, but they all called her Coco.

"How fortunate that you met Hannina and Frederik outside," Madame Ziege said to Emmie, dragging out her vowels in a way that brought at once to Emmie's mind the wife of the Danish draper she had known in Sydney. "I would not like to think I was responsible for your waiting alone."

"Mrs Leslie was not alone, Mama," said Frederik. "Miss Raymond was with her."

"I'm afraid it was rude of us not to introduce ourselves," Hannina said.

"Did you not?" cried Madame Ziege. "Frederik!"

"I don't suppose it is your practice to greet strangers in the foyers of hotels, Captain Ziege," Emmie said. "I promise you, I took no offence."

Frederik expressed his relief with a sparkling smile that reminded Emmie of her youth, as if only now did she notice that receiving such a smile had become a thing of the past.

Walking through the reading room of the Hôtel de Russie in Cannes with Prince Galitsin one day, Frederik had passed behind a chair in which he had observed a lady reading a letter. From the tilt of her head or the set of her shoulders – he was not quite sure which – he realised that it had been Emmie. The Prince had been telling him with relish about a novel called *Salammbô*, which interested Frederik not because it was improper but because it was set in ancient Carthage. He had even read some of it, despite its tediousness.

Now, however, it was the improbable association between the novel and Mrs Leslie that amused Frederik.

"I couldn't help noticing your parasol," Emmie said to Hannina. "Were you in Cannes? I believe I saw it there."

"Then perhaps your paths have already crossed!" said Mr Ker.

"Perhaps," Hannina replied.

"Unless it was one of the Princesses' parasols?" Alma said, dismaying her family: Coco would not have been so gauche.

"The Princesses' parasols?" Emmie asked, because the matter could not now be circumvented; and she understood that they must be referring to Princess Alexandra, about whom it was said that she had not been allowed to bring any Danish attendants with her to England when she married the Prince of Wales – something mysterious to do with the political situation in Schleswig-Holstein – and it occurred to Emmie that perhaps Hannina was a Lady-in-Waiting.

"Knowing that we were coming to Nice," Frederik explained, "Princess Alexandra asked my sister to buy three parasols in Paris. She was to send one to her and keep one for herself. The third was to be delivered to Princess Dagmar, who has been some months at Villa Bermont in the hills behind Nice, where her fiancé, the Tsarevich, is very ill."

"I see," said Emmie, impressed by the ease with which Frederik reported such a delicate matter.

While seconded to the Russian navy, Frederik had looked after the Grand Duke Constantine's yacht and taught his eldest son Nicholas to sail. Although Grand Duke Constantine was not among the Imperial entourage now, acquaintances of Frederik's were at Villa Bermont and it was gratifying for the Ziege ladies to see that he was appreciated. Not that he sought out the company of Russians only: it was he who had made the acquaintance of Mr Ker on the terrace of the club in Nice. And Mr Ker, who liked modest young people with something to say for themselves, and possessed an old man's facility for getting them to say it, soon discovered that Captain Ziege was an experienced hydrographer. Some days afterwards, Madame Ziege had called on Mrs Ker with Hannina.

Although the Zieges' visit coincided with the melancholy drama at Villa Bermont, they could be of limited use to their own Royal family. Madame Ziege was relieved to find that their time was not more taken up with the affairs of the Tsarevich and Princess Dagmar. She wished them well and prayed for them, but it was for Alma's benefit that she was enduring the Mediterranean again instead of enjoying her old age at home. When her daughter Ida had died of fever on board ship on the way to the West Indies in 1849, it felt as if she had herself sustained a crippling injury. But later events made her own wound seem less grievous beside that of her granddaughter, Alma. Ida's death was followed by that of her husband, who was killed in battle. A year after losing her parents, Alma's little sister died. Then, last year, Alma's brother Christian had died in the West Indies at the age of twenty-two.

Brought up by her grandmother and Aunt Hannina in Copenhagen, Alma was thought by all who encountered her to be a girl of exceptional charm. Whether in the school room or music room, at tea with her grandmother's friends or skating with girls of her own age, she had a knack for putting people at ease. She had borne her brother's death with her customary dignity and never stopped being obliging, but no-one could doubt her sorrow. Her dark eyes still sparkled with readiness for fun but there was a new depth to them that seemed in some way connected with her misfortunes. Everyone agreed that something had to be done for the poor girl, who now had no family of her own.

Madame Ziege would have taken Alma alone, but first Hannina said that she would come too, then Clara proposed that her own daughter Coco go with them. She would be company for Alma, and it would be a valuable introduction to the world for Coco after her sequestered upbringing in the West Indies. Coco had always been happiest in the hammock slung between two palm trees in the garden: she would lie there for hours gazing at the scarlet hibiscus and listening to the hummingbirds. But she had never attended to her lessons as her parents wished, nor did she express much interest in other people. It was hoped that sending her to Europe would bring her out of herself.

Only when she had decided to take her granddaughters to the south did Madame Ziege raise the matter with her sons. She did not expect that Christian would be able to desert his new post at the Legation in Vienna for an extended vacation, but it was the company of her older son, Frederik, that Madame Ziege had been hoping for all along. Although she approved of hard work with all the zeal of her Lutheran faith, and she knew that Frederik was a hard worker, she had sometimes wondered if he would ever stop work for long enough to find himself a wife: he was already thirty-nine. He had been away so much over the past few years, and his beautiful letters were dim consolation for his absence. He reminded her of his father, whom she still missed sixteen years after his death and thought of more and more. After a gruelling expedition in Greenland, Frederik had straightaway been commissioned aboard an ironclad after the hostilities with Prussia, and she was concerned for his health. Nor did his lack of resistance to her invitation allay her anxiety.

In Madame Ziege's eyes, it was preferable that Emmie's origins were in Australia rather than in England. As a young girl she had fled from Copenhagen with her family as the English bombarded the city. She still remembered the fire and the sudden, incalculable rubble, the noise of the guns and the screams of the dying, the injured, and the merely frightened; the sea itself had been in flames. And though adult life had thrown her into the company of a great many English who never guessed at her aversion, she was not disposed to favour anyone of that race. Madame Ziege knew that Emmie was a colonial widow but she was keen to discover more. Maternal duty required her to consider every possibility.

They had agreed to reassemble for dinner in the Zieges' rooms, which represented a kind of safety in numbers, Emmie imagined, from the critical eyes of the Italian staff. It surprised her that the Danes all spoke perfect French. The mother and son even spoke passable Italian.

Emmie chose poached fillet of sole to start with, as did Mrs Ker, which would be gentle on the digestion. Captain Ziege chose prawns.

"I do not know how you have the nerve to eat *langoustines* in public," said Hannina.

"Why not? I have shaved off my beard."

"Oh Frederik, you know I was referring to the mess on one's fingers."

"It's just a knack," said Frederik, but his hands remained in his lap.

"I don't understand how anyone could ever eat those – things!" Coco cried, as if the pile of glistening pink monsters might come rustling to life and start across the white tablecloth towards her.

Frederik smiled at his niece and restrained himself from alarming her with accounts of unlikely things he had eaten. Conscious of the advantages of this holiday with his family, he accepted its conditions. If he was obliged to be polite to a number of more or less eligible ladies, in the present circumstances it was a pleasure. Mrs Leslie did not behave with the formality derived from a lifetime spent in nurseries and drawing rooms. It was not just that she had some experience of the world: she didn't appear to wait to see how other people responded before responding herself.

He turned to Emmie, seated on his left. "You will think it impertinent of me, I'm afraid, Mrs Leslie, but I wished to ask how it is that you are friends with Mr and Mrs Ker?"

"We met by chance in Cannes and discovered a shared connection with Australia."

Emmie looked at Mr Ker, inviting him to explain. Leaning forward over the table with a glance towards each end, he said, "We are connected by a stretch of coast in northeast Australia named The Labyrinth by Captain Cook. On the mainland at the bottom of this is a mountain called Mount Ker, after my late father. At the top is a group of islands named in honour of Mrs Leslie's late father, The Hannibal Isles."

"Your father was called Hannibal?" enquired Frederik, which surprised Mr Ker because he had expected him to pick up on his allusion to surveying.

"Yes," said Emmie. "I know, it is an unusual name."

"But not so unfamiliar to us, as it happens," Frederik replied. "My father, while Danish consul in Tunis in the twenties, did a survey of Carthage and published an account of his findings."

Emmie pictured the flat sands where she had ridden with George in Egypt. "I'm afraid I do not know it."

"Know it? Of course not! Why ever would you?"

"To students of ancient Carthage it is an important text," said Madame Ziege. "Especially in France, where it was published."

Frederik beckoned a waiter to refill glasses. "I have always wondered if Monsieur Flaubert knew of it," he said.

Coco and Alma glanced at each other. Miss Raymond feared she was blushing.

"It is not your father's fault if charlatans profit from his work," Madame Ziege said.

Emmie gathered her wits. "You lived in Tunis then?" she asked. It was not that she objected to discussing Flaubert, though she knew nothing about him, but she would avoid the subject if – as it appeared – the Zieges were sensitive about it.

"My father was stationed there for eleven years," said Hannina. "I was born there."

"And were you born in Tunis too, Captain Ziege?"

"Indeed I was not – "

"He was supposed to be born in Rome," his mother said, "but he couldn't wait. He always was inquisitive."

"I was born in a village called Monterosi – and named after it."

"Named after it?"

"I am Frederik Monterosi."

"So *you* are named *after* a place," Mr Ker observed.

"Mrs Leslie has a place named for her too!" Miss Raymond announced. She wished she had contributed this fact earlier, but she had not remembered it.

The company all looked to Emmie for clarification. She nodded. "A friend of mine called Captain Pascoe was charting south of Sydney, near Twofold Bay, and he named some straits the Emmeline Straits. I've never been there. The name will be changed, I dare say."

"I think it must be lovely to have somewhere named for you!" declared Alma.

Madame Ziege thought it peculiar that a respectable woman should have a place named after her. "Was your father a naval man?" she asked.

"No, he was a pastoralist," said Emmie, confusing Madame Ziege further.

"Frederik, if you ever discover somewhere, will you name it after me please?" Alma asked.

"My dear Alma, if the Good Lord favours me with a discovery requiring a name, then I promise it shall be named for you!"

Mr Ker said, "Let's drink to that!" And they all raised their glasses.

It was near the end of the meal. Frederik was offering Emmie a bowl of grapes when he asked, as if continuing an earlier conversation, "And so, Mrs Leslie, what brings you here?"

"I take it you do not mean to Genoa," she said, "for that was Mr Ker."

"For which we are in his debt,"

Emmie acknowledged this piece of gallantry with a smile and a slight inclination of the head.

"I dare say what brought Mrs Leslie is the same that brings the rest of us," Hannina said. "Climate and comfort, health and rest."

Emmie was not accustomed to being spoken for with such assurance, but she recognised that Hannina was providing her with an option to deflect Frederik's question. "Precisely. And is this true of you too?" she asked him.

"Of course."

Emmie decided that his eyes were like dark amber.

*

The next day, Emmie went with the Zieges on a second visit to the Duomo, where Hannina tried to get everyone to observe all the things listed in her guidebook. Emmie looked at the ancient doorways, the bas-reliefs, the dull paintings and the screen dividing the Chapel of St John the Baptist from the nave, but she liked the place no better than when she came the first time with Sydney. The only amusement it afforded was a story told to her by Frederik, about the *Sacro Catino*, a hexagonal dish carved from a single piece of emerald which he said was a gift from the Queen of Sheba to Solomon. It was claimed to be the vessel in which Joseph of Arimathea received the blood flowing from the side of the Redeemer. The Genoese acquired it during the Crusades, since when it had been in the cathedral's treasury. It was brought out three times a year and exposed to the veneration of the faithful; no foreigner was allowed to touch it under pain of death. Despite these precautions, for some time it had been known that it was made of glass, but of such rare perfection that it was still thought to be very remarkable. After the city was occupied by Napoleon the *Catino* was taken to Paris. When reclaimed by the Genoese it was packed so carelessly that it broke on the homeward journey, but the fragments were reunited in a setting of gold filigree.

Frederik enquired of a sacristan if it would be possible to see this revered object and was told that the keys to the cabinet were held by a municipal officer who, for a small charge, might be persuaded to unlock it. This provoked dissension in the Ziege party, for Hannina and her mother wanted to look at the pictures in the Palazzo Rosso and the Palazzo Balbi. Wouldn't Emmie prefer to join them? But despite the uncertainty of Frederik's plan, Emmie and his nieces preferred to go with him − "in pursuit of a broken dish," as Hannina put it with a sigh.

They set off on foot to find the office, passing through the narrow streets with swishing skirts like errant swans. Being with the girls reminded Emmie of her own sisters. They made her feel young, and the candid stares of the citizens of Genoa made her more aware of Frederik's discreet presence.

Instead of making straight for the place where they hoped to locate the key, they took a detour through the old city along the Via degli Orefici, where they were detained by a succession of craftsmen in booths, each of whom had exquisite gold and silver filigree to show them, worked into bunches of flowers, butterflies and every conceivable kind of brooch. At one grimy window, while Coco and Alma peered at the display, Emmie and Frederik bent over the counter inside to examine a tiny golden bee.

"Is he going to buy something for her?" Alma said.

"Not yet!" said Coco, eyeing Miss Raymond, who was hovering by the doorway and seemed not to have heard.

Although Alma knew that her sensible younger cousin must be right, she also now knew that the same unfamiliar thought about their uncle had occurred to them both.

They threaded their way through alleys, up and down shadowed staircases which emerged onto terraces situated above the port like boxes at a theatre. They found themselves among hulking palaces whose sheer walls teased their curiosity. Their shoes became filthy; so did the hems of their skirts, in spite of the girls' best efforts to raise them above the dust and dirt. Emmie assured them that the hotel staff must be used to it: they would clean them if the Zieges' maid could not.

At Romanenzo's Emmie bought some candied fruits, and they stopped for a light lunch at Klainguti. Frederik wondered if Genoa had produced such delicious lemonade in Columbus's time. He said that being in the Navigator's city gave him a funny feeling, for it couldn't have changed much.

The key for the *Catino*, after all, was just an excuse for exploring.

*

In the morning, Frederik, his sister, nieces, Emmie and Miss Raymond arrived at the railway station in two hansom cabs. After inspecting the statue of Columbus, they squeezed into one compartment for the short journey to Pegli and the Pallavicini Gardens.

Coco caught Alma's eye for an instant. Although Emmie and Frederik were seated in opposite corners, it seemed to Coco that the situation must feel rather intimate for her bachelor uncle and the unattached lady, and this intrigued her. Inside her muff, she pressed her knuckles against each other in secret delight. Until this winter, Coco and Alma had not spent sufficient time with their uncle to question the family story that his naval commissions had made it impossible for him to get married. During the last few weeks they had discussed his romantic prospects often, and they were still baffled. He might not be rich, but they could see that he was attractive to the eligible ladies whose acquaintance he made. He was always charming and good-humoured, yet he remained unmoved.

Despite the pure marine sunlight the air was icy, but Hannina had brought her parasol again. Emmie wondered what she could possibly need it for. The sun was pleasant, to be sure, but there was no warmth in it. The girls had their muffs, and Emmie herself was wearing gloves and thick undergarments. A woman with a parasol drew attention to herself, Emmie reflected, and hid herself at the same time. Similarly, Emmie had felt when she was in mourning that people saw a widow, not her, Emmie – which was apposite, for she had experienced a dissolution of herself when George died, a swift vanishing not just of daily purpose but also of the interior fabric by which she was used to recognising herself. All that was left was the visible fact of her bereavement. There was nothing coy about her mourning clothes: they were for her a refuge, and she had been thankful for them.

The Gardens were a place of silent enchantment after the seething city. Sunlight flickered through overhead branches as a sequence of tableaux unfolded among the paths, each with its own centre – an obelisk, a Turkish kiosk, a tiny gilded bridge, a Chinese pagoda. Stray fauns and marble statues held their breath in secluded niches; Psyche surprised them as they came round a corner.

Suddenly they heard a piano playing an English hymn tune.

Emmie recognised it at once. The confident notes of "Let Us With a Gladsome Mind . . ." burst through the crystalline air like peals of bells. The zest of it made her want to weep, as if the notes struck by the piano were an obscure code to unlock her heart. Afraid of her own tears and the confusion they would produce in her companions, Emmie hurried ahead. The path changed direction, and where it ended she could see water. As she drew close, the music became clearer and she saw that the water was a miniature lake, in the middle of which was a tiny Greek temple. The piano must have been inside, for it was nowhere else. With bewildering immediacy, Emmie was transported to her sitting room at Canning Downs, where once she had played the first hymns heard in those wild lands. George had insisted that they bring a piano, but the tide rose in the river while the steamer was moored for the night to the wharf at Brisbane with the portholes left open, and the boat sank. George ordered another piano up to Moreton Bay, which, cushioned on sacks of flour, was dragged on bullock drays ninety miles across the mountains to the house he had built for her. So generous – generous from the start . . . and at the end – for did he not die thinking of her? "Do not retire too much from the world," he had said, "but live in watchfulness . . . May the Great and Almighty God bless and direct and protect you, my own darling. I cannot return to you, but you may come to me. For Oh! After this short life we shall meet, never again to separate . . ." The notion that this music *was* George possessed Emmie; that he had returned after all, that she could somehow reach out to him.

The music stopped as if the air were wiped of sound.

Emmie looked about her.

There was nothing; nothing but the dwindling intimation of a presence in the stillness and the silence.

Emmie turned and found Alma standing at her shoulder, pale as one of the statues, her eyes glazed with tears. She too had felt the uncanny force of the hidden piano. Frederik placed his left hand on his niece's shoulder, a mute gesture of comfort that surprised Emmie by its gentle way with Alma's rush of grief. Emmie smiled, whereupon Alma linked arms with her as they turned their backs on the lake.

They made their way back to the city in silence, a necessary silence whose very ease was a mutual acknowledgement that their intense experience was both shared and also personal. Only Coco felt oppressed. She remarked how odd it was to hear a piano like that, in the middle of nowhere, then added that if they had walked around the lake they would no doubt have seen a boat tied to a jetty. But Hannina gave her a look which said: "Be quiet" – and she was.

The scene stirred Frederik's own sense of undefined loss – of which he felt ashamed because he believed that he had not in fact lost anything. But having reached the age of thirty-nine, he wondered what he was going to do with his life that he hadn't done already. His travels and commissions were undertaken in the spirit of preparation. The very wording of his application for secondment to the Russian navy had expressed this: it was to gain experience that would not be available to him in the Danish navy. But for what purpose? Such conceit! What had he imagined he would be doing now? His rank might be elevated as the years passed, until he reached a position of worldly eminence, but what of that? The real work, the work for which he was preparing himself, of activity, discovery, learning – the work he longed for and which alone seemed worthwhile, wasn't this already behind him, such as it was? Hannina was only two years older than he, but her life now looked set in decline. She had not married, she had no children: if she lived to be a hundred it would still appear that her zenith had occurred unseen five years ago. And if this were true for her, why not also for him – five years ago, when it still seemed that he might achieve so much? Greenland had altered him. The cold had made a crack in him and doubt of his own strength had crept in.

This was not an affliction for which Frederik expected sympathy. It expressed itself rather as humility, a curiosity about – and respect for – the activities of others. So his awareness of Emmie's loss was not limited to her bereavement alone but extended to the perception that her life had fallen away in a landslide where she had proved to be the most stable point. Yet he found that he did not think that *her* life was waning, as he did with his sister and was tempted to do with his own. He sensed that she had started upon a new phase of life altogether.

*

At luncheon in the hotel, when they discussed plans for going on to Rome, Emmie was disconcerted by the realisation that everyone, herself included, assumed that she and Sydney would travel with the Zieges. They had met them only three days ago and already they belonged to their party. She suppressed a shiver of panic. Why not join them, after all? She was independent. She could leave whenever she wished.

They agreed to go to Rome by steamer, via Leghorn, in two days' time. "Very well," said Frederik, "I shall purchase tickets this afternoon. And now, if I may change the subject, please will you tell us about your brooch, Mrs Leslie? It makes the wares of the Via degli Orefici mere trinkets."

Emmie felt herself colour. She reached up to where the brooch was pinned and wondered if wearing it was a mistake.

"One of the figures looks to be a kangaroo," said Frederik.

"A kangaroo!" cried Alma. "Are there really many kangaroos in Australia?"

"I'm afraid they are so numerous, they are a pest."

"Oh!"

"There are millions of them," added Miss Raymond.

"And what are the other shapes?" Frederik asked.

"There is an emu, and a 'blackboy'," said Emmie, touching them with the tips of her fingers.

"'Blackboy'?"

"It is sometimes called a grass tree, as if it were a mixture of the two. It is unique to Australia as so many plants are, but common, like kangaroos and emus."

"But why 'blackboy'?" said Hannina.

Coco laughed, and her aunt said, "Am I being very stupid?"

"It is thought that the top has some resemblance to the tousled head of an Aborigine," Emmie explained.

"So it is a tableau of the Australian bush," Frederik said.

"Yes. My husband had it made for me after we gave up our property."

As soon as it was said, Emmie feared that the Zieges might misinterpret her reply. Although she did not wish to discuss it all in public, nor did she wish to rebuff them. So she pressed on: "I suppose it *is* unusual and of course it has a significance for me, but it is not conventionally beautiful . . ."

She remembered her first sight of the ore from which it was made: her brother Arthur rushing into the homestead at Canning Downs with his boots on – "Emmie! Emmeline! Look!" – stretching out his arm and opening his fist. In the palm of his hand was a dull lump of quartz. "Gold!" he said. And behind him, George coughing.

". . . all the lovelier for being so singular," Frederik was saying, and his family murmured their agreement.

As they drank their coffee, Coco and Alma volunteered to go with their uncle to buy the steamer tickets, expecting that Emmie would come too. But she said that she wished to write some letters, and then it was awkward for them to renege.

Emmie made no move to rise from her chair and Hannina suddenly said that she would join the outing. Madame Ziege appeared to be pleased with this arrangement, for she blessed Emmie with a smile full of creases. It might have escaped the others how Emmie had slipped in with their arrangements, but it had not escaped Madame Ziege.

"Miss Raymond, why don't you go with my son and the girls?" she said.

Sydney looked for a moment at Emmie. "Yes, Sydney, why don't you go, if you would like to?" Emmie said.

So Emmie was left alone with Madame Ziege. They sat in silence for a while, enjoying the anticipation of an intimacy which both knew might not be realised. A waiter brought them more coffee, then withdrew.

"You need not have stayed, but I'm glad you did," Madame Ziege began at last.

Emmie felt complimented by this frank opening. She stirred her coffee. "It must be nice for your granddaughters to be with their uncle," she said.

"Yes. And for Hannina."

"And you . . ."

Madame Ziege inclined her head and smiled wryly. "Of course." She paused, then said, "Please excuse his questions."

"I do not mind them," said Emmie, assuming this to be a prelude to her own interrogation.

"What he said about your brooch was true. It is very fine . . ."

"Thank you."

"Your husband was much loved, I think?"

Emmie had been looking forward to talking about George, but all of a sudden the prospect of being catechised about him by this old lady was unbearable. "Yes," she said. Dod was the name by which she had first known him, the childhood name which his brothers used. A flash of memory brought to her that his family also sometimes used to call him Mains, for some reason. She had not thought of this nickname for years, and the reminder of it also brought to mind her own sister Lucy calling him Peter, after Peter the Rock, and there was a midshipman who used to come up to the house – what was *his* name? – whom she used to call Paul. "He was a kind man," she said. "He died of consumption after a long illness. Eight years."

"That was why you gave up your property in Australia?"

"Yes."

"It must have been very difficult."

"It was."

A headache had developed between Emmie's eyes, like an animal unfurling itself from sleep. Madame Ziege saw beads of moisture on her forehead and said, "Are you too hot, my dear?"

"No, no, I'm sorry, a headache has just come on . . ."

"I'm so sorry to hear it! Would you not like to lie down?"

"Oh dear . . . Please excuse me!"

Declining Madame Ziege's suggestion of a mustard compress, Emmie retired to her room. There she drew the curtains and sat down on the bed. As she took off her brooch, she remembered that when George had left Canning Downs for Sydney to take his seat on the Legislative Council, he had the piece of gold in his pocket to show to his friend Clarke. Found at the Swamp, near the head of Rosenthal Creek, it was the largest of several samples from the run. For a time, two heady months or so, they thought they had struck a real vein of gold. They recalled the stories of sudden, fantastic wealth that had drifted from California and Victoria over the last few years: but that hope too had turned to dust. Instead of returning up-country in triumph, George was taken ill and they went "home"; it was the first time she had left Australia, the land of her birth. And though they returned after two years to New South Wales, the hard work at Canning Downs was beyond him and they never resumed their life there. He took the freak nugget to one of the new smiths in Sydney and had it wrought into a bauble for her. Canning Downs was bought by his cousin, Gilbert Davidson, and then they came back to England for good. Neither of them could bear to live in Sydney, surrounded by so many reminders of their loss. They reckoned it was better to take "home" what they had gained. There at least they could provide properly for Carrie and Charlie Wickham, the children of Emmie's dead sister Annie, a task for which their father, Captain Wickham, judged himself, or Brisbane, to be unfit.

Emmie lay down and drew the eiderdown over her. For an active man like George, she thought, consumption was a cruel disease. First the coughing, then the night sweats, and at last the wasting of strong limbs until the most he could do was to tend his chrysanthemums in a heated conservatory at the back of the Rutland Gate house. Then there was a sudden decline when they were staying with his Aunt Coats at Lipwood, near Newcastle. On the Sunday night before they left, after Emmie had read to him as usual, he said he meant to hear from Dr P. if he thought his case was hopeless or not. Emmie told him that he could only repeat what they had heard before and knew – that he was in a most precarious state, that his disease had indeed assumed a chronic form, but that with God's blessing his life might be spared for many years yet.

George said that he had been wishing for a long time to speak openly to her. Although he knew it would comfort her, he had wished to wait till he felt quite sure that she was not afraid. Now that talking did not agitate him, he wanted to tell her that he often thought he might be taken during the night; that he felt it would likely be sudden, but he was content to live or to die as God saw fit. His words were slow and distinct. He said that he was all sin, but that God's mercy was greater than his sin; he prayed that he was not presumptuous in expressing his confidence. In the prospect of death he had but a single sorrow – leaving Emmie – which was not a sin, since everyone longed for life; he too would like to go on living, though the Almighty had taken away the dread of death. His whole heart poured out with such calm that Emmie could only listen in amazement.

"Do you feel all this dependence on Jesus?" she said when he had finished, reaching out to clear the spittle from his lips.

"Who else do you think I trust to? Without Him I cannot live, without Him I dare not die." There was no hour of his life, he said, not even the best spent, that was not sinful, but God was able and had promised to cleanse him. He trembled sometimes for he had never had an affliction and God tested those whom he loved. Emmie said that his trial was this sickness, and it was God's grace that made him say otherwise. He said that he dared not count that as suffering when he had so many blessings. Had he been beggared, or lost like poor Ernest, or had Emmie died, then he would indeed have been tested. But not now. All was mercy.

"As it is possible I may go without being able to say anything, I must say, my own beloved one, that if I die you have the consolation that I believe you have been the humble instrument in God's hands of turning my soul to Him. It would be useless in me to try to express what you are and have been to me. All I can say: May a great and merciful God bless and reward you for the love and care such as if ever equalled certainly were never surpassed. May the Almighty God and Saviour support you in your sorrow. To think that your grief will not be great would be not to know your affectionate heart. Never was mortal man so blessed in a wife as I have been in you. You have been everything my heart could have desired and a lifetime spent as a true Christian could never express what I feel."

He meant to arrange his affairs so that she should at least have no material cares. Then he advised her to keep Carrie Wickham with her until Carrie was eighteen; thereafter Emmie must decide. It might not be wise to keep her longer; he hoped and believed she would prove to be a dutiful soul. He should like the curate, Mr Clayton, to come to read to him after breakfast.

In faint pencil he wrote on a slip of paper: "Of course I know that you nor anyone else can tell, but do you think the end may be sudden, or a gradual wearing out of physical strength?"

Next day he rallied a little and observed that this house they had rented in Cheltenham for the summer would be lonely after he was gone. He counselled her instead to go to Scotland, to his brother William at Warthill. There she could be as quiet as she pleased, and the kindness and sympathy would be all she could desire . . . there were people about who would also . . .

In winter Rutland Gate would be best, he said, or St Leonards, where his brothers Tom and Walter would be, but this was merely a suggestion. Then he wished that she would continue their subscription to the Brisbane hospital, and not to get out of the Gigoomgan property unless there was difficulty in managing it. "Give Pat my pony – he walked with me the last time I rode her. He is the Prince of Bushmen! Ask Tom to keep her for him till he wants her. I feel at ease, my darling. Sell the carriage horses, a pair will get too fresh for comfort. Get a fine large horse, but keep both carriages. Write to Little to sell all our land except at Port Curtis and King George Sound, at these prices more or less: Murray's Farm at Warwick, £400; Connor's land at Ipswich, £200; ninety-six acres at Bulimba at £12 per acre; twenty-nine acres in Enoggera at £15 per acre; thirty-six acres at the Warwick Boiling Place, £1 per acre. He'll get most for land by getting a good deposit down and letting the bulk lie at interest secured on the land. Insist on a return from Gigoomgan now . . ."

Then nothing till he woke and said he hoped, if it were God's will, that he might know a little while before he was called, because he had some friends he would like to tell that he had not found religion irksome as he had used to think it must be; that religious people made a great mistake in shutting themselves out of the world, for then those who were thoughtless supposed that religion was something remote from them or difficult to practise. He said he wished particularly for William and his sister Mary Anne to be told of his faith. Both had been so kind and he knew William was anxious and his sweet Matilda too, and that Mary Anne had written him such tender letters, and he would like to tell David Fairholme too the blessing the Book had been that he gave him, he had indeed read and studied it as much as he was able.

"Do not think I am sad," he said, "only so thankful." Then they said the Evening Hymn together and soon afterwards he slept.

Next morning, he was seized with a haemorrhage and, after six terrible days of watching, Emmie's beloved husband breathed his last in the most perfect peace and joy in his Saviour.

*

They boarded the Peirano Company steamer at eleven o'clock in the evening, leaving themselves half an hour to get settled before departure. A night-time voyage suited Emmie, for she was inclined to sickness at sea. While she hoped that she might have outgrown this unfortunate weakness since she did the last run from Australia, the evidence of recent channel crossings made her doubt it. If she felt well enough she might venture out for breakfast after they left Leghorn – it was only the Mediterranean, after all. Knowing that neither she nor any of the ladies would be expected to appear before noon was some comfort.

While Emmie said her prayers in her cabin, Frederik was leaning against the rail on deck. The night was cold but clear. When the boat grunted away from the quay, the thousand and one lamps dotted up the hills behind Genoa became indistinguishable from the stars and were mirrored in the sea's moonlit surface. The nuzzling silhouettes of the ships at anchor merged with their own shadows. For a moment the steamer was poised between the embracing arms of the Mole Vecchio and the Mole Nuovo, then it slipped into the open sea. So different from the icy desolation of Godthaab or Nikoalevsk; or the swarming junks off Shanghai and Hong Kong, where the families lived on their wretched vessels. He remembered being taken ashore once in a boat where the woman who was rowing had a swaddled baby strapped to her back, its head shaved except for the beginnings of a pigtail which swung from side to side with the rowing motion. Frederik had watched many cities recede glimmering into the darkness, but he could think of none where the panorama was so soothing as Genoa. Whatever was impressive about foreign ports tended to be enhanced by an accompanying sense of strangeness, whereas what made Genoa so seductive was its venerable walls. Copenhagen was of course familiar, but it was intractable, fraught with toil and yearning. From the Sea of Okhotsk he had longed for it with a passion that at times felt demented, but, during the tedious years of surveying in the Øresund, he had been desperate to escape Copenhagen's claustrophobia. It combined the protection of home with the limitations of school.

In the pocket of his overcoat was a small piece of amber, which he

rolled between the tips of his fingers. A sailor had found it on a Baltic beach, carved an anchor into it and given it to him. Frederik had carried it with him ever since and it had acquired the power of a charm, which embarrassed him for he was not a superstitious man. The gift was made when Frederik's job was dull and he hankered to be elsewhere. He knew that he had never voiced any such thought at the time, but the old sailor had somehow divined it; had respected both the feeling and his restraint in keeping it to himself. And though it was Denmark that Frederik wanted to get away from, the piece of amber would not have meant so much to him were the sailor himself not Danish.

*

It had been night too when they left Toulon. Frederik, with a seven-year-old's clamorous heart, had not wanted to go to bed but clutched the rail at his father's side as the city faded away. Mama took the girls and Christian off to their beds, leaving him to enjoy the swelling sea and the sturdy pleasure of having his father, indulgent for once, all to himself. On the passage to Greece he was kept buoyant by the reflection of his delight in the good humour of the crew and his parents. He was exhilarated by the sun and the salt, the whip of the sails and the gratifying order on board – and above all, by his father's willingness to initiate him into the adult world of the ship. With unusual patience, his father explained about the winds and why the sailors pulled on one rope rather than on another, about the rules that governed the ship and how it was divided into different territories. Not once was Frederik seasick.

Soon after their arrival in the hastily established capital of Nauplia, Tuxen Ziege had contacted Sir Edmund Lyons, whose brother he had known in North Africa. The previous year, Lyons had brought Otho the Bavarian on the *Madagascar* to be king of the new independent state of Greece. He was still in the Mediterranean, maintaining a British presence, and an extra boy was not a burden. His ship was a safer place for the boy than among the precariously reformed bandits that occupied the charnel house of Greece, even though the Zieges privately regretted that it was a British ship.

Frederik's father knew from reports that the violence of the civil war had been atrocious. He had seen a few of its effects when, as Consul in Tunis, he had been drawn into negotiations on behalf of some of those sold into slavery following the capture of Kos by the Turks. But he was unprepared for what he found. As he saw more and more bones strewn about the country, often bearing marks of monstrous cruelties, he came to regard the slaves as the lucky ones. After such carnage it was hard to favour those who called themselves victors: there were those who died, then there were those who remained – presumably by savageries of their own that were better not imagined. And among them, those ridiculous Englishmen, adventurers and adolescents seeking an Arcadia of their fantasy.

While it was possible for Ziege to keep the girls and Christian at home, if a hut in a ravaged Greek village could be dignified as a home, Frederik was of an age when he ought to get educated. The *Madagascar* provided a temporary solution, and after a few months Frederik transferred to a French vessel under the kind supervision of Lieutenant Torné. From him, Frederik learned French, English and – for he dimly recalled speaking it to a fond old man in a drawing room on his return to Denmark at the age of eleven – he must have had some Greek.

A small volume by one of those English philhellenes whom his father so detested was lying heavy as another man's purse in the other pocket of Frederik's overcoat. Edward Trelawny had played a much publicised part in the Greek War of Independence. Everyone knew that he had been besieged in a mountain cave with a Greek child bride, and supposed this demonstrated an attachment to some heroic cause. Frederik's father had never met Trelawny, but the man was infamous among those who had consular dealings with Greece in the aftermath of the war for his posturing and his troublesome alliances: when Tuxen inveighed against the English, he was never slow to invoke Trelawny. Ever since his own trip to the Far East, Frederik had meant to have a look at Trelawny's *Adventures of a Younger Son* for himself. Now the prospect of sailing where Trelawny had sailed with Byron and with poor Shelley galvanised him. In the hotel's smoking room he had read fifty pages, but the boastful delight with which Trelawny related his tales of piracy repelled Frederik. He had stopped in Java in 1858, and just a few hours there were enough to convince him that Trelawny was a liar.

Frederik lit one more cigarette. As he cast his flaring match overboard, for a moment he imagined Emmie at his side watching the silvery water trailing into the darkness. Instinct told him that she would disapprove of Trelawny's book, but her notional presence was sympathetic and companionable.

*

When Emmie woke in the morning, pulling the blankets up around her neck against the cold, she realised with startled satisfaction that she had slept through the night undisturbed by the swell, and she at once looked forward to the day ahead with impatience. Even the calendar was not against her. Only on finding that she felt well did she appreciate how much she wished to be in good spirits for the Zieges. She lay still for a moment, wondering about them. Their family group was disjointed but it had an air of self-sufficiency; they were close, which was a sure attraction for her. And Frederik seemed precise, industrious, amusing and thoughtful.

Emmie turned her head to see Sydney, and cold air stabbed her shoulder. Sydney was huddled up with her back turned, leaving only her nightcap visible and the corner of a book she was reading.

"Good morning, Sydney," said Emmie.

As Sydney twisted round, her hair sprang loose and her book dropped shut with a snap suggestive of a French novel rather than the book of sermons which it was. "Good morning, Emmie. My! You slept well!"

"Didn't I just!"

"Right through Leghorn!"

The task of dressing in the cramped cabin – chamberpots and facecreams, hair, corsets and stockings, petticoats, silks and buttons – was at last accomplished, and they emerged like butterflies from their cocoons. Their dresses filled the passage. A shivering steward helped them negotiate the companionway up to the deck, where they hoped to find breakfast in the saloon. The Zieges were already there, the ladies in woollen shawls. On the table stood a basket of hot buttered rolls, preserves, a dish of cold meats and a pot of steaming coffee. Seeing Emmie and Sydney, Frederik stood at once and pulled out chairs for them.

They all said good morning and Alma smiled a guileless welcome.

"We were afraid you had fallen overboard!" said Madame Ziege, a cup to her lips which hid her expression as she peered at Emmie over the rim.

"Dear me! I hope an alarm would have been raised!" cried Sydney.

"Uncle Frederik would have jumped in to rescue you!" Coco declared.

"Indeed?" said Emmie.

Towards the end of his service as a lieutenant in the Russian navy, Hannina explained, Frederik was serving on a frigate which put into Plymouth. As they left the Channel, a sailor fell into the sea, whereupon Frederik jumped in after him. "Come on, Frederik!" she said. "You tell it!"

"Do Mrs Leslie and Miss Raymond really want – ?"

"Ach, Frederik! Get on!"

"Mrs Leslie – ?"

Emmie laughed, conscious that she was being played to. "Please – go on!" she said.

Frederik frowned. "I'm not so good at telling the next bit," he said, "because I was in the sea and didn't know very well what was happening. My uniform is not so convenient as a swimming costume, even though I had taken off the jacket . . . Anyway, I thought the man was drunk because he was so thrashing and helpless, but it turned out that apart from being unable to swim he had somehow broken his leg on falling."

"Good gracious!" Emmie cried.

"But when I had a grip on him," Frederik continued, "I realised that the ship had not put about. I could see all the sailors' shouting faces, but they were disappearing in the wrong direction. It alarmed me, as you may imagine. In the excitement some blunder was made, orders were given to the pilot, no doubt, but not understood, for the ship steamed on. The sailor begged me to release him – "

"'Let me go! Let me go! We cannot both be saved!'" cried Alma, eager to heighten the drama.

"Poor man, he just wanted you to let him die in peace!" said Madame Ziege.

"Well, I admit I was interfering. In my defence, I believed I was doing the right thing at the time . . . Or rather, I didn't think at all . . ."

"Not thinking, Frederik – that is always your trouble!" said Hannina.

It was plain to Emmie that the Ziege ladies' teasing disguised intense pride in Frederik's exploit. She thought of George organising the bailing on the steamer when they came down from Brisbane in the storm with Carrie. When they started taking on such quantities of water, everyone thought they were lost and the captain sought comfort in a bottle. George threw the bottles overboard and kept the boat afloat. Emmie's own beautiful horse was the only loss.

"But you were delivered," she said.

"As you see. I held on tight and at last the ship came round."

"So you rescued the man," said Emmie. "And earned the respect of the crew, I dare say?"

"When I reached deck, I'm told the mate cried 'Hats off!' and 'Three cheers!', but in truth I was so exhausted that I did not notice. However – I will say it because it will otherwise be said for me – I was later awarded the Russian gold medal for life-saving with the ribbon of St Vladimir."

"The *prestigious* ribbon of St Vladimir, Willi says," Coco added.

"Who would have thought your brother was so impressionable, Coco?" said Frederik. "I should get him something nice for his birthday, to encourage this flattery!"

Rome, April–May 1865

EMMIE'S party attributed the increasing cold to their being at sea: but at Civita Vecchia the porters were wearing overcoats and there was ice on the dockside. They arrived in Rome to find that the fountains were frozen.

Such conditions were well provided for at the Hôtel de Russie. Remembering Frederik's courteous, easy manners from an earlier visit, the management were well disposed towards his family. At the Hotel Possidoni, nearby on the corner of the Piazza di Spagna, Emmie was informed by Signor Possidoni that good, clean fires were maintained in all the apartments, and that hot water was available whenever required. He provided pans to warm the beds and any number of spare blankets.

There was a coach stand outside the hotel. Leaving her maid to organise her rooms, Emmie set out at once with Sydney for the *poste restante*. They tried to recognise landmarks as they clattered through the icy streets: what was that fountain? Where was the Via Condotti? Were they in the Corso now? Before they could name a single feature with confidence they were drawn up in front of the Post Office in the Piazza di Colonna. They made their way among urchins and milling visitors to a counter in the cavernous interior, where Emmie was presented with two letters. One, on which she recognised Mant's meticulous hand, had been forwarded by Fanning in London from Australia; the other was from her sister Kate. There was one for Sydney too, from her sister; and the peevish, groundless notion that it brought news of another birth came to Emmie with a flash of certainty. As always from *postes restantes*, she departed convinced that there were other letters which a semi-literate clerk had failed, or hadn't bothered, to decipher as hers. On the way back, they called at the lodgings of her friends the Reverend and Mrs Walsham How, whom she knew through the Leslies. He was a man with strong opinions on religious matters – and everything, he argued, pertained to religion. In a general way, Emmie admired him, for she believed that everybody, and priests in particular, ought to live by robust and correct moral convictions. In this respect, it was said by many, Walsham How was an inspiration. She stopped to leave her card also with Admiral and Mrs Birch – old friends from St Leonards, in Sussex, who had known George and Wickham – and with one or two other acquaintances from Cannes.

Mant's letters, though insisted upon, were never welcome. That one should have caught up with her here, when she was so free from care, was galling. Douglas Mant was the managing partner in Gigoomgan, a cattle station in which George had invested after selling Canning Downs. Within two months of George's death, Emmie discovered that the third partner, Anderson, had drawn money against her prospective income. However sound his explanations, she knew that he would never have behaved so when George was alive. The problem of protecting her interests was compounded by the distance, but at first her partners behaved as if she wouldn't concern herself with them at all. Her only control was through the regular reports, which she analysed with a thoroughness learned from her years as mistress of the largest sheep station on the Darling Downs. Every three months she had to read ten thousand words about the coupling and diseases of cattle, about fencing and taxes and wages; and about Mant's family. She could picture their situation only too well: the man would come in exhausted, smelly and dirty after twelve hours in the saddle, eat what his wife had prepared from butchered cows and a neglected vegetable plot, then sit up half the night with his account books. Emmie insisted on the paperwork because she had to, but she assumed that she came between Mant and his family, and this upset her. Yet she was determined not to be cast down. She would read this letter now and answer it at once, even though she was tired from the journey. Then it would not be hanging over her at her rendezvous with the Zieges in the morning.

Meanwhile the Zieges made a short excursion, before darkness and hunger forced them back. In the Piazza Navona, they noticed that the fountains' sculptures were encrusted with icy snouts.

When later they were sitting down to their meal, Alma suddenly asked: "Uncle, did you ever get used to the cold?"

Although the question seemed inoffensive, it provoked a titter from Coco. Earlier, the girls' high spirits were thought to indicate delight at their safe arrival in this Cradle of Civilisation, a feeling which was shared by all. But the two of them had not been able to help observing – they were exposed to all eyes, and weathers, after all – the endowments of Neptune and the Moor, which had been magnified by the ice. It was hard not to laugh at stark nature's joke.

Frederik did not understand the cause of Coco's giggles. The sights that delighted his nieces had reminded him of cases of frostbite he had seen (scarcely dining-room conversation); of the corrosive power of cold and the feeling he sometimes had that it had infected his very marrow. He half expected to see a Greenlander's canoe slide from the ice-hung grottoes of the fountains, and the thought made him shudder. He might pursue warmth in the south, but the north still cleaved to him like his own shadow.

"Did you not bring your bearskin, Uncle Frederik?" said Alma.

"I did not expect to need a bearskin in Rome," he said, stripping the meat from his quail.

Alma understood that Emmie had been married to an Australian sheep farmer. Knowing nothing of such things, she imagined something like a Danish smallholding, but worked by convicts and without the civilising proximity of Copenhagen. Since Emmie did not fit this picture it made no sense, and Alma longed to probe. "I wonder if Mrs Leslie has a sheepskin?" she said.

Frederik wondered why Alma said such odd things. "You'd better ask her yourself," he said.

"You appear to regard the climate as an elaborate entertainment for your own benefit, girls," said Madame Ziege. "It is a serious matter for some." She thought it just as well that Mrs Leslie and Miss Raymond were dining on their own this evening.

*

The Tower of the Capitol was their first destination the following morning. Frederik said that it was essential for new visitors to Rome to study the disposition of the ancient city from here and establish their bearings in relation to the modern one. Madame Ziege had heard variants of this speech from her husband, from Thorvaldsen, and from Carsten Hauch, when they undertook to introduce her to the city more than forty years ago. It was still bitterly cold and she stayed indoors with Hannina.

On the Tower, Frederik stood with a map of the city and its environs between his outstretched hands. He looked up, his eyes narrowing against the sun as he considered the horizon. Surrounding the Campagna to the northeast rose the amphitheatre of the Sabine Hills, with Tivoli conspicuous at the right. The low ground was occupied by the Tiber valley, and to the southeast lay the Alban Hills, dotted with villages and towns. Frederik adjusted his hat a little and drew his gaze in closer. Then with one yellow kid-gloved hand he started to point out features:

"The hill at twelve o'clock is the Quirinal. Beyond, in the distance, with the trees on, is the Pincian. At two o'clock is the flat Viminal, a bit difficult to distinguish; there is a church on top whose name I forget. At three is the Esquiline. At four, the Cælian – you can just see the top storey of the Coliseum at the foot of it. At five is the Palatine, covered with the ruins of the Palace of the Cæsars, and beyond it, at six, the Aventine. We are on the Capitoline, of course. I think that makes seven, doesn't it? Rome is said to have seven hills, after all; the Pincian doesn't count. Behind us is the Vatican, but even Catholics do not elevate the Pope's mortal seat to the immortal rank of Roman Hill." Enjoying Emmie's avid attention, Frederik pointed out the Arch of Septimius Severus. "The church beyond is the Santa Martina. A little to the left, on the side of the Quirinal, is Trajan's Forum – you see the Column . . . There is the Via Sacra winding along through the Forum to the Arch of Titus, and that pyramid is known as the Rostra, where the Ancients made their speeches; facing it, the column of Phocas, called by Byron 'the nameless column'; further back, the Temple of Saturn and, to its left, the three columns of the Temple of Concord . . . I'm so sorry – while I am chattering on, you are catching cold!" he exclaimed, as Emmie shivered.

"Mrs Leslie – " Alma blurted into the pause. She had been watching Emmie's response to her uncle as if she could not wholly credit her attention, but believed it must imply some subtler meaning. She had wanted to speak, but now, having made her opening, she could not think of anything to say. What emerged, to her dismay, was, "We were talking last night about how cold it was and I wondered if you had a sheepskin rug?"

Startled, Emmie turned to Frederik for enlightenment. In the movement, the sun caught her eyes beneath the brim of her hat. He thought of a kingfisher, and smiled.

She turned back to Alma. "Do you mean 'Have I brought one with me', or 'Do I possess one'? The answer is 'No' on both counts."

"Why . . . ?"

"I've seen enough sheep in my life so far. I wouldn't be sorry if I never saw another shred of wool again."

In Coco, surprise was revealed by the merest flinch – skin stroked by falling blossom – but Alma looked as if she had been slapped.

"I'm sorry," she said, "I didn't mean . . ."

But she knew neither what she meant nor what she didn't mean. Emmie touched her shoulder with her fingertips and said, "Heavens! Did I snap? I'm sure I didn't mean to!"

Alma's lilac hat tilted up as fast as it had tilted down. Her hair, black as basalt, slipped back over her shoulders and her wide-set, dark eyes implored Emmie for renewed favour.

Later, as they walked down Capitol Hill, Frederik found himself alone with Emmie for a moment. A shawl covered her shoulders, and her black straw hat afforded some protection from the wind. Frederik felt that he ought to apologise again for detaining her in the cold.

"It's quite all right," she said, then hesitated, like someone feeling in the dark with her toe for the step of a threshold, as she allowed to Frederik a confidence which she had just denied his niece: "It sometimes seems foolish to me that, having spent most of my life in the service of warmth – I mean, involved with sheep – I should find myself living in cold England, always feeling cold."

It was the catch in her voice as much as the words themselves which made Frederik feel that she was entrusting him with something personal, to see how he would treasure it.

"I should like to know more about that," he said with care.

"About what?" said Emmie, laughing. "Wool, or my dislike of the cold?"

"Perhaps you should begin with the wool, or rather your family's connection to it."

"Goodness me! Do you really want to hear about that?" said Emmie, pleased by his interest.

"Yes. Despite what you said to Alma, you are wearing a woollen shawl," he teased her.

"Indeed, I was surprised no-one remarked it!" Emmie said, glancing at him, interested that he had observed it and said nothing. It wouldn't have mattered if he had pointed out that she was wearing wool at the time, but he had not, and this created a bond between them which was less frivolous than it seemed. She felt a stealthy tug of complicity. "I can see I shall have to tell you about my father's uncle," she said, as the others caught them up at the foot of the steps.

But though never shy of putting himself forward in life, it was several days before events permitted the long-dead John Macarthur to claim more than a moment of Emmie and Frederik's shared attention.

*

Emmie found that her friend Mr Arbuthnot had called at the hotel to deliver invitations for herself and Sydney to the Bachelors' Ball for that very evening. While she had no objection to going herself, Emmie thought what a fine opportunity it would make for Coco and Alma to enjoy themselves in Society. In her answer, she suggested that the gentlemen might like to invite her young Danish friends if they required more ladies to make up numbers; nor did she omit to mention their uncle, as chaperone, their aunt and grandmother.

Emmie supposed that her pleasure would consist, for the most part, in watching the girls' enjoyment. They looked so pretty in their ball-gowns, and no-one who remembered dancing at their age could fail to share their vivid excitement. She would dance a little and amuse herself, as one did; if Frederik requested her hand once or twice, it would only be polite to dance with him. But from his first modest bow – "Mrs Leslie, may I . . . ?" – which she answered by placing her fingers in his extended hand – from that moment she felt as if a silk thread attached them, coiling and stretching but never breaking, like the waltzes themselves, which seemed to jump the gaps with a lilt and stirring of the blood and send her twirling into the next movement. Far from being vicarious, her delight was the fruit of her own soul, and the richer for being unsought. She was more used to Scottish reels, but waltzing was the fashion in Rome, as elsewhere in Europe, and Frederik was an accomplished partner – light on his feet but firm. Whether the cause was the dance, or his touch, she could not say, but she experienced a kind of joy as she moved that she had not thought ever again to feel, and for which she felt grateful.

Frederik could not identify any one factor that made him want to go on dancing with Emmie. It was not just the vibrant satin at her waist, nor the evanescence at her neck as they turned, nor the sense of her rippling – it was none and all of these – her palpable enjoy-ment was compelling enough. He felt in her an energy, a willingness to engage with the tumble of events that proceeded from strength rather than caprice. She carried with her a fan that she used two or three times, but so deftly that he did not have the opportunity to examine it. A flash of ivory, enough to see that it was carved with Chinese figures, then it was snapped shut.

He wanted to ask her how she came to possess such a fan, and an opportunity looked as if it might arise the following day when an Italian gentleman named Ceccini had invited them both to go hunting. But if Frederik imagined riding through the thawed Campagna beside

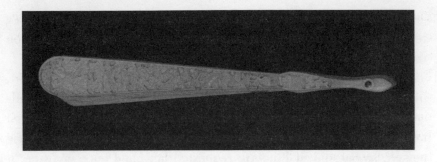

Emmie he was to be disappointed, for Alma and Coco wanted to come too and, the weather remaining cold, it was thought more suitable to hire a carriage at Barfoot's near the hotel and follow the hunt, rather than join it. He reminded Emmie that she was due to tell him about her great-uncle, at which she laughed and said, "He was a profiteer, but a visionary too!" Then there was a wild hallooing and with all those in the other carriages following the hunt, they scanned the low-lying mist for a glimpse of a fox.

"I wonder if anything is out there?" Alma said.

"If not a fox then a ghost," said Frederik, who believed he had seen an apparition one foggy evening many years ago in Paris.

At that moment, sleek and raw with urgency, the fox broke cover. Emmie exclaimed as it doubled back down the line of carriages; Coco and Alma flung themselves against the window beside her. At first mingling with the onlookers' voices, then drowning them out, came the baying of the hounds. Then the pack emerged from the mist and the ululating huntsmen bore down on their frenzied quarry. A pair of American riders, who were accompanying the ladies in the last carriage, headed off the fox, which turned to the open country again. But it was anticipated by other riders coming round in a wide arc. Seeing them, it paused in mid-stride, ears pricked up, then plunged off at a tangent, stretched against the ground as if hoping to slip beneath its assailants. But in an instant it was surrounded, then a huntsman was yelling amid a whirl of hounds, all howling at the scent of fresh blood.

The story of John Macarthur emerged on the day after the hunt, during a visit to the Protestant Cemetery, where Emmie wished to visit Shelley's grave. Just a few days before her tragic death, Lady Mary FitzRoy had given Emmie a small volume of Shelley's poems to take with her into the bush. Knowing that Shelley too had died before his time had helped console Emmie, in her solitude, for the loss of dear Lady Mary. His verses had also comforted her on the steamer voyage from Moreton Bay.

As they walked along paths that were lush with the wild flowers of a late-burgeoning spring, Emmie told Frederik how John Macarthur first went to the southern continent as a lieutenant in the New South Wales Corps in 1790. He was accompanied by his wife Elizabeth and their infant son. For a junior officer in peacetime it was an opportunity for full pay, at least, Emmie said; and despite, or because of, the grim rumours circulating about the new convict settlement, who knew what other opportunities besides? When permission arrived for officers to be given grants of crown land, after the austere Governor Phillip's departure, Macarthur acquired a hundred acres at Parramatta, which he cleared and cultivated using ten convicts supplied, in accordance with regulations, at government expense. As paymaster of the New South Wales Corps he disposed of substantial funds and was able to control the market in valuable commodities. In particular this meant rum, which, in a colony chronically short of coin, was the preferred method of payment.

"He was not dishonest," Emmie added, for she was speaking about her father's uncle, after all; "although in our more stringent times he might not be thought altogether scrupulous."

"He was well placed to benefit from opportunities," Frederik suggested.

"Well, he saw no reason to surrender his advantages to convicted felons or anybody else. Why should he?

"By the turn of the century he owned 1,600 acres, 600 sheep, and 100 cattle. Since I was a little girl, hearing stories about him at my Grandmother King's knee, I knew that he was one of the richest men in New South Wales. He was also one of the most quarrelsome.

He fell out with the master of the ship that brought him in the first place; with Lieutenant Colonel Grose who took over from Phillip; with Foveaux and the second Governor, Hunter; and he was quite ready to do battle with my grandfather, Governor King, who took over from Hunter in 1800. Since my grandfather intended Macarthur to be ruled, a clash was inevitable. It came about as a duel between Macarthur and Colonel Paterson, the senior officer, who was loyal to my grandfather. Seizing the opportunity to rid himself of a nuisance, my grandfather ordered Macarthur to England for court martial."

They were approaching Shelley's grave. Cypresses grew beside it, the same shade of green as Emmie's velvet dress. On the ancient wall above, Emmie read the poet's name and the inscription "*Cor Cordium*".

"I wonder what is the significance of '*Cor Cordium*'?" she said.

"It must be an allusion to the story that when Shelley's body was burned on the shore at Viareggio, his heart was plucked from the fire by Trelawny."

Emmie shuddered. Frederik did not tell her that the plot beside Shelley's grave had been bought more than forty years ago by Trelawny for his own eventual use. It was said that he had earned this macabre privilege by the stories he told his poetic friends about the East Indies. Frederik reflected that he was enjoying a tale which would become part of the way in which he saw Emmie in future, just as Trelawny was characterised for the poets by his stories, whatever their veracity.

"When Macarthur was sent home," Frederik continued, "it must have been during the war against Napoleon?"

"Yes. And he came back via the East Indies, where the British Resident was Robert Farquhar, a cousin of my late husband's mother," said Emmie, turning away from the grave. "The British wanted to prevent the Dutch colonial possessions from falling into French hands. Using a policy of temporary annexation, Farquhar took the chance to improve British command of the spice trade, only to find himself relieved of his post by the authorities in India for exceeding his brief. It was at this point that John Macarthur arrived, on his way home to face British justice. He urged Farquhar to argue his case. Farquhar did so and was shortly appointed by Clive as Commissioner for restoring the Dutch settlements."

"He had influence, then."

"As you will see. And Farquhar's family naturally wished to express their gratitude for Macarthur's support."

"Of course."

"On his return to England," Emmie proceeded, "Macarthur's court martial was thrown out because he had resigned his commission. He was now at leisure to pursue his own interests. These, by good fortune, coincided with those of the King.

"Now we come to wool, which at that time was a most valuable source of revenue. For many years King George had been worried that the best-quality wool came from Spanish merino sheep, and he wished to breed merinos in England. By the time of Macarthur's visit to England there was an established flock at Kew and the surplus sheep were being sold off at auction to approved buyers. The man responsible for the King's merino flock was none other than Sir Joseph Banks, whose interest in New South Wales dated from his arrival at Botany Bay with Captain Cook. His advice had been critical in founding the colony. Macarthur must have wondered on the journey back to England how to approach him, for he would need his support to get some merinos. At St Helena, he bought some natural history specimens and obtained a letter of introduction to Banks, but even so his prospects were not good. For Paterson, his duelling opponent, was a friend of Banks, and had just been elected a member of the Royal Society, of which Banks was President. Moreover Governor King, my grandfather, was also a friend and regular correspondent of Banks, and had lately written to him that Macarthur's fortune was made at the public expense, at the cost of great discord and strife.

"Nevertheless, when Macarthur returned to Sydney in 1805, he had with him eleven of Banks's precious merino sheep, purchased at Kew. He also carried a letter from the Secretary of War, Lord Camden, instructing Governor King to allow Captain Macarthur a 5,000-acre land grant."

"So how did he manage to get round Banks?"

"He passed him by. Robert Farquhar's father, Sir Walter, was a fashionable physician – to the Prince of Wales and Pitt, among others – people whose interests and opinions Lord Camden was well advised to note. Banks might have the ear of the King, but so did Lord Camden. The King might listen to Banks pleading my grandfather's cause, but a jumped-up naval officer in his dismal Antipodean roost, even if he was a loyal fellow, could not be allowed to stand in the way of the brave soul proposing to breed sheep on a decent scale whom Lord Camden described."

"So Banks was overruled?"

"Yes. And Macarthur named his new estate Camden Park, a snub to my grandfather and pious tribute to his benefactor. Nor was it coincidence that Macarthur was accompanied back to Australia by Robert Farquhar's first cousin, Walter Davidson, as well as his own nephew, Hannibal, my father. My father, by the way, did not take after his uncle in character, although his life was shaped by that apprenticeship and by his early friendship with Walter Davidson. Davidson's influence is also still felt in my family."

"And Governor King," said Frederik. "Was he a relation of your Uncle King, whom you mentioned the other day with Mr Ker?"

"He was his father."

"Then the Macarthurs and Kings must have mended matters . . ."

"John Macarthur never mended anything with anyone. In fact his feud with my grandfather was repeated with the next Governor, William Bligh. Not a man celebrated for his tact, Bligh began his term of office by informing the most powerful colonist that he was not interested in his sheep. Then he shouted at my grandfather in public, in front of Macarthur – allegedly reducing poor Grandfather to tears – that he was a fool for letting Macarthur get away with his knavery. Within months, Macarthur broke Bligh's authority and Bligh was bundled – trussed – out of office. For this, Macarthur was once again recalled to England, accompanied by my father and Davidson. This time, he was kept away from New South Wales for several years. My father – after collecting my mother, who was Governor King's daughter – returned. Davidson never did, despite

– 44 –

having acquired property there – but that's another story."

"Did Governor King not object to his daughter marrying a nephew of John Macarthur?"

"I suppose he must have liked my father and recognised that he was different from his uncle."

"And what became of John Macarthur?"

"His interests were looked after by his wife, Elizabeth, most capably. He was erratic and even more ungovernable after his final return, and ended his life in a straitjacket – 'a colossal wreck', perhaps – but his fortunes flourished. I'm afraid it is rather my father's works of which 'nothing besides remains'."

A figure in black had been approaching them along the path, arms swinging from side to side. As they drew close, they saw that it was an English parson, who raised his hat in greeting. "Good morning! Such a fine one!" he said, and his sweeping arm seemed to welcome them to the vernal cemetery.

Frederik raised his hat. "Indeed," he said. But he did not wish to be diverted.

*

The end of the Roman hunting season was marked by the Races, which took place in the grounds of a farm on the road to Frascati. Many of Emmie's friends were present, including all the Zieges. The cold had at last given way to a sweet warmth, which blessed the countryside with the scents of spring. A small orchestra near one of the tents was playing adaptations of Rossini overtures so that it seemed that everybody, not just the horses, was heading pell-mell for a finishing line. People switched from one conversation to another like bees among flowers; they shouted greetings and congratulated one another for no other reason, it seemed, than their continued existence.

For Emmie, the original Races, from which all others suffered by comparison, were those inaugurated by the Leslie brothers at Moreton Bay. She had heard how, before her own arrival on the Darling Downs, George and Walter used to arrive in a gig with top hats and canes like young bucks about town – and yet, as everyone knew, they had come ninety miles by dray over roads that broke bullocks' backs, leaving their station for days at the mercy of God knew what, for the sake of the sport and the sociability. And the Leslie horses were always at the front.

Emmie favoured a fine black horse with a white streak on his nose because he resembled her old friend Cap-à-Pie. He belonged to Signor Ceccini and he never won, as she knew he would not. It was Coco who showed the greatest flair for picking winners, despite her complete ignorance of horses.

"I ought to let you have my pocketbook," Frederik said to his niece. But he did not let her have it. Nor, Emmie noted with approval, did he make any bets of his own. She had not minded George playing whist on board the *Vimeira* with Governor FitzRoy, but otherwise gambling was a vice for which she saw no excuse.

Emmie was determined to go to St Peter's on Easter Sunday. This shocked Sydney, and, by way of compensation, she insisted on going to the Anglican service outside the Porto del Populo on Good Friday, trusting that the Good Lord would understand the consistency of her intentions on Easter Day while forgiving the blasphemous practice required for friendship's sake. When they had first discussed the matter at the Races, Madame Ziege said that if they wanted to go to a Roman service then they should go to Santa Martina.

"Why to Santa Martina?" Emmie asked.

"It is because of the link with Mr Thorvaldsen, the sculptor," Hannina said. "It contains the model which he used for his statue of Christ."

A sense of unreality settled on Emmie. What had she missed? She looked around at all the people jostling for position and wondered what she was doing there. "I don't think I quite follow," she said, but her words were lost in a crescendo of cheering as a race came to its end.

The next evening they went to see *La Traviata*, where Emmie was again disturbed by thoughts of George. As the stricken heroine lay dying, she could not dispel the image of his patient suffering and the peace he had at last achieved with his Maker, which he said he had learned from her but which she knew had welled from his uttermost soul. Witnessing this mysterious, blooming certainty of a better life had deepened her own faith.

As they were driven back to the Piazza di Spagna afterwards, Frederik remarked that the opera made him think of the poor Tsarevich at the Villa Bermont.

Huddled in a fur coat, a fox pelt encircling her throat, Madame Ziege said into the darkness, "I wanted to tell you about Thorvaldsen, Mrs Leslie." Her accent endowed her voice with an authority that forestalled the question of why she was thinking of him. "He was a sponsor at Frederik's christening. As I believe I told you, Frederik was born very quickly. It was early August, and it was hot. Excessively hot. We were returning to Tunis after some leave in Denmark. I had started with my three daughters on the journey from Leghorn to Rome, where we were to await my husband's arrival from Denmark – he had been detained, I forget why. A few days into our journey I was obliged to halt at a village called Monterosi, which had little in the way of conveniences for travellers. My plight was evident – there was no concealing it – and we were taken in by the innkeeper and his wife. It was all most biblical, I do assure you. Frederik was born at seven o'clock in the morning, whereupon a sort of preliminary baptism was performed by some women of the village. After washing him in a big water jar, they surrounded him with images of saints. It appeared to me that they had no expectation of the baby's survival, though I had no notion why. Of course, it was impossible to remain there, the *vetturino* had some mattresses arranged in the carriage and I, with my new-born son, was carried into it. We proceeded at a very slow pace to Rome, where it was said there was fever. Two days after our arrival, my husband arrived and Frederik was baptised properly, Carl Frederik Monterosi. Thorvaldsen and the writer Carsten Hauch were his sponsors. A few days later, both Frederik and I were taken ill, and we made haste to Naples. My husband feared for our lives, but we were saved. We returned to Tunis in October."

When Madame Ziege announced that she would join Emmie at the

Vatican on Easter Sunday, Emmie was not surprised. The experience Madame Ziege had described might have no direct bearing on her Lutheran beliefs, but an obscure sympathy for the women who had assisted at Frederik's birth could explain her readiness to worship at St Peter's when in Rome at Easter, in spite of her dutiful advocacy of Santa Martina on Thorvaldsen's account.

*

A cannonade on the castle of St Angelo announced daybreak on Easter Sunday.

At eight o'clock, the Zieges collected Emmie and Sydney from their hotel, and together they went to St Peter's. Despite arriving more than an hour before the service, they found that the great church was crowded. The best seats available were in a block near the back of the nave. Frederik sat with his nieces behind Emmie and the others. He knelt and offered brisk prayers for his family, for the forgiveness of his sins, for the safety of all those at sea – and another for patience this morning. Then he sat back in his chair and sighed. The warmth and the groundswell of voices were soporific. He hoped his mother would endure the ordeal. At her age, it was surprising that she should undertake it, and he was proud of her. He sat back and lifted up his eyes to the distant cupola, where the image of the Almighty looked down on His servants. There would be time enough to study the figures below Him and the words running round the base of the dome. He let his eyes drop. Just over Emmie's shoulder, he saw her open fan.

It was the one that she had at the ball, an ivory brisé fan whose ribbon ran through slots well below the ends of the rounded sticks. Fine vertical ribs formed a background to intricate carvings. Above the ribbon were individual figures. Below, on the guard, he could make out a dragon, a tree, and human figures. As before, the fan puzzled him. Emmie did not strike him as the sort of person to buy such a luxury, but she had made no reference to having connections in China. He wondered if Hannina had noticed it.

Emmie had taken this fan to the ball on an uncharacteristic whim.

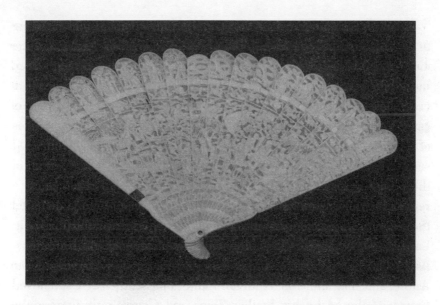

Had she wished to impress Frederik with it in some way, or to provoke his curiosity? It was too exotic, she now realised, a badge of vanity which he would find distasteful. For this morning's service, however, there was no doubt in her mind about taking it, for it had belonged to her mother, a wedding present from Walter Davidson.

At first, Emmie supposed that the vastness of St Peter's must distract worshippers from their prayers. An atmosphere more different to the sober focus of the congregation at St John's, in her childhood, was hard to imagine. She thought of the children gathering in their Sunday best at the landing-stage below the house and crossing the Parramatta River with their parents and Grandmother King, who were laced into their Sunday faces. They walked up to the church in a group; always laughing, but not too much because it was Sunday, and in church how grave they were! Foster, who later drew her likeness for Leichhardt, would have been there too. Sitting for the picture had seemed momentous for, though betrothal was not mentioned, her father's permission had to be secured before her image might be presented. Her young heart was reassured when her father accepted this strange man as a suitor for her. Within two years she was married to George, however, and there was never any doubt of her parents' approval.

But now only God could advise her, Emmie thought, endeavouring to pray. And when at last the service started, her heart rose with the music: she felt engulfed by the majesty of the advancing procession, the solemnity of the Pope on his portable throne, wearing the triple crown and brilliant robes. In front of him were carried seven golden candelabra and two huge fans of ostrich feathers, in which the eyes of peacock feathers seemed to be set. It didn't matter that she could see very little after this, or understand the Latin, for the grandeur of the place and the music's billowing resonance sustained her in a reverie, like a child, or an ancient votary. In the frescoes she fancied the dead were passing before her, a gallery of cameos: Mr Leichhardt; Lady Mary; her own unborn, unnamed child – familiar night visitor – its blood glistening on dark, intrusive, agitated hands; her dear sister Annie, and James; the old tenth laird and his wife; then at last beloved George, followed by his brother Tom, and George's tiny namesake nephew; then her father. But clearest of all was her mother, whose fan she now held tight. That Davidson, who gave it, had proved so ruthless and unnatural made it a strange treasure, but his wickedness served only to enhance its association with her mother's trusting nature. At this Easter service, Emmie felt as if she were holding a tiny, private symbol of the redemption that sinners might receive through intercession and the suffering of others.

By the time Hannibal had married the former Governor's daughter and returned to the colony to breed sheep, Davidson was set up in Macao with Portuguese citizenship. He sent a present for Maria, Hannibal's bride – a case of trinkets that were not to be found in the penal colony's stores. Among them was a fan, which she could stir her tea with for all he cared, provided she was impressed by it – which she was, but not in quite the way he anticipated. Maria was a modest lady, conscious of her duties and without the least inclination to frippery. It was not the objects themselves which pleased her but the gesture, which she interpreted as a disinterested act of kindness from an acquaintance in a distant land, and her new isolation at Parramatta heightened her appreciation. Not that she minded isolation: she was born on Norfolk Island, after all; and her marriage was happy. As one pregnancy followed another, and her life and the world seemed to settle into affluence, she would sometimes use the fan and be reminded of youth and adventure. She never cared for adventure herself, but initiative and the spirit of discovery were things she admired in men above all virtues, except Christian behaviour. Davidson's wedding gifts seemed to exemplify these, and they were rare enough in Australia – or so she supposed – to ensure that she would think well of him. But it was her mother's good fortune, Emmie reflected, to believe that the man in whom worldly and spiritual virtues had attained perfection was her own husband. She expected a man to achieve things in the world, and Hannibal did so, but he remained, as he began, a family man, a bulwark for her to lean on in her tribulations. For despite the blessings which God granted her through her family, her lot was not an easy one.

All her eleven children, including Emmie, thought of her as a kind of saint. While the childhoods of the older ones were haunted by the sickness of her pregnancies, the younger ones had the image of their mother's suffering instilled into their earliest consciousness. Their temperaments were seasoned by their mother's headaches, ruined digestion, and the nervous collapses brought on by her years of childbearing. Still she never complained: and as each child's sense of pain matured into an adult's, they awakened to a sense that her resistance to the dispiriting tendencies of her trials was akin to a miracle. For rather than depressing people with her ailments, her presence had invariably inspired merriment.

Emmie had nearly twenty years of her own frequent indispositions behind her now, but she had no children and could only speculate on how much heavier was her mother's burden. Her life was tormented by the presence of death as her mother's seldom was, but her discomforts must be negligible in comparison. Memories of her mother's cheerfulness, the strength she gained from her family and her faith in God, impressed Emmie. Her mother had accepted her sufferings with meekness, bowing to His will and trusting in His mercy, just as the congregation were now commanded: however magnificent St Peter's might be, that message was the same. Emmie recalled her mother's last letter, received when she and George were in England, written from the Inn at Ipswich on the Brisbane River while the cottage at Woodend was being prepared: *Dear, dear Emmie, what shall I say! that I miss you, that I think daily of you, you may indeed believe! When once I hear of you and good tidings I shall be happy and oh! a hundred things will interest me to hear, but to hear that you are both well will be the best assurance I can desire. All the arrangements dear George made tend to make us comfortable* – Yes, Mama had borne that trial too with fortitude, turned out of her home of thirty years, where she had raised her family, to start again as the wife of a provincial police magistrate, a job Papa was fortunate to get. *May God bless and preserve you both. That we may meet again is my fervent prayer.* But that prayer was not answered in this world, for the post soon brought a letter from Emmie's brother Arthur, a memorandum of her last days. On the day before her death, he wrote, Mama had dreamed of Emmie, whom she had told she would die: but Emmeline should not mind, for God ordered all things for the best; their mother was quite happy. She spoke to Papa of her want of faith and he told her that she should look upon the forgiveness of her sins as a certainty through Jesus Christ. She said that she believed His mercy was infinite; she was overshadowed by the spirit of the Almighty. After a short sleep she woke in pain, and soon afterwards, with Arthur and her husband at her bedside, she passed away.

Death had been a rare visitor during Emmie's childhood: she knew of no other large family where it had been so shy. Sometimes, she fancied that her mother had exercised some mysterious influence, as if her constant pain was payment for her children's rude health. Emmie did not imagine her own mourning to be evidence of love, nor in any way ornamental to her existence. She regarded inflated grief in others as vanity. She had longed to be free of it herself and now, perhaps, she was. How could she be lonely when she still had so many friends and brothers and sisters in the world?

There were others who were far more savagely tested by death, Alma for one. Emmie could not see her, but she became aware again of Madame Ziege at her side, intent on the high altar, where two deacons stood facing each other like angels at the Sepulchre while the choir sang the Sanctus. The sound swelled to its titanic climax and reverberated, before fading through long echoes to silence.

A fanfare of silver trumpets followed at the consummation of the sacrifice and Emmie's tears flowed. She fumbled for her handkerchief but was anticipated by Madame Ziege, who pressed her own into Emmie's hand. Emmie looked up and saw that Madame Ziege's eyes glittered behind her black lace veil. She sensed that they had been privy to something intimate in one another but, instead of feeling intruded upon, Emmie was grateful. After dabbing at her eyes, she handed back the handkerchief and pressed Madame Ziege's hand. Then she spread her fan and cooled herself.

The pomp and splendour with which Christ's resurrection was cele-brated affected Frederik like a revelation. Christ was risen indeed! And afterwards the crowd was dazed, like people returning from an arduous journey. Emmie turned to Frederik and her face shone. She smiled, shedding her remote world like a mantle. He was reminded of their visit to the Pallavicini Gardens and thought how odd it was that he should have shared two such experiences with her.

After the fatiguing service they lunched in the Zieges' rooms before Emmie and Miss Raymond retired for a rest. Frederik accompanied them to their hotel. On his left walked Sydney and on that side, he noted, he felt blank, while Emmie's presence on his other side was like a deep current, pulling and holding him with marvellous, steady buoyancy. Seeing the pins holding her hat in place, he imagined her slim fingers removing them, and the way she would shake her hair when she was upstairs in her room.

"You will join us for the Illuminations, I hope?" he said, as he took his leave.

With a smile, Emmie laid her gloved hand on his wrist. "Of course!"

Returning, Frederik wondered why Emmie captivated him so. They came from such different worlds! She couldn't even speak Danish! Yet the remoteness of her origins was part of her appeal. He had the impression that they valued similar things; that life might be lived afresh with her, and their pasts be a source of strength to one another.

If she did not know Denmark, now she was at least acquainted with his family. He urgently wanted to learn about her, to chart the route by which she had come to these shores, to feel the tides she had ridden and see the views she had seen.

He called for a cup of coffee and went to the smoking room, where he sat back in a leather armchair with his legs stretched out. As he lit his cigarette, he wished his brother Christian could meet her and help to clarify his thoughts. Nobody was more adept than he at judging ladies. If the gossip he had heard was correct, Christian's liaisons included the wife of the former Austrian ambassador in London and the Queen of Spain. Frederik checked himself – the thought of such affairs made him thankful for an instant that Christian was out of the way in Vienna – yet he longed for him, for his heart was loyal and his understanding swift. As for his sister, Clara, what would she make of Emmie? Her years in the West Indies had produced in her a lively sense of misfortune – as if she had been kidnapped rather than respectably married, and bore a grudge against those who had been elsewhere – and this inclined her to be sharp about others. She would find a way to mention Emmie's age and to note that she had no children, but she could not fail to find her amiable.

Frederik stubbed out his cigarette and drifted into sleep. When he woke half an hour later his legs were stiff and he had a headache. He stood up and lit another cigarette, which he soon threw into the fire. He recalled what he had been thinking about before he went to sleep and felt a prickle of excitement. His thoughts had run in this direction before, but never with such force. The situation had emerged so suddenly, and was so improbable, that he was afraid of having misapprehended it.

Later that evening in the Piazza, Hannina reassured him that he had not. Placing her hand in the crook of his arm, she followed his gaze. Emmie was not composed and grave as she had been in the morning, but alert for fun. Her eyes were large and dark in the twilight as they swept back and forth across the massive building, impatient for the first sign of a flare. She had linked elbows with Miss Raymond and Alma.

"My dear brother!" said Hannina, pressing her nose against his shoulder, and Frederik understood with a shock that she was congratulating him on the movement of his heart, as if it were evident to the world before he was aware of it himself.

All of a sudden the clock struck. Light blazed on every surface: each statue and column, each cornice and frieze – even the dome itself – ignited in a stupendous firmament of fire. To the very summit of the cross the building was so instantaneously lit up with lamps that it seemed the work of enchantment. Before the clock had finished striking eight, the gigantic architecture stood out against the dark sky like a fantastic celestial citadel.

*

When Emmie did not reappear for three days after Easter, Frederik feared that he had been too quick; his hopes were unwarranted, his desires misguided. He did not know what to do with himself and strode about the city in a fury at his own folly, dourly attempting good humour when called upon to accompany his nieces. Then a note was sent from Madame Ziege, at Hannina's instigation, asking Emmie and Sydney to join them on a visit to the Pantheon in the morning, with lunch afterwards at Spillmans. The invitation did not unsettle Emmie, for she was already unsettled: she had kept away from the Zieges on purpose, hoping that a little detachment would benefit her. She had been sightseeing in the Forum with her friends the Walsham Hows on one afternoon, and on the other she went to see the Coliseum with Mr Arbuthnot and Sydney. She was not naïve about her circumstances: she was a widow, no longer a young girl. If she read the situation correctly, a second chance had appeared in her life – for which she thanked God. Yet she was afraid, for Frederik was so very unexpected! Not in himself, for it was a mysterious sense of inner recognition that drew her to him, but in his worldly self. It was pleasing and reassuring that he was a naval officer, but Denmark – Russia – hadn't Greenland been mentioned? – all this would be a chasm in his past, illuminated perhaps by anecdote and incident but remaining substantially unknown. Her life at present might be unhinged from purpose and passion in the world, but it was tolerable, steady, and not without affections. To abandon such a condition for the moonshine hope of earthly joys might seem foolhardy, even greedy, but she could not leave Frederik out of account. And if she was not afraid to admit to herself that she liked him, allowing more than that would surely lead to a commitment that would jeopardise the modest happiness she now enjoyed.

After some thought, Emmie sent a note to Madame Ziege saying that she would meet them. Then she spent the evening writing to her sister Kate, who was still in England. She told her about the Easter festivities and how she thought of their Mama; she told her of some of the sights she had seen, and the Ziege family, and how strange it was that this girl from New South Wales should spend Easter in Rome in the company of Danes – so far from their dear old home! She made no mention of her predicament, but it was a comfort writing to Kate, for the bond she shared with her was like no other. When George first took Emmie to the Darling Downs, Kate was already there with Pat. Though pointed there by Cunningham, it was Patrick who had opened up that stretch of country. His Uncle Davidson saw to it that he could not enjoy it, but he and Kate made the best of it and were still remembered there as the first pioneers. Tiny, frail Kate had married a man whom everyone thought was about to be rich, but never in the trials that lay ahead did she flinch. Kate, even better than Emmie, knew the far horizons of virgin territory, the rigours of huge flocks and the brittle humours of exhausted men.

As Emmie wrote, the memory came to her of riding up to the Goomburra homestead with George one day, when Kate's back was so bad, and seeing her struggling to hold a half-broken horse while Pat was yelling at her to keep it still as he grappled with an injured hoof: George had wanted to strike his brother for treating Kate so. And even though the boys' uncle had hounded Pat to the brink of ruin, while George had made good, Emmie still felt the deference and trust due to Kate both as elder sister and as precursor.

Emmie's sleep that night was fitful. By morning her head ached and the cursed monthly pains dragged through her body so that she could not bear to go out at all. Sydney took an apologetic message to Madame Ziege. She said that Emmie hoped to see them in the next day or two but today she was quite laid up. She returned at once with a reply in Hannina's hand, which assured Emmie that they understood and wished only for her speedy recovery. Having no Danish, Sydney knew nothing of Hannina saying that she hoped that Emmie was not declining to be drawn. "I shall go and see her later," she said to her mother, for she liked to thrust forward her brother's purposes if she could do so unobtrusively, despite the little claw of envy in her heart: it was Frederik whom Alma adored because he had been so kind on the ship when her mother died (and would not *she* have been kind?) whereas it was she, Hannina, who had borne the burden of bringing up the girl. And then she added in English, "Miss Raymond, I take it *you* will not refuse us?"

Emmie slept through most of the morning. When she woke she was much better and embarked on a long letter to Mary Anne Ferguson, George's sister. She ordered a bowl of beef *consommé* to be brought at lunchtime, and afterwards she was surprised by a visit from Hannina.

"Frederik was taking the girls to look at some churches," Hannina said in her mild drawl. She noticed that Emmie took her cloak and hat herself instead of passing them to her maid, and hung them on the hat stand. It was the sort of gesture that she knew her brother admired for being natural, for some reason, and of which she herself was incapable. "Kind Miss Raymond was worried about leaving you, but I said she should go with them," she said. "Myself, I have no wish to stand about in cold churches. I would prefer to keep you company, Emmie, if you want it."

"I am delighted." Emmie indicated a chair near the fire. "Do sit down. Shall we ask for some tea?"

"That would be very nice."

Hannina observed Emmie's arrangements as she crossed the room to sit down. It was not large, but it was comfortable and clean. It was papered in dark green, which matched the upholstery of the chairs near the fire. Two windows gave plenty of light, even though the shutters were half closed. A *chaise longue* with a discarded green rug stood near the wall between them, and beside it was a table with a jug of water and an empty glass. A fire burned in the grate, although the weather was warm, confirming the impression that Emmie had been indoors all morning. An open writing desk occupied a space to the right of the door, with a blotting-pad and an unfinished letter. In the wall facing the fireplace, an open door led to the bedroom.

"You are well looked after here?"

Emmie replied that she was; and, as Hannina pulled her chair up near, Emmie noticed her fan, which she was toying with in her lap in such a way that Emmie wondered for a moment if she had been intended to see it. She said, "How fascinating! Please, excuse me – "

"Please!" said Hannina, handing it to her.

The slim sticks were of finely carved sandalwood. Above was a scene in gouache on paper of a Chinese lady with her servant beside a river. "It's just – no, it's not the same . . . I have one very similar at home . . ."

"It was given to me by Frederik," said Hannina.

"By Frederik?"

"Yes."

"Has he – I did not know he'd been to China – "

"Oh, he has been everywhere! But I believe he bought this for me in Irkutsk."

Emmie did not know where Irkutsk was. She opened the fan, enjoying the picture's swift revelation and the rattle of the paper as it whipped taut between the sticks, then she closed it again and handed it back.

"Where did yours come from?" Hannina asked.

"It was sent to me by one of my brothers-in-law who worked for the trading firm of Dent in Canton."

"Ah. But you have another, much finer one," said Hannina. "Frederik noticed it."

"Frederik noticed it?"

"On both occasions. You had it at the ball and again in church. Even in church, one notices such things."

Emmie suspected that she was being teased but she did not mind, so that Hannina was pierced by a little stab of resentment, even as she schemed on Emmie's behalf, because she saw that she would take Frederik away to a life of breakfast on the balcony with one's spouse, and children, and she would not care about the desolation of those whom he abandoned. Emmie told Hannina that the fan had belonged to her mother, and that having it with her in St Peter's had a special significance for her. "It sounds foolish when I hear myself say it."

"But," said Hannina, "I understand."

As Emmie described her mother a little, she elicited a sequence of approving nods from Hannina. "I think she would have been friends with my mother, do you think?"

"Do you know, I think she would!"

"You should tell Frederik about your fan, it would interest him," said Hannina.

*

After breakfast the following day, feeling much better, Emmie threw her shutters wide to the sunshine. Frederik was crossing the Piazza di

Spagna towards her hotel. He wore a new hat with a wider brim, almost like a wideawake, and he carried his cane. His gait was purposeful but light, that of a man on holiday with things to do. He was wearing a bow tie. He grinned when he saw that she was pleased to see him – such a smile, all roses and joy, could never be artificial – and privately blessed his sister, who had encouraged him to visit Emmie.

"Good morning!" he called, lifting his hat and spreading his arms.

Although instinct told Emmie that this was a moment she would remember for the rest of her life with pleasure, she moved away from the window.

"It is Captain Ziege," she told Sydney, who was reading about some scandal in a three-day-old newspaper at the breakfast table. "I shall go down to him."

As Emmie arrived in the foyer, Frederik stepped forward.

"Good morning, Mrs Leslie. You are better this morning, I hope?"

"Thank you. Much better."

"Then it is indeed a fine morning!"

No sooner had he uttered this compliment than he looked away, towards the street, as if to distance himself from his remark and draw her attention once again to the sunshine. Then he turned back. "We were planning a visit to the Villa Borghese this afternoon," he said, "and I wondered if you would care to join us?"

When she first saw Frederik approaching, Emmie had assumed that she would find herself going out with him at once. Now, though she was pleased enough with the invitation, the sudden prospect of an empty morning was an abysmal disappointment. He must have seen this, for he added, "Until then, if you care to continue discussing the weather or anything else, I am at your disposal."

Emmie laughed. "Thank you, I should like that very much!"

"Splendid!" he said, with a slight bow from the waist. "Shall we walk then?" He had an errand to run for Hannina which might form a destination, he explained, but otherwise they could please themselves. He would have to tell his family, so that they didn't make a plan for the morning which depended on his company, but Emmie might appreciate a moment to collect herself. He would return in fifteen minutes for her.

Emmie hurried back upstairs to inform Sydney. Retaining the dark blue skirt she was wearing, she exchanged her white blouse for another with narrower sleeves, which would enable her to wear her braided cream silk jacket. She put on a circular hat with a stiff crown and she carried her parasol.

Their progress was slow as they paused before each window with bronzes and mosaics in the Piazza di Spagna. Frederik told her how, when his father was excavating in Carthage and found a mosaic, the English consul, Sir Thomas Reade, was so jealous that he had it smashed in the middle of the night.

"Oh!" cried Emmie. Peering through a window at some sprightly mosaic fauns, she said, "It would be most distracting to have such things on one's floor, don't you think?"

"My ideal for floors will always be wood. Inlaid woods in geometric designs. Pearwood, rosewood." He had once been in the palace at Oranienbaum. Afterwards he was questioned by a fellow officer about the riches inside, the gold and silver and precious stones, but the thing he remembered above all else was the beauty of the floors.

"I favour wood too, but long polished boards. The dining room in my childhood home had the longest boards I have ever seen in a room, made from New Zealand pines. That is the standard against which I measure floors!"

In the Via Condotti they stopped at Miller's, the hatters, where Emmie examined an elaborate lilac confection with trailing tulle. She said she would buy it, and asked for it to be delivered to her hotel. But at the last moment she resisted squandering money on something she would never wear. "I would spend my life contemplating, or tripping over, a vast hat box – a monument to my folly!" she said to Frederik as they regained the street.

"You would give it away – "

"Am I to buy it then, knowing that I shall give it away?"

"But one must have a new one sometimes," said Frederik, tipping the brim of his own new hat.

"My dear Captain Ziege, permit me to say that your new hat is the very pinnacle of gentlemanly elegance!"

In this idle fashion they proceeded to a studio in a side street on the other side of the Corso. The studio belonged to a Monsieur Bergeret, whose speciality was painting on porcelain. Hannina had heard that he gave lessons in this art, and Frederik had promised to investigate. When they arrived, they found their way up a narrow staircase and were directed into a long, open room on the first floor, flooded with light, where Monsieur Bergeret, one foot on a rostrum, was even then regarding with despair an assembly of Roman ladies seated at tables, busy with paintbrushes. All around were stacked and hung hundreds of pieces of porcelain and majolica: plates, bowls, jugs, tureens, serrated dishes, sauce boats, all in varying states of decoration. Disengaging himself, Monsieur Bergeret raised his eyebrows high by way of interrogation, and Frederik presented his enquiry in Italian. Monsieur Bergeret's faltering answer prompted Frederik to address him again in French. This appeared to secure him a new friend, for the artist embarked on a peroration in which, Frederik later told Emmie, he declared that he would be only too delighted to share his modest skill with a Francophile lady.

Their task accomplished, Emmie and Frederik made their way back, so gradually that it seemed as if neither wanted to bring their outing to an end. Passing the door of Emmie's hotel, they continued up the Via del Babuino, all the way to the Piazza del Populo. There they wandered round the church, and Frederik pointed out the cloister in which Luther had stayed when in Rome. Then they returned down the other side of the Via del Babuino, still talking, where they were diverted into an establishment belonging to a cameo artist. Together they watched him scratch away at the image of a man with a nose like a hawk's beak. His answers to their questions were so concentrated round his prices – 100 francs in shell, 1,000 in *pietra dura*, 200 in marble – that they wondered if he was deaf, and departed. And at last, exhausted, Emmie went back up to her room.

It was during the afternoon, when they were sitting on a bench with Hannina in the gardens of the Villa Borghese, that Frederik remembered the sandalwood fan. He was sitting between the ladies, who each had their parasols up, though the bench was in the shade. Leaving

Coco and Alma to explore inside the villa, they had come outside to sit down because their legs were tired. Madame Ziege was already asleep in a nearby chair.

They had been silent for several moments, almost ready to doze in the warm, still afternoon, when Frederik said, "Hannina tells me that you have a fan like hers, Mrs Leslie. Do you have a link with China too?"

"Yes," said Emmie, "as a matter of fact, I do. Walter Davidson."

"Cousin of the man Macarthur met in the East Indies, who went with your father to Australia?"

"I congratulate you, Captain Ziege. You are most attentive!"

"Well?"

"You surely cannot want another of my stories?"

"I depend upon it!"

"Well . . ." she said. "Allow me to gather my thoughts," and she cleared her throat and placed her hands carefully on her lap, fingers pointing towards her knees like a sequence of rods that she would use as structure for her words. "Davidson was less interested in sheep than in the prospect of linking New South Wales to the China trade. The East India Company had a monopoly on all commercial operations in the Indian and Pacific Oceans, of course, but he took that for an inconvenience, not a prohibition; as also the regulations against shipbuilding in Australia. At any rate, the Pacific was a long way from interfering eyes.

"Davidson tried to run sandalwood from Fiji to Canton in partnership with Macarthur. My father was involved in some way too. I know that he went to China at least once. But the business did not work out as intended, and Davidson decided to cut his losses. He made a speculation in land along the Hawkesbury River, then joined John Macarthur when he was sent back to England. I believe they took their remaining sandalwood with them and sold it to an unsuspecting American sea captain at Rio de Janeiro.

"When he got to London, Davidson used his connections to get Portuguese citizenship. This enabled him to operate independently of the East India Company at Macao. Assisted by the loan of a thousand pounds from Alexander Riley, another Australian merchant, he founded a firm with a Mr Dent that traded successfully between Calcutta, China and London. Davidson did not forget Australia, however. In 1814, he sent a ship down to Sydney with tea. That's when he sent wedding presents to my parents, including the ivory fan."

"I was trying not to peer over your shoulder in church, but it seemed a very beautiful fan."

"Thank you."

"I imagined that you had a more recent China link."

"I did, but alas – no longer. It is the same one. I don't mean Davidson – though he is still alive – but it is the same enterprise. Davidson eventually retired to England, a rich man, but he was succeeded in China by two of his nephews, my husband's brothers: William, who did very well before going back to Scotland, and then Tom, who became ill, and died three years ago."

"Oh dear!" said Hannina. "What a tragedy!"

"Yes," said Frederik. "But there is more to this Davidson than meets the eye, I think."

"There is!" cried Emmie with feeling.

Frederik stroked his moustache with his right index finger. "Was he the cause of your husband and his brothers going to Australia?"

"Yes. The prospects for getting on in New South Wales were thought to be better than in Scotland. Davidson arranged for his nephews to be sent out to my father – apart from the eldest, whom he took with him into Dent's. But you still haven't told me how you got the Chinese fan you gave Hannina."

"Hum . . ." Frederik was not fond of talking about himself. It always felt like conceit. "I bought it from a Chinese merchant in Irkutsk," he said, recalling the fantastically caparisoned caravans coming in from Kyatka; snip-eyed gentlemen with points on their hats and points on their beards, indifferent to climate, borders, oddity, everything but their commerce; the reek of their tussocky ponies laden with bales of silk and bundles of artefacts; the shafts of perfumes and colours as leather flaps were unstrapped and cloths thrown aside.

"And where is Irkutsk?"

"Oh. In the very south of Siberia. It is a clearing house for Russian trade with China."

"And what – if I may ask – was a Danish naval officer doing in Irkutsk? It must be an awfully long way from the sea."

"It is. But its river runs into Lake Baikal, which is the biggest inland sea on the globe."

"And does the Danish navy often do manoeuvres on Lake Baikal?"

Frederik laughed. "It does not. I was working for the Russian navy. When my ship froze into the Pacific harbour, I travelled back overland to St Petersburg."

At that moment, Alma and Coco reappeared. They woke Madame Ziege and found hansom cabs to take them back to their hotels.

*

On the 22nd of the month the Zieges gave a dinner for their friends in Rome. Emmie and Sydney were there, of course; so too were the Walsham Hows, who enjoyed dinner parties, and Admiral Birch and his wife. Madame Ziege disliked the vicar because he was a prig. It mystified her that his compatriots found his company edifying. She supposed it was because what he represented conferred respectability: and not indifferent to that quality herself, she feared that failure to invite him and his wife would be ungracious. She found the Birches more congenial. They were critical of Nelson and they had played some good rounds of canasta with herself and Madame Mostraven.

"What else could one need besides the navy and the church?" said Madame Ziege, to which Emmie was still hunting for a reply when Alma cried:

"An artist!"

But there was an artist for Alma too, a Danish painter by the name of Bloch, whom Frederik had encountered in the Caffé Greco. The Muller family came, acquaintances from Copenhagen; the de Calsens, who had sometimes kept Madame Ziege company while the others went out; the Mostraven boys and their mother; and a Russian Count with whom Frederik had made friends.

Madame Ziege did not care for rich food, but she wanted to do things properly. The service was just as important, and in this regard the Russie staff were very amenable. A small dining room was reserved for her use, with good silver candlesticks and engravings of the ruins of ancient Rome; ten waiters were allotted to her party. It was the sort of occasion at which Frederik's unobtrusive efficiency was most in evidence, for those inclined to observe. Emmie noticed the grace with which he attended to the guests' comfort. His voice was never tedious, his tone never rough as he nourished lean conversations and intercepted loneliness farther down the table. While listening to Madame Mostraven on his left describe the wonders of the Sistine Chapel, he noticed that her son was tongue-tied before Coco's reserve: when his neighbour drew breath, he remarked to Coco, "Madame Mostraven reminds me that we have not visited the Vatican yet; they were there all morning yesterday!" And as Coco politely enquired of the youth how he had found it, Frederik's attention was once more devoted to Madame Mostraven. It was a trick that Emmie watched him repeat many times in different ways. Meanwhile, he managed the meal discreetly: turtle soup was followed by roast partridge with little deep-fried artichokes. The Reverend Mr Walsham How held one speared on the end of his fork for Frederik's particular appreciation. "Exquisite!" the parson pronounced. The occasion was seamless, and what made it so was Frederik's guiding hand. He had just signalled for the dessert to be served when he heard a genial but vehement opinion expressed by Carl Bloch.

Bloch was seated next to Alma. The two of them had been enjoying one another's company to the virtual exclusion of everyone else. But when Alma alluded to the lessons that her aunt had been receiving, Bloch turned to Hannina, who was sitting opposite him, to ask her opinion of them. Pleased by his interest, she told him about the procedure at Bergeret's studio, and such as she knew of his methods, the composition of his paints and the effects on them of different oven temperatures. He asked whether she herself had succeeded in producing anything and she said that only today she had painted two plates with scenes from Hans Christian Andersen's tales.

"Andersen? But he is a buffoon!" declared Bloch.

"Opinion is divided on that point," Hannina retorted.

Bloch shrugged. "A vain, semi-literate vulgarian!"

"You are young to hold such an opinion of someone forty years your senior. However, I believe my brother agrees with you."

The exchange was in Danish and, as Bloch turned to Frederik for support, Frederik laughed as he might at a favourite old joke and said to Emmie, "They are having a disagreement about the merits of Hans Christian Andersen." Then, in Danish, he added, "Some people choose to regard him as a sort of holy fool. I have always thought that his most revealing tale is 'The Emperor's New Clothes'."

"Hoorah!" said Bloch, raising his glass, and Frederik winked at him.

"My uncle says that Grandfather's cousin knew him, and thought he was an idiot!" Alma remarked to Bloch.

Madame Ziege leaned forward. "Mr Bloch," she said, "let me tell you. It is like this: Mr Andersen says in one of his books that when he was a boy, his singing used to be appreciated by his neighbour, Mr Ziege, his wife and their guests. But Andreas was a Councillor of Chancery and a Councillor of Justice, while Andersen was a pauper, so what does 'next door' mean? Andreas remembered a boy coming to the door sometimes who sang. They thought he was a halfwit and used to give him coins. Another of my husband's cousins was married to Christian Colbjörnson, Privy Councillor and President of the Highest Court of Justice. She gave the young man introductions, hospitality, and a blue Werther coat. So you see, in our family we agree to differ on this subject."

Everyone laughed politely, but Frederik was seized with mirth by Admiral Birch's immoderate bellow: he checked himself with a frown and said to Emmie, "Do you know Hans Christian Andersen's tales?"

"I hesitate to venture into this snake pit," she replied. "Didn't he write a story about flax?"

"I'm sure if he hasn't, he will. Perhaps he already has. What happens in it?"

"I cannot remember. I just remember that there is one about flax."

"I wonder why you remember that one?"

Emmie was uncomfortable, as if she were being asked for a solid explanation of something whose significance to her was circumstantial. Now that it was being scrutinised, she felt self-conscious. "It's a long story," she said. "Another one." And she rolled her eyes in self-mockery.

"Ah! But how delightful!" Frederik exclaimed, so that for an instant Emmie was afraid she would be obliged to tell it at once. But he forestalled her: "Don't forget it!" And her anxiety was transformed into pleasurable anticipation of a moment when he would ask her to tell it to him alone.

An opportunity occurred sooner than was to be expected. It happened that Sydney and Emmie were the last guests to leave, and Frederik accompanied them on the short walk back to their hotel. When they reached the foyer, while Sydney went up to bed, Emmie asked one of the staff if it would be too much trouble to bring Captain Ziege a nightcap, if he would like one? In two minutes she was sitting opposite him in front of the drawing-room fire. Her silk dress gleamed a deep, silvery blue in the light of the flames. He raised his glass of Madeira to her and said, "Your good health. Now, tell me about the flax."

Emmie set her cup of arrowroot down in its saucer and began: "It is a story I grew up with."

"So much the better!" He lit a cigarette.

She smiled. "Much more, in a way, than the ones about John Macarthur and Walter Davidson, which still touched raw nerves when I was a girl. They were spoken of in hushed tones, if at all, and never outside the family. Whereas the story about flax was a favourite of my Grandmother King's, who lived with us in her old age. Visitors would often question her about the colony's early years. If the opinions they expressed were misguided, which in her view they usually were, she would say, 'Pray, Sir,' – whenever she began like that, one knew she intended to tease – 'Pray, Sir, why do you think a colony was founded here?' When the answer referred to convicts, as it would, she turned to one of us for her answer. 'Flax!' we would say, and she would smile slyly, as if to press home the point that even the children knew the answer. 'Flax?' the unsuspecting guest would echo, whereupon she would deliver her oft-rehearsed lecture on the history of New South Wales."

Emmie took a sip of her drink. When she looked up at Frederik again, he nodded.

"'While sailing up through the Pacific in the *Resolution* on his second voyage in 1774,'" Emmie resumed in a quavery Devon voice, imitating her grandmother's, "'Captain Cook discovered a rock about a thousand miles east of Botany Bay, which he named Norfolk Island. It was noted that quantities of splendid pines and flax grew there.' I will dispense with my grandmother's voice if I may," she interrupted herself.

Frederik understood that the observation about Norfolk Island was not trivial, for the navy needed flax for making sails, and pines for spars; flax could also substitute for hemp in rope. As a naval power, Britain depended on these products.

"The scheme to form a colony at Botany Bay was first presented by an American loyalist, one James Matra, who was seeking fresh pastures for dispossessed Americans. When the French blockaded the Baltic, threatening Britain's flax supply, it was recalled that Matra had mentioned that flax was available in great abundance on Norfolk Island. Not that he had ever seen it there, but he had seen it in New

Zealand because he had sailed on Cook's first voyage on the *Endeavour*, and this gave weight to his view. It was supported by Sir Joseph Banks, who added that the flax was tall, its fibres nearly three times as long as those of Baltic flax. The scheme was widely ridiculed – it would in any case be in breach of the Company's monopoly – but when harnessed to the humane solution it offered to the convict crisis, it soon became politically expedient. Norfolk Island was small, only thirteen miles square, but unlike New Zealand it was uninhabited, so better for cultivation. It was to be hoped that the seeds might be transplanted to Botany Bay, where the space for developing the crop was unlimited. Chances for success might be remote, but the potential rewards justified the investment. If nothing else, it would stop the French settling there first."

Mention of the French reminded Frederik of a half-remembered point. "Didn't the French arrive there at the same time?" he said.

"Yes," Emmie said. "It is extraordinary, more fantastic than any story book. It was eight months since the Fleet had left Europe, two since they had seen another ship; they thought they were alone on the outermost rim of the world. They had got as far as establishing that Botany Bay itself was quite unsuitable, and while Governor Phillip went to investigate another site mentioned by Cook further up the coast, the rest of the Fleet was amazed to see two ships on the horizon. These turned out to be French, on a voyage of exploration commanded by Capitaine La Pérouse. Word came back quickly that Phillip had found the 'finest harbour in the world' – Sydney – and the Fleet hurried up to rejoin him. On the 1st of February, 1788, the day after they landed, after a terrible storm had torn into them during the night, Phillip addressed himself to the matter of flax – 'the next point in his monarch's instructions', according to my grandmother – and the establishment of a sub-colony on Norfolk Island. For this task he chose his aide de camp and protégé, Philip Gidley King, my grandfather."

"And what of the French, if I may divert you for a moment?" Frederik asked, as Emmie drew breath.

"It is no diversion," she replied at once, marvelling at her own fluency, which seemed to spring not from herself but from some quality of his concentration, his eyes that were at once so keen and so gentle. "Before preparing for this new expedition, my grandfather – the only officer who knew French – was sent in an open boat back to Botany Bay to speak to the French commander. He found him to be affable, grateful for the assistance proposed by Phillip, and talkative. Among his instructions from the French government, my grandmother claimed, was a specific command to carry home flax plants from the South Pacific. His expedition, nearly three years out from Europe, had just been at Norfolk Island but couldn't land because of the surf: he defied King to do so. It was, he said, fit only for eagles and angels. Then King left the French, taking back with him a few runaways who had escaped from Sydney through the bush – fortunately for them, as it turned out, for La Pérouse's expedition vanished. Thirty years later, it was discovered to have been wrecked off an island in the South Seas. The crew had been eaten by cannibals.

"My grandfather did succeed where La Pérouse failed. He landed on Norfolk Island with a party of twenty-two, fifteen of them convicts, nine men and six women. The ship then returned to Sydney. For seventeen months thereafter no-one called at Norfolk Island except to make one further delivery of convicts. During that time the settlement struggled against rats, parrots and gales. Priority was given to the cultivation of food, but, in any case, scant flax was found, and the two convicts who were supposed to be able to dress it proved helpless with this Antipodean variety. When two ships arrived from Sydney in March 1790, they brought news that the colony on the mainland was in a bad way. No relief had yet come from England. Instead of helping my grandfather, they brought him hundreds more convicts to feed. Governor Phillip had also taken this opportunity to rid himself of Major Ross, the officer in command of the marines at Sydney Cove, who had shown themselves to be tireless only in their sustained obstruction to Phillip's authority and refusal to co-operate with his plans for the colony's survival. Ross was to relieve my grandfather who, in the absence of any ship from England, was to take news of Governor Phillip's desperate situation back to the Admiralty.

"The French Revolution had occurred since King was last in England. But when he made his report to the Admiralty he was assured that the colony had not been neglected as he supposed, for a ship had been sent in 1789 with stores for two years: but she had struck an iceberg near Cape Town and was abandoned. Another convoy had been sent, which King unknowingly crossed with. As well as a new military force for the colony (including Lieutenant John Macarthur), it carried more than two thousand new convicts (of whom more than two hundred died on the way). Among them were skilled flax dressers, destined for Norfolk Island.

"My grandfather – promoted to Lieutenant Governor – was ordered to hurry back. Detaining himself only for long enough to get married, he was on Norfolk Island again in the autumn of 1791. Conditions had deteriorated so drastically under Major Ross that my grandfather described the island to the Admiralty as 'an exact emblem of the infernal regions'. The population was now near a thousand, and they were surviving on a diet of sea birds. Many convicts were too debilitated to work, others preferred to die, and the few free settlers were set in determined opposition to the military as well as to the convicts. Nevertheless, they were all drawn up in ranks in their rags and tatters to greet the Governor's Lady, my grandmother."

"I suppose she was as exotic as a giraffe to the assembled multitude."

"I don't expect it was noted that her dress was already a year out of date."

"And the flax?"

"The experts sent in King's absence had produced – guess . . ."

Frederik shook his head. "I cannot."

Emmie smiled. "Two yards of cloth. The coarsest my grandmother had ever seen, and quite unusable."

"Does it still exist, I wonder? It must be one of the costliest lengths of textile ever manufactured."

"Wouldn't it be amusing if it still exists? I don't expect my grandfather was amused though, for he attached the utmost importance to this aspect of his task; difficulties were no excuse. A new solution occurred to him when he recalled Cook's comment that the natives of New Zealand knew how to process their flax. In due course, the Admiralty approved his idea and Vancouver, who was bound for the Pacific, was instructed to kidnap some natives and deliver them to Norfolk Island. Accordingly, in April 1793, two frightened Maoris were landed on the island. They were further confused when presented with the flax. My grandfather realised that something had gone wrong with his plan and did not try to cajole them. Instead, he attempted to communicate and at last discovered that one was a priest and the other a warrior. On New Zealand it was the women who dressed the flax."

Frederik burst into laughter. "Oh! How dreadful! So the noble enterprise ended in farce!"

"Thirty years later, my grandmother certainly saw the funny side of it. But I cannot believe my grandfather ever did. I'm afraid the only consolation for his futile efforts and hardships on Norfolk Island was knowing he had carried out the King's orders to the best of his ability."

Frederik blinked and set his empty glass on the table beside him. His own experience as a naval officer assured his sympathy with Emmie's grandfather.

"Anyway, now you know why flax featured in my grandmother's conversation," said Emmie. "Her life was shaped by the quest for it. It is no wonder my family took note when Hans Christian Andersen wrote a story about flax."

"Yes, I do see," Frederik said, and threw another cigarette end into the fire. "What a sorrowful tale!"

Emmie stifled a yawn. "Excuse me!"

"What became of the Maoris?"

"They were returned."

"There are a hundred more questions I should like to ask," he said, "were it not for the lateness of the hour."

*

When Frederik took his family and Emmie to a concert in the Sala di Dante behind the Trevi Fountain, he knew only that it was an evening of Bel Canti, including several items by Rossini, because the tickets were bought in haste through the hotel and he had not inspected the programme in detail. He was therefore taken by surprise when he heard the opening of Paisiello's "Il Mio Ben Quando Verrà". Like a ship slipping anchor and drifting with the current, he was borne away on a wave of recognition to another concert hall, in Irkutsk, which existed for him in an imaginative place so separate that there never was a way to give it voice. The song was moving because of its self-possession. The sweet melody moved in gentle, steady circles, lifting to vast sighs, then settled back with heart-rending dignity. It caught the measure and depth of sadness by containing it within a rounded

 cycle of emotions. He closed his eyes and crossed his wrists, touching each cufflink with the tips of his little fingers. Made from cuts of tree agate and surrounded by diamonds, they were a gift from Mouravieff, Governor General of Eastern Siberia. They have since been stolen.

Frederik filled his lungs with a gulp, then pulled himself in and glanced at Emmie's profile in the dim light to see if she understood the words. What would she think if she did? "When my beloved comes to see his unhappy love the sunny shore will be covered in flowers. But I do not see him, alas, my beloved is not coming. Gentle birds, when he tells the breezes of his passion and his lamentations, he will teach you a sweeter song. But I do not hear him. Who has heard him? My love has fallen silent. Thou pitiful, weary echo of my tears, return to him and he will softly ask for his bride. Hush, he calls me, hush . . . alas! No, he calls me not, O God, he is not there." Emmie's innocence of the song's meaning seemed to Frederik to augment its poignancy. The sound of the music might play on her as the wind on an Aeolian harp, and it would find chords already marked out, harmonies already tuned. A fully formed world was contained in the gentle cast of her face, with infinite stories, and perhaps secrets, to which he had found some access. He wanted to know more, always more, to hear her voice, to see the freight of her life and meet its people. And he was unnerved by his own curiosity, for knowledge generated responsibility.

The Paisiello song reminded Frederik that he had yet to visit the Villa Volkonsky. When he mentioned in Russian at the Embassy that he had known General Mouravieff in Irkutsk, invitations were thrown at him on behalf of every Russian in Rome, and he was urged to go at once to the Villa to present himself to Prince Volkonsky. The "Siberian Princess", they told him, had herself visited her cousin at the Villa. Frederik knew that the old Princess Zenaida, to whom the Villa once belonged, had died three years before, and he knew that Maria Volkonsky, about whom he had heard so much in Siberia, had also died. But he had not expected to discover her traces in Rome. As he felt the pull of the huge welcome, he recalled the stupefying conviviality he had witnessed in Russia; and even as he thought how pleasant it would be to let it overwhelm him, he foresaw the loneliness that would inevitably follow and shied away. He wanted just to walk with his family and Emmie in the Villa's grounds. So he wrote his application and sent it through the Embassy.

The Villa was only open for two days each week and they spent the day waiting for the permit's arrival in the Vatican museum. So they were ready for a morning's exploration of the sculptures and antique statues of the Villa's formal gardens. A magnificent view of the Campagna opened from the terraces, which was bisected by the Claudian aqueduct. It being spring, the air was not hazy and Frederik could distinguish the arches far into the Alban Hills. He thought of his father's watercolour of the aqueduct on the plain behind Carthage, only six inches high but unwinding to a width of more than five feet, with each intact and semi-ruined arch precisely represented. It exemplified his father's passionate devotion to detail.

A huge bust of Alexander the First stood between two lines of low shrubs at a focal point of the garden's symmetry. Hannina said it was out of place in a classical context.

"Scarcely classical," Frederik said in Danish. The garden was imitation Renaissance and it annoyed him that his sister should describe it as classical. Had she learned so little from her childhood? "Anyway, it was built by a Russian family, and they still live here."

"Which is why we are here, I take it," she answered.

Frederik had been going to tell them about the Volkonskys. Now he was peeved. There was an implicit rejection in Hannina's tone, as if his Russian experiences were no concern of hers. And though she upbraided him for not speaking more about them, he now felt loath to share with her the scrap that he had been on the point of offering.

"What was that?" said Emmie.

Frederik was at once ashamed of himself. "I rudely told Hannina that the garden was Russian neoclassical, not classical."

"Is there so considerable a difference?" said Emmie, straightening up, for she had been sniffing a rose.

Coco's eyes widened. It was not a question she would have asked her uncle, though all he did was shrug and say, "Perhaps not!" Then he laughed and continued, "What I should have said, Hannina dear, is that I don't believe a bust of Alexander the First is out of place in a Volkonsky garden."

"You must explain a little, Frederik dear," Hannina replied.

"If I am not mistaken, a Prince Volkonsky was aide-de-camp to Alexander the First."

"How do you know these things, Uncle Frederik?" Alma asked.

"Well . . ."

They had gathered on a terrace, where Frederik sat in the middle of a bench. In a long, single wave of doubling fabric, Emmie and Hannina sat on each side of him, then Alma came in beside Emmie, while Coco perched herself on the bench's arm beside Hannina, her back straight, her hat tilted very slightly forward.

Frederik removed his hat and held it by the crown against his chest while he ruffled his hair with his other hand. Then he replaced it and said, "I was reminded of the Volkonskys at the concert the other evening. One of the songs, by Paisiello, was a most beautiful lament for a vanished love. I had heard it before in a concert hall in Irkutsk, which was built by Princess Maria Volkonsky, known as the Princess of Siberia. I came across her name and that of her husband many times while I was there. He was the younger son of an aristocratic family, who joined a plot to reform Russia. On the first day of Nicholas the First's reign, 14th December, 1825, the conspirators staged a disastrous rebellion. Together with about a hundred others, Volkonsky was stripped of his title and his immense riches and sent to hard labour in Siberia. His wife followed him, despite the disapproval of the Tsar and her family. She was one among several wives who lived as best they could outside the prison. Many, including her, had left children behind, and many now had new ones. It was the women, and none more so than Maria Volkonsky, who helped sustain the group's spirits over the years. The commandant allowed his unusual prisoners special latitude as he grew used to them, and he trusted them to abide by an unwritten code. Provided they adhered to all the formal terms of their sentences and sought no direct contact with the west, they and their wives could come and go around the prison. He managed it as a sort of closed community. In due course the prisoners' hard labour came to an end and they went off to their places of exile. Volkonsky was sent west to a place called Urik, about twenty miles from Irkutsk.

"Twenty years had passed when they were astonished by the appointment of a man called Mouravieff to the post of Governor General of Eastern Siberia – "

"Was he the man . . . ?" began Hannina.

"Yes, he was the man I stayed with," Frederik replied. "What was remarkable about his appointment was that he had a number of cousins among the conspirators, including one of the men – boys really – who were hanged. Mouravieff did not have the power to release the prisoners, nor would he have wished to. He did not share their beliefs. His concern was to develop Siberia, and his genius was to recognise that among these men and women was a fund of knowledge that could be put to use. He enabled them to contribute to the communities in which they lived, with their knowledge of local languages and medicine, a hundred things that were valuable. An example of the way this could work was produced by the death of Maria Volkonsky's mother.

Suddenly she was to come into a lot of money which ordinarily she would not have been allowed. Mouravieff understood that she would spend it in ways that would benefit Irkutsk. So he let the money through and she built a foundling home, then a hospital, then a concert hall. She was a public benefactress and, like the rest of the exiles, she was revered by the people of Siberia. The story ought to end there, but it does not. After Tsar Nicholas died there was an amnesty. Many of the so-called Decembrists had died by then, but most of those who were alive, including the Volkonskys, came back. Twenty-nine years had passed in which all trace of them was supposed to have vanished. But they had become legends.

"I met many people who knew the Volkonskys. Not so much Prince Sergei, but the Princess and also the son, Misha, who was selected by Mouravieff to work for him. That was typical of the man. Although the children of the prisoners were intended by the Tsar to remain uneducated serfs, they were the best-educated children in Russia. Misha was not free to leave Siberia, so Mouravieff said, 'He's just the man I need!' But by the time I was there, three years after the amnesty, he had left.

"I was told at the Embassy that he got engaged here, in Rome. The next year, his mother came to visit her husband's cousin, Princess Zenaida, who lived here. She was a famously eccentric character. She converted to Roman Catholicism, which angered the Tsar, and she made her house a gathering place. She gave very generously to charity – even her clothes in the street once, it's said. She was Maria's most faithful correspondent through her years of exile, sending her music, seeds, books and so on. It is odd to think of the two of them walking in this garden. It's only three years ago, and since then both of them have died. They are figures from a different world."

Coco had not moved, but she had long ago stopped listening. The idea of exile made her think of her own upbringing in the West Indies, where her father had been governor of the Danish possessions. The caress of the warm garden and the sight of flowers made her think of the garden in St Thomas, fenced off from the outside world and too often forbidden from within, as her parents made her do her lessons in the house. Even now she missed her nurse, Valeria, who taught her to embroider so that a bower grew in her lap of violets, roses and lilies; and the cook who once, long ago, hid her in the laundry when her mother was looking for her. It had astonished her to find a friend in the cook, and she did not understand why she wanted to protect her from a punishment that Coco knew she deserved. Coco did not now recall what she had done, but she did not doubt the necessity of her mother's strict regime any more than she ever had.

Coco took the others' silence to indicate that they had not been listening either, but she was mistaken. Alma was thinking of the noble women, bereft of their children, sacrificing themselves for their sad, heroic husbands; of her countryman who wrote a whole book about Abraham and Isaac, although he was said to be an atheist; and she wondered what Bloch would have made of this story – perhaps he would paint a scene from it.

Hannina did not see why they had been subjected to this rambling story of seditious Russians. Russians were always excessive in their behaviour. Nor was there any precept or intent in it, so far as she could divine. "Frederik," she said at last, "your stories are always about other people. It was a wonderful story, most romantic, but I do not understand why you told it."

"The Paisiello song was said to be a favourite of the Princess Volkonsky's," Frederik said, and Alma wished she could hear it again. "That's why I heard it in Irkutsk, and why I recognised it here."

"Well, but what of it?" Hannina insisted.

A picture had formed in Emmie's mind, vague as a loose formation of birds that flew up from beyond the terrace, of Frederik wrapped in a bearskin, listening to strangers, his agate eyes absorbing everything as he went about his business – whatever that was – and generating in his mind a web of images and tales which could emerge again through any number of different stories. His presence shone through his story like the light behind the arches of the aqueduct, both as listener and again as teller. The characters and events of the story meant nothing to her except as extensions of his own experience, and she declared to Hannina: "But it *is* about him – about your brother!"

"Is it?" Frederik said, and pulled out a handkerchief to wipe his face. He had been on the point of telling about the cufflinks, but now decided not to. Emmie hadn't noticed them, and the story would probably seem out of place.

*

Frederik had formed the habit of walking out early each morning. Thirty years' naval service had made sleep impossible after five-thirty, at which hour the ladies were still fast asleep, so he could please himself. Sometimes he read before getting up. Often he walked up to the Pincio, perhaps stopping on the way at a barber in the Piazza di Spagna; or he might go down to the Caffé Greco. But he was always at Piale's reading rooms when they opened at eight o'clock, and there he would read the newspapers until his family expected him back.

It was at Piale's that he learned of the Tsarevich's death. The report said that Princess Dagmar was with him at the end. Frederik hurried back to inform Hannina and his mother. The death was not unexpected, but there would be repercussions. The question of Dagmar's marriage would be raised once more. Princess Alexandra would wish to visit the continent if the constraints of pregnancy and British diplomatic protocol allowed. Frederik was also anxious to alert his family to another, more immediate and personal point concerning the cause of the Tsarevich's death. While he understood that it would be impossible to avoid discussion of the tragedy, he relied on their delicacy when referring to it with Emmie, for her husband had also died of consumption. Madame Ziege and Hannina did not miss the implications of this remark and enjoined Coco and Alma on no account to speak of the Tsarevich's death with Emmie. To one another they spoke about little else. Telegrams were despatched to Nice and to Princess Alexandra; letters were written to Christian in Vienna, to Clara and the Bagges and the Meldals in Copenhagen, and to Bille Brahe.

Emmie found it strange that the Zieges' response to the Tsarevich's death was so muted. Perhaps they were not so close to the royal family as she had supposed.

Piale's was located on the corner of the Piazza di Spagna, a few doors from the Hotel Possidoni. As Frederik and Emmie wished increasingly to be alone together, they found it a convenient meeting place. It was a large establishment where Emmie's arrival excited no remark. Knowing that Frederik was comfortable there on his own meant that she could join him at her leisure. He would be sitting in the same green leather armchair, screened by a newspaper but vigilant. She would pause for a moment to see if he registered her presence. He might not have looked up at someone moving a few yards away, but he noticed the stillness of her figure so close.

Less than a week after the news of the Tsarevich's death, Frederik was waiting for her with some nervousness, for he had come to a decision. His mood was confused, however, by a report in the newspaper, and he failed to direct their conversation as he had intended. When Emmie arrived she indicated the paper and asked if anything had happened. Instead of evading the question, Frederik answered, "The commander of the *Beagle* has killed himself."

"I beg your pardon?"

"Captain FitzRoy has cut his own throat, apparently."

"Oh! How dreadful!"

Talking was forbidden in the reading room. Already newspapers were being rustled in objection. Without further ado, Frederik collected his hat and they went together into the street.

"I thought for a moment you meant Wickham, my brother-in-law," Emmie resumed, as they turned into the Via Bastianello. "But he died last year."

"I'm sorry. But I don't understand what has he to do with the *Beagle*."

"He was First Lieutenant under Captain FitzRoy, and when FitzRoy gave up the command it was given to Wickham."

"And he was your brother-in-law?"

"He had remarried. My sister Annie died long ago."

"But you knew FitzRoy?"

"I only met him once, as a girl," said Emmie. "To tell the truth, I had forgotten he ever commanded the *Beagle*. When I was younger, the *Beagle* meant Wickham."

"Because of your sister?"

"Partly. Annie was engaged to him before he took up his command and went off to finish our uncle's survey of the north coast of Australia. He was away for two years and sent letters to Annie when he could. We heard about the discovery of the Victoria River and the Timor Straits, and the cache of Aboriginal art – the so-called fetish objects – on Depuch Island. Our family naturally took a great interest in what he was doing."

"It was FitzRoy who commanded the voyage that Charles Darwin wrote about."

"Oh, yes. Mr Darwin. I believe Captain FitzRoy invented a storm-warning signal system as well."

Frederik laughed. He had read Darwin's account and he had presumed that Emmie's connection with one of the most celebrated modern voyages would guarantee her interest in its commander, but she seemed not to be interested in him at all. "I believe he did," he answered, "though I wasn't aware of it until reading the paper this morning. Nor did I know until today that he was a man of strong faith. It is said that he was much distressed by the ways in which Darwin's discoveries are thought by some to undermine the truth of the Bible."

"He is a tragic character," Emmie agreed. "As for Mr Huxley, I should be vexed to recall that he came to visit us at Canning Downs. But he was an entertaining man – he did a charming sketch of the house – whereas Captain FitzRoy, according to his brother whom I knew well when he was Governor of Australia, was not entertaining at all," said Emmie.

They were climbing up the steep steps to the summit of the Pincio. They were both rather out of breath and Emmie had to hold up her dress with both hands so that she didn't catch a toe in the hem. Frederik was ready to give support, but it was awkward. Both regretted not having taken an easier route.

When they reached the top, Emmie said, "Will your family not be wondering what has become of you?"

"I am sure they will be able to amuse themselves this morning," he said.

They approached a stone balustrade from where they had a view of Rome's rooftops in the morning sunshine. "They will think you have deserted them," Emmie said.

Frederik was leaning forward with his arms crossed on the ledge. Now he turned back to face her and smiled. "They will not," he said.

"You are very sure of that."

"I've no doubt that my mother and Hannina will guess what I am about."

"And will they approve?"

"I believe so."

But the question of precisely what Frederik was about remained unstated. As it hung in the air, Emmie realised that with her last rejoinder she had implied her understanding of what was happening.

"Yes," Frederik said, standing straight before her. "I have a question I want to ask you."

"Is it not a marvellous view from here? There is the Capitoline – "

"A question – "

"I believe I can see the Via Condotti – "

"A question," he repeated.

Suddenly turning her back on Rome, Emmie stared at him, as if he had pinched her. "Oh!" Her eyes were huge and liquid.

Frederik braced himself, as if he were about to ski down a long, steep slope without any means of control. In Greenland, he used to discern bumps by looking at the shadows ahead. If necessary, he would snap out of the skis and throw himself into the snow, leaving the skis to run away by themselves. Now he felt that he was past the point where he could jump clear. He just had to hope. If the first question – whether there was any reason she knew of why she could not have children – was unaskable, he would have to plunge on to the second.

"I wanted to speak of love," he said. "I had been coming to doubt whether I would ever find myself speaking of it to anyone. Now I find it surprisingly easy. God has brought you to me, Emmie, and I love you. Please will you be my wife?"

"Oh!" she cried again, and gave him her hand.

PART TWO
Marriage

Malvern, September 1865

FREDERIK had a first-class compartment all to himself on the midday train to Malvern. His head rested against a board upholstered in a pattern of red flowers, which matched the seats. Despite the floral confusion – the flowers were both rose and carnation and yet neither of them – he was comfortable, and more content than he could remember ever having been. After so many years of dissolving horizons, he was fast approaching a resolution in his life: marriage, stability, a future – perhaps children; at any rate, a union with Emmie, the idea of whom, it now seemed to him, he had carried within himself since boyhood. In three days' time he was to be married. In the rack over his head were two leather bags containing those of his belongings that were not in his tin uniform box and his trunk in the guard's van. Besides a few oddments long in the care of his mother or his brother, this was the sum of his worldly possessions. Crockery and furniture – chattels – were not part of a sailor's life. What could not be transported was an encumbrance. He was looking forward to setting up home with Emmie, but he imagined it as a place where they unpacked their luggage together rather than the deposit of a lifetime's accumulation of objects.

When he had taken leave of his family in Copenhagen two days ago, summer had surrendered to autumn. Here in England it was fighting a valiant rearguard action, which Frederik interpreted as a sign of God's favour. He had never seen the English countryside at this season and it was wonderful to him. He felt enfolded and warmed by the soft contours, as if the earth itself had breathed in the summer air. The lush hedgerows divided the landscape into neat views: cows, sheep and horses mooched in the green fields; snoozing labourers lay curled like puppies in the shade of a haystack. Even the wild flowers along the railway line offered themselves to the traveller like posies in a lavish Eden. It was no wonder, Frederik thought, that the English were so complacent if this was their home – and yet how different from the frenzy of London!

He had been suffering from a cough in Denmark, which worried him enough to seek reassurance. The doctor had tapped his chest and assured him that it was a result of the unseasonal dampness. Instead of reminding the man that he was used to moisture in the air, Frederik paid him gratefully and took his leave. London had exacerbated the complaint, yet he remained confident of its being soothed by the mild country air. He was happy; as avid for the future as a young cadet – and had been so since meeting Emmie in Genoa. That he had not seen her now since the end of May caused him no anxiety, for he was sure of her and of their decision to marry. The relative ease with which they found time to be alone following their engagement reflected that they were both of an age and station where supervision was not appropriate.

For Alma's and Coco's sakes they had not wanted to cut short the tour. Emmie came with them to Sorrento and Naples, where it gratified Frederik to witness how truly welcome Emmie was in his family. After they arrived in Marseille, however, their intention of getting married in the summer was thwarted by a telegram which arrived from Copenhagen informing the Zieges of the death of Frederik's paternal uncle, General Anton Ziege. Frederik was obliged to hurry back to Denmark with his family, while Emmie returned to England with Sydney. She proceeded to Malvern with her ailing sister, Lucy Master, and her husband, where the three of them took the hydropathic cure while awaiting Frederik's return.

Relations between Tuxen and Anton Ziege's families had sometimes been uneasy, but there was no question that the General's funeral must be attended. There was some concern over the fate of certain things in his possession. As eldest son, Tuxen had inherited anything of family significance from their father, but so much of Tuxen's life was spent abroad that Anton had become *de facto* custodian of an assortment of objects and papers. When at last Tuxen came back to live in Denmark in 1840, he had been too preoccupied with the task assigned to him by the new king, Christian VIII, to reclaim everything at once. After his death, his family had deferred recovering what was due to a more suitable time. Now that Anton was dead, Fru Ziege believed that his family had things which belonged to hers. Frederik doubted it. He had always understood that his father's collection of coins and antiquities, his pictures and diaries – which the family would have treasured – were entombed in the Royal Archives. Because Christian VIII valued his work, Tuxen assumed that later kings would do so too, and he had donated everything, neglecting his family's inheritance for the sake of an imagined contribution to the royal good, which was equivalent in his mind to the public good. Frederik had not looked at his father's papers. He was certain that they would reveal a man of stupendous diligence but he was afraid too that they would show his father to have been deluded. For what had his hard work achieved? Not much for his family, to be sure.

Yet Frederik only felt fonder of his father's memory because of that. For though Tuxen Ziege was a diplomat, his sphere that of the Court and international affairs, he was not a worldly man, and his older son resembled him in this. Frederik was not afraid of anyone thinking that he was marrying Emmie for her money, but he regretted that he had nothing to share with her; nothing but himself – and then it helped to consider his own identity in terms of his family. It was this desire to share that now made him remove from the inside pocket of his frock coat a small case which he had persuaded his mother to part with. Inside was a gilt and blue enamel propelling pencil with a diamond set in the top. A useless article, altogether unsuited to writing, let alone in a train where he might be robbed of it.

The precious curio reminded Frederik powerfully of his father. He knew that it had been given to him by the French King's son, the Duc d'Aumale, Governor at the time of French North Africa, following an expedition in 1837, but he did not know for what he had earned this

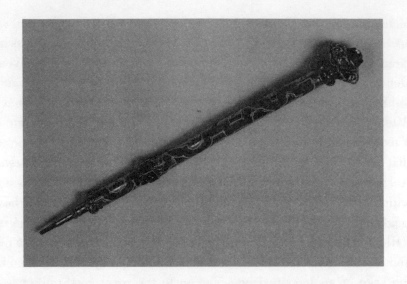

valuable gift. If the Duc wished to reward him, there were more conventional forms, and indeed the class of his Légion d'Honneur was raised in 1841. It was odd that there should be so much obscurity about his father's activities when he himself was so precise. When they were in Naples, Frederik had heard his mother tell Emmie that his father had first been awarded the Légion d'Honneur when the Emperor Napoleon and Josephine had visited the Danish frigate on which he was serving in 1814. A strong wind was blowing as the Empress negotiated a swaying gangplank, causing her some difficulty with her skirts, but the prompt action of the alert Midshipman Ziege saved her from embarrassment. Madame Ziege said that he was awarded the Légion d'Honneur, fifth class, for this intimate service. It was a ridiculous tale which would have been anathema to her husband, for the award was plainly made in 1833 after the publication of his book, dedicated to the French King, about his Carthage excavations. Frederik did not altogether discard the tale, however: it was more amusing than the truth and, in some mysterious way, it captured a pleasing aspect of his father. For his father had been an observant and energetic man, attentive to everybody's comfort save his own: in this story he was conjured to life as a young man in a way that his naval record failed to reveal.

In 1837, in Paris, his father had founded "La Société pour l'exploration de Carthage". His partner was an Englishman called Sir Grenville Temple, whom Frederik's family supposed – because of his sensible alliance – to be exempt from the offences of his countrymen. He had sufficient money to finance a joint expedition, and he had himself travelled in the Tunisian interior as far as the holy city of Kairouan in 1832, relieving the country of monuments whenever possible, after the example of the ignoble Lord Elgin in Greece. Accompanying a French military expedition to Algeria, he and Ziege witnessed the capture of Constantine and then proceeded in a French schooner via Bône to Tunis. They did some archaeological work on the way which they wrote up together in two reports. It emerged that Temple had informed Sir Thomas Reade, the British Consul General in Tunis, of their intentions in advance, with the predictable result that Reade obtained from the Bey of Tunis a monopoly for himself over excavations in the centre of Carthage. When Reade destroyed one mosaic, Ziege took Temple to the site of another, larger one representing a willowy naiad lying on a galloping sea horse, and left him in charge of the excavation. Later, he learned that the mosaic had been ruined because Temple thought himself too grand to supervise the workmen personally. Ziege could forgive the flaunting of wealth and even indiscretion, but not incompetence, and so he left Temple behind to deal with Reade's agents and continue the destruction of ancient Carthage by himself. Other than that his father disappeared into the hinterland, Frederik had no certain knowledge of what he did for the next two months.

He had an impression of his father riding slowly over baked and stony ground in the company of his dragoman; reaching for his notebook and pencil to draw the arc of a hill in the distance; dismounting to scrape sand from an antique funerary slab; transcribing Punic or Latin inscriptions; doggedly pacing and measuring a ruined temple; bargaining in Arabic with a knot of Bedouin for some ancient coins; recording, by the light of a campfire, recording every detail, always recording, for the benefit of his Crown Prince. Frederik thought he remembered the dragoman, Sidi Rais Ali, from when he was a boy.

He was the janissary and interpreter at the Danish Consulate then, a benign old Mamluk who indulged the Ziege children; his swathed and turbanned figure was the genie of their story book. The news that he had accepted an invitation to work again for his old master came in a letter from their father which announced that he had purchased three horses and some baskets for the trip, as well as salt, cotton handker-chiefs, perfume and gunpowder as gifts for the Bedouin; also supplies of tea, sugar and coffee for gifts as well as for personal use, together with medicines, roasted barley flour mixed with aromatic and fresh herbs which they thought was good for mixing with dirty water, and of course spirits for use in a lamp so that he could heat water. There was no aquavit or wine since they were in Muslim territory; his uniform had been altered so that it looked like that of the Bey's cavalry.

When Frederik's train stopped in Oxford he bought an apple from a hawker on the platform, who passed it through the window. It was the first Frederik had eaten this season and it was crisp and sweet. As he ate, it occurred to him that his image of his father when trav-elling derived from letters resembling shopping lists, but he had never regarded them as inadequate. As for what his father was actually doing on that trip, he supposed the answer was in the Royal Archives for posterity, unless the Prussians one day marched into Copenhagen and burnt them all.

Just as Sidi Rais Ali was working for two masters – the Bey, as well as Ziege – so was Tuxen Ziege. Promises had been made to the Danish Crown Prince concerning the artistic and scientific trophies which he expected to find, but similar promises had also been made to the French government. In 1833 the French Ministry of War had praised Tuxen Ziege's "Recherches sur l'Emplacement de Carthage" for its topographic, statistical and military value, and Ziege now advised them that the purpose of his excursion into the interior was to continue the triangulation of the country, which he had already begun with observations in various measuring stations. When apply-ing for a travel permit from Ahmed Pasha Bey, however, he merely stated that he wished to examine traces of ancient peoples in the terri-tory under the Bey's control. The resulting official document was addressed to all fifteen governors of the Tunisian provinces. It bade them take good care of Monsieur Ziege, Danish Knight; to honour him and protect him from anything that could harm him, as he was a guest of the country. The Bey might have been less hospitable had he known of Ziege's researches for the French.

Ziege was accompanied not only by his dragoman. The Bey provided him with a kind of policeman called a Hanba, and Ziege also took with him a Moorish servant and two boys to oversee the luggage and the horses. All six of the party were armed and mounted. Riding alongside the Carthage aqueduct – of which he made drawings in the saddle – they reached Zaghouan on the third day, where he carried out trigonometric surveys and read the barometric pressure. Then he sketched the temple and drew a plan of it. Bad weather prevented him from climbing the mountain for two days, but they began on 2nd April, 1838, at 6.23 a.m., accompanied by two local peasant guides. They reached the top at 10.55 a.m., where the Sheik of Zaghouan, Sidi Qasem el Fadel, visited him an hour later but was unable to provide names for the surrounding mountains. On 7th April they reached Kairouan, but Ziege declined to enter because the city was forbidden to non-Muslims. Unlike Temple six years before, Ziege felt unable to enlist his companions in such a deception. Nevertheless, he managed to draw a map of the town and its environs and wrote in detail about everything he could see from outside, in particular the town gates and the citadel, including its three cannon – the Bey having removed the others after suppressing a revolt.

Ziege continued to make detailed notes, sometimes minute by minute, about the landscape and vegetation as well as the ruins along the way south. He described every monument, giving local names where possible, and applied himself to larger Roman towns with particular attention, measuring and observing with obsessive fervour. At Kasserine he performed more trigonometric surveys, read the barometric pressure, observed the latitude; then drew a map, made watercolours and sketches of the important monuments including the mausoleum of the Flavia family; copied a large number of inscriptions; and finally acquired a Roman lamp and vase which duly found their way into the Crown Prince's collection. And so it went on.

In October 1838, Ziege presented his findings to Pelet, the Minister of War in Paris. Pelet encouraged him to write them up, though without assurances as to payment. There was talk of sending him back to North Africa but Ziege demurred, saying that he wanted to be at home with his family. Yet he stayed in Paris throughout the following year, studying the work of Daguerre. He only returned home in March 1840, following the death of Frederik VI and the accession of the Crown Prince as King Christian VIII.

Frederik did not need to understand all of his father's achievements in order to respect them. He recognised his application and his energy, and he knew that he had inherited his commitment to detail, even as he knew that his brother Christian had inherited his mother's urbanity. He understood what it was to travel with open eyes and yet long for home: hadn't he too written such letters – from Ajan, for example, on the shores of the sea of Okhotsk; on the sleigh journey to Yakutsk . . . on the bottom a thin mattress, which could be rolled up, and on that a bearskin and two blankets. Behind was his carpetbag and a pillow; on top of it all, himself, wrapped in furs. In the storage compartment at the front was a box, divided into compartments, in which was tea, sugar, a small cask of aquavit, rusks, cheese, spoons, knives, forks, glasses, plates; also his black inkwell, cream jug, butter. He carried an axe, a big knife, a tinderbox, gunpowder and shot, three books, a frying pan, a little tea kettle and a pot. His gun was hung inside the sleigh so that he had it ready at any moment to shoot pheasant or grouse, which were said to be numerous and were not frightened off by the reindeer bells. He took beef, pork and the ingredients for cabbage soup – pepper, salt, bay leaves, onions, potatoes. The best of the meat was cut into pieces and put in the soup, and the whole was frozen into a block stored in one of the baggage sleighs, together with ham, smoked fish, potatoes and preserved delicacies in tins. A piece of the frozen soup could be cut off with the axe and in fifteen minutes over a fire it was ready to eat. Besides all these, there were pickles, vinegar, mustard, pepper, salt, oil, butter, sugar, coffee, sweets, jam . . . It was customary to take more provisions than were necessary for the benefit of others when the traveller had to halt longer in a post house during a blizzard. *When the good Lord brings me back to my beloved home I will often look back on the days I have spent in this beautiful valley among the wild, snow-covered mountains. There are just twenty or thirty little wooden houses here, with forever smoking chimneys. Behind them, a short way up the mountain, there is a church with a green-painted roof. Every evening after sundown, according to the Russian custom, the bells ring. The chimes are multiplied by the echoes from the mountain, and the ringing makes a deep impression which moves you spontaneously to prayer. I don't need to tell you the object of my prayers since you know it as well as I, my dear mother . . .*

Frederik rolled the pencil back and forth between his fingers. The smoothness of the enamel and the roughness of the gold filigree mimicked on his skin the rhythm of the train on the tracks. He could not bring material things to Emmie, but she neither sought nor needed them from him. Whatever quality she valued in him, he believed he must have inherited.

Taking a notebook from his pocket, Frederik turned to some jottings about his family that he had made for Emmie in Copenhagen, supposing that she would want to know about the family she was marrying into, about her new name and its origins. She might object that she was marrying *him*, not his ancestors, but he did not wish to impose the information, only to make it available. For what was he, if not a product of his ancestors? In the same way, an acquaintance with her family background was indispensable to his understanding of her.

"Johan von Ziege, born about 1613. Renowned Juris Consultus from Zerbst in Anhalt & Intimate Counsellor of Anhalt, died in Halle 1692, leaving Joachim." Using his father's pencil, Frederik added on the facing page, "All families seem to bloom spontaneously at some epoch. The soil from which we sprang is close to the western border of Brandenburg-Prussia, a sovereign principality with about 20,000 inhabitants at that time, about sixty miles SW of Berlin. Halle is about thirty miles SSW of Zerbst.

"Joachim Ziege, 1666–1734, Halle. Postmester (Mayor) in the service of the government of Poland and the Electorate of Saxony.

Married Juliane Dorothea Levin (1662–1742) daughter of Johan Levin, Government Secretary in the Electorate of Brandenburg.

"Christian Ludvig Ziege, 1699–1760. Principal Clerk in the office of the Paymaster General in Copenhagen; became Clerk of the Chamber, then Assistant Paymaster General, finally titular Councillor. Married 1739 Engelke Mouritzen, daughter of the Rector of Hobra."

Frederik wrote: "The Danish King Christian VI married a Princess of Brandenburg, and under her influence many Germans were brought in to fill high positions of state. Perhaps Johan Levin used his influence at the Brandenburg court to get a job for his grandson in Denmark. The name Levin suggests Jewish origins, but there is no independent evidence for this. His grandson married the daughter of a Lutheran pastor.

"Christian Ludvig had six children: Johan Christian, who had eight children; two (both called Frederik Augustus) who died in infancy; Carl Vigant; Ferdinand, who had two children; and finally Ulrik Anton, who had five children: Engelke, Christiane, Johanne, Tuxen, Anton."

Frederik added: "Ferdinand took command of the Fortress in Copenhagen after the English bombardment, from which my mother recalls fleeing as a girl. Confusingly, he was known as Frederik, the name given to both his older brothers who died as babies. It is to one of his sons, Christian Andreas, that Hans Christian Andersen refers in his autobiography (this was mentioned in Rome one evening)."

Frederik put the pencil back in his pocket. Five generations of a family – accommodated within two pages! Yet Frederik imagined that an echo of each individual could be heard in himself – however different his life might be from theirs. And though none of his family would be at the wedding, he found he did not mind, as if he had always known that he would marry abroad and had long ago accepted the implications to himself of it being most unusual for people to travel long distances to weddings other than their own. There had been talk of Hannina making the journey but Frederik discouraged her himself on the grounds that she was needed at home by his mother, who was not well. The true reason was that she would have been a burden. It was enough to know that his family were with him in spirit, even his father. Perhaps it was no accident, after all, that he should be marrying someone met when travelling with his family, for Emmie knew him as he needed to be known – as a man with a family. In this respect their situations were more nearly symmetrical than at first appeared, for though she was not with her family while they were in Italy, he understood from the way that she spoke of them that neither time nor oceans would ever wash them from her heart. It was only fair that he should be without his family now, while Emmie, who had only Miss Raymond on the Continent, should be joined by members of her own dispersed tribe.

From his waistcoat he extracted a small silver pocket knife. He passed the pad of his thumb across the blade, testing its edge. Then, pressing the notebook open on his thigh, he cut out his notes to give to Emmie at a suitable moment. As he tucked them into his pocket, he raised his head. The train was approaching a town, which must be Malvern: his heart surged with such violence that for a moment he thought he might be sick, as the strangeness of events rushed in upon him – why Emmie? Why England? Why not a placid Danish girl? A Martinique planter's daughter? A Tartar? A Russian in Irkutsk, St Petersburg? An Italian? A Greek, met while staying with de Jongh in Smyrna – or a Turk, or a Greenlander, for heaven's sake? So often, while proposing eligible Danish ladies to him, his family must have wondered if he would not bring back a bride from his travels. And in the end it was Emmie, whose life could scarcely have been set on a more distant trajectory if she were Polynesian, or so it would have seemed eighteen years ago when she married her first husband! God's mystery was wonderful!

*

Frederik waited in the front pew, facing the altar. His shoes were shined, his hair was brushed back flat from his broad forehead, his hands were motionless at his sides. He was concentrating on the thought of Emmie walking up the aisle behind him and on the moment when they would step forward together and make their vows before

God. No thought of past or future disturbed him now. The Reverend Mr Walsham How – less bumbling than he was in the unfamiliar habitat of Rome – was standing on the chancel steps, facing the congregation. It could only be a matter of seconds before the music to accompany Emmie's arrival began. Frederik was aware of a hush, and the stir of crinoline twisting from the waist, but he did not himself turn. He had done so a minute earlier and to do so again would appear nervous and undisciplined.

Apart from the vicar and his wife, nobody in the church had met Frederik until the previous day. He expected that everyone would be disposed to welcome him for Emmie's sake, but they would not be slow, among themselves, to pronounce him unsuitable should he not meet with their approval. Only two of Emmie's ten siblings were in the church, Kate and Lucy, and the only one from Emmie's Scottish family, her first in-laws, was Patrick Leslie, Kate's husband, who was best man. The few others consisted of Lucy's husband Bob Master, his sister Fanny, and their parents. It was Colonel Master who had the honour of giving Emmie away, for the friendship he had shown to Emmie's father in his declining years had made him the most suitable man in the country, if not the world, to act *in loco parentis*. Otherwise, there were some friends Emmie had made when staying with the Masters at Knole, not far away, and some strays – Mr Burton, Emmie's solicitor, had rather surprisingly made the journey from London with his wife. And there was Mrs Walsham How, in a substantial bonnet. Frederik anticipated that letters in which he was minutely described would be dispatched soon after the wedding. It was only right and proper that those who loved Emmie should care what he was like. So he did not turn round, for it was expected that a man should keep his eyes to the front.

Frederik was not in uniform. Although still a serving officer, he did not intend to be on active service after his marriage and he did not wish to give the impression that Emmie was committing herself to the semi-abandonment of a naval wife (God forbid!). Marriage was to be a new estate from which he did not wish to be distracted, and the wearing of a civilian frock coat confirmed this.

Beside him stood Patrick Leslie, whose indifference to frontiers seemed to have seeped into his beard. He had not worn a cravat with any degree of comfort since youth, yet the wildness in him, which had struck Frederik as soon as he saw him, proceeded less from the beard – Pat's was not such an unusual specimen, after all – than from the blue eyes, although whether it was their colour which startled or some other quality was hard to say. To describe them as cornflower blue was to purge them of surprise. They suggested some yet nameless flower, to be found only in a remote cleft of a distant mountain range, unseen by anyone but Pat. They projected strangeness, as if the world seen through those eyes was unlike that seen through anyone else's; as if he had looked on things and places which were not visited by ordinary eyes. There was an intensity to them not unlike that of a religious zealot, except that they were also kind: and Pat's fervent kindness had been directed at Frederik with a grace that could only come from the heart.

*

On arriving at his lodgings, Frederik had immediately sent a message to the address where Emmie was staying with the Masters, together with Kate and Pat. If it were not inconvenient, he wrote, he would come to find her in half an hour.

His plan was arrested within ten minutes by a banging on the door and an unknown Scottish voice telling the landlord that he had come to see Captain Ziege. Frederik looked out of his window to see Pat, top hat aloft in a knotted fist that looked more suited to cracking a whip than lifting a hat. When he saw Frederik, Pat's beard parted in a wide smile and Frederik recognised that he was being greeted not as a brother's usurper but as a much-loved sister's new husband. It was Emmie who had suggested Pat as best man. Frederik's first reaction was to think it an odd idea. His choice would have fallen on his brother, or Meldal or de Jongh. But Christian was in Vienna, Meldal was on the high seas and de Jongh was in Smyrna. There was nothing much for the best man to do since the wedding was so small, but an alternative had to be found. That Pat, as George's brother and as the husband of Emmie's sister, should consent to be his best man was a token of good will that Frederik counted a blessing.

It was not only curiosity that had impelled Pat to seek out Frederik. It was also a restlessness, an urge to prod things along. Sometimes his impetuosity was attractive, as it had been to Kate (and still was) when she had refused the persistent attentions of her rich cousin William in favour of her dashing, impoverished Scot. But as Kate knew to her cost, it was responsible too for many of the setbacks in his life that resulted in their having lived for the last few years in England. For Pat suffered from an acute sense of displacement. For him, "real life" was on the sheep stations of New South Wales, riding and driving stock, carving a domain from the bush; performing feats of physical prowess that were talked about far across the land. On the neighbouring stations would be his brothers George and Walter with their wives and children . . . wasn't it all set to be theirs for ever, their principality? But George was dead, Walter was like a shade, his only thoughts now to pop at grouse on the moors and afterwards wrap up his knees in plaid, and spend the coming winter in Pau. The land on that fifty-mile stretch of the Condamine on the Downs, which Pat had been the first to claim, was sliced up and divided among others, and the only child was his own feckless Willy Norman. Never mind life, never mind "for ever": after just ten years, he was living a ghostly, suspended existence in lodgings in Norwood with Kate – his beloved Kate, who had slept under a wagon when she first went up to the Downs, to whom he had given *such a country* . . . ! And Emmie belonged in Pat's real life: she too had been part of that hallowed existence on the Darling Downs. She understood. And because he knew that she loved it, and that she had loved his dear George with a devotion that was both a joy and a torment to behold as George waned to a strip of dry skin and then perished – because he trusted her love more than anyone's on earth except that of his own Kate – he trusted her now with Frederik. If Frederik nursed a tiny worry that Pat might regard Emmie's new marriage as a betrayal, no such notion existed in Pat's head. The fact that Frederik was a foreigner and a man accustomed to the faraway only made Pat better disposed towards him. Had Emmie settled to a life of ease with a gentleman in Cheltenham, then Pat might have been less enthusiastic, but her choice displayed faith and courage, a thirst for new adventure. She had found a way out of a life which looked set to be a living tomb – and in doing so, she was an inspiration.

As Pat walked, trying not to run, to Frederik's lodgings, his mind was not focused on the quiet Malvern street but on the memory of another meeting nearly eighteen years ago when the hard work had seemed to be almost done, and Eden all but attained. He had been looking after Canning Downs while George was in Sydney getting married, and the plan was that he should take the new phaeton all the way to Brisbane to meet them on their return. Drays pulled by teams of bullocks managed it, with some cajoling from their drivers, so why should not he? But he did not bargain for the rain. It came down with the sudden fury of a thunderbolt, flooding the rivers in minutes. He was trapped on the Downs, frantic and powerless. The violence of nature was a feature of that country, they all knew that, but you could not plan for it (although George should have had the nous to check that the portholes were closed on the steamer at Brisbane before leaving it for the night). Kate insisted that Pat couldn't leave until the rain let up: the whole countryside would be immobilised, so he would not miss the newlyweds. He had so looked forward to meeting them and to whisking them back to their home across the mountains! It fitted his idea of himself, and his relationship with George – but when he set out three days late it was with the anxiety that he had let them down. He knew they would manage, George always did, but he wanted to help, to be part of it. He imagined that they would stay put, but it turned out that they had taken Wickham's little buggy up to Ipswich, stopping the night at Dr Simpson's hut on the way. The next day they pressed on, hoping to reach the inn at Fassifern where they expected to find Pat, but they were stopped at Warrill Creek where the riverbed had been so washed away that the horses could get no footing. Pat was not there, but Hodgson was there by good fortune, on his way to Brisbane, and he and some other fellows turned out to help the travellers. Pat had often heard how they found Emmie and her maid standing in the soaking wet grass, wrapped together in a huge red blanket with a great umbrella overhead, holding a tallow candle between them brought by a shepherd. They were each placed upon a horse with a man on foot on either side of the saddle and another pair holding the bridle, and escorted across the torrent. It was only the following day that Pat had managed to get to the inn, exhausted in body and miserable with his failure. But George and Emmie quickly soothed him, explaining that it was their own impatience which prevented their waiting for him in Brisbane: marriage had robbed him of good sense, said George, laughing – as if good sense ever deserted him! And if good sense had prevailed on them to stay put, Emmie observed, should it not have done the same with Pat? George had said that Pat would be struggling on towards them, she added, so they had undertaken the journey in the spirit of a race. And here they all were, met halfway, and what could be better than that?

The rain stopped and the sky swarmed with birds like a million scintillas struck from a rainbow that spanned the land, as if its great arch would not hold the intensity of its own colours. The air smelt heady and rich with scents triggered by the rain. Pat told Emmie that this was the very smell of Creation.

They all agreed that the tracks were truly impassable, so they were obliged to stay for several days and oh! what a joy it had been then to see Emmie's excitement about her new life. Knowing Canning Downs and how Kate had been preparing for Emmie's arrival, Pat was confident that it must surpass all Emmie's hopes in comfort, beauty and prospects. Sweet secret! One warm evening, as they were sitting on the veranda, the distant sound of a cornopean came to them through the raucous chattering of the cockatoos. That must be Mackenzie! said George, and it was, for he had heard of their difficulties and had come over from Coochin Coochin with Mr Burgoyne to pay their respects to Mrs George Leslie. They were joined too by Mr Fairholme and his cousin Mr Pinnock, and in the evening Mr Burgoyne sang, to the delight of all. At last they all set out again, but progress in the carriage soon became impossible and eight oxen were harnessed to it. When they reached the mountains, Emmie was told she must ride. She did not quite understand why at first, other than that there was some suggestion of danger. However, she did what she was told and when she saw the carriage being dragged almost perpendicular up a rock, she was mightily relieved to be safe aboard Butterfly. When one of the men requested her to ride a little further ahead, if she wouldn't mind, she said she would mind it very much, as she wasn't accustomed to riding solitary in unknown mountains. Seeing some awkwardness in this exchange from his position following, but not hearing, Pat rode up to join them and heard the driver explaining that the beasts wouldn't pull the carriage up the pinch unless the drivers swore at them, which they didn't like to do while she was in earshot, whereupon Emmie laughed and rode on ahead in Pat's company, admiring the parrots squabbling in the vast trees and the country as it opened out before her. And the next day, passing through miles of wild oats and purple vetches as high as the carriage wheels, she came into her new life.

*

As she walked up the aisle, Emmie saw Pat's broad, comforting back. Nearer, ready to turn towards her, stood Frederik. It still seemed so improbable, so frankly incredible that she should be getting married again that, until Frederik's arrival in Malvern the previous day, a doubt remained in her mind, which amounted to no more than amazement at her own good fortune; and even now she felt that if she took her eyes from him for an instant he might vanish, and the parson would shrug and wring his hands and say that man's estate was full of woe – but wasn't that a reason to grasp at joy and make the most of it? No doubt Frederik contained man's share of woe, but he offered a new life with the conviction of love; and – this she knew, for she was no stranger to love – what more could be wished for? The answer was seeded in the question: it made her tremble with wonder, as it had so often in recent weeks, just as it did in that other life so long ago. She was older than most women who had children, but if there was a reason why she could not, she did not know it.

It was the side of Emmie's veiled head that Pat saw, and the finely wrought lace cuffs and lappets, which he knew at once.

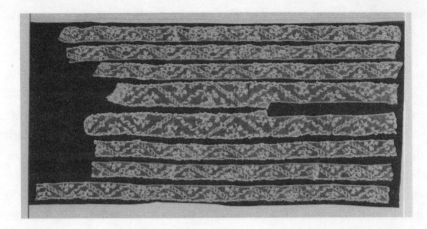

He should have been expecting to see the lace, he realised. Turning on impulse to Kate, he saw from her complicit smile that it was no surprise to her: and in the reach of Pat's eyes, Kate saw their own wedding day, when she had worn Grandmother King's lace, and the pain of their losses, which somehow were always fresh with Pat, as if he had never quite understood how they came about. She wanted to touch him and tell him it was all right, she still loved him, but he was too far away; and he was not a child, he ought to know it. His eyes, moreover, had moved on.

Beside Kate stood Lucy, who had surely also worn the lace at her wedding. Watching her now, weak and pale and huddled beneath a woolsack of shawls, Pat recalled her all those years ago, the youngest girl in that great happy house that became his second home. He had asked his mother to send her a doll from Scotland. It took nearly a year. He had been up-country at Colleroi when the box arrived and it was decided to wait for his return to Vineyard before presenting it to Lucy. How proud she had been of her Scottish doll, how she had boasted of it, and how pleased they had been that he had taken such trouble! He had seen all the sisters wearing this lace – Kate, Lucy, Libby, Mary, Annie – all except Emmie. A superstitious man, Pat thought, might have drawn conclusions from that.

Kate knew that Pat was brooding, as ever, on his inability to recover what was lost. Not that anyone ever expected him to, or that the slightest possibility ever existed: her father had gone bankrupt because he was personally liable for the Bank of Australia. But it was George and Hugh Gordon, Mary's husband, who had bought things from the Vineyard sale, because they had some spare money, which she and Pat had not, nor ever would have. It was of this that Pat would be reminded when he saw the lace. He was troubled not just by nostalgia for Vineyard but by the eternal self-reproach that he had not managed to rescue her parents – forgetting, as George would never have done, that lace, being classed by the bailiffs as a woman's property, was exempt from the sale. It was only Emmie's because Emmie was the one to care for it.

While Pat's unfailing, naïve tendency to see the best in people, especially women, served to sustain Kate's love of him, Kate was aware that her sister was more demanding. Charm and an improvident temperament might secure Emmie's affections, but never her love. She needed a husband who was bountiful, of course, but she needed him also to be mindful of costs, as George was. Not that Kate hadn't often begged God to make Pat more mindful of costs, but thrift was never a condition of her love. George's outrage on seeing Kate holding a horse while Pat inspected its hoof, when her back was causing her such pain, affirmed him in Emmie's eyes. Yet though Kate had seen that he was in the right and Pat in the wrong, it made her love Pat and regard George, for all his virtues, as a little inflexible. The incident had come to mind the previous evening during dinner at their lodgings, when relief at finding that Frederik was not only tolerable but also likeable ensured that an evening which might have been tense was one of conviviality.

They were eating jugged hare. The landlord claimed to have shot it himself, which prompted Bob Master to ask Frederik if he did much shooting.

Frederik set his knife and fork down on his plate. "I shoot – of course! But sailors are at a disadvantage before you landsmen," he said.

It seemed to Kate that Frederik ate almost invisibly, whereas Pat's elbows were always going in one direction or another. He had never learned how to cut a potato cleanly or to chew without looking as if he were grinding bones. "I expect you are a good shot, though," she said.

Frederik recalled an Englishman in Hong Kong who, hearing that he was bound for the Amur, said, "What marvellous shooting you will have there!"

"I will tell you a story about a good shot I once made," Frederik said, "if you wish."

There were murmurs of assent.

"When I first went ashore with a gun in De Castris Bay," he said, " – that is the Pacific coast of Siberia – I hadn't been walking five minutes along the edge of the pines before I saw a pair of swans take flight. They were moving out of range, but the instinct to shoot and the excitement of finding myself at last on this wild coast made me fire nevertheless. One of the birds fell like a stone. When I had stuffed it into my game bag, the bulk of it against my coat made me feel enormous." Frederik sat back and curved his arms in front of his stomach to demonstrate his increased girth. "Some few hundred yards farther on, I came to a Yakut hut made of silver-birch bark, with a bear-skin flap for a door. Inside, around an open fire, sat an old man smoking foul tobacco, a youth fletching an arrow and a woman sewing hide with a bone needle. The top of the hut was open. It was supposed to work as a chimney but did so imperfectly, for the interior was thick with pungent smoke. The old man did not look surprised to see me and motioned me in, but the swan made it difficult to get through the narrow opening. I had to unbuckle the bag and pull it in awkwardly beside me. Through the gloom I saw a baby in a cradle full of broken bark, and there were two flintlock muskets. The old man asked in broken Russian why I had killed a swan. I had no ready answer – I had done it without thinking – and I said I would eat it with my friends on board ship. The man shrugged and said that foreigners had strange ways:

people – he said this in such a way that I took it to cast doubt on whether I qualified as a person – *people* usually ate fish or reindeer." As Frederik's audience chuckled, the shame he had felt in the ragged Yakut hut was renewed, and he added, "I do not know if my crime or my strangeness affected the man most. What I could not explain, because it excused nothing, was that it was an exceptional shot!"

"I'm sure it was!" Pat cried.

Emmie smiled at Pat.

"And do you ever shoot for trophies, Captain?" Colonel Master asked.

"I confess I have shot sable, but I do not enjoy pursuing trophies," Frederik said. Then, lest inadvertently he offend the gentlemen present, he added, "After all, you need somewhere to *display* your trophies – a castle, at least! – unless you are to set up in business as a – what do you call it? A stuffer of animals?"

"A taxidermist," Emmie said.

"Unless you miss all the time," said Bob Master. "That would be a solution."

Frederik laughed. "Indeed it would!"

"And what about shooting in self-defence?" said Emmie. "Were you not threatened by a polar bear in Greenland?"

"Nothing worse than cold and boredom. In Siberia I was warned many times to look out for bears, but I never saw a single one."

"Bears indeed!" exclaimed Pat. "The worst I had to contend with was bushrangers."

"Huh!" cried Frederik, pleased to shift the attention from himself. "Now that does sound dangerous!"

"They were a danger, I don't mind admitting!" said Pat. "Almost as soon as I went out to New South Wales, I wrote to my father asking him to send me a pair of long-barrelled pistols. He was shocked. He did not always appreciate how New South Wales differed from the Garioch. But I believed that if I were known to have the means of defending myself and my property, I would be less vulnerable. And so it proved. I carried guns for years, for use against my fellow men, but I never had to hurt a man."

"It was understood, then, that you would use the gun if pressed," said Frederik.

"He would have!" said Kate, though she realised as she said it that she did not know for a fact that he had not. Organising a property two hundred miles into the bush with ticket-of-leave men and the constant threat of bushrangers was not achieved by observing the manners of society drawing rooms.

"Of course," Pat said. "Circumstances make you do things that you never expect to do. I'm sure you have found the same, Captain Ziege?"

"I never expected to ride a reindeer, but I did – and became rather competent," said Frederik cheerfully.

Everybody round the table roared with laughter. Even Lucy, whose head was aching. She was impatient with Pat's Australian reminiscences, jealous of his experiences there and those of her sisters; jealous even of the worlds that lay open to them while her own hopes were so shrunken. "Pray – do tell us!" she said.

"Well," said Frederik, pleased to elicit a positive response from Lucy. "It's a bit like riding a very large, smelly duck, only a reindeer is more capricious and has horns. The saddle looks like a miniature of what a circus rider stands on, but it has no stirrups. It sits on the hump behind the animal's neck, over the forelegs. The reindeer has a halter with reins to one side, and instead of using a bit between its teeth you guide it on the other side with a stick. I was the only European I know of who could balance firmly on a reindeer, and I did it first time. The others fell off. I don't know why, perhaps there was some vodka being passed around, and I missed it. But the animal will suddenly pull its head right back so that the horns lie alongside the rider's thighs, which are over its neck, just above them. And you have to be wary of touching the horns. The reindeer doesn't like it."

And Kate thought of the time when she was found, in agony, holding the horse for Pat, and she wondered how Frederik would have behaved. It seemed to her that he would have intervened with less sense of his own correctness than most men, and less severely than George (who had trained himself to a swiftness of judgement according to a set of principles which all agreed were reliable, and for which all had cause

to be grateful). She had the impression that Frederik tried to understand women in a way that would not have occurred to Pat or George.
She could not quite say how she knew this any more than she could
surmise how he had learned it, but it made her feel happy on Emmie's
behalf.

*

". . . in sickness and in health, to have and to hold, from this day
forward . . ."

As Frederik repeated the words, a vague image of Emmie ill in bed
flitted across his mind; and of an old and decrepit Emmie, still looked
after by himself, white-haired by then and sparsely whiskered yet fit
in body. Or would it be he who grew ill first? He would not – no, he
would not impose *that* on her. Everything crowded in on him with an
amazing intensity: Emmie beside him smelling of – what was it? –
gardenias? her face upturned to his; the intricate lace lappets that
had materialised (from where?); Mr Walsham How smelling of soap,
his hands soft and white; the congregation listening greedily for the
vows that would reassure them of love's continued existence, providing hope to those who had not met love and a shine to hearts where
it had dulled. Frederik was aware of the polished pews and the cold
stone floor, the window embrasures with great pots of foliage and lilies;
of the light streaming through the stained-glass windows, casting a
purple patch onto the vicar's surplice; of the high-beamed roof and
the church, sedate in its yard . . . Would his family be imagining
something like this? Did his father, in his grave, know of it? He
pictured his cameo on the headstone in the Holmens kirkegård – could
he *see* Emmie, in her dress the same colour as her ivory fan? Endowed
with an extraordinary vitality by the situation, Emmie startled Frederik
into thinking of the children they might have, *their* children.
Committing himself so completely, before God, to another person –
and hearing Emmie make the same vow to him – thrilled him with an
immediacy he had never suspected possible.

". . . till death us do part," Emmie repeated, as once she had repeated before, a girl in lace with a head full of hopes and blithe expectations.

Making this weighty promise for a second time must be different, he thought. It gave her words a resonance, a self-consciousness, that made them all the more precious. Her lips did not quiver, nor did her blue eyes stray from his, but he could sense that her whole forearm was trembling. He felt so overwhelmed with love for her that he gasped and he had to snatch up his free hand to stifle a cough.

Emmie's serious countenance dissolved into a smile. His agitation had been making her nervous but now she felt a tremendous surge of relief. It had happened. It was done. This man whom she knew but little, but whom she trusted – she had given herself to him.

"I now pronounce you man and wife," said the vicar.

Emmie and Frederik turned together, and there was Kate, her eyes bright with tears. Emmie saw Pat touch his wrist and his collar with a knowing smile, and she nodded, glad that the lace had been noticed. It was a reminder that her past, though entrusted to Frederik's care, had its own identity, however she was reshaped by marriage.

But signing the register, aware of her cuff against the page, Emmie thought of her hand in Frederik's and wondered if her grandmother's lace was, after all, an unnecessary encumbrance.

Bournemouth, November 1865

FREDERIK and Emmie took lodgings in Bournemouth in a red-brick house on a cliff overlooking the sea. There was no garden to speak of but this disappointed Emmie less than if it had been spring. It was a calm place for them to go and get used to one another. A honeymoon, perhaps, when they could make decisions about where and how to live. For while it was understood that Emmie's income was sufficient for Frederik not to have to work, there was no good reason for them to live in London – in any case, her house in Rutland Gate was let; nor in St Leonard's-on-Sea, where she sometimes lived because the Leslies liked to visit. They had come to Bournemouth on the recommendation of Colonel Master, who belonged to a club there. It was as good a place as any in which to start married life. So it was from Bournemouth that Frederik wrote his first letters home as a married man – "home", after all, being wherever he sent letters to his mother, currently an apartment in the corner of Kongens Nytorv where she had recently moved with Hannina.

The sitting room overlooked a harbour where pleasure boats were moored already for the long wait till next season. On the desk stood a clock with a Réamur thermometer.

While Emmie took an afternoon siesta, he wound the clock before beginning his letter, like a hunting man checking that his hat is secure, a habitual, steadying gesture as he pondered how to reassure his mother . . . Finding that he could not think of what to write, he realised that in fact he did not want to write at all. He sketched an image of himself dancing with Emmie, in which his broad back obscured all

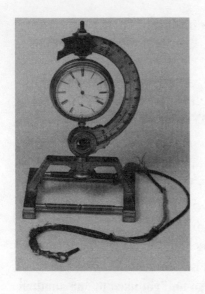

but her face over his shoulder, and her skirts. As he drew her hand on his shoulder, he experienced a tremor of the actual sensation. Emmie stirred next door; he settled back in his chair and gazed out across the grey bay. He sighed with contentment. He heard the clock's tick, a soothing guarantee of the present, and promise of the future.

"I'm afraid I shall be dismal company today," said Emmie one morning after eight weeks of marriage. She had felt unwell since waking. Now she observed with revulsion the silver coffee pot and the warm rolls, which the previous day had been so welcome. After breakfast she retired at once to bed, urging Frederik to go out and enjoy himself without her.

Not wishing to leave her alone, Frederik sat beside her to read aloud from Ecclesiastes. His distress that she felt unwell was made febrile by his uncertainty of the cause. The same thought must have occurred to them both, but he was wary of admitting to it first. He sat on a hard chair, half turned towards where she lay propped on three pillows. She was watching him with grave, wide eyes; her left hand rested in his. "The words of the Preacher, the Son of David, king in Jerusalem," he began. Disengaging his hand from hers, he reached out for the cup of coffee on the night table and took a sip, then resumed reading.

A faint buzz still lurked in his chest; nerves, he supposed, on account of the unspoken thought between them. " . . . The wind goeth toward the south, and turneth about unto the north; it whirleth about continually, and the wind returneth again according to his circuits."

Frederik coughed, fist pressed over his mouth. Emmie said, "My dear Frederik, it is most kind of you to read to me, but are you sure it is a good idea? You have a cough."

"So it appears. And I am only disturbing you."

"I like it when you read to me, you know I do. But I would sleep now."

"Sleep would benefit you more than my splutterings," Frederik said. His articulation of the awkward syllables was exaggerated, so that Emmie laughed in spite of herself. The only thing about his perfect English that ever betrayed him as a foreigner was the care with which he spoke it: now he knew it sounded funny and did it on purpose.

"What will you do?" she asked. "Will you go for a walk?"

"Yes. Then I shall attend to some correspondence. Can I fetch you something while I'm out?"

Emmie thought of the day-bed on the veranda at Canning Downs, where she had spent whole days prostrated by nausea. Pray God it would not be like that! On the crude bamboo table beside her, a small Canton jug of cordial – but what kind? "Some fruit, I might eat some fruit."

"Any particular kind?"

Emmie's hand flopped onto her stomach. "Dear me! I do feel peculiar!"

"Are you sure you would not prefer me to stay?"

"No, Frederik dear, I shall sleep. Bring me back an orange!"

Frederik reached beneath the bed and moved the chamber pot where Emmie could reach it with ease; she smiled lopsidedly.

Now that Frederik was gone, Emmie found that she had not sufficient energy even to alter her position. She felt as if a knot of eels had occupied her stomach. She sank back against her pillows. There could be no doubting what it was, she had been waiting to see if it would strike for two weeks now, dreading it both for her own sake and also for its effect on Frederik; hoping that she might be spared it this time, hoping nevertheless for the reassuring proof of its grip. She could not doubt that he had made the inference too, for she had seen the gleam in his eyes. Yet sure though she was that a child was what she and Frederik both wanted, terror clawed at her.

Unable to sleep, she lay as if pinned by a vaulting memory of the sickness that had squeezed each day at the limits of her endurance.

Every day she had thought it could get no worse, but it did, and she endured because there was no choice: struggling into the heat to lay out her shrubbery, hoping that the distraction would bring relief, praying for respite and that the station hands were not watching. And the heat, oh! the heat augmented the nausea tenfold! Now, at least, she did not have to contend with that. It had taken nearly a year for her to conceive then. She had begun to wonder if there wasn't something wrong. It never occurred to her that knowing she was with child could ever be anything but a cause for joy. Nobody told her – how did you tell a girl such a thing? The relentlessness and the queasiness could not be understood unless felt, and what benefit was there in frightening the happy bride, poor eager innocent? With what clarity she then saw her mother's years of travail! To think that she herself had coveted that condition again despite the months of futile sickness – and never gained it, until now, eighteen years and a world and a husband away! What had been wrong? She could only be amazed at herself that now, so soon, she was prostrated. But for all the thrill of it, she could not dispose of the fear, the sense that she was already in thrall to the process, like a fish thrashing on a deck, and how could she not be afraid when all those years ago it had been a succubus bloating her entrails? *My dear Mrs Leslie, I have not been feeling at all well of late, DV I shall have some happy news to report in my next*, but there was not and there never was, and the thing was dragged out one suffocating evening as she screamed for George, who was shearing late, by the Aboriginal girl whose hands kept rummaging until she pushed her away; and she lay half conscious, bleeding and sweltering into the night and the promise of death. But there was no death: instead she swam through clay to her barren recovery, her only offspring fruit trees, apples and magnum borrum plums, greengages, pears, quinces, oranges, lemons; white Japan honeysuckle, English and Portugal laurels, cypresses, white and pink moss roses, spine roses, white China tea rose, laburnum, gardenia, laurustinus, rhododendron, magnolias, bay; anemone bulbs, purple and yellow crocus, violets, white foxglove, asters and pansies, petunias, nasturtiums and various campanulas, dahlias ditto. *My dear Mr Leslie, I wish I could show you a splendid bunch of Muscat grapes we have gathered. It is so pleasant to gather the first fruit in one's garden! Next year we shall have a great many vines in bearing. The vine does so well in this climate.*

Poor orphans.

It was a year before she could ride a horse. The day after her first canter along the river beside George, she planted some vines at the foot of the gum trees on the lawn, and let them grow wild.

And what if it all happened again? George had tended her through the misery: she hoped that Frederik would do likewise, but what a weight to hang on a man! Imagination or a sense of duty could support much, but how could they alone span the abyss which separated him from her solitary pain? And after all the suffering, the disappointment at failing to conceive again, as if something inside was blocked, George had made her laugh at her own lack of logic. Perhaps she should laugh now at her own fear, for assuredly this was what she wanted. At least – dared she hope? – it might be. Women repeatedly subjected themselves to the agony. Their logic, to be sure, was mysterious. But would a man not feel afraid too?

Anxiety for Emmie curtailed Frederik's stroll along the waterfront. Soon after his return she did sleep, and he sat at his desk to examine the correspondence over Gigoomgan, which now, by law, was his, together with the rest of Emmie's property; undreamed of by him nine months ago, unseen, and as far away on the planet as could be. In the accounts and returns of June, he noticed the sale of thirty heifers for £105 which did not appear in the cattle return. He would have to query this with the trustees, Pat and Mr Aylmer; also the £3.12.6 which showed up for some time past in the balance sheet as a liability. The loss of twelve bulls in May . . . ? Perhaps he had misunderstood something? Yet if he felt its interest – the advisability of boiling down more or fewer sheep this year for tallow – this was because the place was Emmie's. It was moving to see her reflected in the letters from Mant, the distant manager at Gigoomgan: her resonance in the minds of others – her Australian family, as well as Mant – amplified his love for her.

As one day of sickness was followed by another, excitement smouldered in Frederik's heart. Each day, as he wound his clock, he felt a fresh shoot of happiness for all the time that lay ahead for them to share.

*

"My dear, if this is what we think it is," he said one day, giving voice to their thoughts, "then we must proceed most gently, but we shall never forget that it is a blessing. Although I am new to these matters, I am at your side and ready for direction."

When a doctor confirmed that their prayers had been answered, joy expunged all but superficial regret for Emmie's discomfort. Since his thermometer advised that the day was no warmer than usual, Frederik attributed his slight sense of fever to the news. Taking into account Emmie's age, together with the question of her delicacy, the doctor counselled as much rest as possible, so that Frederik often found himself at the broad desk with its sweeping view down to the sea, picking out the figures from Mant's abundant reports or contemplating his clock alone while Emmie tensely ticked off the days before the future claimed her, as she burrowed, bearlike, into slumber's consolation.

Frederik was not accustomed to such a leisurely pace of life. Emmie was afraid that he would grow bored, but he protested that if his happiness were eroded by such an affliction then its foundations were poor; the happiness she had given him was of more solid stuff. The doctor's insistence that Emmie rest was no disappointment to Frederik for he was aware that this period of stillness, when they had only themselves to please, must come to an end when the child was born: and he meant to treasure it. As he wound the clock, he felt as if his usual relation to it were reversed. Instead of measuring what was inevitable, he seemed to be controlling the passage of time, dealing it out by winding the mechanism. The corollary was that time would cease if he did not wind the clock, a notion which seemed almost plausible when Emmie rested and he gazed at the merging of the grey sky with the Channel. He had to remind himself then that a horizon existed, that the land

– 116 –

came to an end as certainly as pregnancy. He wondered if his father had experienced a comparable sensation of suspense when he waited in Paris in 1839. Perhaps he had bought this clock then precisely because of its demands on him, as if by frequent manipulation of time he could hasten its passing.

Frederik's mother had told the children that their father needed to stay in Paris in order to get paid. And though there was some truth in this, it was much later before Frederik understood how irrelevant it was to the case. The real cause was contained in one of those letters, whose arrival would be announced by the footman, *a letter from Africa, Fru Ziege*. It waited on a lacquered tray on a round table in the hall, untouchable and alluring in the eyes of the children, addressed in their father's impeccable handwriting, redolent of the distant haze and dream of their infancy. When Mama was ready she would collect the packet. A tantalising delay followed – the tray empty – and no allusion was made to the missive. A whole day might elapse before she summoned the children to the drawing room. They would find her seated in the centre of the sofa, the sheets of closely written paper unfolded on her lap. Hannina, Clara or Ida would sit on one side of her, Frederik or Christian on the other, always a boy and a girl, and when they were all gathered she would raise one of these sheets, *Your father writes from Tunisia. He is well, God be thanked.* They never knew what she left out: it did not occur to them that a passage that they did not hear might reach the ears of anyone else. But it must have happened because it became known – so Christian discovered some years later, and duly informed his older brother – that, in a letter written while accompanying the French campaign in Algeria, their father reported that a countryman by the name of Dinesen, who was fighting with the French forces, claimed that wherever the French turned up in North Africa, the wells dried up, the trees disappeared, the inhabitants fled and all that was left was the desert. With such defeatist remarks he brought shame on himself and, by extension, his country, Ziege wrote. Frederik did not understand how this comment from a private letter to his wife had become public. However it was, Dinesen had got to hear of it. Dinesen was a bully and notoriously mean – in the end, it was this which impressed itself on posterity rather than the unwelcome opinions of the French that he brought out of Africa. Frederik had heard that his children were obliged to gather round the dining table to share a single reading light, while he sat in splendour with burning lamps on every side. Nevertheless, his unpopularity made the threat of a duel no less serious. So Ziege, now in Paris writing up his trip, stayed there throughout 1839 and into 1840 rather than risk his life against Dinesen in Copenhagen. To the children, and anyone else who asked, his protracted stay was said to be a financial matter, and there was substance in this too, for Ziege had not been paid by the French for his endeavours. He needed to be on the spot, to be a constant embarrassment to the Ministry of War. Frederik now imagined his father wistfully examining clocks, thinking of home, and then becoming fascinated by this unusual specimen with its curved thermometer and neat design, whose workings were not hidden away but open to view behind a pane of glass. Reminded perhaps by the swivel and screw of a sea clock's bearing, he had bought it for his older son, who had just qualified with distinction as a naval cadet. Once interested, he would have made it his business to examine the work of other clockmakers. It was thus that he encountered Daguerre. In April 1840 he commissioned from Giroux, a clockmaker on the rue de Rivoli, the seventh in a new series of instruments designed for applying Daguerre's technique of transferring images to silvered plates. He did this not on his own account, for he could not afford it, but on instructions from the Danish Crown Prince, whom he had apprised of the development. When the Crown Prince acceded to the throne later in the same year as Christian VIII, he made a representation through the French Ambassador about Ziege's poor remuneration, which resulted in a "gift" of more than 3,000 francs and a bejewelled pencil from the Duc d'Aumale to the newly upgraded *Chevalier* – making it seem as if Ziege's continued presence in Paris was purely to do with his work for the French. A further result of the King's accession to Ziege's family was that Dinesen was persuaded to accept an apology: Ziege averred that he had been ill, had expressed himself poorly. If so, it was a unique instance, but he did not rue his apology for he found that his years of work for the former Crown Prince were rewarded on his return to Denmark by his elevation to the rank of Kammerherr. As for the new King, he was pleased to have Ziege back to organise his collections at Amalienborg.

In recent years, Frederik had often had cause to think about his father in Paris because the clock, which he prized, had one short-coming so far as his own life was concerned. He wondered if his father, whose working life had been spent in the heat of Africa, Greece, Italy (and perhaps it was hot in Paris that summer too), had considered that it might ever matter to his son that the lowest temperature on the scale was 0°? On his first arriving in Yakutsk, Frederik was told that it was −44° Réaumur; he had not taken the clock to Greenland. But here it was now, on his desk, and it was telling him the time (2.45 p.m.) and the temperature (12°).

He coughed, and the sound of it penetrated Emmie's dozing next door. She surfaced, feeling disorientated, thinking of George and wondering why. She turned, and bile rose in her throat so that she thought for a moment she would be sick. Raising herself against her pillows, she pressed her fingertips against her lips in distaste. Then she heard Frederik cough again and the sound transfixed her like a blow to the back from an unseen assailant, for it was George's cough. She stared at the wall where hung a watercolour of boats in a regatta. Her gaze locked on one vertical of the thick wooden frame, splitting her focus as she listened for the sound again, straining between incredulity and horror. When it came, recognition burst through her mind like a lesion, as she realised that it was indeed the once famil-iar, dry rasp of a consumptive man. Her chest lurched; she arched her neck over the side of the bed and vomited.

Frederik shoved his chair back and hurried to Emmie's side. He was too late, but he seized the chamber pot and brought it to her quiv-ering jaw. Her white hands pressed against the florid roses on the porcelain; the tip of her left index finger was skewed over the lip like a thorn. With the thumb and little finger of his free hand, Frederik hooked back her hair where it hung loose across her sweating temples.

After a frozen moment Emmie allowed Frederik to guide her back against her pillows, but as the nausea ebbed she shook him away. "Thank you. You needn't have come. Do call Mary," she said.

Frederik was not surprised at her manner. Apart from the plain fact that she must feel ill, he imagined that she would feel miserable, even angry at him for having witnessed her being sick. But these emotions would retreat, and he saw that it was his duty meanwhile to clear up the mess and attend to her comfort. As ever, he was secure in the accomplishment of duty. In any case, it was easy: he loved her and wished only to relieve her suffering. It was a pleasure to demonstrate his love.

Following Frederik's call, Mary's footsteps could be heard hurrying up the uncarpeted steps from the kitchen, then stopping at the threshold as she knocked at the open door. Her hands smoothed her white apron apprehensively. She was in her mid-twenties, with dark hair pinned into a bun, which emphasised the point of her nose and the weakness of her chin. She liked her employers and was eager to oblige. It did not worry her that she did not understand them, for she did not expect to do so. Although he was a foreigner, he was a gentleman; she was a little in awe of him.

"Thank you for coming so promptly, Mary. Will you help Mrs Ziege get comfortable while I see to this?" said Frederik, indicating the rug.

Mary plumped up Emmie's pillows and resettled her, then she brought a clean, warm face flannel and a glass of water with a bowl so that Emmie could rinse her mouth. Frederik returned with a pail of water and a cloth, and wiped some splatters which had not been caught by the rug. "Well!" he exclaimed. "No-one daunted, I hope?"

Mary smiled at him. She had expected that she would have to clear up.

But Emmie did not meet Frederik's eye. "All right, my dear?" he added.

"Yes, thank you."

Although Emmie acknowledged Frederik's solicitude and efficiency, she found herself consumed by fury with him, which only increased as the sound of his coughing reached her again over the splashing water in the kitchen. It annoyed her that he had taken it upon himself to clear up the mess instead of leaving it to Mary. Even though she recognised the kind thought behind the action, she could not help thinking that it was *he* who ought to be soothing her. His calm, which ought to be admirable, was maddening.

"Mary, would you go and fetch my husband, please?"

Shutting the door behind him, Frederik was perplexed to see Emmie's face collapse into tears. In three quick steps he was at her side and he held her close. "My darling! My darling Emmie!" he murmured. "It is all right!" And he plucked at a loose thread from her shawl which threatened to get entangled in his watch chain. He told himself that the emotions of pregnant women were like melt water over rapids, and he was braced. "Emmie, my darling, I am here, it is all right," he repeated.

"All right?" she burst out, pushing away so that he could see her blue eyes inflamed with tears and dread. And seeing his incomprehension, she said, "I believe you do not understand! Oh, Frederik!" And her fingers flexed on his frock coat as if she would as soon beat him.

He stared at her, bewildered; aware that he had mistaken the cause of her distress, not knowing where to clutch at.

"Your cough, Frederik! Don't you understand – have you not spoken to a doctor about it?"

It dawned on Frederik that Emmie thought she was embracing a dying man.

She must be mistaken, he thought. But in his mind's eye he saw his clock next door. Who would wind it in future, if not he? Would his unborn child be its guardian, or would it cease with him? Then again, if his life could be measured in the revolutions of the clock's hands then it were better not to wind the device, for doing so must hasten his end.

Summer 1866

IT was a scene Frederik never tired of watching: Emmie, seated at a dressing table, brushing her hair. During the day, it was pulled back over her ears and secured, by means of pins, with the thoroughness of a sailor lashing a cargo to the deck before a tempest. But in the evenings it was released and a swag of black unfurled over her shoulders, which she proceeded to brush in long sweeps with a silver-backed hairbrush, making it fan out against the light. He marvelled at the straightness of her back when her head turned, at the white arc of her throat. The rhythmic sound reminded him of feet on snow.

Being watched by her husband at her dressing table was a novel experience for Emmie. George had just wanted her to be ready. At Canning Downs he never had time to observe her like this: had he done so, he would have fallen asleep. Later on, when there was time, he found something else to do while he was waiting – a letter to write, percentages to calculate, papers to read; her toilette was none of his business; in any case it was just Emmie brushing her hair and whatnot, the same thing each time. It had never occurred to her to regret this in George, nor did it now. Yet she liked Frederik's attention because it was appreciative, which, as she grew colossal with pregnancy, she found reassuring. His presence elevated mere routine into a ritual. Perceiving a bloom to the cheek or a mark of exhaustion, a thickening of the waist, he enjoyed these alterations as natural to his healthy wife. On the other hand, he shied away from the subject of his own health.

Dressing tables came and went according to where they were staying but, against the hotels and lodgings that constituted the backdrop of

Emmie's life, her dressing case remained a fixture. Whether open in front of her or tucked into a cupboard, it was a guarantee of familiar comforts whatever the surroundings. Made of mahogany, the box was thirteen inches wide, ten inches deep and six inches high, with a brass plate in the top with her monogram, E.M.L. Inside, standing in a line at the back, were five bottles with monogrammed silver caps. One contained rosewater, another *sal volatile*; another a swan's-down powder puff with a pink kidskin button handle. Emmie kept her jewellery in the cavity below the tray. Also accessible from here are four tiny drawers, which fit beneath the back row of glass bottles; these are empty now. Fitted into the lid's underside is a heavy mirror, backed in red leather, which can be removed and stood alone by means of a folding prop, like a portable shrine.

The box was given to Emmie by George Leslie on her first visit to London, a gift from a bush pioneer to his wife as she adjusted to her new status as the wife of a gentleman of leisure.

*

After ninety days at sea on the *Vimiera*, she had gone ashore with George on the pilot boat at Portsmouth so as to stay with Lucy's brother-in-law Henry Master and his wife, and to meet her cousins the Delacombes. They went to church to give thanks for their safe arrival, and there she was struck by the fresh complexion of the women. The next day they took the train for London, her first railway journey: slicing through the green countryside that had been in her mind since consciousness of "home" was first implanted in her as a girl – the trees so short, but the land so cultivated and charming. In London they were met by Patrick Ferguson, George's brother-in-law, who acted as cicerone among the astonishing multitudes, rushing them about to all the sights. The city was scarcely more familiar to George than to Emmie, for he had visited only once, at the age of seventeen, when he and Walter stayed with their Uncle Davidson en route from home to Portsmouth, bound for Australia. One day George said he had some business to attend to and Patrick took her to St Paul's Cathedral. It turned out that George was ordering the dressing case in Bond Street.

They travelled to Newcastle after a fortnight in London and thence to Haydon Bridge, to stay with George's Aunt Coats. Then it was up to Aberdeen, to be met again by Patrick and Mary Anne Ferguson, who took them the thirty miles in their carriage to Drumrossie. George's parents were living there, now that his brother William was married and had taken over Warthill, the family house. Emmie had been eight when Pat Leslie first came to Australia and stayed at Vineyard, telling them all about his own family in Scotland. Since then, the Leslies had become a second family to her. She had imagined and reinvented them in their Scottish home through sixteen years of correspondence, and images from the novels of Walter Scott. Kind she knew them to be, but you could not know someone until you looked them in the eye. Now here she was for four hours in a carriage opposite Mary Anne, and she feared she was grinning like a maniac. Mary Anne beamed back in the most amiable fashion, like a sensible helping of raspberries and cream. Arriving at Drumrossie, she at last met the old laird, swathed in whiskers, and her mother-in-law. The laird's resemblance to George was striking and a little unnerving: both had a narrow face, with agile brown eyes, and they had the same brisk manner. But while the old laird wept when greeting the son whom he had not seen for thirteen years, George – who had resigned himself years ago never to seeing his aged parents again – was dry-eyed. Emmie knew well how he cared, but she was astonished that he could be so composed when she herself was fluttered and choked with the joy of the meeting; hugging dear Mrs Leslie and the laird in turn and rushing all over the place with her new-met sisters-in-law, Mary Anne and Meg, and Matilda, William's wife, whom she pleased to call sister-in-law too, and Matilda's sister Caroline; visiting the Hays and the Dalrymples and the Fairholmes . . . George's sense of homecoming was intense, but she could not help wondering, as she observed him with the tenants, so many of whose sons had gone out to work at Canning Downs, or deep in conversation with his father, whether his pleasure was not tempered by the melancholy fear that it was he, not his ancient parents, who was closer to death.

Emmie could not forget the delicacy of George's health, and there were frights to remind her in case she should do so. The laird had insisted that she could not come to Scotland without a taste of real Highland scenery, and so they made a party of a trip from the Don to the Dee. William, Matilda and Caroline came in his open carriage with George, while Emmie travelled with Meg and a Miss Lumsden in the old laird's closed carriage with post horses. They stopped for lunch at the Forbes Arms in Alford, where they were detained for two hours by a heavy shower, then they continued to Kincardine. Afterwards, Emmie felt angry with herself for not sharing George's vehicle. She wondered whether he had got wet, or what had occurred. For no sooner had they put up at the Head Inn in Kincardine than George had a violent fit of coughing. All night he lay sick. Early in the rainy morning he spat blood again, but he said he felt better when the Fergusons came from Inchmarlo to join them with their children. When the Fergusons went home, he continued with the rest of the party. But the following night he was worse again and Emmie sat up, dabbing his temples with rose-water from a bottle in her new dressing case. The next day, while William and Emmie stayed with George, the other ladies went to Balmoral where they had an introduction to Mr Robertson, Prince Albert's Commissioner, who showed them the grounds and castle. In the evening a Dr Reid visited George, and two weeks later Emmie went with George to Edinburgh to consult with a Dr Duncan.

*

When Frederik's condition was confirmed by a Bournemouth lung specialist he did not even feel unwell, so the diagnosis was received with incredulity; and the cosmic injustice of being struck down when he had only just married, when he was about to become a father, seemed grotesque. His God was not a vengeful one. But it was not Frederik's place to fathom His purposes, only to be His instrument. So his outrage was inconsequential; and when he recalled the fogs coming in off the Greenland seas, he shuddered and knew, deep down, that the doctor was right. Never mind that the thermometer had said it was warmer than Siberia in those infernal bays, the damp was like an infestation of lice and he longed for the crisp tundra. Even so, he did not quite accept that he was under sentence of death for it was well known that consumptives might live out the term of their natural life in tolerable health, for all that some, like the unfortunate Keats, might succumb very rapidly.

Emmie was also sanguine – despite her initial horror – about Frederik's prospects. She was given to understand that the disease was not far advanced in him, and tales of indefinitely stayed execution were common enough. It had taken George eight years to die after his first haemorrhage, and she had always believed the speed of his decline to have been due to his restlessness. During that year in England, everything had still seemed possible – or almost everything, for she did persuade him to give up Canning Downs. But it seemed that rest was something to be found in the disposition rather than circumstances, and recovery eluded him. There was no reason to suppose that Frederik's illness would follow the same pattern. Walter had had it for years and showed no sign of worsening; though it had to be admitted that his brother Tom was not in good health, nor was her own sister Lucy. Poor Ernest Dalrymple had faded very fast, but then nobody but Walter really knew what happened out there in the bush, nor how long Ernest had been ill before he perished. It was certain that he had no respite from work until he was carried to his final bed in Brisbane, with Walter as his nurse.

It was one thing to lose a husband from consumption, but to have it happen twice – such a thing, Emmie told herself, *could not be*. But there came a night in Nice when, woken by Frederik's coughing, six years slipped away in the stupor of interrupted sleep as she reached out to find that he was clammy, and she murmured, as she had used to do, "Would you like some rosewater?"

"Rosewater?" Frederik gasped into the darkness.

Recovering from her confusion, Emmie explained that she could massage his temples and forehead with rosewater. The bottle she kept in her dressing case for George was still there, untouched since his death.

*

Following the advice of Frederik's doctor, as soon as Emmie felt well enough they travelled to Nice, where the change of air brought a marked improvement in Frederik's health. In June they were in London again, and Emmie gave birth to a son in lodgings in Grosvenor Square. She was advised to recuperate in Malvern, whose comfortable dullness would cushion them against the anticipated shock of their duties as parents. Moreover, it was thought only fair that Norah, the Irish nurse whom they engaged, should begin her service in the relative familiarity of England.

Norah was short and broad, with lush black hair, pink face and, when she chose, a generous smile. Emmie and Frederik took to her at once. In due course they found her to be possessed of the same unstinting devotion as Mattie, the convict gardener at Vineyard. Norah had looked after William and Matilda Leslie's baby, George, who, after two years of rude health in her care, had died of pneumonia soon after her departure. His death followed his grandfather's by a few months, and the new laird took it hard.

It was in Malvern that Emmie at last met Frederik's brother

Christian. Only now had he obtained leave from the Legation in Vienna. It would not have surprised him more if Frederik had brought back the daughter of a Chinese merchant from Igoon than that he should choose to marry an Australian widow. Although Frederik had often complained that the Danish ladies were limited, his letters had always been so full of longing for home. There was the perpetual refrain that it was time Clara came back from the West Indies, but hadn't he declared from his Greenland misery that they should all stop travelling, and that Alma should not be allowed to try her wings? Why, when he was now in a position to go home, would he commit himself to permanent exile? Christian understood that there was a medical aspect to the question, but he did not suppose it could be decisive. Besides, it seemed so improbable that a colonial's merits should be greater than those of a European.

Arriving in London, Christian was irked to find a message instructing him to proceed to Malvern. He did not relish the prospect of a week in a dowdy provincial spa. He was appeased, however, by the discovery that his nephew had been baptised Christian.

Christian was not tall, but he was handsome, with a well-groomed, fashionably pointed beard and busy brown eyes. The trace of a scar slanting across his exposed forehead, legacy of a Prussian sabre at a clash over Schleswig-Holstein in 1849, gave depth to what might otherwise have been a bland face. He had a limp too, from Prussian shot at the battle of Isted a year later, which had caused him to be invalided out of the army at the age of twenty-two and to enter the diplomatic service. His manners were impeccable, like his brother's; but where Frederik's were unobtrusive, Christian's were more courtly: Frederik would pull a chair back for a lady neatly, without superfluous words, but the same action would be performed by Christian with a little flourish and accompanied by a compliment. Emmie could not help being impressed by him. Twenty years previously – even ten – he would have seemed an exotic character to her.

She could not have been better disposed towards a new acquaintance. Mutual good will and curiosity ensured that they had plenty to talk about and, though she was older and less fashionable than

Christian might have hoped for a sister-in-law to be, he saw that she was beautiful, and a person of substance. But by the afternoon of the third day Emmie began to tire of his charms and to suspect that he did not see in her the qualities he found admirable in a woman. The day was still and sunny. They were having tea in the garden of their hotel. A table was set up in the shade of a yew, laden with scones, cakes and a large china teapot. Emmie occupied a comfortable chair with her baby on her lap, while Frederik and Christian sat to one side on folding chairs. Norah was a little apart with some needlework, ready to take the baby if Emmie wished.

"I don't understand why you came back to England to have the baby," Christian said to Frederik. "I thought the doctors had told you to stay in the south."

"My dear brother!" said Frederik, tipping his hat towards the shimmering sunshine. "In winter, perhaps – when it is damp – but . . ."

"You mean you quit the south of France for the sake of the sunshine here? That would surprise the good citizens of Malvern, I dare say!"

Emmie laughed, and thought of cloudless Australian skies.

"I appreciate that it would have been more convenient for you to visit us in France," said Frederik, "but we thought it preferable for Emmie to be here."

It seemed to Emmie that Christian suspected her of dragging Frederik to Malvern against his will. She felt assessed and cast aside, her wants deemed legitimate only as they accorded with Frederik's; otherwise they were female whims, to be ruled rather than argued with. "We both wanted it," she said.

"Of course," Christian said.

A waiter had been advancing over the lawn with a silver platter. As he approached the Zieges and it became apparent that the offering was destined for them rather than one of the other groups in the vicinity, they turned from their conversation as from sour milk.

"Please excuse the interruption, Captain Ziege," said the waiter with a slight bow. "A letter has come for you."

Frederik thanked him and opened the envelope. "It's from Oscar!" he said.

Emmie supposed he must mean a cousin, whom she had not met. He was something in the Danish Legation in Paris. He had a brother who was stationed in the Danish West Indies and had married a Creole, if she was not mistaken.

"Prince Frederik is in Paris for two weeks," Frederik announced after reading the letter. "Oscar says it would be a good opportunity to see him."

Christian turned to Emmie. "Oscar is Secretary of the Danish Legation in Paris," he explained. "He is referring to the Danish Crown Prince – "

"Yes," said Emmie, feeling her skin prickle with anger.

" – though I see I am telling you what you already know," he added smoothly. "How rude of me! Our royal family is so overshadowed by those of mightier nations – "

"Christian," Frederik interrupted, "you forget that Emmie spent several months with us – with Mama and Hannina – last year."

"Indeed I had not forgotten!" he cried. "Anyway," he continued for Emmie's benefit, as if in confidence, "although our monarchy is not so wealthy, it has retained its authority while some of its European counterparts have not. Subjects who enjoy its patronage are mindful of their good fortune if they have no independent means."

Offended by this speech, Emmie did not reply.

"Will you go, do you think?" Christian persisted.

"Good God, Christian! Are you in league with a travel agent?" Frederik cried. "Anyone would think you were trying to sell us tickets on commission!"

Emmie spluttered into her sleeping baby's face in an unconvincing attempt to disguise her laughter in a nursery game. Then she lifted her eyes to Frederik, whose smile awaited her, brimming just for her for an instant; and in his flash of humour she saw answer and understanding.

"We shall certainly go back by Paris, Crown Prince or no," she said to Christian, as Norah took the baby. "I would like to meet Oscar, after all."

Emmie was pleased when, later that evening, after dinner, Frederik followed her soon to bed. During Christian's visit she had retired early, knowing that the brothers must wish to talk. But on this occasion she felt troubled by the exchanges with Christian, afraid that she had misunderstood him. Ordinarily, the idea that she might be a subject of discussion between the two of them would not have worried her, but she did not wish it so tonight. She needed Frederik's reassurance that she had not disgraced herself in Christian's eyes.

Although the lives of the two brothers only permitted occasional meetings, Emmie knew from experience that this need not reflect the strength of their bond. Their correspondence was regular and she had no doubt that they were devoted to each other, as she was to her own distant siblings. Christian would by nature feel protective towards Frederik and therefore wary of her. She was unprepared, however, for her reaction to him. She expected men to be direct and active; to have solid beliefs and to act in accordance with them. Even Mr Huxley could not be criticised for failing to defend what he professed to believe was the truth. It wasn't that she doubted Christian's courage – he bore the marks of it, after all – but she found him self-serving. She felt ashamed for thinking it, for his ability and his loyalty to his country were unimpeachable. Nor could she say that he was anything other than scrupulous in fulfilling his obligations towards his family. But there was something too polished about him, too fastidious. Imagine him shearing a sheep!

But whatever her feelings towards her new brother-in-law, Emmie was aware that they counted for nothing. For Frederik's sake she was bound to be on good terms. In any case, she was unlikely to see Christian often. Of more pressing concern was her own family's health. Glad as she was to come to England for little Christian's birth and enjoy the comforts of Malvern, the south of France was more suitable for Frederik, and she was determined to go back there as soon as she was recovered. She said as much to Frederik as he came into the room, watching him in her mirror as she brushed her hair in readiness for bed. "Of course we will go by Paris and visit the Crown Prince. But," she added, laying aside her brush and turning to face him, "why did Christian find it necessary to make explanations to me?"

Frederik drew up a chair to the fire. As he sat down, he unbuttoned his waistcoat. Emmie was pleased to see more colour in his face. "Oh, you don't want to take too much notice of Christian," he said. "Do you mind if I smoke?"

"Not at all, my dear."

He took a cigarette from his case. Finding that he had no more matches, he picked up the tongs and reached into the fire for an ember, which he raised towards his face. "Ah, the things one can do without a beard!" he remarked through the puff of smoke. He inhaled, then blew the smoke out through his nose, hunched forward a little, with his hands on his knees. "There is no doubting Christian's loyalties, which is a fine thing," he said. "But he may not be so sure of me, because he interprets them more narrowly."

"You mean he thinks you have betrayed your family, or country, by marrying me?"

"I hope he is not so harsh. But I believe some such notion worries at him."

"Was that meant to comfort me?"

Frederik smiled. One of the reasons he loved Emmie was that she didn't want or ask for hollow comfort. That made it easier to go to the core of a matter and find whatever true consolation was to be had. "Christian is very sure he knows how the world works, and perhaps he does," he said. "But if he does not always give credit to others for understanding, it is because he does not fully appreciate that they might value things differently. This applies as much to me as to you."

Puzzled, but too tired to seek elucidation, Emmie picked up the bottle of *sal volatile* from her dressing case, then she stared at it as if unsure how it came to be in her hand.

*

After she had met the Danish Crown Prince, Emmie recalled Frederik's remark and realised that she had missed its full meaning. Contrary to her expectations, the occasion was not elaborate, unlike when she was presented at Court thirteen years earlier. Then, quite apart from the care devoted to her gown and hair – she remembered her determination to carry a bouquet with a shiver of embarrassment – it was deemed necessary by the Dowager Lady Farquhar, her sponsor, that she even learn to curtsy in a particular way. She had taken great delight in being the first Australian-born lady to be presented to the Queen.

Leaving Norah in their hotel with the baby, Frederik and Emmie made their way to the Danish Legation, a tall, narrow building of classical design in the rue Saint Augustin with pretty wrought-iron balconies. She had worried about what she would wear, but Frederik discouraged her from ostentation and she wore a dress of grey silk trimmed with lace, long gloves, and her Australian kangaroo brooch.

Oscar was waiting for them in the hall. Although his forehead was higher and his nose more aquiline than either Frederik's or Christian's, Emmie noticed his resemblance to his cousins: the firm jaw-line and dark eyes. But he was more fleshy, as if the comforts of Paris had made a willing convert. He kissed Emmie's hand and greeted Frederik with a hug before accompanying them upstairs to a salon furnished in Empire style. Prince Frederik entered a minute later without any of the pomp Emmie associated with royalty, already smiling. He was of medium height with an owlish, intelligent face. Dressed in a dark frock coat with frogging and a pale grey waistcoat, his appearance gave no clue that Emmie could discern to his rank.

"Enchanté," he said, taking her hand in his as she curtsied. As she rose, he added in perfect English, "I think I can say this since we are in Paris? I am truly delighted to meet you, Madame."

Then he turned to Frederik and, gripping both his hands, addressed him warmly in Danish before turning back to Emmie, still holding one of Frederik's hands, and declaring to them both, "This is truly a pleasure!" And the conversation proceeded in English.

When lunch was announced they moved to a dining room of unexpected intimacy. The round table would have accommodated another four people, but it was too small for more numerous parties. Emmie supposed there must be another, larger dining room. The paintings on the walls were views of Copenhagen – sober merchants' houses arranged along wharves and streets that would be silent on Sundays apart from the clang of church bells, and swarming with industry again on Mondays. But between two windows there was one exception, to which Oscar drew Emmie's attention, a strange aquarelle of a ruined pagan temple with a headless statue in a niche, situated on the edge of a hill above a desert. Oscar told her that it was the work of Frederik's father, no stranger to this building.

Sole colbert and iced champagne were followed by tender fillet of veal and creamed endives. Later, Frederik told Emmie that the Prince had enquired beforehand, through a note from Oscar, what she liked to eat. There were even fresh strawberries, though they were not as good as Scottish ones. It was like going to lunch with a friend of Frederik's; a friend of some importance, to be sure, but he was kind to her and interested in little Christian. He thanked her for making the effort to visit him because, he said, he had been most anxious to meet Frederik's wife. And he urged her to come to Denmark as soon as possible so that she might see what kind of people her husband came from.

"And then you will see the stuffed eagle that your husband sent me two years ago."

Emmie wasn't sure if she had heard correctly, and she turned to Frederik for confirmation. "A stuffed eagle?"

"Yes, yes! Stuffed eagle!" the Prince repeated with delight.

"Yes," Frederik said, and he sighed. "An old Greenlander brought it to me one day. It was so cold there, and so boring, that the appearance of this . . . creature . . . quite unseated my reason, and I bought it at once. It was beautiful. And the man . . . the man needed to sell . . . Only afterwards did I wonder what I might do with it, for my mother would not want it in her house. I couldn't send it home so it stayed with me, occupying a quarter of my living space, for the entire winter. In the end I sent it to the Prince for his collections."

"You suggested that it sit on top of a tiled stove."

"Did I?"

"Yes. Naturally I followed your advice. I hope you will come and see it *in situ* one day soon," he said to Emmie.

"I should like that very much," she said.

"And was there not a bowhead whale?" Frederik asked. "I recall its skeleton being stowed after we had disembarked in Greenland."

"Yes. There have been problems with its reassembly. Unfortunately it was not well labelled." There was a pause before Prince Frederik said, "Your time in Greenland is mysterious."

"There is no mystery at all, Sir," Frederik replied. "Porridge twice a week, rice soup once, ollebrod once, sweet soup once, yellow peas once and meat soup once a week. Afterwards, either salted meat or seabirds – fricassée, roasted, or prepared as steak from the wings and breast; or dried fish, usually cod; occasionally, reindeer or grouse. No vegetables, only prunes and dried apples. Sometimes we ate seal pup: when the meat was fresh, it was preferable to the seabirds, but when old it tasted of cod liver oil . . ."

Everyone laughed as Frederik delivered this list.

It was understood in Copenhagen that Frederik had not enjoyed his Greenland expedition, but this surprised nobody. He had done his duty, which was the important thing; and he had not complained, which would have been a disgrace. However, his second-in-command, Lieutenant Bluhme, had published a report which exposed Danish abuses in the colony. In the drawing rooms of some of the Zieges' acquaintances, this was regarded as downright seditious. It was whispered, in mitigation, that the hardships had somehow affected his judgement. With futile distress, Frederik realised that this reflected well on himself, for having shared whatever hardships Bluhme might be thought to have suffered, he was considered to have borne his trials with proper fortitude.

"But what really happened there?" said the Prince when the merriment had subsided. He was aware that Frederik had not aired his views about Greenland, whatever they might be, in public. "I read Bluhme's report."

"It would be comforting to believe that he exaggerates, but he does not," Frederik replied.

"I feared so. It would be foolish to condemn the man for his honesty. Still, the public nature of his attack is regrettable."

"Indeed, Sir."

"But you share Lieutenant Bluhme's impressions?"

Frederik rubbed his eyes with the thumb and middle finger of his left hand, then glanced at Emmie. She knew nothing of his Greenland experiences and he had no wish to share them with her. However, it seemed for the moment that he had no choice. "It is not easy to speak of such things," he said to the Prince, "for they are thankfully so removed from the circumstances in which we find ourselves that any approximation to the truth must sound like exaggeration. I take it Bluhme chose to proceed in the way he did – with a public broad-side – because he assumed that if his observations were presented through proper channels they would somehow be disregarded." Frederik hesitated, uncertain just how frank he ought to be. Then, as if judging from the Prince's expression that his true opinion on this matter was precisely what the Prince had summoned him for, he continued: "The first point to make is that there *are* no proper channels for such unwelcome information. Had Bluhme – perhaps through me – come directly to you, then you would have taken appropriate action, but I had no warning of Bluhme's intentions."

The Prince nodded. With his elbows on the arms of his chair, he placed his fingertips together and said, "And the second point?"

"You referred to Lieutenant Bluhme's 'impressions'. This, I submit, is not quite the right word, for it implies that the substance of his report might owe more to his interpretation than to what he observed – the facts themselves. And I do not dispute Bluhme's facts."

"But you dispute his interpretation?"

"No. I regret his presentation, and I regret the facts themselves, but I dispute nothing."

When Frederik said no more, the Prince turned to Emmie. "Lieutenant Bluhme says that native Greenlanders suffer because nobody sees their welfare as their responsibility," he said. "It is a grave charge against a government."

Emmie took it as a compliment that such a remark should be addressed to her, but she assumed too that the Prince was hoping to draw Frederik out through her. "Indeed," she said.

Frederik laughed, delighted by Emmie's evasion. Seeing that the Prince was amused too and admired her loyal silence, Frederik relented and offered a single example: "The Administrator at Godthaab used to grumble to us about the natives' hopelessness. He said that they stole like ravens, though in our experience they were honest enough. He had been there fifty years, so he ought to have known, but he had learned nothing – wilfully, I believe. He had been married to a Greenlander woman, who had died. He had two daughters whom he treated abominably, the older one was a servant in her own home. I often used to find her weeping."

"Not much of an example," Oscar observed.

"Exactly so," said Frederik, with an air of finality that indicated to the Prince that he preferred not to discuss the subject further in front of Emmie.

The Prince sighed and shook his head. "You see, Madame," he said, turning to Emmie, "how we need your husband?"

Emmie was not sure how to interpret this, whether as an allusion to the desirability of Frederik's appointment as a Colonial Administrator in Greenland – for which she thought he would not thank the Prince – or to his commendable practice of telling the truth. In any case, the Prince's good will towards the Ziege family was apparent to Emmie. Only afterwards did it strike her that, while he treated Frederik as a friend, almost no mention had been made of Christian.

San Remo, Winter 1866

IN the light of dawn the stone walls of the Chalet Poncarte were leeched of colour. The mottled surface reminded Frederik of the lichen that the reindeer used to scratch up beneath the snow in Yakutia.

In the evenings of late summer, when they first arrived in San Remo, the house had appeared gilded, as if it had sucked up each day's sunshine. It stood above the village; it was hard to imagine a more promising aspect. The lawn was partially shaded by two umbrella pines, so that Emmie and Frederik could sit outside in comfort and watch the fishing boats in the little bay below. Along one side was a border of lavender, reaching like an unruly curl from the back of the house where it spilled over the wall behind in a great fringe, from a rippling field of purple.

On reaching Chalet Poncarte, Emmie's dressing case was put away in a cupboard, emptied of the things she required for daily use. These were ranged in a tidy crescent on the pretty, lace-fringed dressing table. Trunks and boxes were unpacked and stored with relief: there were no social engagements or business matters to disturb their peace other than those they chose. Norah was now able to settle Christian into a routine of sleeps, feeds and periods of play which were integral to his parents' lives. At last they were in the situation they had craved: they were at home – or what counted as home – with their baby.

Emmie and Frederik were old enough to have seen the impact of children on people's lives and to have understood that their own lives would be changed too, however Norah might shield them. They welcomed the inevitability of change, as they welcomed one another: each of them had set out on the unfolding terrain of their future with faith, aware that at times it might be rugged. It was liberating to feel that they were now entered upon the real purpose of adult life. Having spent so long waiting and preparing for this goal, they shared a sense of having earned what others perhaps stumbled upon too young fully to appreciate.

Frederik would rise early to walk along the shore. If, before leaving, he heard Christian crying, he would loiter in the hall, hat in hand, and wait until the plaintive sounds were halted by Norah. Then he put on his hat and stepped outside. At the garden gate, a branch of climbing rose threatened to catch his shoulder. He pushed it aside with his Malacca cane, noting each day that it needed cutting, but feeling disinclined to do so, for he enjoyed the sense of parting a curtain before coming out to the path. Then he would set off either to the left towards the shore where the fishermen might be landing their catch, or down to the right, through the pines towards the headland.

Wearing a dark suit of heavy cloth (it was still chilly at this time of the morning) and a bow tie, he looked from a distance much like any other gentleman to be found along the coast. He noticed the swell of the pale sea and how the sky and air changed from one day to the next, though others might swear that the weather was the same each day. After he had walked for twenty minutes towards the headland, he came to a spur of rock which he had to scramble round in order to continue. Occasionally he would do this; more often he would stop and sit in its shelter, on a log of driftwood, and smoke a cigarette before returning. Sometimes he encountered a man in a shabby hat, seated on a canvas chair in front of an easel. He had a gaunt face, restless eyes and a grizzled beard. At first they just raised their hats in greeting, but after a few days Frederik approached him.

The artist planted his paintbrush in a jar, then extended his right hand. "Algernon Smith," he said.

Frederik shook hands. "Frederik Ziege. What brings you out so early?"

"I like to catch the early morning sunlight. Besides," he said, "I find it easier to paint before the sun makes me sluggish."

Frederik offered him a cigarette, which he declined.

"And what brings you here?" enquired Mr Smith.

"I am a naval man, recently retired and married."

"What navy?"

"Danish."

"Ah! A Dane!"

After a pause, which Frederik expected to be broken with a remark about Princess Dagmar's recent marriage to the Tsarevich, Mr Smith declared, "How dull you must find this coast!"

"Not at all," said Frederik. "It is tame, certainly, but that is the beauty of it."

"And do you say it is beautiful because it is tame?"

"No. A man may find many things beautiful, though his mood might dispose him to appreciate one better than another at different times."

Mr Smith nodded before asking, "What is the wildest coast you have visited?"

Frederik considered for a moment, drawing on his cigarette. "I spent the winter three years ago doing a coastal survey in Greenland," he replied slowly. "That is a most desolate place. But I think the wildest was sailing north from the Sea of Japan. When you see the area on a chart, it is usually drawn up very small, but you can see the mountains of Manchuria and Japan from a distance of twenty miles, and the sea itself is much rougher than the North Sea. You pass through into De Castris Bay, which is long and treacherous, and the charts are hopelessly inadequate so that you are in constant danger of running aground. The coasts on either side – Tongusia and the island of Sakhalin – look bleak and inhospitable . . . But God knows! They too are beautiful!"

"Don't you look at the sailors here, and the sea, and think them like children?"

"No!" Frederik protested. "The landscape may be calm, but the sailors are as skilled here as anywhere."

"I should like to travel, but alas! I shall not. I am consumptive."

Frederik wondered whether Mr Smith's confidence was prompted by recognition of a fellow-sufferer. "I'm sorry," he said, looking him in the eye without pity. "I trust you will have many years of tolerable comfort left to you."

Mr Smith shrugged.

"In any case, when you are travelling, you want to go home. When you are still, you want to travel," Frederik remarked.

"Are you not content, then?" Mr Smith said.

"Most certainly I am!" said Frederik, as if Mr Smith's question was an accusation. He crushed his cigarette underfoot. "I have no desire to go back to sea!"

Frederik stood up. He felt that the painter wanted him to ask the same question in return, but he regretted what he had already said. "It has been a pleasure meeting you, Mr Smith. Doubtless we shall meet again."

But Frederik did not go that way again until he was persuaded that the painter had left the area. Instead, he went down to the beach to observe the fishermen handling their craft and their nets. He had seen natives spearing fish through the ice in the frozen rivers of Siberia, and the practices here seemed no less marvellous: he watched knowing that he could not do what they did, and he felt angry with the English dauber who had wanted him to admit to some superiority he did not feel just because he had travelled far in a ship.

Before returning to the house, Frederik would make a detour into the village where he bought bread at the baker. He knew that Emmie thought he ought to leave this to Signora La Broussa, the housekeeper-cum-cook, who expected to do it, but he enjoyed the feel of the warm loaves and the sense that he was not returning empty-handed from his walk. He found the signora on his return one morning with her arms in a huge, sweet pile of lavender. It emerged that Emmie had mentioned her wish to distil lavender water from the crop in the garden. An empty bottle from her dressing case, which she would fill with the liquid, stood waiting. Emmie had been looking forward to doing the job herself – she only needed the signora's advice – and was disappointed to find the job almost done: she took it as evidence of the signora's sensitivity towards Frederik's blithe usurpation of her bread-buying duty. Frederik said that if he wanted to buy bread, he would. The signora could buy more bread, if she must, and feed it to her pig.

Norah would bring Christian to join them for breakfast, which was taken at a round table in the morning room, a comfortable room with a bay window facing east. Fed, fresh, pink and blond, Christian presented at the best of times a charming image of felicity, sugges-tive of an eternity of tranquil, sunny days. At worst, he wheezed and wailed with grim, nerve-shredding tenacity.

Arrangements had to be made for washing clothes and cleaning the house; for looking after the garden and guaranteeing a supply of fuel for the winter. Signora La Broussa could give them advice and tell them what the usual practices were for the house, but Frederik and Emmie liked to make sure for themselves that such matters were disposed of in the best possible manner. Thus Emmie interviewed two other local women before agreeing to the washerwoman recommended by Signora La Broussa, while Frederik overruled her choice of dairy after finding that supposedly fresh butter was rancid: taking the trouble to visit its source, he discovered a filthy cowshed supervised by a slovenly oaf who resented his inspection.

The morning was the time for considering Emmie's Australian affairs. Having examined several folders of documents, George's shrewdness was evident to Frederik. He had demanded detail from those accountable to him and, if a margin could be increased by careful management, or an interest rate improved upon elsewhere, then he would write the necessary letters. Uncertain of her own abil-ities but determined not to let George down, Emmie had sought the advice of her brother-in-law William, who had given up his partner-ship with Dents in Canton. But though his advice was said by Emmie to be invaluable, Frederik could see that it was in practice often superfluous: for Emmie herself was economical and efficient by upbringing; she was well acquainted with the nature of the concerns she had inherited from George and she was not afraid to express herself. However, the death of her other partner, Mr Anderson, after a short illness, highlighted the risk of investing in so distant a venture, for his widow would doubtless sell her share, upsetting George's arrangements.

Until the weather began to turn cool in November, they ate lunch outside beneath a vine-threaded trellis. Afterwards they would rest or read until late afternoon when, accompanied by Norah, they took Christian for a walk in his pram. Frederik fretted about his son more than did Emmie. He always had an opinion about whether the boy was dressed to suit the tiny variations in climate, and he knew exactly what other clothes were in his cupboard to choose from. His attention was not felt by Norah as interference but as care, and it pleased her. Emmie was not altogether surprised by the interest Frederik took in domestic life because she had expected it of him, but it delighted her nevertheless. In each detail of nourishment and clothing, Emmie felt a confirmation of the bond uniting them.

Their sense of themselves as a family was reinforced in November by the arrival of Fanny, the daughter of Mary Anne Ferguson, George's sister. Fanny was a sweet-tempered, intelligent girl of eighteen, with the pale skin and auburn hair of her Scottish ancestors. She was thrilled by her Aunt Emmie's invitation to spend the season in the south, while Emmie – who was anyway extremely fond of her – looked forward to making welcome a member of the family who had always been so kind. This was reason enough for Frederik to be hospitable to Fanny, while nothing could indicate more clearly that he himself was accepted by Emmie's family than that Fanny should be permitted to stay with them. Fanny doted on the baby and, to Emmie's amusement, she seemed in awe of Frederik, whose combination of amiability and experience was quite new to her. His knowledge of the world, his command of languages, his manners – everything about him seemed glamorous to her, but especially the fact that he had fallen in love with Emmie. And if Fanny saw Emmie in a different light because of Frederik, then Emmie was bound to be pleased.

One morning soon after Fanny's arrival, a man came to the house in a brougham drawn by two handsome bays. Emmie and Frederik were out, leaving Fanny to her self-imposed hour of French study. She jumped up when she heard the carriage and looked out of the window.

She saw a short man descend, leaning with care on a slim silver-tipped cane. He had magnificent whiskers, like her own late grandfather, but, when he was shown in with a grimace by Signora La Broussa, Fanny was unnerved to discover that he spoke not a word of English.

"Enchanté," he said, and added something about "Monsieur le Capitaine Ziege" as, with a bow that Fanny was convinced must make him overbalance, so top-heavy did he seem, he handed her a card engraved with a Russian name. Though small of stature, he was very sure of himself, and Fanny felt all her French unravel: "Monsieur Ziege est içi mais il n'est pas içi."

The man considered this news with astonishment, then directed a further volley at her.

"Il va — vient — I mean il va revenir," she tried.

He brought out an enormous watch from his waistcoat pocket and tapped it. "Quand?"

"Bientôt!" Fanny told him with a triumphant smile.

He seemed to derive some satisfaction from this, and bowed and left the room.

"Monsieur! Monsieur!" Fanny cried, pursuing him out of doors, afraid that he would leave without seeing Frederik.

"M'selle?"

"Il va revenir bientôt, très bientôt," Fanny uttered, "Monsieur Ziege va revenir très bientôt . . ."

"Oui. Je comprends," he said, but he plainly didn't expect her to understand because with a brisk little mime he indicated that he would wait for Monsieur Ziege in his carriage.

As she went inside, Fanny thought with chagrin that she had revealed herself to be an ignorant bumpkin. The Russian gentleman would tell them what sort of reception he had met with, and she would be disgraced.

When Emmie and Frederik returned, the man kissed Emmie's hand and embraced Frederik, addressing him at length in Russian. Frederik nodded, smiled, then replied with a few words in Russian and at last invited him inside. The man explained himself all over again to Emmie when he was inside, in a language that Fanny recognised to be French but which still remained obscure to her. It was with relief, verging on hilarity, that she realised that Emmie had no more idea of what the man was talking about than she did herself. After his brandy, he stayed for lunch, and didn't depart until after three o'clock. Although he continued to talk in French for the ladies' benefit, his accent was so quaint that they depended on asides from Frederik to comprehend him.

Besides a message, the man had brought a package for Frederik.

As Fanny watched Frederik unwind a long piece of cloth, she had the sense that something wonderful and dramatic was about to happen. His hands moved firmly, not rushing but not hesitating. In the middle was a heavy dagger with an ivory handle, like an Orthodox cross, which he unsheathed before handing it to Emmie.

Fanny expected that an explanation for the visitor's gift would emerge, but Emmie volunteered nothing and Fanny felt that it would be impertinent to ask. When they took Christian for a walk, Frederik asked her instead how her French studies were progressing.

"Not very well," she answered. "I'm afraid I really didn't understand your friend at all!"

"Had I been looking after you as I should, I would have stopped your ears!" said Frederik.

Expecting him to proceed with some discussion of what had occurred, Fanny laughed, but instead he asked, "Do you have snow in Aberdeenshire at this time of year?"

"Now come along, Frederik," said Emmie at last, when they were sitting down in front of their soup. She had changed into a blue silk evening gown and pinned her hair tight over her ears, so that her long coral earrings glinted in the candlelight. Her blue eyes were intent on him as she chided, "You have kept us in suspense long enough. Fanny and I have been most patient, and now it is time for you to put us out of our misery."

"Misery?" Frederik said. "Am I responsible for misery?"

"It is too cruel."

"But what do you wish to know? I have received a gift from Constantin Nicolaevich – "

"Oh, Frederik! Do stop being so mysterious! Fanny will go home saying that you have assignations with peculiar little Russian men and – "

"Will you, Fanny?" Frederik said.

"I hardly know what to say, but I admit I am curious!"

"Ah!" Frederik raised his eyebrows in such a way that Fanny still wasn't sure if he was surprised.

Reaching to the middle of the table, Frederik picked up the salt dish and pepper pot, one in each hand. They were both cut glass: the salt dish was flat, the pepper pot cylindrical with a silver top. "There are two aspects: the Danish, and the Russian," he said, setting them down in front of his place. With his left index finger on the rim of the salt dish, he continued: "My cousin, Ida Bille Brahe, accompanied Princess Dagmar – or Marie Feodorovna, as I believe we should now call her – to Russia in September, where she has by now met a number of acquaintances of mine, as has the Princess." Then he touched the pepper pot with his right index finger. "Among them is the Tsarevich's uncle, Constantin Nicolaevich, whose son Nicholas it was my duty to teach to sail some years ago." He took a sip of soup before proceeding: "Mutual friends are a conversational boon: my name was mentioned. News of my marriage – " Frederik inclined his head to Emmie " – and of Christian's birth, was duly conveyed. Good wishes from the ladies and a token of the Grand Duke's good wishes were thought to be appropriate, and they were entrusted to the buffoon who visited us today because he was heading to Nice for the season. He travelled by way of Germany, where of course he was detained, and it has taken him all this time to reach us."

"Your modesty is infuriating sometimes!" declared Emmie.

Frederik shrugged. "I am just telling you the facts!"

"You know perfectly well what I mean!" said Emmie, pretending to be cross. She knew that Frederik would not tell stories if there was any hint of boasting in them, and she admired him for this: but she felt that Fanny deserved to have a story to take home with her. "The yacht," she said, "what of the yacht?"

"It was a schooner, called the *Opecit*," he said, "based at Strelna. Every now and again I would receive the order that the young Grand Duke was to come aboard, and he would spend the day with us."

"And you taught him to sail?" asked Fanny.

"Yes, I taught him how the schooner worked."

"How old was he?"

"Nine."

"That is very young."

Frederik smiled. "It is old enough," he answered.

"What was he like?"

"He was pleasant, but not greatly gifted I'm afraid."

Fanny considered this for a moment; then, as if proffering a gift with caution, Frederik said, "The strangest thing about his days on board was the presence of all his kitchen staff. He wasn't allowed to eat food cooked in the galley – he had to have everything specially prepared."

"Good heavens! Why on earth?" Fanny cried.

"They are all terrified of being poisoned."

"It must have been bewildering having him suddenly appear for a day, and then be without him – what did you do in between?"

"It's just like any other naval vessel – the officers alternate watches and ensure that it operates smoothly."

"Were the other sailors all Russian?" Fanny asked.

"All the sailors were, and most of the officers."

"Did you speak Russian with them all?"

"How funny. I recall my mother asking me that too. Yes, I did not wish to give anybody the opportunity of regarding me as a foreigner, more than was unavoidable."

After they had gone to bed and were alone, Frederik teased Emmie. "I don't understand why you and Fanny wanted to know all those dull details."

"They are not dull," she said. "It was interesting hearing about the background to the dagger."

Frederik evaded direct questions and Emmie was glad that he did not discourse on his past life. She did not need to know every particle about him in order to appreciate him, but she was grateful for the slivers afforded in the rare anecdotes he granted to others. Even if the dagger was no more than a trivial memento to him, as she supposed, it represented a phase of his life which was now brought within the orbit of home.

The idea of a domestic idyll was essential to both Emmie's and Frederik's conception of happiness. She had a clear memory of it from childhood, and sometimes she liked to believe she had attained it in her first marriage. Frederik, on the other hand, had never been more than a pilgrim to the shrine of his mother's Copenhagen hearth. Settling down together with their baby, albeit in a rented house, was a departure for them both, but, in their separate ways, they were skilled at coping in unfamiliar territory. When Frederik took command of the *Boyarin* in De Castris Bay because the captain was ill and the second-in-command was crippled by arthritis, he kept two small boats on permanent alert ahead of the corvette in the mist, taking soundings. It took two weeks to travel a hundred miles but, alone in the squadron, the *Boyarin* avoided running aground. Frederik even enjoyed himself, although he was exhausted when they docked in Nicolaevsk.

Life in Emmie's childhood home, Vineyard, was safe and ordered, but danger and exploration were the currency of nursery and dinner-table stories alike. Emmie would never forget her brother Jack's half-starved, shattered appearance when he returned from his expedition with Strzelecki to Gippsland, nor the lesson that it was Charlie Tarra, his blackfellow, who kept them alive by catching koalas. There was Annie's news from Wickham aboard the *Beagle*, and older tales from her cousin Philip King, who was a midshipman when the *Beagle* charted the South American coast, first under his father and then under FitzRoy. Baron von Hügel was a regular at Vineyard, also Cunningham and others . . . Then there was strange Mr Leichhardt, to whom she was the last woman to bid Godspeed as he departed from Canning Downs in 1848 before vanishing in the interior. Two years before, when she was still Miss Macarthur, he had complimented her in a letter on her "silver-ringing voice" and told her that he "had learned by heart the outlines of her fair countenance". Success at Canning Downs depended partly on routines, but life appeared more as a succession of confrontations with the unpredictable – the ruthless elements, disease among animals, ticket-of-leave men, Aborigines. Contending with new and difficult circumstances was not just a way of life for Emmie, it was life itself, and a preparation for the time when God would judge them. Yet domestic felicity remained her ideal as it did Frederik's.

They were not complacent in expecting to be able to navigate the present. They knew they would be surprised. And so they were – above all, by Christian. At first, he could be banished to the nursery in case of prolonged bouts of crying, where Norah would soothe him. Since it was assumed that he was healthy, there was no cause for unusual concern. It was Norah herself, upset by his gasping over Christmas, who insisted that "the babby must see the doctor".

"But the doctor has often seen him," Emmie said, referring to Dr Wright, who came over from Menton once a month to check up on them. Although his visits were demanded by Emmie as a precaution for Frederik, and he did alleviate her own persistent complaints, they felt more like social calls. His top hat mattered more to him than his stethoscope, and when he inspected Christian, he did so in the manner of an indulgent godfather.

"It don't seem right, Sir, that he should be gaspin' so," Norah explained.

The doctor looked at Christian in bemusement and turned him up the other way to see if he yielded any further symptoms when facing to Australia; tapped him on his chest and on his back, gingerly applied his stethoscope.

"Yes, he is a little short of breath," he pronounced at last. "Very common among infants. Nothing much to be done, alas, other than keeping him where there's plenty of fresh air to be had. Which you are doing very nicely as it is."

After Christian's examination it was Frederik's turn. When the business was finished, Frederik proposed some refreshment before the doctor's return journey.

"I would appreciate that mightily," said the doctor.

They settled next door, as usual, each with a glass of port. Dr Wright lit his pipe with an air of expanding comfort while Frederik provided himself with a cigarette and considered what was on his mind with trepidation, as if the act of voicing it would give substance to his fears.

"Do you think there is any connection," he began at last, "any connection between my son's condition – and my own?"

Dr Wright continued to puff as if he had not heard the question, his benign gaze directed to the garden.

"Not, perhaps, that much might be done, yet I should like to know," Frederik struggled.

"Knowledge is often a dangerous thing."

"It is said in some parts of the Mediterranean that consumption is infectious . . ."

"Oh, dear me, no! That is peasant lore. It has no more foundation in science than has the efficacy of rain dances!"

"But I understand it to be a persistent belief."

"So, I fear, is the trust in rain dances among the Aborigines of Australia. Medical research, however, indicates that consumption runs in families."

"So you think it possible that there is a connection?"

The doctor inclined his head.

"Yet there is no other instance of consumption in my family."

The doctor shrugged.

"I see," said Frederik.

"It is important not to reproach yourself. The only thing to be done is to ensure, so far as possible, that he benefits from a good climate, as you have done yourself. Christian's health may be delicate, but there is no certainty that the disease will develop in him."

Reflecting on this discussion after Dr Wright's departure, Frederik told himself that the doctor's opinion was just that – an opinion. But the fact remained, at least in Norah's view, that Christian was delicate. Had he been suffering from a broken bone or any disease with a known cure, a solution would be found. As it was, Frederik could only shudder at the baby's preciousness. He decided not to tell Emmie about his conversation because it would worry her to no purpose. Probably she had made the connection herself, and they would find themselves talking about it in due course.

Emmie had wondered whether to speak to Dr Wright on her own account, but she did not see what he could say. She grew sicker, however, and still had no period, so he examined her on his next visit and told her that she was expecting another baby. The moment then had been missed for Frederik to tell Emmie about Dr Wright's diagnosis, for she would agitate herself over the new baby too – and there was nothing to be done, and anyway Dr Wright might be mistaken.

Late in March they were due to travel to Denmark for Alma's marriage. Emmie had been looking forward to the trip, to being shown Copenhagen by Frederik, to showing his family how glad she was to be among them. But she was not well enough to travel. Her disappointment was the more acute because she liked Alma; and the match of their circumstances – Alma was marrying Carl Bloch, the artist whom she had met in Rome when they were there together – made her feel a particular sympathy. No occasion could have been more auspicious for her first visit, but sickness left her with no choice but to stay in San Remo, persuading herself that Frederik's family would think she did not care to mix with them. Since she was staying at home, Christian did so too, and Frederik went alone.

Happy as he was to be with his family and friends, and to enjoy the many other consolations of Copenhagen, Frederik discovered that he missed Christian. If it had once seemed that home was where Emmie was, he found now that this definition was no longer adequate. Home, it seemed, was also where their baby was, and their unborn baby too. He looked forward to returning with unequivocal excitement, anticipating a similar sense of euphoria to that which had overtaken them both the previous September.

Copenhagen was damp and overcast. As Frederik travelled south again, the weather cleared and the temperature rose. The railway carriage from Paris was stuffy and he was troubled by a headache. When he reached San Remo, it was a hot spring day and he regretted not having dressed in his lighter suit that morning. Still, the sunshine was uplifting and he put his slight dizziness down to the excitement of seeing Emmie and Christian.

As soon as Emmie heard the carriage arrive she hurried outside. Frederik had dismounted already, was approaching, and she was in his arms. Her lavender scent rushed upon him as he felt the relief with which she submitted to his embrace; from his touch, she knew his pleasure at being with her again. But when he stepped back and, with her elbows in his hands, they looked at one another, they were shocked by what they saw. From the bags around her eyes and a slight puffiness around her mouth, he could see that she was tired; while to his skin there was a uniform, waxy pallor, redeemed only by a hectic patch at each cheekbone.

Norah was on the threshold with Christian. When Frederik saw her, he advanced with outstretched arms and she surrendered the baby, whom he hugged. "Ah! How I have missed you!"

"You will need a rest, my dear Frederik," said Emmie. She determined to wait before telling him about the letter she had received from Mant during his absence.

"A rest? I have been sitting in a railway carriage for three days!"

"But you must be tired!"

The driver had unloaded the luggage and was waiting to be paid.

Frederik handed Christian to Emmie, settled with the man and thanked him with excessive zeal.

He was reaching out for Christian again when he was seized by a violent fit of coughing. It did not cease until he was sitting on a chair in the hall, elbows on his knees, a handkerchief pressed to his mouth.

Recovering himself, he turned towards Emmie, trying to smile. But she was not looking at him. She and Norah were transfixed by the scarlet bloom on his handkerchief.

Frederik was conscious of the gravity of what had occurred, but in the days that followed, as he lay in bed obedient to Dr Wright's instructions, it was not his own tiresome crisis that he dwelled upon. He was plagued by the feeling that he had betrayed Emmie, as if there were something he had failed to resist, or neglected to offer. An intruder was in the home: a Sword of Damocles hovering over them, which was not the illness itself, which they knew about, but an unknown realm within their marriage that was disclosed by it. What would it be like to travel where there was no guide? Frederik wondered.

Emmie watched impatiently for Frederik to recover. She needed to discuss Mant's news with him. Despair, however, brought restraint, for she knew that it was already far too late to do anything, and had been too late long before she had any inkling – even before Mant had sent the information from the other side of the world – that 3,000 head of cattle had, allegedly, vanished.

Switzerland, Summer 1867

O NCE he was sure that Emmie was comfortable in one of the saloon's spacious private booths with Christian and Norah, Frederik came on deck to feel the soft flutter of the air and look at the parallel shore. Travelling by steamer over Lake Geneva's glassy surface made him recall crossing Lake Baikal in winter, when he was pulled in a tarantass by tough Siberian ponies across a white landscape that stretched to the horizon. The contrast could hardly be greater. There, the traveller was exposed to raw nature: here, nature seemed so gentle and ordered. But where a sailor's life was for the most part featureless routine, despite surface excitements such as crossing Lake Baikal, his life now was not so empty of events as at first appeared. Married life, it turned out, was one of constant activity. Already this year he had been alone to Denmark, then back to San Remo; now from Montreux, where they were staying for July, they were making an excursion to Vevey to visit Emmie's old friend David Fairholme. Next week they would be in Lucerne. Meanwhile Christian had learned to crawl; he was coming alive to the world more marvellously than any flower; and beloved Emmie was *enceinte* again. Who would say that this was monotonous? If ever he was wistful about his bachelor days, it could only be for their placidity.

Dr Wright had advised them to go to Switzerland for the summer because the air was so much better than on the coast. They were further encouraged by the prospect of visiting Fairholme, who had sold up on the Darling Downs some years ago to return to Scotland. Finding it less to his taste than he recalled from boyhood, Fairholme had let his property near the Leslies in Aberdeenshire and retired with his Swiss wife to Vevey. Always devout, he had turned to God with renewed conviction here, finding the serene atmosphere suited to contemplation. But it was less for his religious attitudes – much as they admired them – than for his business experience that Emmie and Frederik needed to see him. He had been on the Darling Downs with the Leslies almost from the start, in the early 1840s. Emmie remembered him arriving with his cousin Mr Pinnock at the Fassifern inn when George first took her to the Downs. He was a regular visitor at Canning Downs, and he had kept in touch since Emmie's sudden departure with George in 1852. He knew the sad history behind her remaining Australian possessions and he was sympathetic. Only Pat was better informed, but he and Kate were in New Zealand now, and anyway his judgement was not always reliable. It seemed odd to Frederik that they did not talk to Walter, since he had been George's partner during the early years, but Emmie insisted that he would not trouble himself about Australian affairs nowadays. Even if he relented, he was twenty years out of date.

Frederik identified the tall, awkward fellow at the landing-stage from fifty yards. His round-brimmed hat bobbed above the crowd as he scanned the deck and his massive beard dragged back and forth across his chest. Emmie's eyesight was not so keen and it was a moment before she recognised him. When she did, she waved with sudden fervour and cried out, "David! Mr Fairholme!"

Fairholme's hand shot above the crowd. Bouncing up and down, waving his hat like a lasso, he was an unruly sight, indifferent to the attention he attracted.

When they were ashore, Emmie hurried forwards as fast as her condition would allow and grasped Fairholme's outstretched hands.

"Well I never! Well I never!" he uttered, munching his words as he rubbed her fingers. "Who would have thought indeed, Emmie, Mrs Leslie, Mrs Ziege I should say – so here you are, who would have thought? Well!"

When Frederik appeared at Emmie's side, Fairholme turned to him without releasing Emmie's hands. His mouth was still open, allowing

Frederik to see that he had very few, rather hefty teeth. Fairholme's blue eyes were wet with tears and Emmie – to Frederik's amazement – did not shy away from his display of emotion: she was also weeping as she smiled.

"Captain Ziege!" Fairholme cried, letting go of Emmie's right hand at last. But when he tried to shake hands with Frederik he found that his left arm was in the way because he still held Emmie's other hand. Although he let it go at once, he was in a muddle now, and embarrassed. "Please excuse me!" he said. "I'm afraid I am overcome . . . Captain Ziege, it is an honour, I am so grateful to you for coming all this way with your dear wife! You are a lucky man!"

"I am delighted to be here," Frederik said.

"Your journey was bearable, I hope?"

"It was – "

"Oh dear me," said Fairholme, noticing Norah with the baby in her arms. "And this is the wee boy – Christian, is it?"

Although Frederik was aware that Fairholme had known Emmie when she was first married to George, he realised now how strange it must be for him to see her with a baby. He wondered whether he knew about her miscarriage.

Having greeted the whole party to his satisfaction and recovered himself, Fairholme led them to a waiting carriage, which took them to his house. There they went through the introductions all over again with his wife, a friendly lady who had not been in Australia.

"I am so sorry not to meet your sons," said Frederik.

"They are at school in England," she replied in a German accent that complemented her husband's Scottish one.

"Yes, my dear, they know that," Fairholme said, trying to usher Frederik and Emmie upstairs.

"Mrs Fairholme, do you think we might feed Christian before we eat?" asked Emmie, who had spied through an open door a table being laid for lunch. "Norah – "

"Of course!" said Mrs Fairholme, grateful for the reprieve from Australian affairs. "Follow me, Norah." And they departed down a corridor.

From the broad windows in the drawing room there was an unob-
structed view of the sparkling lake vanishing to the horizon. Frederik
realised why someone who had spent years in Australia might want
to retire to Vevey. A man whose gaze was accustomed to the long view,
and was not restless, might find some peace here.

"Now," said Fairholme, when Emmie and Frederik were seated and
a decent interval of small talk had elapsed. "Now, tell me what has
happened at Gigoomgan."

Emmie sat up straight in her uncomfortable, ornate armchair. Her
head was inclined forward as she spoke, but she looked straight at
Fairholme. She knew that men tended to be impressed by her grasp
of business. "My husband and I were in the process of extracting
ourselves from the partnership, which had become unsatisfactory," she
said. "Mrs Anderson, the widow of George's original partner, takes
little active interest, and I therefore find myself with very little control
or check on our managing partner, Mant. Not that I have ever had
reason to mistrust him. But in spite of my links with Australia, my
home is now in Europe and I believe that our capital, and income,
should be closer to home."

Emmie paused, and Fairholme said, "There is good sense in that."

"About a month ago I received a letter from the manager," she
continued, "which quite alters the way things stand. He tells me that,
at the last muster, three thousand head of cattle were missing."

"Three thousand! And do you believe him?"

"I don't know what to believe."

Fairholme stood up and went to the window. "What do you think,
Captain Ziege?"

"I was interested by your first reaction," Frederik replied. "You did
not immediately say that Mant must be a swindler, or mad. Either of
these must be possibilities, but my wife and you are better able to
assess the further possibility that he may be telling the truth."

"I have told Frederik that such things can occur," Emmie said,
"and we are informed that the droughts have been severe. Both my
brother Jack, who is still in that part of the world, and Fanning in
Sydney, confirm this."

"Unfortunately there can be no question of going to see for ourselves," said Frederik, "at least until the baby is several months old – "

"By which time it will be too late," Emmie added.

Fairholme pressed his great hands together. "Hum. Hum hum. What a conundrum! It is true," he said to Frederik, "that such disasters can occur. The climate is unpredictable – floods and drought will do terrible damage. Fortunes are hard won and easily lost."

"And Mant knows that Emmie is aware of this."

"Quite so. He gave some account, I suppose, of the missing cattle?"

"He says there were unusually heavy fatalities following the last inoculations."

"That is possible," Fairholme said. "Nevertheless – three thousand! Even a large run would be strewn with corpses. Do you have the stock returns for previous years?"

"I do," said Emmie. "I should very much like to show them to you, but they are in London – "

"In the camphorwood chest?" Fairholme enquired with a smile.

"Oh!" cried Emmie, right hand pressed to her bosom. "You remember the camphorwood chest?"

"Of course I remember!" Fairholme cried. "George used to keep all his business papers in those splendid drawers. You still have it, then?"

"Why would I not?"

"Because . . . you have brought it round the world . . . And it is the way for things to get lost . . ."

"Oh, come now, David," said Emmie.

"The camphorwood chest, as I recall, was brought by Walter from Canton?"

A knock on the door interrupted Fairholme. A maid entered and announced in German that luncheon was served.

"Very well, Jeanne. Then we shall come."

The camphorwood chest, Fairholme explained to his wife and Frederik as they sat down, arrived at Canning Downs in 1849. "Wasn't it a belated wedding present from Walter, Emmie?" he said.

"I believe it was intended as a wedding present. Although we had been married almost two years by then, and Walter himself did not turn up until several weeks later."

"It was most peculiar," Fairholme said. "Here was the finest piece of furniture anyone had ever seen on the Downs, and it came from Walter, who seemed to have abandoned us. Beautifully made, very practical, a really first-rate piece, and I can still remember its smell. It has a very particular, resinous smell, doesn't it, Emmie?"

"It does still."

Fairholme put down his laden fork. "Walter," he said. "We always thought something happened to him – " Fairholme pointed to his temple " – when Ernest Dalrymple died. It was around the time I bought Toolburra off them. Walter was no less a pioneer, no less of a worker than everyone else at the start. After Pat staked the claim and went back to marry Kate it was Walter who lived alone in a slab hut for six months, with the wind whistling through the gaps between the timbers, while George brought the stock up with Ernest. And for five years Walter worked alongside George. Not so able as his younger brother, but he pulled his weight, you had to. And then poor Ernest, who had always found it hard – he came out with George and Walter from Scotland, I think, and followed them in everything; he was devoted to them – he was on the point of leaving for Ceylon, to start afresh, when he got ill. It was Walter who nursed him in a Brisbane boarding house. He died in Walter's arms. Then Walter suffered from some kind of nervous collapse himself. He went to China to see William, the oldest of the Leslie brothers. It was thought that this change of scene would sort him out. The idea was that George would go home to Scotland on Walter's return, leaving Walter to look after the station for a year. They had got through the hard years and things were going pretty well. But Walter was no better when he got back from Canton, worse in fact, so there was nothing for it but to send Walter back home. There was some concern about whether he would even make it, I think. Didn't Tom and William fetch him from Malta?" Emmie nodded. "And while Walter was at home he forgot all about Canning Downs. He wouldn't answer George's letters – which was a nuisance, because he was George's partner. George needed his consent, his signature and so forth. It was assumed that he would go back and take up the reins, giving George a break. And eventually he did go back, in a leisurely sort of way, via Canton, where he bought the camphorwood chest, which he sent on ahead while he kicked his heels in Sydney, and poor George never got his rest . . ."

Mrs Fairholme cleared her throat. "David, dear, we are all waiting for you."

"Oh dear heavens! Have I been running on so?" And he applied himself to his food, elbows clamped to his ribs as if they had been strapped there when he was a child to teach him to eat politely.

"Poor Mrs Fairholme, you must find this Australian gossip dull," said Emmie.

"I have little to contribute, but I do not find it dull," she answered. "It is a great part of my husband's life and there is not much opportunity for him to talk about it. This is a treat for him, Madame Ziege."

Emmie smiled. She thought Mrs Fairholme's response was very gracious.

"And how did you take to the gift?" Mrs Fairholme resumed.

"We were very pleased with it," said Emmie, but her tone suggested that their feelings had been more complicated. She said nothing about how they felt Walter had taken advantage of them, how his handsome present seemed like an insult in the light of his behaviour. "It was less a wedding gift, in the end, than a parting gift," Emmie said. "He arrived at Canning Downs as the men were shearing, but he did not exert himself. George had no option but to buy him out."

"First partnership terminated," said Frederik.

"Second, if you count the one with Pat," Emmie corrected him.

"Oh – Pat!" cried Fairholme, as Jeanne removed his plate.

"Speaking of Ernest Dalrymple," said Emmie, "did you hear how his brother Hugh has opened up the Rockingham Bay area?"

"I heard something about it, yes. Port Hinchinbrook. Seems like every week another adventurous chap claims a new piece of the continent for civilisation."

"What will the young men do when the whole world is claimed?" said Mrs Fairholme. "Thank you, Jeanne, yes, we will have the fowl now."

Frederik laughed. "What indeed?"

Another maid set half a guinea fowl on a plate before each of them, and Jeanne handed round a bowl of little roast potatoes.

"It is a different world now," said Fairholme, shaking his head. Then a memory came to him, which he fancied illustrated his point: "Do you remember the fellow who came to George with a snake bite?" he said. "George collected his powder flask from a table nearby and blew the finger off!"

"Oh!" cried Mrs Fairholme.

Frederik wondered if Fairholme had undergone dentistry at the same surgery.

"It's true," said Emmie. "He saved the man's life. He said, 'Thank you, Sir. Alas that it's this finger because I am a shoemaker by trade.'"

"How terrible for the poor man!" said Mrs Fairholme.

"On the contrary," said Emmie, warming to the subject. "Snakes were a great danger and you had to take action rapidly. I was once standing in a pergola of grape vines with my hands clasped behind my back when I felt a fierce sting. I rushed to my husband who was seated at his writing table and said, 'I am bit by a snake!' There were two tiny drops of blood on the ball of my thumb – just there," she said, laying down her knife and stretching out her hand to show a small scar. "He seized a bundle of quills with the usual pink cord around it, shook the quills out and bound my wrist. His candle was alight and, his lancet being near, he held it in the flame a moment and lanced my hand. A black who was at the stable was called in. 'My word! Corbon saucy fellow that!' he said, meaning it was a big snake, and he sucked the wound. I was not allowed to sleep that night but made to walk up and down till the danger of stupor was past. The snake was found the next day and killed."

Frederik wondered if he would have had such presence of mind. He felt ashamed of his thoughts about Fairholme's dentistry. "Goodness, what a lucky escape!"

"It was!" said Emmie.

There was a pause, as if in deference to Emmie's bravery. Then Mrs Fairholme said, "I expect you have had some narrow escapes too, in your time, have you not, Captain Ziege?"

"I have never been threatened by a snake," Frederik said. "Any dangers I have encountered are trivial beside those faced all the time by serving men – and pioneers – and their wives," he added with a little bow to Emmie, just teasing her, and everyone laughed.

"Going back to your problems with Gigoomgan," Fairholme said. "As I understand it, you would like me, a poor second opinion to Emmie, to say whether a stock return reporting a loss of three thousand head of cattle could be truthful?"

"Just so," said Frederik.

"Well then, my answer is that it *could* be truthful. But at the frontiers of the known world you find people who are beyond the frontiers of the law. Every kind of chicanery is possible."

"In short, having removed them to a neighbouring station, for a consideration, he may be relying on Emmie's knowledge of local conditions to believe that such a quantity of beasts have died?"

"He may be gloating over the proceeds of a speedy sale even now. Equally, he may be tearing out his hair on your behalf, suspecting that they have been spirited away by rustlers, and him unable to prove a thing."

"If we do not go out there, it will seem as if we have accepted it all without question."

"I'm sure that I would wish to go if I were in your situation, however small the chance of reclaiming anything."

"That is our feeling," said Emmie, "but I dread the voyage – for Christian's sake and my own. Frederik will be all right: he is used to ships."

Frederik shrugged. "Emmie is concerned about the risk of fever on board." Although he had watched his sister, Ida – Alma's mother – die of fever on the way to the West Indies in 1849, he remained convinced that the danger from fever on board was no greater than on land.

"Oh, don't!" cried Mrs Fairholme. "I keep thinking about that boy, Ernest Dalrymple, so far from his poor mother, feverish and dying . . ."

"Indeed, but he is gone to somewhere better, Mrs Fairholme," Emmie reproved her. "We may find comfort in that."

Mrs Fairholme continued to look sorrowful, as if she knew she ought to find comfort in Emmie's pious reflection, but did not. "Jeanne," she said, "I think we shall move on now, we are all finished."

They went upstairs again to the drawing room, where they sat for half an hour drinking coffee in Canton cups with a motif of Chinamen that Fairholme had bought from George Leslie. Emmie had a matching set: William had sent down a set of eighteen, and they had let Fairholme have six. Then they strolled with Christian and Norah along the waterfront until it was time to catch the ferry back to Montreux.

*

A week later, Emmie was sitting between her mother-in-law and Carl Bloch at a round table in the window of the dining room at the Hôtel

Fayard, Lucerne. Lunch at the *table d'hôte* was drawing to a close. Beside Madame Ziege sat Frederik. Beyond him was Alma, beside her husband, completing the circle. It was obvious that they were newlyweds, Emmie thought, for there was a deep, suggestive radiance to Alma. Her effusiveness was such that you could not help but feel warmed by her if she was talking to you, but there remained a sense that you only had her attention on loan from Bloch. From her own place on Bloch's left, Emmie could see when Alma turned to him that the shine of her eyes, even the lustre of her black hair, acquired a new intensity. Her face, which Emmie had thought of as round, now seemed heart-shaped. Two years ago, she had sometimes been referred to as "poor" Alma: now the epithet would seem ridiculous.

As Alma wiped her fingers on her napkin, having just eaten a pear, Emmie noticed her glance at a dish of plums. It struck her that Alma had just eaten an enormous lunch – a quick mental list yielded soup, *mousse de jambon*, cutlets, vegetables, bread, ice cream, fruit and more fruit: anything, in fact, that she could lay her hands on.

"Alma, have a plum," said Emmie, steering the plate towards her.

Alma beamed and her eyes seemed to caress the fruit. When she reached out, the new diamond on her finger sparkled.

Alma's vigorous health persuaded Madame Ziege that her grand-daughter must also be expecting a baby.

Madame Ziege was wearing her black hat, with the little net veil pinned back. She did not mind Emmie and Alma being bareheaded, but she felt uncomfortable without a hat in public and had no more intention of altering this practice than that of wearing a black satin dress. Only the shawls and jewellery changed. Today she had a cameo brooch at her throat, but no shawl indoors because it was July. Her expression gave little away: wide eyes, whose steadiness implied experience and a habit of absorbing detail; lips which were often pinched into a pout; a network of fine wrinkles that seemed to Emmie to have spread since she saw her in Rome. But Madame Ziege was delighted to be where she now was. This was understood well by everyone except Bloch, who was nervous of her. Knowing that Bloch wished to take Alma south, when Madame Ziege heard that Frederik intended spending the summer in Switzerland, she suggested to the Blochs that she and Hannina accompany them on a diversion.

"Now who will join me for a walk this afternoon?" Frederik said, opening wide his arms to include everybody in the invitation, then rubbing his hands together with slow, abrasive twists. His face was flushed, his voice resonant, and his smile happy; Madame Ziege reminded herself that he had always responded well to company.

"It's just like it was in Genoa or Rome!" cried Alma, as they walked along the broad street outside the hotel, two couples abreast.

"I don't think Coco would wish to hear that she had metamorphosed into Bloch," said Emmie.

Alma giggled as she translated for Bloch. "We used to go for walks without Granny," she explained. "It felt like playing truant!"

"Does it feel like that now?" Frederik said.

"No," Alma answered, squeezing Bloch's arm.

"How could she be playing truant when she is with Bloch?" said Emmie, and Alma smiled.

Passing a parade of shops, Frederik drew Emmie to a halt outside a window in which there was a dressmaker's dummy wearing a short, black velvet jacket with white embroidery. "Isn't that the sort of thing you need?" he asked, referring back to a conversation from several days before.

"Yes," she replied, inspecting it through the glass. "But I don't like the embroidery."

"They might have others. Let's go in and see."

They were welcomed by a thin woman with a taut face. As she asked if there was anything she could help them with, her hands fluttered around as if to indicate infinite possibilities in the cramped, upholstered premises. Three full-length mirrors erupted with green, announcing to Emmie that Alma had followed them into the shop, and the lady's hands repeated their little dance.

"Do you have other jackets like the one in the window?" asked Frederik.

"Oh, no! Each one is tailored to fit!"

"But do you have any similar ones that might be altered?"

"Is there something amiss with that one?"

"It is the white embroidery," Emmie answered. "I would prefer black on black."

"Black on black?" the lady repeated.

"Perhaps it can be unstitched," Alma suggested, "if it fits."

The woman looked as if she had been slapped. Unperturbed, Frederik asked if they might look at it. "If it isn't too much trouble," he added, with a charm that she was evidently not anticipating. She was about to fetch it from the window when Emmie asked how much it cost.

"Fifty francs, Madame."

"Fifty francs!" cried Alma.

"In that case we will trouble you no further," Emmie said.

"It is indeed too much if the embroidery has to be unpicked," said Frederik.

After they had dressed for dinner at the hotel, Alma spoke of the jacket again. The gentlemen were already downstairs waiting with Madame Ziege. Alma was sitting at Emmie's dressing table while Emmie helped her with her hair. "You could have a jacket like that made in Copenhagen for much less," she said.

Emmie said nothing. She wasn't going to Copenhagen. She was seeing if her own bone hairpins would help restrain the wilful cascade of Alma's locks. Reaching down for another pin, she touched Alma's fingers as she passed one up to her.

"Thank you," Emmie said.

"It's very kind of you to do this."

"It's a pleasure."

Alma took a bottle from Emmie's dressing case, removed the top, and sniffed. She looked in one of the little glass boxes. "Is this kohl?"

"Yes," said Emmie. She was concentrating on Alma's hair. "I don't know why I have it, I never use it."

"What's in the other one?" Alma asked, putting the first one back.

"Gypsum."

"Do you use that?"

"I used to, from time to time." George had liked her to use it when they went into society. Just because she was a native Australian, he teased her, there was no need to frighten people with the colour of her skin. But she was paler now, under European skies. "You should try it," she said.

"Oh, do you think I have too much colour in my cheeks?"

"Of course not," Emmie said, though she did think so. "There, that's done."

Emmie straightened up and Alma looked at herself in the mirror, her fingers pressed against her cheeks. The startled look in her eyes reminded Emmie of how she was when they had first met two years ago. Emmie pressed her shoulder and said, "We ought to go down."

*

When she woke in the morning, Emmie decided to stay in bed while Frederik went downstairs for breakfast. She felt unwell – the familiar reward of her condition. She had to be severe with herself not to envy the good health that some ladies were said to enjoy when they were pregnant. Her disappointment was aggravated by the suspicion that her brother-in-law, who was due to join them that day, would be unmoved by her ailment.

Emmie's estimate of Christian's sympathy was not put to the test, however, for Frederik brought news on his return that undermined their plans. Coming into the main lobby by the reception desk at seven o'clock, intending to go for his customary walk before break-fast, he had been intercepted by the hotel manager. Generally, nobody was about at this hour but the night manager.

"Good morning, Captain Ziege, you have had a good night, I hope?"

"Yes, thank you," Frederik said. The manager was short and stout. Across his waistcoat was a watch chain. Frederik had observed that the watch attached to it was very beautiful, since the manager had frequent and ostentatious recourse to it. Now it was in his pocket, stifled and ignored as he wrung his hands.

It had been known for two days, he explained, looking up at

Frederik, that one of the hotel's guests, a German living on the top floor, was ill. Such things happened, and no grounds were given for alarm, but he had taken a sudden turn for the worse during the night – had passed away, in fact. And now two more guests were ill. To his immense distress and regret, not omitting infinite apologies for the inconvenience entailed by the catastrophe, he was left with no choice but to inform his esteemed guests of the circumstances and assist them with whatever arrangements they deemed appropriate.

Frederik's habit of rising early stood him in good stead. He was able to pre-empt the stampede that must occur when the other guests came down for breakfast. It turned out that the staff, whom Frederik now recognised to be manning the reception desk like troops at a rampart, had done some useful preparation. At first they recommended other hotels in Lucerne where there were vacancies, but when Frederik said that he believed his family would wish to remove from the place altogether, they were ready with suggestions. A boy was ready to run to the post office and telegraph other hotels in the region to establish whether they had room. It was a question of weighing the facility of travel arrangements against the desirability of the destination. They should leave with minimum upheaval, thanking God that they were not the afflicted ones and praying to Him to relieve the sufferings of those who were. The clerk said he hoped that all the guests would show similar understanding, and there was a very comfortable hotel near Thun, where he believed space might be found for the Ziege party at short notice. Road conditions were good and it could be reached by evening if they set out soon. He mentioned the views and healthy aspect, the fine food, the spacious rooms and the excellent service which Madame Ziege would assuredly appreciate. From the corner of his eye, Frederik saw an English couple whom he had talked to the day before come downstairs. The manager approached them in the same way. If he stopped to consider all the options, there would be fewer left, he thought, and asked the clerk if he would be kind enough to send the boy to the post office to make the necessary reservations.

By the time Frederik rejoined Emmie, the arrangements had been made. Two carriages were ready; they ought to leave within the hour; he would go and alert his mother, Norah, and the Blochs, before returning to help her pack. As Frederik's news and the hideous prospect of a day's jolting inside a carriage took shape, Emmie began to feel worse, if anything, than when she first woke. Feeling grey and fugged with nausea, she raised herself on her elbows – but all she said was, "What about your brother?" for he was already on his way from Vienna.

"I shall have to leave a message at the desk here for him to follow to Thun."

When Frederik left the room, Emmie pulled herself out of bed and began to organise herself with brute determination. She did not want her son to be exposed to the risk of staying here a moment longer than necessary. The man had said it was a fever; no further detail was needed to know that it would be contagious and fatal; Frederik was wise not to have delayed, and to have chosen a destination as far as was attainable within the day. She would have to make the best of it.

Madame Ziege appeared in the lobby without any sign of haste, packed and breakfasted and ready to take her seat in the coach. The Blochs waited with her, panting with excitement. None of them behaved as if there was anything to justify alarm. It was Norah, in the end, who suffered most from their enforced departure. By now she was used to discerning signs of anxiety in Emmie and Frederik, and perceived at least in the briskness of their departure some evidence of it, but she felt that nobody was showing proper concern for poor baby Kiki. Emmie asked her if she would be comfortable breastfeeding Christian as they travelled and Norah, pleased not to be taken for granted, replied "Yes, Ma'am." What agitated Norah was the lack of fuss. The little angel was in danger of getting the Fever! Didn't anybody care? When Emmie took Kiki to wait with his grandmother, Norah's chest started heaving with emotion. Instead of directing the porters what to carry, she charged off with bags and trunks alone, with the result that she strained herself. She cried out, dropping the end of the trunk that she was dragging down the hotel steps. She insisted that she wasn't injured and would have lifted it again had not Frederik restrained her and escorted her into a carriage. Once they were travelling, it was plain to Emmie and Frederik, whose carriage Norah shared with the baby, that Norah was in pain, and it grew worse when she tried to feed Christian.

They stopped at an inn to change horses. Norah's condition was such that Emmie wondered if she was able to continue. The innkeeper said that she could stay, but the nearest doctor was in Thun so she might as well go on. Norah would not hear of stopping anyway, so she stayed as she was, propped up with cushions and covered with rugs as best they could, while Emmie fed Christian on rusks and cooked carrots which she had procured at the inn. She had also filled a bottle with some boiled milk from the inn, but Christian would not take it and the milk splashed over Emmie's dress. Exhausted by his uninterrupted yelling, Norah tried to feed him again in spite of the pain, but now he would not take to her.

"Poor Norah, it is time he was weaned," Frederik said. He took the baby from her and attempted to distract him. The mountains and valleys rang with his howls until at last, half an hour before they came into Thun, he slept.

The two carriages had kept together during the journey until they were approaching Thun, when Frederik was pleased to see the other one pull away. Although the ghastliness of the latter half of their journey was not known to those in the first vehicle, it was some relief for those in the second to find their arrival expected. Alma took Christian on her lap in an armchair, where she gazed at his serene, sleeping face with voluptuous devotion, while Emmie and Frederik helped Norah upstairs. Having guessed that Norah would be in need of attention, Madame Ziege had already organised a maid to warm her bed. She had also asked the manager to call a doctor, who was expected presently.

Emmie was convinced that the doctor would diagnose some sort of internal rupture. She was already considering how best to look after her and cope with her own crisis over Christian. Then, as she stood braced against Norah's side, with her arm round her stooped back while Frederik supported her under her arms, Emmie felt Norah shiver;

and her own heart skipped a beat. Norah shivered again, and Emmie's anxiety ballooned. She told herself that Norah had just caught a chill, in spite of their efforts to cover her up in the carriage. She felt a desperate surge of responsibility for her son's valiant nurse, who had entrusted herself to their care. At the same time, Emmie's mind was flooded by the implications for them all if Norah had come away with the fever. She was grateful for her mother-in-law's foresight.

Frederik left the room when he had seen Norah safe to her bed. He knew that she felt humiliated to be seen in her dishevelled state. Her corset had been loosened in the coach so that her jacket had unexpected bulges and her robust bosom sagged. Her black hair, which was normally so neat in its rolls on top of her head, had spilled over her left shoulder. When the door was shut, Emmie sat beside her on the bed and helped her undress. As a nightgown was slipped over her, Norah shivered again with a violence that made it seem more like a convulsion.

Emmie was terrified. "Are you cold, Norah dear?" she asked, hoping it had been a shudder of relief, and she drew the blankets and a thick eiderdown over her. She heard the tremble in her own voice and hoped that Norah would not recognise her terror.

"A little," Norah said. "You are so kind, Ma'am." She gave a gentle smile and blinked.

"Nonsense, Norah," said Emmie. Norah's cheeks, which were usually ruddy, were pale: they would be burning red if she had the fever, Emmie thought. "Would you like me to rub a little camphor on your temples?" she asked.

Norah smiled. She knew that Emmie kept a little stock of pads infused with camphor in one of the glass boxes of her dressing case, for she had prepared them herself. Emmie believed that the sharp aroma benefited Christian when his breathing was difficult and sometimes rubbed a little on his pillow, or directly on to his chest. "Like a baby," Norah answered, and nodded.

Glad to have something definite to do, Emmie hurried from the room. A porter had taken her dressing case, but she didn't know which was to be her room, so she had to go downstairs to find out and then return all the way to a room two doors down from Norah's. She was not surprised to see Frederik lying on the bed, for he often lay down for half an hour in the evening. He raised his eyebrows, asking after Norah.

"Is Kiki all right?" she asked.

"Alma and my mother are with him. He is asleep."

"Then I will stay with Norah until the doctor comes."

"Of course. Poor Norah!"

Emmie unlocked her dressing case. Now she took out the box containing the camphorated pads and returned to Norah. Sitting on the side of Norah's bed, she removed a pad and held it against Norah's left temple, then moved it in a soft arc over her forehead and held it to the opposite temple for a moment. Norah inhaled. "Mmm," she murmured with closed eyes.

The more Emmie sensed Norah's nerves ease under her touch, the more she wanted to continue the soothing motion of her fingertips on Norah's temples, until she was overcome by drowsiness herself.

She was interrupted by a knock on the door announcing the doctor.

His examination was careful and considerate. At the end, he declared that there was nothing the matter with Norah which a few days' rest would not repair; she might have a mild chill, but Emmie should not fret. Leaving Norah to sleep, Emmie put Christian to bed in her own room. Frederik ordered a light supper to be brought up to her which, to her own surprise, she consumed hungrily before putting herself to bed. As soon as he was able to disengage himself from his mother and the Blochs, Frederik joined her.

*

Arriving at dusk, preoccupied, they had formed no sense of the landscape surrounding the hotel. The following morning, Frederik found it to be nestled in a sheltered gully, overlooking a valley that swept from rocky peaks to pastureland below. The grass there was lush and verdant, and the sky above the mountainous horizon an untainted blue. Wildflowers offered themselves up to the sunshine in splashes, reds and yellows and purples; the distant snow glittered. A lawn sloped down to a broad terrace suspended over the panorama like a ship's prow.

After breakfast, Bloch seated himself on the terrace and sketched, while Frederik watched over his shoulder. Alma was chatting to her grandmother, who was in a deckchair with a rug over her knees. When Alma saw Emmie at the hotel door, she waved. Feeling better this morning, Emmie carried Christian down the slope; he was wearing a floppy white sun hat. At the bottom, where the grass evened out towards the terrace, she put him down. After a moment's hesitation he pulled himself up by her skirt, as she had expected he would. Then he saw Alma, who was crouched down on the terrace with her arms stretched towards him.

"Come on, Kiki! Come on!" Alma cried.

Christian grinned, then let go of Emmie and tottered several steps towards Alma before his legs buckled and he fell to the grass.

"Frederik! Look! Look!" Emmie cried. "He's walking!"

Frederik turned. He only saw Christian sitting bewildered on the grass, but the ladies' excitement was sufficient to persuade him that his son had indeed just walked. "Oh, poor Norah!" he said. "She will be so sad not to have seen!"

"It is always the way," said Madame Ziege. "Babies always jump through hoops for fly-by-night entertainers like Alma."

The rest of the morning they vied with one another in trying to make Christian walk to them, as if the favour he seemed to bestow by doing so amounted to a state of grace more coveted by the adults than anything else in the world. The exercise exhausted him and he fell sound asleep after his lunch, not waking until his uncle arrived in a mood that had been cooking inside his carriage since leaving Lucerne.

Christian Ziege, Special Envoy from the Kingdom of Denmark to the Imperial Court of Vienna, did not doubt that his family had done the right thing in fleeing Lucerne. But his journey from Vienna had been arduous enough without the final day-long trek to Thun. If someone had shown a little more foresight then he could have been warned; then he might have cancelled or adjusted his arrangements.

It was a sign of the times that the idiot hotel manager's greed prevented him from alerting his guests earlier. And then Christian felt irritated by the good humour prevailing in Thun.

"Oh dear, poor Norah," he said when Frederik told him of their adventures the day before. "Put it down there," he commanded a waiter who was handing him a cup of tea, indicating the table beside his chair. He had been up to change, and now was downstairs in the drawing room with the rest of the family. He was wearing tweed breeches and a matching jacket. Emmie noticed that he had groomed his moustache.

"You should have got Alma to massage Norah's head. She's the expert," Christian said to her.

Emmie was taken aback. Frederik must have told him about her own efforts.

"She used to massage our heads whenever we had headaches — didn't you, Alma? Especially Frederik's," Christian added.

Alma blushed, afraid that her uncle was making fun of her. In front of Bloch, she did not know how to respond.

"Hush, Christian, leave Alma alone," said Madame Ziege.

"Isn't it true, Frederik?" Christian repeated.

"I'm sure Bloch is well aware that Alma is the best antidote to headaches in all Denmark," Frederik said lightly.

Bloch laughed. "How could I doubt it?"

Kiki had been standing in front of Alma, swaying as she held his hands above his head. Suddenly he slipped her grasp and scuttled the four steps to his uncle's table, where he reached up and grabbed at his cup of tea. There was a crash and everyone turned to see his mouth open wide as he sucked in air for a yell that resounded through the hotel drawing room.

"Aaahhh! You — !" Christian snarled, then pursed his lips and seized his nephew away from the hot tea and broken china.

No sooner did Christian have Kiki on his knee than Emmie swooped down and relieved him of her child. Checking that Kiki had not scalded his hands, she took him from the room in her arms.

"My fault — I expect I shouldn't have put it there," Christian groaned.

He sensed that the incident somehow put him in a bad light. Looking around in his resentment for someone to blame, he found justification in Emmie's abrupt departure.

Frederik noted with sorrow that Christian's presence at dinner cast a shadow. He didn't understand why because his brother was witty and urbane. When Christian was at home in Copenhagen, everyone was merrier. Frederik's love for his brother was undiminished by the separation of their lives. While he heard the asperity in some of his remarks to others, he did not regard it as a true reflection of his brother's nature. It was a sign of tiredness, he explained to Emmie when they were alone later – and why should he not be tired, for he had heavy responsibilities in his work? – or an expression of his caustic sense of humour. Perhaps it was their own fault for failing to inspire him.

"You make it sound as if his own family should feel honoured that he pays them any attention."

"That is ridiculous."

"So I believe. I do not think that we should be held to account because Christian is out of sorts."

"Very well, but I think we might have tried harder to be appreciative."

"We, Frederik? Do you mean me?"

Frederik did not think he had meant to single out Emmie, but now that she suggested it he wondered if that was in fact his hidden purpose. "Your behaviour is impossible to fault," he admitted, "if frosty."

Emmie knew that Frederik adored his younger brother and she believed it would be wrong to claw at this privilege of blood. Nevertheless, she felt it only fair to say that she felt uneasy with Christian. "Perhaps it's because I do not completely understand his European ways," she suggested.

"Oh, Emmie! You can do better than that!"

"I expect I can," she answered, "but I think we should sleep."

Frederik laughed.

She sat on the bed in her dressing gown, arms raised as she removed the pins from her hair. He stood in front of her, receiving the pins in one cupped hand.

"How are you feeling?" she asked, looking up at him. In the candle-light, the clear shadows on his face that were cast by his features obscured the greyness. His cheekbones stood out, his straight nose and the sweep of his jaw; and she thought how handsome her husband was.

"You fuss too much," he replied.

"I might say the same to you."

"And what about you? Both of you?" and he touched her stomach with the back of his hand, where she held it.

Cannes, September 1868

INSTEAD of returning to San Remo when they left Switzerland, Emmie and Frederik took a house in Cannes. In view of Emmie's imminent confinement it was thought wise to be within close reach of a doctor; Frederik's health was not referred to. The house was called Villa Louisette and it was in town. Being larger, it would accommodate more servants than Chalet Poncarte. They had engaged a cook and a lady's maid in Thun, where the season was winding down. They had travelled in a separate carriage together with a nurse, who was expected to assist Norah for the time being, and take on the duties of wet-nurse when the baby was born.

Within a few days of arriving, Frederik received a letter from Christian in Copenhagen which mentioned the trouble he had gone to in accompanying their mother back home. The arrangement had been agreed on many weeks before as the only sensible option. Alma and Bloch were bound for Italy: the duty fell to Christian – he being a relatively free agent despite his weighty obligations – but it seemed that he felt put upon, though he did not suggest what alternative had been passed over. Frederik felt hurt, as Christian must have known he would; and since Christian would surely not have wounded him on purpose, it followed that someone had put him up to it. Frederik discounted the possibilities that his brother might not have considered his feelings, or that he did, but didn't care.

Two weeks later, Frederik received a package with a letter from Hannina. He picked it up in the late afternoon from the *poste restante* during an unsuccessful mission to buy a proper milk jug. He opened it on his return, when he was light-headed from the unexpected heat. In the package was a jacket similar to the one they had seen in Lucerne. But somehow the embroidery was white.

As soon as Frederik saw it he felt cross. Now he would have to mediate between Emmie, who would still want to unstitch the embroidery, and Hannina, who would be offended. Patient discussions and long letters would be needed. He had enough problems without this being foisted on him. And how could they have been so stupid as to get the colour of the embroidery wrong?

When he read the accompanying letter and saw the lengths to which his family had gone to please Emmie and himself, instead of feeling ashamed, he felt held to ransom. Alma, it transpired, had lovingly drawn the jacket from memory soon after seeing it. She had observed Emmie's other clothes and gathered clues to her taste from Norah and Frederik himself. She had written detailed instructions for the fabric, buttons and collar; estimating Emmie's size after having the baby, she had suggested measurements for bust, waist, shoulders and length. Wishing it to be a present from them all, she had given a little money of her own via Madame Ziege, which was augmented by Christian and Clara. The remainder was supplied by Hannina. A great deal of thought and trouble had gone into the gift.

Frederik felt squeezed by his family for a response that was not there — for the fact remained that the garment was useless. Had Hannina's letter been limited to the jacket, his mood might have relaxed, but she went on to write how disappointed she was not to have seen him and Emmie over the summer, and she proposed a visit to Cannes in November. Frederik took this as veiled criticism for not accompanying their mother home, and immediately assumed that she had instigated Christian's objectionable remarks. He wrote his reply trembling with an anger that was in itself upsetting because he knew it to be inappropriate even as he felt it. Did Hannina not understand that he had commitments of his own? Why, for that matter, had she not come to Switzerland herself? It was intolerable that she meddled in his affairs. Did she not understand that Emmie was having a baby in November? How could she be so block-headed as to imagine that she would be welcome then? October or December might have been all right, but if she wished to pester them with demands then he would thank her to stay at home. *Go to the heaths of Jutland if you want a holiday. Do not bring your gloom to our sunny home.*

Frederik sealed his letter with a thump. He left it on a pewter tray in the hall, ready for posting, and then went up to the nursery to play with Kiki before his bedtime.

When he went into the dining room for dinner, he saw that his letter was gone. One of the servants had taken it to the post. Suddenly he was aware of the monstrousness of what he had done.

He did not tell Emmie about the jacket or about his response until the following day, by which time he had written another letter to Hannina asserting that his barbaric rudeness was a symptom of nervousness about the forthcoming birth. Not that this excused his behaviour, he added, but he felt he owed Hannina any available explanation. One of the most distressing thoughts to him was that she might think his otiose manners were a reflection of some ungraciousness on Emmie's part. This, he assured her, was far from the case, for Emmie did not know about the gift yet and he had not the least doubt but that she would be touched. For himself, he would remain sick with shame until his dying day that he could treat his dear sister so, and would be tortured with worry until he heard a word of forgiveness from her.

Hannina received both letters by the same post. Although she read them in the order in which they were written, when she gave them to her mother after lunch to read, she gave her the second one first.

Madame Ziege read without comment, until she had finished them both. Then she laid them aside on the sofa, looked over to Hannina who was seated in an armchair, blew out her cheeks and said, "Well!"

"It is so unlike him!" said Hannina.

"I expect he *is* nervous about the birth."

"No doubt."

"He seemed so well in Switzerland," his mother recalled. She supposed he was afraid for Emmie, and for himself. Gripped by sudden fear that his children might be made orphans, a man might do anything. "Poor Frederik. You must try not to take it to heart."

Knowing that she had done nothing to justify the first letter, Hannina could only suppose that something else had inspired it. Although she knew that Emmie was not responsible, she had the sense of something unyielding in her sister-in-law which made her suspicious of her influence on Frederik. In spite of his apology she noted that he had not referred again to the idea of her visiting. He described his home as sunny, but his hysterical tone made it sound rather less appealing than the chilly landscape of Jutland. And if his home was not sunny, but a place where freakish storms were generated in her gentle, subtle brother, she could only assume that Emmie must, in some way, be responsible.

*

On 10th November, with a miraculous absence of complications, Emmie gave birth to another boy.

They called him William Frederick, in honour of the Leslies and his father. Frederik knew that his family would not be pleased with the English name. There had been remarks from his mother during the summer, which he sidestepped, when she discovered that he spoke to Kiki in English or French rather than in Danish.

Soon after the christening, they were surprised by a visit from an old friend of Emmie's. Retired from active service, General Blomfield still had a military bearing. The rim of hair on top of his head had turned from iron grey to white, but he had the same mutton-chop whiskers and his complexion was as florid as ever. His eyes twinkled with fun in just the way that had endeared him to Emmie and her sisters when he commanded the garrison in Sydney. Emmie had seen him from time to time over the intervening twenty years but the meetings always made her sad because he reminded her of happier times, before God and the world made claims on her family. Now she was eager to display her new life to him. He would see that the Macarthur spirit, which once had so beguiled him, was strong here after all.

When they were settled in the sitting room with cups of China tea and slices of the fruit cake that Emmie had discovered was part of the cook's repertoire, General Blomfield produced a pretty silver rattle. It consisted of a bundle of little bells suspended from the stem of a whistle, with a coral mouthpiece. The present was greeted with emotional thanks from Emmie and she handed it to Kiki, who rushed about, waving it with glee. It made a rustling sound.

"It's a whistle too, old chap," said Blomfield, reaching out so that he could demonstrate.

"Kiki, dear, give it to the General," said Emmie.

Kiki swerved out of his reach with a yelp, into his father's outstretched arm. Frederik plucked the rattle from him and passed it to Blomfield with a smile.

While Kiki whined and tried to grab it back, General Blomfield put it to his lips and blew a rippling peep from it, which woke the baby who was sleeping in Norah's arms. "Dear me!" said Blomfield, lowering the rattle to his knees and turning with an apology from Norah to Emmie. The baby snuffled and settled again at once.

Blomfield's moment of inattention enabled Kiki to snatch the rattle away.

"Kiki! Give it back to the General! You must not snatch like that!" cried Emmie.

"Good heavens!" said Blomfield. "All power to the boy for being quick!"

But Kiki could get no noise from the whistle and he started to cry, until Blomfield snapped his fingers in front of the boy's face and tickled the bells with his fingertips. The manoeuvre was accompanied by a momentary expression of daft surprise, pop-eyed and rubber-lipped, which made Kiki giggle.

Emmie and Frederik laughed too and Frederik said, "You have the gift of playing the clown for children . . ."

Blomfield shrugged. "I am fond of children." And he snapped his fingers again at Kiki, with the same result.

"Some people can do it, some cannot."

"General Blomfield is an old hand at amusing children," Emmie said to Frederik.

The General smiled. "The man who had the greatest gift with

children I ever saw," he said to Emmie, "was your old convict gardener at Vineyard."

"Mattie Kempsey," said Emmie.

"Was that his name? I don't know that I ever knew it."

"Yes, Mattie Kempsey." And there flashed into her mind an image of spying on him with her brother Jack from behind a eucalyptus as he leaned into a flowerbed with his hoe, his short body curved over the tool, his rough cloth jacket and trousers hanging loose. He must have known they were there, but his kind face was impassive beneath the broad yellow hat. On a whispered count and a giggle, they would launch their pebbles at him and then run, at which he would – do what? Roar? Give chase? She could not remember exactly – only that he always made them laugh. But this was the province of children: it was unthinkable that Mattie would perform for them in front of adults. "I can't think how you knew," she said.

"Why?" said Blomfield. "Because you had already outgrown that when I came there? There were other children too, there were always children at Vineyard!"

"No, I mean Mattie would have buttoned his lip in front of adults. He even did so with us when we were older, to a degree, though we had always known him."

"Oh, I see, you thought it was a secret. It was one of my favourite pleasures to spy on that fellow!"

Frederik laughed. "I like the thought of the distinguished General peeping over the hedge at the gardener!"

Blomfield mimed the action, using his hands as the hedge. "Boo!" he cried at Kiki. "The wonder is that the gardens weren't infested with other adults crouched down hoping to catch him."

"I have a picture of him," said Emmie. "Not here. In London. It is a thing I prize. My cousin Philip King was in the garden one day with his watercolours, and he did a sketch of him while he worked."

As General Blomfield departed, Emmie felt an undertow of nostalgia drag at the pleasure of his visit, from which she had hoped that the fresh momentum in her own life would protect her. Her own children should have sustained her above his wave of recollections about the "happy home" in Parramatta – the regimental band playing on the veranda while they danced indoors; evenings at Government House with the *Rattlesnake* midshipmen; a picnic at Clovelly with Leichhardt and Laura Trevelyan and so forth. She had looked forward to demonstrating to Frederik that she did not have to be sentimental about her childhood. Instead, General Blomfield had mentioned Mattie Kempsey;

and from feeling buoyant with confidence that her children would manage very well without Australia, secure in the benefits of Europe which she herself never had, she was pierced with distress to think that they would not grow up in that great garden with Mattie as playmate, clown, guardian and friend. She even missed the picture of Mattie, which was in a drawer in her camphorwood chest with so many other things, unsmiled on, in her house in Rutland Gate. And though she tried hard to believe this Villa Louisette was now her home, for it was where her loved ones were, still it did not have Mattie or her picture of him.

It seemed natural to Frederik that Emmie should miss New South Wales. When a life was divided into discrete epochs, as hers had been, it was to be expected that memory should isolate each one and endow it with an impression of stability. Perhaps the grim contrast between the apparent security of her worlds with their actual collapse made her more open to nostalgia than she might otherwise have been, but he did not think her prone to it. She thought she had an interesting upbringing, and he agreed. She did not use it to devalue the present: she had a talent for making a life of the present. He once asked her what she imagined they might have done had he been fit, and she answered without hesitation that they would be doing as they did now

– bringing up their children. When he pressed her, she would only add that if he had been a little more adaptable to climate then more time in Denmark or Scotland might have been agreeable.

If Emmie had mixed feelings towards visits devoted to reminiscing – she was both thrilled and repelled – Frederik was often frustrated by them. His curiosity about Australia had been roused, but it was always talked about as a land beyond reach, so that all hope of satisfying his curiosity, all speculation, must be futile. He wanted to go there and see for himself, get a context for this part of his new life – Emmie's past – which was broader than a parlour anecdote; perhaps take issue with it. The feeling was the more acute because he liked all the people he met who were associated with it. Although he understood that part of what drew Emmie to him was that he belonged to a different world, he felt that he would not truly belong to her life until he was acquainted with her former world.

Emmie and Frederik used often to take Kiki to the Woolfields' garden, which Lady Woolfield had insisted that they use. Leaving the baby at home with Norah, they would take a hansom cab to the entrance and walk between the beds of glorious plants to the head gardener's hut. The gardener gave Frederik the key to the chicken run, where he would take Kiki to gather eggs. Sometimes he gave Emmie a basket of flowers or vegetables to take home with her, according to season.

They were about to leave the house one day when she discovered that she had mislaid her hat.

"Where's Mama's hat?" she said, finding it neither on the hat stand inside the door, nor on the table, nor in the hall wardrobe.

"Where Mama hat?" Kiki repeated. "Where Mama hat?" And turning tail, he rushed to the stairs, which he climbed with great stomps of his little legs. Emmie raised her eyebrows at Frederik and they smiled at one another, enjoying their son's intelligent response. At the top of the stairs, Kiki scuttled along to Emmie's bedroom while his parents waited below, intrigued to find out if he did know where Emmie's hat was, and whether he would deliver it to her.

When he didn't reappear after a couple of minutes, Emmie decided to check up on him. She walked up the stairs holding the banister, listening; the silence was ominous. "Kiki?" she called, "Kiki dear?"

The sharp chink of glass shattering on her bedroom floorboards was followed by a loud cry. Emmie hurried along the landing where, in a moment, Kiki careered into her skirt. "Kiki, what have you done?" she said. He was yelling and clutching at her.

Emmie's hat lay abandoned on the floor. Beside it were strewn the remains of not one but – she soon discovered – two of the bottles from her dressing case. The room was already filled with the stinking fusion of *sal volatile* and brandy.

"Christian, I . . . How *could* you?" she cried, and burst into tears. "It is really the *end* . . . Frederik! Christian, you are im*poss*ible! You *must* not play with Mama's things! You might have *hurt* yourself!"

When Frederik reached the doorway, Emmie was holding Kiki by the upper arm while he wailed, and she dabbed at her eyes with the back of her other hand.

"I think we shall need a dustpan, Norah," Frederik said, as she arrived behind him.

Norah nipped around him. She had one already.

"He has broken two bottles from my dressing box!" Emmie lamented.

"Oh my dear Emmie, I am so sorry!" As he took her hand he noticed that her lace cuff was crumpled.

"Norah, do leave it alone," said Emmie. Norah was crouched among the glass and spilled liquid. "Maxine will do it."

"Oh, that's all right, Ma'am, unless you want me to take Kiki."

"No," she said, renewing her hold on the boy, which gave new bite to his cries. "Now do stop that, Christian! Mama is very cross!" And, withdrawing her left hand from Frederik's, she smacked Kiki on his dangling hand.

"Yaah! Yaah!" he cried, unable to get free because Emmie was holding his arm, and he jumped up and down as he screamed, furious at his powerlessness.

"Stop that!" cried Emmie, smacking him again.

Kiki lunged for Emmie's wrist and bit her.

"Ow! Don't you dare, you little monster!"

As Emmie rounded on Kiki in fury, not knowing what to do, Frederik intervened. He took hold of Kiki's shoulders and said, "That will do now! Do not *ever* bite people! Now, go to Norah – Norah, if you wouldn't mind, for a few minutes please."

Kiki took Norah's hand and followed her from the room with alacrity.

Frederik turned to Emmie. "I am sorry about the bottles, Emmie, but you know – they should not be left out!"

"He should not be playing with my things!"

"He is a small boy with a healthy sense of curiosity."

"I am sure we would never have played with the things on *my* Mama's dressing table."

"He is in here often. He sees you touching the bottles and using them. I'm sorry, but it is unfair to blame him."

"I'm sorry," she said.

There was an appeal for understanding in her streaming eyes. Compassion welled up in him and he hugged her. He knew why she was upset about the broken bottles, and he knew that she regretted losing her temper with Kiki.

"I have something for him," he said, "which I have been keeping."

Emmie tipped her head back so that she could look at him as he held her. "What?" she said, trying a smile.

"I'll go and get it."

When they were gathered in the hall again, ready to go out, Frederik knelt down in front of Kiki. "It is Papa's whistle," he said. He blew on it softly and hung it on a cord round Kiki's neck.

Kiki's blond head bobbed down to see what was lying against his chest, giving him a double chin. Then he took the whistle and blew a clear, shrill note. His face burst into a grin. "Papa wissa!" he cried.

As they climbed into the hansom cab, he kept it between his lips, blowing repeatedly.

"There's no need to blow it all the time, Kiki dear," said Emmie.

Kiki glanced at his mother but, not caring for what she said, turned away to the window and delivered a few long, satisfying notes. "Papa wissa!" he exclaimed with pride.

Frederik caught Emmie's eye. Together they stole a look at Kiki, who was filling his lungs for another happy blast. Frederik raised his eyebrows.

Emmie covered her face with her gloved hand so that Kiki should not see her smile.

If she thought she was hiding something from Kiki by doing this, or maintaining some hold over him, she was mistaken. He knew where he stood with regard to this whistling, and he made the most of it. Jiggling in his seat, he blasted and phooted and chirped and peeped all the way to the Woolfields' garden.

Trusting that the chickens would be sufficient distraction, Frederik demanded on their arrival that he surrender the whistle.

Kiki realised he was being cheated. Apart from a few minutes while they gathered eggs, he bellowed news of his betrayal to the world as he slunk behind his parents: "Kiki want Papa wissa! Kiki want Papa wissa!"

"Oh, let him have it! It's only fair," said Emmie, as they took their seats in the hansom cab for the journey home.

Frederik reached into his pocket and Kiki stopped howling, as if a pipe had been cut. For a moment, they could hear the horse's hoofs. Then Frederik handed back the whistle and a new onslaught commenced. By the time they reached Villa Louisette, Frederik and Emmie felt that the single shrill note was seared into their brains.

They asked Norah to take charge of Kiki while they went to have a rest.

"Where does the whistle come from?" Emmie asked as she removed her skirt.

Frederik was already lying on his separate bed, having removed only his jacket. "I had it in Greenland," he replied. "I rather wish I had left it there."

"Perhaps it can be lost."

"I expect so."

Emmie settled herself under her eiderdown. She was worn out, but in spite of Kiki breaking George's precious bottles, in spite of her own reaction, and in spite of the dreadful whistling, she felt happy. She fell asleep at once.

Lying back with his hands clasped beneath his head, eyes closed, Frederik considered the irony of Kiki's performance: weak lungs had not prevented him from driving anyone within earshot to distraction. It was strange to think of giving away the whistle as a toy when it had once been such a vital part of his equipment. He had carried it in Greenland whenever he left the settlement, and insisted on all the members of his team doing the same. Its note could be heard more clearly than a shout in the skin-stripping wind, when disaster was just a slip away into the chilling waters, or the limitless snow and ice surrounding an injured skier. Working in small boats in a sea cluttered by icebergs and islands, a perpendicular wall of frozen snow at the water's edge, was never the simple activity of hydrography textbooks. Frederik usually took Nielsen with him to work on the outer edges, leaving Edvard Thomsen to work with Bluhme between the islands and the coast. Had he left the inept and surly Subgunner Nielsen under the troubled Bluhme's supervision, nothing would have been achieved. So he forfeited Edvard's company for the sake of efficiency. Everyone understood why this arrangement was necessary, but it did not make them happy; and maintaining it exerted a constant strain on Frederik.

Letting Kiki have the whistle might seem to trivialise the dangers from which it once offered hope of rescue, Frederik reflected, but it also had the effect of easing the weight of those weary months. He might take his gift to Kiki as a covert admission that his past was indeed a kind of play, in which dangers were courted for the sake of their conquest; a bachelor's frivolity, useless to him now.

The unexpected thought startled him, for why should he need help? If he was looking for symmetry, he had it upside down: now that he no longer anticipated the need for rescue, the whistle was redundant. Why look for anything more complex? He loved Emmie and his boys, wanted nothing more – was it not mad to imagine troubles? Just because he could see that a man in his situation – an experienced naval officer, moored and renewed as a husband – might suffer regrets, it did not mean that he was such a man. Not that he would deny losses, but they might have more to do with ageing than with marriage. There were moments when he missed the adventures, the thrill of skiing alone on the barren Greenland slopes, or the shipboard industry, or the fascination of exotic places: but age would have made him unfit for such things if illness had not done so. He had just passed from one age of man to another, and the whistle belonged to the earlier one.

Having always had the sense that people tended to like him, Frederik had lately begun to doubt the impression he made on new acquaintances, as if some vital part of him had withered while he wasn't attending. Whether rehearsing amateur theatricals in St Petersburg or as an officer at sea, he knew, without being told – had always known – that he was liked. Now he felt more distant from those he met, set apart by marriage and anyway less interested in them, and consequently less likeable. This detachment generated its own loneliness, different from the loneliness of a winter in Greenland, or the isolation of Eastern Siberia, which was compensated for by a sharpening of the senses. Even now he could recall the settlement at Ajan with striking clarity, the slope dotted with twenty or thirty small wooden houses, their smoking chimneys wispy fingers reaching for the vast firmament. The chimes of the church bells, multiplied by the echoes from the wild, snow-covered mountains that reared up behind, cast an enchantment over that station on the edge of the world that must draw the most hopeless unbelievers to prayer.

A life without regrets, Frederik considered, was an absurdity for a human being: for who, equipped with the dissonant faculties of reason and desire, could block awareness of possibility? It was the pollen of life, and applied as much to the past as to the future. The trick was to maintain a clear sense of balance. In his own case, this ought to be easy, because any regrets he might have would always be outweighed by his feelings for Emmie and the boys. Without them the future would be hard to endure, if he were spared to face it. Yet knowing this did not prevent pleasure in the children slipping, like a weight on a worn cog, to anxiety. He wondered if his and Emmie's worry about the children's health would have been so great had he been healthy himself. The futility of the question did not quite silence it. Besides feeling responsible, he felt so sorry that Emmie should have to carry this burden. Only the children redeemed his sense that he was instrumental in trapping her into a hideous replay.

As Christmas came and went they were less absorbed in the care of the children than seemed, in moments of reflection, to be the case. In December, Frederik was introduced to some acquaintances of Emmie called O'Neill, an old couple who were wintering there with their son, Henry, who was just a year or two younger than Frederik. The connection, as so often, was Australia, though Frederik never grasped the precise nature of it. Henry was a naval officer on half pay, for whom the pleasures of Cannes society were sufficient compensation for the lack of a commission. Frederik enjoyed his company, and when Sydney Raymond came to visit in January, then Carrie Wickham in February, his visits were regular and much appreciated. The Galitsins were also in Cannes, and the Tresckovs – relatives of Alma's father, who had welcome news of Copenhagen. They were much more occupied than they had been in San Remo, but they found it a strain.

They were invited to go to the opera with the O'Neills one evening, and accepted before knowing that the work in question was *La Traviata*, which they had enjoyed together in Rome.

"I wonder that respectable theatres should choose to stage that opera," said Emmie. "I suppose its vulgarity makes it popular."

"I do not want to die in Cannes," Frederik announced without warning.

Emmie thought for a moment of San Remo. Their time there now seemed like an idyll, so free of worry compared to the last year. "Perhaps we should go to Paris." She dreaded morbidity, but she knew that Cannes must grow frustrating for a man used to activity.

Frederik gave a wry, tired smile, crinkling his eyes.

"Poor dear, you are weary," said Emmie.

"I was thinking of the opera," he said. "The removal to the city."

Emmie recalled how the courtesan fled to the city after informing her lover that she could not marry him because she was consumptive. She reached for his hand. "But we must do something."

Frederik nodded and looked out of the window. The night was warm, hinting at spring, and the starry sky invited speculation to vault from the tiny cell of Cannes. And after a moment he said what was on his mind: "Let's go to Australia."

PART THREE
Journeys

La Hogue, Summer 1868

O N a latitude somewhat lower than Ascension Island, Frederik lay on his berth, lulled by the ship's easy motion. His head still throbbed, but he was getting used to it on this voyage and he knew that a rest, out of the sun's glare, would help it pass. He thought about the goggles which he had worn when travelling in Siberia. They were in a tin trunk at his mother's Copenhagen apartment now, together with other equipment and mementoes from his former life. The crew and his fellow passengers, including Emmie, would think them ridiculous if he wore them here. And what would he have thought five years ago had he seen a figure such as himself wearing goggles on deck? Yet his mind kept reverting to them, for he knew that if he could only shield his eyes, then the pain that he had been suffering from the bright marine sun would abate.

Madeira was a hulk on the stern horizon before the Zieges had walked together on deck. Emmie had warned Frederik that she was prone to sickness at sea, and for the last few days she had only left her cabin for an occasional white-faced scurry into the saloon with the children, or to totter on deck, alone or with Frederik, hungry for air. A sailor had caught a dolphin two days before, and Frederik had watched him land it on deck with Kiki, who was delighted by the spectacle. The dolphin was said to be yellowish in the water except for its fin, which was dark blue with bright blue spots. Out of the water, it changed to all colours of the rainbow, a thing of great beauty according to Frederik, and Emmie very much regretted missing it. But that day she felt better. At breakfast, following his constitutional on deck, Frederik had reported that the breeze was good, the air bright and clear. The Captain confirmed that they looked set for a fine day's run; the awnings would be hoisted soon, in preparation for entering the tropics.

Emmie had been clinging to a vision of herself on deck with her family, in which Frederik impressed Kiki and the ship's company with his nautical expertise. Though otherwise comforting, the promise of awnings, which would block the clear view of the masts and rigging, threatened this unexamined daydream of Kiki and Frederik peering and pointing. So she announced that they must all go on deck at once and take advantage of the break in the weather. "It is allowing some respite today," she added, and smiled at Norah, who was so dependable with the children – not in apology, but in recognition of her own incapacity. In the cuddy's aqueous light, Norah's cheeks were still rosy, which was more than could be said for Frederik, who was ashen. Her own colour, she knew, was pale – it always was – but with a suggestion of pink in the cheeks instead of the yellow that seeped in when she was not herself.

"The break is in your reaction to the weather, not the weather itself," Frederik observed, surprising himself. Complaints about the weather at sea irritated him, for they implied some failure on the part of the weather to adapt itself to the requirements of delicate travellers: in his view, travellers had no business to complain. Moreover, looking at the food on the table before him – ham and kidneys, bread and quince jam – he found he had no appetite, and the coffee made him queasy.

"You are so literal-minded, my dear," Emmie replied. "Besides, it is not my attitude to the weather that is in question, but my reaction to the sea; and over that, alas, I have no control." Her tone suggested that it was Frederik who had raised the matter in the first place.

One thumb plugged in his mouth, Kiki allowed his father to lead him by his other upraised hand along the promenade. The only light came from the hatchway ahead, in a shaft that splashed to their feet and vanished behind them into gloom. Its radiance today, and the way in which it highlighted the straight edges of the planks, indicated that it was bright outside. Sometimes the ship rocked so that their progress here was an ungainly stagger, but this morning there was only the soft undulation of a gentle swell. At the companionway, Frederik let Kiki go ahead, so that he could catch him if he fell back. Still sucking his thumb, Kiki put one foot on the bottom step and reached out, swaying, for the rail. "Both hands on the rail, Christian." Frederik had to check himself from repeating the lecture he had given so many times already, about the importance of rules on a ship, Be careful on the companionways. They are dangerous, you can slip and hurt yourself. Use both hands.

Passing on rules to his own son at sea gave him a sense of vertiginous incredulity, like finding a pencil in his pocket and recognising it to be one that he had used to draw when he was eight, sitting on a spar with his back against the *Madagascar*'s mast. He remembered his father showing him about the ship on the way to Greece: here he was doing the same for his own son, the action linking generations. The individuals faded against the age-old drama of a father showing his son the ropes. Torné on the *Madagascar* used to tell him that he would remember the lessons he learned then for life. And so he had.

Emerging on deck, Frederik felt the sunlight attack him. It was not the heat – it was not yet nine o'clock – but the glare that troubled him. It bore into his eyes like air through a furnace's vent, making a blaze inside his skull. With half-closed eyes, he led Kiki along the deck towards the mainmast from where he hoped to play with him at spotting sailors in the rigging, or if there were none to be seen then they would just watch what was going on. But when he looked up, his vision seemed to explode as if the lattice of ropes against the sun were shatter-lines on glass, and the sky itself were about to fragment. Raising his hand to protect his eyes was a huge effort, impossible to sustain. His arm dropped so heavily to his side that it seemed to pull him with it. Afterwards, he was not quite sure whether he was in fact over-whelmed by dizziness, or if he sank to his knees to avert his collapse. But while such a distinction might mean something to Frederik, it meant nothing to Emmie and Norah, who were following and saw him crumple; nor to Kiki, who stared at him open-mouthed for a moment before starting to wail.

Emmie shrieked and rushed up as fast as the drag of her heavy skirt would allow. "Frederik!"

"My head . . ." he mumbled. "The sun . . ." He was sitting on the deck, thumb and middle finger splayed across his forehead.

Emmie knelt beside him, one hand on his shoulder to support him. "What happened?" she asked.

A sailor who saw him fall was kneeling on his other side. He was an Ethiopian, with a silver cross at his neck.

"I'll go below for a little . . . a lie-down. It is nothing."

Like everyone else on board, the sailor knew that Frederik was a retired naval officer. "The Captain – he not well," he said. He winked at Kiki who, secure now in Norah's grasp, returned an uncertain smile from behind his thumb. Norah held the baby in one arm, and her other hand was on Kiki's shoulder as he leaned back against her.

Frederik blinked. His mouth was open wide, as if frozen, and his lips were almost the same colour as his waxen face.

"Please – help me get my husband to his cabin, would you?" Emmie said to the sailor.

"Yes, Ma'am." And with a hand under each arm, the sailor lifted Frederik to his feet and steered him to the companionway. Emmie preceded them to the promenade, where she guided Frederik's feet from below while the Ethiopian eased him down from above. Directed by Emmie, he helped him to his cabin.

"I am most grateful," said Frederik as he sank back on his bunk. "I am sorry that it was necessary."

"Me too, Sir," replied the sailor, and departed.

*

Exposure to bright sunlight brought on the excruciating headache again the following day, and then again, so that there was no mistaking the cause and effect. These headaches were new, and they frightened Frederik – partly because of the pain which it seemed he must suffer during the voyage, if not beyond; and partly because they revealed that something inside him had deteriorated. Four years ago he had been second-in-command of an ironclad warship. The idea of a sailor suffering from sunlight would have struck him then as ludicrous; it did so still, yet the pain was there, vivid as a split watermelon. It was a bitter disappointment because he had looked forward to being on board ship again.

Having made the decision to travel, the listlessness that had gnawed at them in Cannes had vanished. They went to Paris in March, where they spent two weeks staying at the Hotel Castiglione with his mother and Hannina, and the misunderstandings of the previous autumn were resolved and forgiven. Then they were in London until June, in lodgings at 77 Sloane Street, arranging their affairs for a prolonged absence. They had a view over the gardens in Cadogan Place, and they could walk up the road to the Park with the children. The lease on Emmie's Rutland Gate house was extended to the tenant for a further five years; letters were dispatched to Australia in advance to prepare for their arrival, and there were numerous matters to settle with Mr Burton, the solicitor. Having let their Swiss servants go, a new lady's maid had to be engaged who would travel with them. There were purchases to be made and people to see – above all, Leslies who would have packages for Meg, their sister. Since her marriage to Mr Rolleston, she was the only one now living in the Antipodes. It was Rolleston who, as Commissioner for Crown Lands, had signed the Leslies' original squatting rights, but he had been promoted to work in Sydney, so they expected to see him and Meg. After booking passage on the *La Hogue*, a triple-masted vessel of 947 tons, Frederik made a trip to Denmark. He returned in good health after two weeks, keenly anticipating the voyage to Australia. The discovery that he was no longer fit to enjoy it was a harsh blow.

Many times when Frederik lay down with a headache, worrying, his mind returned to the goggles. A label inside the case said "St Petersburg", but his friend Carstensen gave them to him when his ship, the *Vojevoda*, joined them in De Castris Bay off the Siberian coast. It was clear by then that Carstensen would be going south again to Vladimir on the Manchurian coast, where a Russian colony was to be erected, and thence to Japan and China, so the goggles he had brought in case he had to travel through Siberia would be superfluous. Frederik, however, had already left the *Boyarin* and was on the steamer *Constantin*, bound for Ajan on the Sea of Okhotsk. It was sheer luck that he coincided with Carstensen, for the *Constantin* had made a detour down De Castris Bay to deliver some freight, before going north to Ajan.

Frederik recalled how obliging Carstensen had been: as soon as he heard of Frederik's decision, he had urged the goggles upon him, saying he had heard that it made all the difference to a long journey by sleigh, with snow on all sides as far as the eye could see. Frederik had not considered this, but he found it was the case: sometimes the whiteness seemed even to penetrate closed eyelids, making it hard to sleep. Just thinking of it made his head hurt worse. Grevenitz, who travelled with him as far as Irkutsk, was amused by the goggles but conceded their efficacy, while for Arsenieff, his companion to Moscow, who travelled the route regularly as a courier for Mouravieff, goggles were essential. Frederik had tried to give Carstensen some money for them, but he would not hear of it, and Frederik had instead given him a larger sum, so that he might buy some scissors for Hannina and cups for Christian, also some Chinese curios for Julie Festitit. Carstensen assured him that he was delighted to have some commissions because it gave him an excuse to go shopping – otherwise, he said, he would only spend money of his own that he could not afford on things which he would later regret. And, warming to the impromptu market that had gathered round him in the *Vojevoda*'s mess, Frederik had bought some embroidered Chinese slippers for Alma and Coco and several yards of gorgeous grey silk for his sisters to make into dresses.

Remembering how valuable they had been in Siberia against the snow, he had taken the goggles with him to Greenland too, though he did not intend wearing them when sailing or working. And he did not regret it. He had not expected to ski there – he had never done it before – but it was a welcome diversion from the claustrophobia in the small colony during the winter months when they could not work. Bluhme and Nielsen would not take the goggles even though he offered to lend them, complaining that they restricted their vision. It was true that the goggles did restrict peripheral vision, but Frederik still believed that vanity made them refuse. In any case, they never managed to ski successfully, whereas he and Thomsen were able to go downhill with the speed of trains, and very exhilarating it was too, with the wind behind you. The one bright memory in the whole grim venture.

It even started badly, with the wretched brig *Tjalfe*, which took them to Godthaab. Poor Thomsen and Nielsen shared a cabin just five feet by eight, divided from the main hold only by a few stinking boards. They dubbed it the Lobster-pot. The entrance, Frederik remembered, was via the aft hatchway, which was closed as soon as they went down, and they had to sleep on the floor because there was no space for bunks. They had the choice of staying down in the Lobster-pot or going up on deck to stretch their legs and breathe some air and, since the passage was very rough, they would immediately be soaked on deck. The lurching and pitching generated a terrible stench which was far worse in the Lobster-pot because of its proximity to the hold. There was sludge everywhere, making it look as if everything was smeared with stove polish. Even their hands and faces were black when they emerged. As for Bluhme and Frederik himself, their conditions were only marginally improved by having bunks. Although the smell and the grime in their cabin were not so bad, they could not escape it. They were officers in his Danish Majesty's Navy, but they were worse off than passengers in steerage to Australia. Yet even as he thought this, Frederik thought of the hold rocking beneath, which now held a cargo of rails: on another trip, it might take emigrants, or, until lately, convicts, who would stay there throughout the voyage. And he knew that it would be worse than on the *Tjalfe*. But it was so *unnecessary*. A matter of minimal expense and an injection of efficiency – hard to achieve in Denmark, it seemed, when it came to their benighted colony.

Over the next few days the weather was calm. There was concern because they appeared to have lost the south east Trade Wind; the passage was in danger of delay. But Emmie had found her sea legs and resolved to do her best with Kiki on deck. Together they watched the sailors taking down the light sails, which were stowed below, and replacing them with heavier ones for the stronger winds ahead. A cape pigeon was spotted, then an albatross attached itself to the ship for a spell. Although they were surprisingly far north, these were taken as encouraging signs of progress. Then one day after breakfast a great squall came on with torrents of rain. The top-gallant, main and mizzen sails were furled and, as the wind moved round to the north, the topsails were reefed for the first time since leaving England. In the afternoon, the wind dropped, the rolling seas went down and it became quite fine. The reefs were shaken out in the evening and Emmie and Frederik went on deck. There was a full moon and, in the heavy swell that was the legacy of the day's turbulent weather, the play of light on the waters was beautiful. Ribbons of silver were wreathed about the ship, glimmering off into the far distance where the ocean dissolved into the jewelled canopy overhead. The ship was at the centre of an orb illuminated by a constellation of coloured points.

"The sun almost seems superfluous, like this," said Frederik.

Emmie turned to look at him as he gazed over the flecked water. His eyes were wide now, as she had not seen them for days; and though he was calm, he seemed to be sucking in what he saw with the intensity of an emigrant looking back at his homeland shore. He had come up without a hat and the dark curls by his collar fluttered in the

breeze. There was a play of light across his face, a humour and animation that made something active out of his watching, which was so
true of him that she wanted to weep, for she was afraid that by day
this truth was fading.

"I have a pair of goggles at home," he said all of a sudden. "At my
mother's home, I mean."

"Goggles?"

"I wore them in Siberia, and in Greenland. If I had them now,
perhaps they would protect me."

"God knows best," she said.

Frederik looked straight at Emmie. Her hair was drawn up from
her nape, braided higher than usual, to the crown of her head, so that
her neck and earlobes were clearly visible in the moonlight. She wore
pendant earrings, clusters of tiny diamonds, which sparkled. A double
row of pearls was fastened around her neck, whose line was echoed
by the woollen shawl around her shoulders. The colour of her eyes
was swallowed in the darkness, but they retained their candour and
their kindness. Believing that they were not observed, he made to kiss
her, but she pulled back with a nervous smile and a frown. Her tongue
clicked in token reproof.

"You are a strange mixture," he said, "of resignation and resistance."

"Frederik! Whatever do you mean?"

"Where necessary, you accept things with Christian piety: at other
times you are ready to fight . . ."

"Frederik, we are in public!" she said in half-whispered rebuke.

Frederik laughed.

Emmie straightened her back and pulled the shawl closer round
her bosom. She knew that he was being serious, which pleased her.
If she was also being teased, she could enjoy that too, but she had
her dignity to preserve. "And you would make yourself look foolish
by wearing goggles," she said.

The following day, as the wind got up once more and the sea began
to heave, it was Emmie who lay in bed, feeling nauseous, thinking
about the goggles. Not that they interested her: she didn't know why,

as she dipped in and out of sleep, they kept tormenting her. Since she had never seen them and they held no associations for her, their image in her mind's eye was vague. They taunted her. It was their oddity which made Frederik's reference to them linger, for he was fastidious about his appearance. The ship pitched and her stomach lurched: how disappointing to find that she had not got her sea legs after all! Now, as they neared the Cape, the passage would become rougher, and continue so as they sailed with the Roaring Forties all the way to Australia.

In the afternoon, as the sea grew higher, the deadlights were put in. Like the goggles, thought Emmie, protection from the elements. Yet calm as she knew the scene in the cabin might seem from the outside — the lady on her bed in the soft illumination of a lantern — she did not feel calm. The light guttered crazily and the gale outside swelled like the turmoil within her. The thought of the goggles blanketed her mind. She wished Frederik had not mentioned them because they confused her: instead of being a screen to shut out the sun, she found herself thinking of them in reverse, as if they stopped something inside from escaping. Were they a device to prevent agitation from the outside, or to trap it within? The question presented itself as a riddle that must be solved before the refuge of sleep would open to her. She thought of Frederik's gaze — was it rapacious, was he trying to cram himself with sights, crunching up as much of the world as he could before . . . before the end? He was observant, that was all — but maybe that was why the thought of him wearing goggles was troubling. Any suggestion that his vision should be dimmed prematurely was upsetting. Silliness! She eased herself over, trying to accommodate herself to the ship's motion, afraid that any sudden movement would make her sick. The deadlights blocked the sea from coming in through the portholes but they also prevented the stale air from escaping: the cabin felt tight about her.

The sickness she was feeling ought to be seasickness because she was at sea in a gale, but it felt different — more intimate, more profound, the turbulence of a pool created by a spring rather than an invasive spill from elsewhere. As with all pain and unpleasantness, it was better to try not to think about it. But she was unable to sleep or to find solace by reading in the scriptures, as she usually tried to do, and a fugitive thought floated to the surface of her seething consciousness, announcing with the calm authority of a belatedly consulted engineer the possibility that she was pregnant. During the following days, as the sickness persisted and her period did not come, the truth seeped into her like water into hard earth. Frederik kept her company for hours, reading to her when he felt up to it, sometimes just sitting with her in silence, holding her hand; a stillness of which George would never have been capable save in his last days. She called on Julia, the maid she had taken on in London, to attend her, but she found her sullen. Sometimes Emmie would make her way to the saloon to be with the children, more rarely up to the deck. Norah accepted the increased dependence on her with grace. While regretting her employers' suffering, she did not begrudge it. She was devoted to Kiki and Willy.

As the ship bucked through the tumultuous seas round the Cape, a strange calm descended on Emmie despite her constant nausea. This was a surprise even to herself, for while common sense told her that this pregnancy was inopportune, she found that she did not feel it to be a disaster. She was afraid for herself, as she had been before, but when Frederik sat beside her she found that her fear vanished behind a new awareness of the trust she held for him. Instead of lamenting that the child might be fatherless while it was still young, she rejoiced that she carried a further legacy of Frederik. It would be her own last chance of having a child too. After George's demise she had assumed that she would have no descendants, but God sent Frederik to her and she was bound to welcome their issue as a divine dispensation. Moreover, she perceived in her present ordeal a further revelation of His mysterious design. There was something very *fitting* about finding herself in this condition on the way to Australia, like her mother, her grandmother, her aunt Harriet and so many more before her, as if she were joining a pattern that was only now apparent to her.

After Emmie's father met her mother, fresh from Mrs Enderby's Clapham schoolroom, and took her back to Australia as his bride, she was surely pregnant on the voyage. Her grandmother certainly had been when she first came from Devon to Norfolk Island with her husband in 1791. And what sort of clue did she have to the stupendous grimness that awaited her? At what stage did her husband tell her about his two sons by the convict, Ann Inett? Did he tell her before they were married, or as they ploughed the Southern Oceans when she had no option but to accept the news with what grace she could? Back and forth and back she went, until her final return around the time of Emmie's birth, to spend her old age with her daughter and son-in-law and their eleven children at Vineyard. Of all the memories Emmie had of her, two recurred most often: the first, herself as a small child, sitting on the floor of the carriage on the way to church, cocooned in her grandmother's skirts. She knew her parents would not have allowed it, but they did not know, or pretended they didn't. It was a secret shared with her grandmother, though why she was the only one with her grandmother, Emmie could not say. The other image was of a benign old lady in a lace cap sitting in a wing-backed armchair by the fire in her room, where Emmie would climb up and make herself comfortable in the folds of black silk and listen to her gentle voice telling tales of the past, or reading Bible stories. She did not live to see Emmie married; nor, thankfully, the collapse of her family's new fortune.

And when Uncle Phillip came out to Sydney with his wife, Harriet, was she pregnant? He had been commissioned to fit out an expedition to chart the Australian coasts, taking up where Flinders had left off many years before. It was Flinders who had introduced him as a youth to the people at the Admiralty, one of the few things he had time for between his release from captivity in Mauritius and his death. Although some ten years before her own birth, Emmie remembered frequent allusion to these events. While her uncle went off in the *Mermaid*, performing feats of skill and endurance which were the pride of all those who had made Australia their home, Harriet stayed at first with Emmie's parents in the cottage at Parramatta. Sons bloomed from her at the rate of one a year and she soon moved to her own home – it was scarcely credible, Emmie thought, that she had so many children so fast when her husband was most of the time away. For those first five years he came back for a brief respite, to refit, resupply and hire a new crew – and to make the acquaintance of his last son and beget another. Emmie thought that Harriet must have been pregnant too on her first outward voyage. She wondered if she had suffered. What in her Devon upbringing had prepared her for her future? Nothing, that Emmie knew of, and yet she appeared to have adapted so well. One might discount the sufferings of others if they were not spoken of. Confined within the reeling ship, listening to the smashing of the waves and the howl of the wind, the grinding of the boards and the creak of the masts, Emmie wanted to know how Harriet had felt. And her first return to England had been on the *Bathurst*, following her husband's final circumnavigation of the continent; a boat not designed for a lady and her children any more than it was designed for long ocean voyages. How had she managed, squeezed up in that heroic barque like a crab in a pot – perhaps pregnant again?

Yet the worst journey of all was surely her Grandfather King's. A story often told in the nursery, in hushed tones, but only once related to her in proper sequence by her grandmother. Emmie was not sitting in her lap – she was too old now – but in a chair by a window in her grandmother's sunny room, from where she could look out across the lush garden, past the Norfolk pine, to the welcoming finger of the jetty protruding into the river, signifying arrival to visitors from Sydney and beyond. It was from that place that she first saw George Leslie. News of the *Royal George*'s arrival had been announced by flags from the signal post at Parramatta. Captain Harding had gone to meet them in Sydney, and Emmie could still recall the excitement at Vineyard as they listened for the splash of oars. "Ssh!" gasped Libby or Kate, if she or Lucy or Arthur uttered a squeak; Mary and Annie did not need to be told, they had been tremulous for days at the prospect of the boys' arrival. Jack emulated the manly silence maintained by James, while Pat was behaving just as he fancied his future father-in-law believed he should, thoughtful and affectionate as ever, spreading good humour around with the grace that made her father describe him as "one in ten thousand". At last the splash and knock of a boat were heard – then Harding's voice, "Ahoy Macarthurs! I have visitors for you!" Followed at once by a strange voice, deep but youthful, "Pat! Eh, Pat! Is Patrick Leslie here?" A Scots voice, George's voice. Her father had gone down to the landing with Pat, James, Jack and Captain Wickham. The older girls followed at a proper distance, and even though it was long past their bedtime, she and Lucy were allowed to go down too. There was her brother Charlie, returned from his trip to England; and another youth, already slightly stooped and looking lost, who turned out to be Ernest Dalrymple. It was clear which were the Leslie brothers, for each of Pat's long arms embraced one. George disengaged himself first and, grinning, faced the host of Macarthurs. He looked at each of them directly as he was introduced – Emmie could see his intelligent eyes registering everything, and when it came to her turn she curtsied and he laughed and said, "Ach, Emmie! Ye widnae stand on ceremony with me, wid ye?" but instead of feeling embarrassed, she felt put at ease. He was short, but he stood square on to the world, chest out, without a trace of Walter's nerves. Dark hair brushed back, dark brown eyes, a compact but well-defined face in which could be seen the energy, resilience and toughness that he soon demonstrated were his. And so young, barely nineteen.

His early years of toil in the bush were broken up by visits to Vineyard, and she had already watched for his arrival many times when she said to her grandmother, "Grandmama, please will you tell me about Grandfather's journey to England, before you were married?"

"Good gracious, dear, why ever do you want to hear about that?"

"I have always known about it," Emmie replied, "but only in scraps. I would like to know what actually happened."

"But I was not there, I do not know – "

"You know better than anyone else."

The old lady hesitated, peering at Emmie through myopic eyes as if uncertain whether to decline her granddaughter's request because she was too young or because it was unsuitable – only to conclude that neither were adequate responses. "Well dear," she began, "you know that he was summoned from Norfolk Island by Governor Phillip?"

"Yes. He was to go to London with news of conditions. There was not enough to eat, and no relief ship had arrived."

"That's right. But the *Sirius* had run upon a reef off Norfolk Island, and though the stores were salvaged and the people saved, the ship was wrecked. So when Grandfather departed for Europe in the *Supply*, the colony was left without any ship. The plan was for the *Supply* to sail to Batavia, then return with provisions in company with another chartered vessel to Sydney while Grandfather took passage in a passing ship for London. Sailing in a wide arc round the Barrier Reef, which had nearly sunk the *Endeavour*, they reached Batavia in mid-July, only to suffer the same calamity that afflicted Captain Cook."

Mrs King paused. In her stillness, she seemed almost part of the furniture, but for her animated eyes which plucked the next word from Emmie.

"Pestilence."

"Indeed. It carried off half the *Supply*'s complement, and when at last your Grandfather took ship, a month later, it turned out that it was foul with disease. Within a week, six men were ill. Then fever struck the captain, the surgeon, the two mates, and all save four of the sailors. Before the captain became delirious, Grandfather obtained permission to construct a tent on board so that he and the survivors should not have to go into the putrid air below decks except where essential, when Grandfather ordered them to wrap themselves with the utmost care. With the help of a few men – and he told me that even they were raving much of the time – he got the ship to Mauritius in less than a month. There it was cleansed and a fresh crew entered, which was composed of all nations. Of the twenty-six sailors who came from Batavia, only four completed the voyage. The rest were either dead or left at the hospital with little hope of recovery."

Emmie shifted in her chair, drew up one leg and smiled, hoping that her grandmother would indulge her with the conclusion.

"Very well. Grandfather reached home just in time for Christmas. After interviews at the Admiralty and with Sir Joseph Banks – and with William Blake, with whom he left a pair of watercolours of the natives – Grandfather hurried down to see his mother in Launceston. While there, he called on me, and we became engaged, as you know. We were married at St Martin-in-the-Fields in London on 11th March and four days later were together on board the *Gorgon*, bound for New South Wales. Our journey was enlivened by the company of the ship's commander, Captain Parker, and his wife, Mary; also Captain Paterson of the New South Wales Corps, and his wife Elizabeth. We continued then to Norfolk Island where, a month after our arrival, your uncle Phillip was born, named in honour of Governor Phillip."

"And what was it like?"

"What was what like, Emmie dear?"

"Everything."

"Oh, there's no point thinking too much about it," she answered. "Very different from life in Launceston, that much I can tell you. But if your grandfather's spirits were sometimes depressed, as they were, I had only to remind him of the journey he had survived in 1790 to make him feel that God had not quite forsaken him. And when news reached us of the wreck of the *Pandora* on the Barrier Reef after catching some of the *Bounty* mutineers, we again had cause to thank God for His mercy. There were always things to remind us that our situation might have been worse."

It was strange, Emmie reflected now, how her female forebears who began married life with such discomforts and privations seemed to flourish in their marriages. Her own brothers and sisters, whose lots, on the face of it, were easy in comparison, had all been beset by difficulty. Though unacknowledged until now, this mysterious fact had been contained within her, waiting to be unlocked.

Perhaps it was a dim intimation of this that had impelled her to marry a sailor – who now had brought her to the same condition as her ancestors: engulfed by sickness, day after day, as the ship crashed through desolate oceans that were first crossed almost within living memory, if you excluded Tasman, Dampier, and some maverick whalers. And as the ship grappled with the winds and the waves, week after week, and each day she shuddered with sickness as if snagged on the cold claw of eternity, she had the sense that they were still probing at the world's limits. Yet this distant continent was her birthplace, was once her home. The sense of displacement was more acute when she turned from her daytime reveries to find Frederik seated at her side, for he belonged to a life she had left behind in Europe. Sometimes she stirred with the words to call for George already formed, as if in sailing back to Australia she were going to rejoin her former life. She would think guiltily that she must disturb him from his book, or drag him from the whist table to bring her a poultice and a bowl, picturing the willed patience on his brow. Realising that it was not George but Frederik induced a momentary sensation of unreality, of being untethered from the world in which she thought she had woken. Then she registered her courteous, ailing husband, who longed for goggles to assuage the burning in his head, and her mind settled down again into the life that was hers, with the velvety knowledge that she had forfeited nothing yet.

Australia, 1868–9

AN ivory workbox. In the centre of the lid is a medallion on which is written in relief the name Emmeline. Every other surface, apart from the underside, is carved with scenes of Chinamen at leisure: cruising in a boat, playing music, picking fruit in a garden, eating. Within is a cylindrical case with similar ornate carving, which is for storing needles, and a little rack in which sit spools for thread. Everything is made of ivory except the box's catch, which is steel. It is typical of the nineteenth-century China Trade. No Chinese lady would have owned it, but from the eastern seaboard of America, via the estancias of South America, the towns and bush homes of the Antipodes, the hill stations of the Raj, the sitting-rooms and drawing rooms and bedrooms of Europe and back to Nantucket – all round the world, ladies who thought of themselves as Europeans or Western would have been grateful to possess such a box. An exotic symbol of affluence.

The box belonged to John Macarthur's youngest daughter, Emmeline, now Lady Parker. It was bought by Walter Davidson on his first trip to Canton in 1808 as a christening present for his mentor's new child. Although Emmeline was not born before his departure, he was confident that the evidence of his foresight would sweeten the gift. The box had a blank medallion: he found someone in Sydney to carve the name. Lady Parker was Emmie's first-cousin-once-removed, also her godmother. At thirty-five she married late, but the match was deplored: first, by her mother, because Parker's prospects were uncertain – he was secretary to Governor Gipps – and anyway it was most inconvenient of Emmeline to get married; secondly, by the Vineyard Macarthurs, who detested Governor Gipps because of his attempts to limit the size of squatters' runs, and because he had hanged men for killing Aborigines. By marrying Parker, Emmeline aligned herself against the interests of the squatters, prominent among whom was George Leslie, whose chief duty on the Legislative Council had been to fight Gipps. Gipps was beaten: but in the end George died and it seemed inevitable that Emmie would die childless. In due course, Parker returned to England with his wife, where he was knighted for his political works, but Emmeline remained without children.

From the exile of her marriage, in England, Lady Parker found herself thinking more and more often of Camden Park, the home of her youth, where she knew she would never return. Following her father's death in 1834, the estate passed to her brothers, but for years its future was uncertain. Many people viewed with relish the fact that, having established his family's fortunes so triumphantly, the ruthless John Macarthur's inheritance should prove problematic. He left an estate of 28,000 acres of prime agricultural land and a fortune solid enough to survive the crashes of the 1840s that ruined so many, including his nephew Hannibal. But of his seven children, only James produced a child who could be regarded as a suitable candidate for inheriting, and that was a daughter. Bessie, that daughter, had married Captain Onslow in 1867, and produced an heir who was named James in honour of his grandfather who had just died. The relief at Camden was enormous, and when Lady Parker received the tidings in England, it ranked with the news of the previous three years – of Emmie's remarriage and the birth of her two children – as a source of true joy. Here were things of real value salvaged from the wreckage. It was natural that she should wish to entrust to Emmie a present for the new baby, but she also wanted to give something to Emmie herself. And then she remembered her ivory box, which she knew was still at Camden. Nothing, she felt, could be more appropriate.

Lady Parker had always been fond of Emmie. The divisions that existed between their families, first in youth and later in marriage, were not of their making, though both ladies were loyal to their families and

to their husbands. Lady Parker regretted the dispute between Pat Leslie and Davidson, which cast such a shadow over relations between Camden, her own home, and her cousins at Vineyard. She did not know the rights and wrongs of it because nobody had ever thought to explain it to her. Only her brother William had not followed the family line, although he had more obvious cause to dislike Pat Leslie since, in the midst of the feud with Davidson, Pat succeeded in marrying Kate, William's only love. The others all favoured Davidson. In due course, the Vineyards' unassailable loyalty to Pat suggested to Emmeline that her family, and Edward in particular, were wrong to be so partial, for Davidson's intransigence towards the Leslies vitiated relations with the cousins: two of the Vineyard girls had married Leslie boys. When Emmie was born and named after her Camden cousin, Pat Leslie was still a child, and at Vineyard there was still every reason to regard Davidson as a friend. But the closeness that was promised by that naming was prevented by Davidson's cruel procedure against Pat, and now there was nothing in the world that Lady Parker wished to give Emmie more than the box she had received as a baby from Davidson, laying to rest those evil shadows with this memento of their shared name.

Word of Emmie's arrival reached Camden, where it was known that she and her family were to stay in Sydney for a few days with the

Rollestons. Everybody had things to do in Sydney. No doubt they would wish to come to Camden, however, and a gracious note from Bessie, stating that they were welcome whenever it suited them, was left at the Rolleston house. Two weeks passed before she received an agitated reply from Emmie saying that they were going to a house somewhere out on the South Heads Road. Bessie's husband had it from his barber, or somesuch, that they were being assisted by an ex-convict, which was puzzling. He assumed that Emmie's new husband must be one of the incendiary young men reputed to infest Europe nowadays: so very disappointing for poor Emmie. Irritating, too, because there was the box to give her and, according to Aunt Emmeline's letter, Emmie had a package to deliver for the baby. Bessie mentioned Emmie's mysterious letter to her uncle, Sir William, who still lived in one wing of the house. Having corresponded with Emmie occasionally on botanical matters – he had sent some orchid speci-mens to a Mr Ker at her behest – it seemed improbable to him that she would be guilty of simple rudeness. He made his own deft enquiry, and the information it yielded made him urge his niece to don her bonnet and get out to Double Bay at once.

*

It had been early morning when they rounded South Head and began the approach to Sydney. Frederik could feel it in the ship's motion, as the heaving to which he had been accustomed now for almost four months subsided, and a lightness crept through his flesh.

Emmie was far from well, but she came out on deck with the others after breakfast. The prospect of this moment had troubled her during the long periods of solitary, queasy reflection in her cabin. She knew that the town of her childhood had long since been replaced by a city. Even in 1853, after an absence of just two years, she had returned with George to find the place transformed. Then, despite the ranks of new buildings bunching up to the water and spreading into the surrounding countryside, they were struck less by the physical aspect of the place than the atmosphere. Gold had changed everything. They couldn't even get a hansom cab to take them to an hotel, except at an extortionate price.

Emmie knew that a ship's imminent arrival was signalled to Sydney as soon as it was spotted from the Heads. It was a system she had seen in operation countless times in her youth: when the information was received in Parramatta, there was still plenty of time for someone to go the few miles down to Sydney to meet the new arrivals. She expected to be met now by Rolleston, though she could not be sure of this since the journey had taken much longer than expected because of their having lost the Trades before the Cape. Rolleston might have had to leave town, but he would have made alternative arrangements if necessary. As they passed Inner South Head, Frederik marvelled at the extent of the water ahead. He said that he had heard that the fleets of the world could be hidden here in perfect safety, and he saw that it was true. Emmie felt a native's thrill of pride; and the clear sunshine of an Australian spring day lifted an unseen weight from her spirits. In Watson's Bay she pointed out Clovelly, the cottage on a cliff which her father had built. Sir Henry and Lady Parker had bought it from him and rebuilt it. The new owners seemed to have added a curved portico. There on the north shore was the place where she and George had been landed after their terrible steamer journey from Brisbane. Now numerous houses were built there, and a landing-stage where a ferry-steamer was pulling away. There was Shark Island and the broad sweep of Rose Bay; the sails of small boats ducking into Double Bay, houses dotted on the green slopes between the rugged headlands.

Emmie peered into the haze ahead. "Pinchgut!" she cried.

Frederik narrowed his eyes, quick with curiosity. His head felt clear this morning, as if the proximity of land softened the light just below a critical point. Nowhere had he seen such a broad reach of sheltered water, with so many coves and inlets fingering into the greenery on either side. Where Emmie was looking ahead there was a little island which had some kind of fortification on it.

"They've knocked down the old buildings and built a fort!" she said. "It used to be where convicts were locked for solitary confinement."

Frederik shivered at this reminder that he was entering a colony founded on the toil of convicts, and he shivered again as he recognised the fort for what it was.

"I expect it was built because of the Crimean War," he said.

Emmie had heard about the fortification of Pinchgut Island, but had forgotten about it until now. "It seems strange to think they were worried the Russians would come here," she said.

"But they might have. Had the war not ended when it did . . . There was a Russian squadron in the Pacific, after all. I was attached to it."

"What a thought!"

Frederik recalled the tale he had heard of a handful of British troops landing on Kamchatka. The Russians he had met in the East had been convinced that the British would try to land again on the Pacific coast, supplied from Australia. Mouravieff had used the fear to justify his aggressive policy in Manchuria, knowing that the Chinese could be relied on not to resist. A transparent excuse for their massive land grab perhaps, but the Russians were not blind to Sydney's discreet menace.

Government House was still visible, but landmarks became more obscure as they grew closer. It was all very well, Emmie thought nervously, arriving somewhere unfamiliar when you had made preparations, or if you were a small party – in the days when it had been just George and herself, for example – but now there were the children and Frederik to think of, not to mention Norah and Julia. Responsibility for them all in Australia was hers, she felt, just as she would expect Frederik to arrange things for them in Copenhagen. But she realised now that she had done nothing, leaving it all up to Rolleston. He had promised in a letter to secure a house for them, but suppose he had not?

Just then, Julia approached her and asked if she might have a word in private. Although fresh-faced, she looked tired. She wore one of her two grey dresses, buttoned to the neck, and thick black shoes. Emmie had taken her on in London on the recommendation of a friend who employed her sister, and she had not warmed to her during the journey. Off Tasmania, she saw on deck a look between Julia and the second mate, which confirmed what she had suspected since passing Kerguelen, that Julia was carrying on with someone. By then it seemed wiser to say nothing. Julia could not be said to neglect her work and she would be miserable enough in Sydney at the inevitable parting from the man, without Emmie adding her own reproaches.

Emmie was holding Willy so that he could see the ships and the distant city. Beside her, Frederik held up Kiki, who stared in silent awe at the first human world beyond the ship that he had seen since leaving the Cape. Other passengers pressed about them. The deck was cluttered with baggage. "What is it, Julia? Can you not say it here?" Emmie asked.

"If you please, Ma'am," Julia repeated. Her blonde hair was loose about her shoulders, which she knew Emmie disapproved of, and there was an obstinate steadiness in her eye.

"Really, Julia, can't you see that it is not convenient?"

Julia stayed where she was, waiting for Emmie to see that she must change her mind.

"Very well, if it is really so very urgent that it will not wait," Emmie grumbled, passing the baby to Norah.

Julia's progress along the crowded deck was confident and nimble. It occurred to Emmie that she was going too fast on purpose, to make her feel awkward. Well, she was twenty years younger and had not been suffering from months of sickness. Emmie reminded herself that in order to be in effective command of someone else, you had first to be in command of yourself. If Julia wished to say something to her in private, then it was right that she should give her that opportunity.

At the top of the companionway, Julia had to allow passengers to ascend, a procession of hats bobbing towards her. When Emmie caught her up, they waited together in silence and Emmie could see from Julia's refusal to meet her eye that she was anxious. Seeing them above, a gentleman retreated and halted the stream, allowing the ladies to come below. Emmie went first and headed for her cabin. Two trunks stood on the floor, which Julia had helped to pack. On the bed were further cases and boxes, including her dressing case and a hat box. The rest of the luggage, which they had not used on the voyage, would be brought up from the hold in due course. Emmie stood beside the trunk and waited for Julia to speak.

As soon as she was in the cabin, Julia's courage deserted her. With a heave of her shoulders and a snort, as if a valve had been unscrewed, she burst into tears.

Solicitous now, Emmie moved behind her and closed the door, then took her hand. "Dear me, Julia! Whatever is the matter?"

"Oh, Ma'am, please forgive me! I am so sorry! I am to leave you!" Julia said through her tears.

"Leave me, Julia? What can you mean?"

"Me and McCafferty – we are to be married!" she cried, as if Emmie already knew all about her and McCafferty.

"Married, Julia? McCafferty? Who is McCafferty?"

She suddenly felt disgusted by the girl's self-pity and by her stupidity. The assumption that Emmie knew could not be withdrawn, and Emmie's sympathy, which she had been so ready to extend, wilted.

"He is the second mate, Ma'am. I am engaged to be married to him."

"Well why are you engaged to him, for Heaven's sake, if it causes you such distress?"

"I am upset at the inconvenience I am giving you and the Captain, Ma'am!"

Julia pressed the heels of her hands against her eyes. When her nose started to stream as well, Emmie extracted her own embroidered handkerchief from her sleeve and mopped at the girl's face. She regretted being so harsh. Julia was miserable and muddled; she needed her help. She only wished she felt stronger herself. "When we are all safely ashore and established we shall discuss it. I will speak to McCafferty then if you wish."

"But, Ma'am, I can't go with you! McCafferty wants me to go with him!"

After four dismal months on board, Emmie was missing the moment to which she had so looked forward. It was tempting to go back on deck at once and let Julia suffer the consequences of her silliness if she chose.

"I'm sorry to keep you, Ma'am, I know you want to be on deck."

"Yes, Julia," Emmie replied, relenting. "And I should have thought you would wish to be on deck too. Sydney is said to be the finest harbour in the world." Emmie wondered what, in fact, was keeping them below. Since Julia couldn't really be proposing to leave at once, there was no need for further discussion now. "Come along, let's go up and watch the ship coming in."

Julia stared at Emmie, amazed that she could believe anything was resolved. "What about my pay, Ma'am?" she said.

Emmie felt her insides lurch, as if a huge wave had appeared from nowhere and rolled beneath the ship. Julia's demand was impertinent, but Emmie was shocked by the sudden, clear perception that Julia's intent was fixed, and the duty this entailed for her. Disregarding her own intense desire to be on deck with Frederik as they floated into Sydney, and in spite of her own volatile condition, she would have to take issue with Julia and do her utmost to dissuade her.

"Julia, think! You are proposing to disembark into a country on the other side of the world from your home with a man you hardly know – for a most uncertain future, if I may say so; forfeiting your passage home . . ."

"I know McCafferty as well as I need to know him, Ma'am."

Obstinacy, Emmie reflected, was an estimable attribute in certain circumstances. In others, it was a perfect devil. "How could you know him, Julia? It would be most exceedingly rash of you . . ."

"Begging your pardon, Ma'am, but how long had you known your husband?"

Emmie was speechless. The insolence of the girl! What could Julia possibly know of her courtship? Yet she had unsheathed a point with some edge. "And what would you do?" she asked, ignoring the question.

"We shall go to Melbourne and open up a confectioner's shop. McCafferty knows a man who will lend us . . ."

"Julia, this is moonshine!"

Julia's tears started again, but they were the product now of frustration and anger rather than anxiety at broaching the subject with Emmie. "Ma'am, it is all settled!"

"How can it all be settled? We have not so much as come ashore yet!"

Even as she spoke, they heard the rumble of anchors being lowered, and Emmie thought with scalding frustration of what she was missing on deck, the sight of the crowding boats and the friendly faces waving. Frederik would be wondering where she was, and she wanted to be with him.

"Ma'am, I – "

"At least, Julia, stay with us until you have had further opportunity to consider. It will be for the best."

This was a suggestion that Julia herself had made to McCafferty, but he had told her to get her pay and leave at once. Hearing it now from Emmie distressed her further.

"Julia, you are not in the family way?"

"No!"

"Well, why such haste then?"

"Ma'am, I am to leave and there's an end to it. If you please."

Emmie sighed. "Well, I have said what I think." She could not keep the girl against her will, but she was unwilling to abandon her. "You had better come and see my husband. He will give you your wages." As she left the cabin, she added, "If you are really determined then there is nothing for it. But at least make a note of our address, so that you may contact us if necessary. You must understand, Julia, that you may come to us if you wish. You may find you need your reference, at least."

"Thank you, Ma'am."

Coming out on deck, Emmie saw that the ship had anchored in Farm Cove. She could see the Botanic Gardens and, beyond the narrow peninsula on which stood Government House, the tall masts of ships moored in Sydney Cove. The sails had been furled and the deck was crowded with excited passengers and their baggage. Some were gawping over the side, others milled about trying to gather themselves into family groups, concentrating towards the side where small boats were already pressing to meet the passengers and take them ashore. Shrieking children ran about, pursued by the cries of parents and nurses. A dog plunged back and forth, barking frantically. Threading her way with Julia at her heels, Emmie found Frederik where she had left him earlier. He was relieved to see her. Both the children were crying noisily, Kiki in his father's arms, Willy in Norah's, whose impassive face expressed a clear reproof to Emmie for deserting them at this juncture.

"Is everything all right?" said Frederik.

"Julia has chosen this moment to leave us," Emmie replied as she took Kiki from him. Kiki's arms draped round her neck and she could feel his teary cheek against hers, comforting her. "Please would you settle her wages, Frederik. There is nothing more to be said."

Frederik inspected Julia with astonishment. She did not meet his eye but looked at the planks beneath their feet. He wondered what could have occurred, but Emmie had made it clear that he should not ask. "Very well," he said. He disliked paying her in public like this, but there seemed to be no choice and so he reached into his coat. "Two weeks and three days since the beginning of the month," he said. "I will give you a guinea. No more," and he handed her the coin. "I do not know why this is happening and I see I should not ask. But it is a betrayal and an inconvenience."

For the first time, Julia looked up at Frederik, her mouth open in surprise. But seeing no prospect of appeal, she took the money and bobbed a curtsy. "Thank you, Sir. Ma'am." Then she nodded to Norah and hurried off across the deck.

Emmie saw that McCafferty was waiting for her on the other side, leaning against one of the saloon skylights. He had been watching the whole performance.

"She says she is going to marry the second mate," said Emmie. "They are going to Melbourne, where they will open a confectioner's shop."

"Or so she believes."

"Quite."

Emmie sighed and shook her head. She was upset and weary, and she knew that Norah would feel cross at having witnessed the scene. She felt as if she had mismanaged things, but she did not see what else could have been done.

"Now," she said, attempting to rally herself; then, "Oh, please!" as Kiki plucked at her hat, a pretty black straw one with a blue ribbon round the crown. She pulled Kiki's hand away and adjusted her hat. "Now," she repeated, looking towards the crush where some people were boarding and others leaving the ship. "Rolleston, where are you?" She wanted to get to the house, wherever it was. She was not feeling at all well.

A vast man suddenly stepped clear of the crowd. He stood for a moment and looked around, rubbing his hands together. Seeing Emmie, he spread his arms wide in greeting and came towards her. The line of his grin was matched by the curve of his hat brim, and his waistcoat stretched over the expanse of his belly like a sail before the wind.

"Missus Zeegy! Missus Zeegy!" he bellowed in delight.

"Mick!"

Distracted by the need for Rolleston, Emmie watched him raise his tall hat high before offering her hand, which he pummelled in his enveloping paws. Then she smiled and introduced him to Frederik.

"Mick O'Shea, Sir, at your service Mister Zeegy!" and he shook Frederik's hand with enthusiasm.

"Mick used to work for us at Canning Downs. You run an hotel now, don't you, Mick?" said Emmie. As a ticket-of-leave man he had dug ditches at Canning Downs. She had encountered him in Sydney with George fourteen years ago and was pleased to learn that he had started an hotel with his wife.

"Five hotels, Ma'am, five hotels! The gold rush didn't make all the diggers rich, but it did no harm to those of us lookin' after them!" And he roared with laughter, slapping his stomach as if its bulk alone were proof that he was a man of consequence.

"I'm very glad to hear that you have prospered, Mick," said Emmie. "And what brings you on board? Are you meeting somebody?"

His grin was invincible. "I'm meeting *you*, Missus Zeegy Ma'am!" he cried. "What a joy it is to see you with the little ones!"

"But – "

"Mr Rolleston has had to go up-country last week, Ma'am, and Mrs

Rolleston thought I might be of more use to you if I met you than herself, so – "

"How very kind of you! But how did you know that we were coming?"

"My ears may be further from the ground than other fellows', but I hear most things about comings and goings. I called on Mrs Rolleston and said I would be glad to meet you, for old friendship's sake, and what with her being alone at home with the children and knowing my respect for her dear departed brother, your late husband – " O'Shea raised his hat again, momentarily solemn – "she was kind enough to allow me – "

"Well, it is most kind of you, Mick!"

For the second time in Emmie's life, Rolleston had failed to arrive at a critical moment. At her marriage to George, Captain Hoseason had had to stand in as best man; now Mick proved himself a valuable friend. He had organised a wherry to take them ashore, where two hansom cabs were waiting with others at the wharf, together with a cart for the luggage. After escorting Emmie to the first cab, with the children and Norah, he bade her go at once to the Rollestons.

"I thought we were going to a house Rolleston had rented on our behalf?" said Emmie.

O'Shea scratched the side of his head, making his hat wriggle. "Where would that be, then?" he said.

Emmie did not know. She felt foolish at her ignorance, and O'Shea was embarrassed.

"I only know Mrs Rolleston was expectin' you, Ma'am," he said.

"Perhaps the house is near to theirs." Emmie was anxious to be on her way.

"That'll be it, Ma'am, that'll be it!" O'Shea said. Then he slapped the driver's box and returned on board to Frederik and the luggage.

Frederik was about to suggest they engage a porter when O'Shea hoisted a trunk onto his back as if it were a summer jacket and strode off through the swarming travellers to dump it on the wherry. On his return, he intercepted Frederik with a suitcase and told him to stay with the luggage. "You don't want any thievin' fingers at your chattels, Sir," he remarked. Frederik did not know whether this was a ploy to make him give up without loss of face or whether the threat was genuine, but the message was clear enough and he left all the carrying to O'Shea.

There was a moment's awkwardness when they finally arrived at the Rollestons' as Frederik made to tip O'Shea, but from the collapse of O'Shea's grin he immediately realised that he had offended him, and he apologised.

"Forgive me, I was dreaming. You have shown such kindness, and it is a precious quality!"

"No offence, Sir. Honest to God, 'tis a pleasure to be of service."

While Frederik assumed that O'Shea's readiness to help reflected a desire for something in return, Emmie was never in doubt that the true reason was his devotion to George. Few free labourers had been tempted up to the limitless spaces of the Darling Downs in the early days: the stations relied on convicts and ticket-of-leave men, for whom, in their constraints, the activity and the space had some appeal. While these men were obliged to be obedient to the gentleman squatters, their real loyalty was only won by the example of hard work. Among the squatters, Scotsmen like the Leslies proved most capable of this. It was well known that Pat had obtained a pardon for the Dublin lifer, Peter Murphy, who accompanied him on the pioneering journey which opened up the Downs. Pat liked to say that a good lifer was worth two ordinary men. A convict by the name of Jack Sheldon had walked nine hundred miles to be with Pat again after being shut up following a bout of drunkenness at Dunheved, the estate owned by Phillip King, which Pat had leased before going up to the Downs. When he arrived, Pat said, "But Jack, you have bolted, and you know what that means!" "Yes," Jack replied, "but you will make it all right with the Captain." And Pat did.

Meg Rolleston lived in a spacious bungalow in Balmain, looking towards the Parramatta River. A parakeet with brilliant blue tail-feathers flew out of a gum tree on their arrival, causing Kiki to shout and point.

Meeting Meg at the end of her journey back to Sydney was a strange reversal for Emmie. She had first met her when she visited the Leslies in Scotland with George in 1853. Then, Meg was the daughter at home, looking after her ageing parents while her brothers were making lives for themselves across the globe, and her sister Mary Anne was already married to Patrick Ferguson. Now Meg was the only one at home in Australia and Emmie, once again, was the visitor. It had nothing to do with the places, it seemed, but was a condition of the person, as if Meg carried within her an intrinsic stability, which Emmie lacked.

"Now, Emmie dear, you will want to go and collect yourself, I dare say, after your journey," Meg said, when the children and Norah had been introduced and they had all greeted one another. Meg had three children, two girls and a boy, who said "How d'ye do?" to Emmie with unabashed curiosity.

Meg had grown stout in the intervening years. The plainness of her youth had been transformed by marriage into something more appealing: the set of her mouth was benign, her dark eyes – George's eyes – were intelligent, and there was an efficient economy to her movements. Although no older than Emmie, she looked as if she had already settled into middle age with relief. Australia had not weakened her Scottish accent; nor, Emmie judged as she observed the extreme good order of the house, had it brought a lapse in the rigorous standards of housekeeping learned at Warthill.

"Thank you, Meg," Emmie replied, grateful for the offer of a moment's respite before they moved off again. "Is the house nearby?"

"Ach," said Meg, "I was coming to that. I'm afraid . . . Because of your delay, the rascals got cold feet and reneged, and Rolleston hasnae found ye another. But I promise we'll make ye all comfortable here for as long as it takes to get ye fixed up."

"Oh, how very tiresome! I am afraid we shall be a great inconvenience to you, Meg."

Emmie was exhausted. She felt nauseous again, and there was a pain in her lower abdomen more insistent than ordinary pressure on the bladder. She wanted her own space, without obligations, where she could rest or venture forth as she chose.

In the privy, when she lifted up her skirts she saw at once that her white petticoat was smeared. She put her hand to her mouth and bit into her index finger, near the knuckle, as if to get a grip on something as she felt herself swept up in a flood of panic. She had not even told Meg that she was pregnant. Why hadn't Frederik arrived yet? She would have to stay in bed, but she hadn't even anywhere to live. What of poor Kiki and Willy, what would they do while she was confined? Was Frederik well enough to manage? He had seemed so delicate lately! And the baby – ?

"Norah!" she called.

Emmie's tone made Norah hurry, still holding Willy, while Meg followed with Kiki.

"Norah, please tell Mrs Rolleston that I must have a doctor!"

Norah turned for a moment, her cheeks flushed. Seeing from Meg's eyes that she had heard, she put the baby in her arms and explained, "Mrs Ziege is expecting." Then she hurried to help Emmie.

Kiki started to cry. Pushing past Meg's long skirt in the narrow passage, he tried to pursue Norah, but Meg caught his arm and steered him back. She was not perturbed when this made him scream, nor when Willy joined his brother. "Yer mother and Noorah are busy for a moment," she said. "Come with me and my boys. We'll see what birds there are in the garden. Jane!" she called for her maid, who came running, "Wid ye go and fetch Dr Mitchell, please? He is tae come at once, if he would be so kind."

Frederik arrived a few minutes later. He could hear Kiki's squeals of delight and the squawking of birds as Kiki chased them around the garden.

Meg came out to greet him. Stating only that Emmie had been taken ill, she ushered him through to the bedroom where Emmie lay beneath a sheet. The bleeding had stopped, but she was pale and she looked miserable, despite her relief on seeing him.

*

When Bessie Onslow found Emmie, she was in a house in Edgecliff on the other side of Sydney. Meg Rolleston had done what she could to accommodate the Zieges, but the prolonged bed-rest on which the doctor insisted for Emmie made the situation untenable. Some time previously, it had been arranged that Emmie's eldest sister, Libby, should come to Sydney. It was expected that Emmie would by then be well established with her family in the house found by Rolleston. Instead, because of the ship's delay, Libby came just two days after their arrival. Frederik had already made preliminary enquiries and been to see two houses, but they turned out to be expensive and unsuitable. Libby declared that the difficulty of finding good accommodation in Sydney was notorious, but she knew just the thing. There had been some development lately on the hill behind the house which her husband had rented near the shore in Double Bay. The owner of one of the plots was an acquaintance, Libby said. She believed the houses were good, with spacious rooms, while the air was sure to be clean and the outlook pleasant. She would be but a short distance away and could be both nurse and maid to Emmie while she needed her. Now that her children were grown up, she and her husband had been talking about buying a house in Sydney, so it would suit her to stay.

Frederik went out to Double Bay at once with Libby. A hansom cab took them up to Edgecliff. The coast's enticing inlets and long views, which had so delighted Frederik from the deck of *La Hogue*, were now an irritant, as if he had already been seduced and betrayed by them. How was it possible to live in a city so chopped about? But it was spring, and the road up to Edgecliff was lush with mimosa; the red-brick house that he was shown was decent, and it offered a solution. Libby did not need to point out the benefits of its proximity to her; she arranged for a bed to be brought up immediately.

But by the time of Bessie's visit two weeks later, the house had already become abhorrent to Emmie. The tearing frustration and discomfort of being forced to stay in bed was aggravated by the drains, which turned out to be inadequate. Then Willy was not well. Three days of repeated vomiting had wrung the flesh from him, and Emmie was convinced it had something to do with the house. On top of these setbacks, Frederik's first visit to Emmie's Sydney agent, Fanning's partner, confirmed that the position at Gigoomgan was irrecoverable. On succeeding days, many hours were spent discussing whether there were grounds for proceeding against Mant, or whether their interests might be better served in the end by staying in the partnership. While the affair itself remained obscure, the outcome, which had still seemed uncertain from London, now looked liked a foregone conclusion: they would have to extricate themselves, salvaging what they might. Once the papers were drawn up, only a signature was required.

"And so, my dear Bessie," said Emmie, "you find us much tried since our arrival."

Bessie sat on a low ladderback chair beside the bed on which Emmie reclined with her head and shoulders propped on a bank of pillows. She had arrived unannounced and was disappointed to find Frederik out.

Emmie had last seen Bessie when Bessie was a prim fourteen-year-old. Now a mother approaching thirty, she had filled out somewhat. Her lips were full, her skin pale, and the hair that peeped from beneath the bonnet which her Uncle William had urged her to wear was dark, with curls. Her eyes were alert. She knew the anxiety Emmie must be feeling for the baby she was carrying, and her intense disappointment at finding herself laid up.

"I have brought you something," she said, reaching into a basket at her feet. "My aunt Emmeline wrote, asking me to give it to you."

"And good heavens! I have something from *her* for *you*!" Emmie cried, as Libby entered with a tray of cups and fresh tea in a porcelain pot. Libby was short like her sister Kate, and dark like Emmie, but she was broader than all her sisters. She moved with the measured pace of a happy woman who had always managed to achieve what was necessary without hurrying.

Emmie made to get out of bed, but Libby rebuked her. "Tell me where it is, Emmie dear. How many times must I tell you to stay where you are?"

The slight movement made the skin below Emmie's ribs prickle. With a sigh, she sank back. "It is a small package in brown paper. I think you put it in that drawer," she said, indicating the lower drawer of a chest under the window. Directed by Emmie, Libby had unpacked most of Emmie's cases.

Taking the box held out by Bessie, Emmie recognised it at once as the one shown to her a lifetime ago by her grown-up cousin Emmeline, in a sunny sitting room at Camden, on a rare visit with her sisters and mother. "It was a christening gift from Papa's old friend Walter Davidson," Emmeline had said, drawing Emmie's attention to the name they shared on the lid.

"Uncle Davidson," Emmie groaned.

Although not understanding why, Bessie realised that the gift was a mistake.

"Uncle Davidson," Emmie repeated, and tears slipped down her cheeks.

"Emmie! Emmie!" Libby reproved her. "You know it is given with the kindest intentions!"

"Of course! I know!"

Libby handed Lady Parker's gift to Bessie. Inside, Bessie found a silver mug engraved with her baby's name. She held it up for the others to see, and was startled by a fresh torrent of tears from Emmie.

After Bessie's departure, Emmie asked Libby to hide the box. "Perhaps I'll feel differently about it when I am better," she said.

In the course of the next three weeks, the drains became more offensive as the weather grew hotter. The house was exposed and, while the wind brought noise and clouds of dust from a new building site a hundred yards away, it was powerless to disperse the smell. Trees had been cleared between them since they had arrived. Although Willy seemed better, both Kiki and Frederik were coughing again and Emmie was unable to do anything to help them. Every time she exerted herself, she bled, and the doctor told her to stay lying down.

One evening late in November, cramp gripped Emmie's stomach. Dr Mitchell was sent for. By the time he arrived the cramp had abated, but Emmie was complaining of cold although the night was warm. He examined her and said there was no immediate danger, but he advised Libby to sit with her during her fever. Libby did so throughout the night, mopping her sister's face and neck while Frederik walked in and out, unable to sleep. Snatches of agitated chatter reached him, interspersed with Libby's soothing tones. She could not be ill, Emmie said, for she needed to care for Frederik. Was it not cruel that he should be afflicted too? In this life, it seemed that all that was given to one to love must be taken away, nothing should be taken for granted. It was hard to bear, but God knew best.

"Hush, do not fret yourself, Emmie."

Did Libby think about Vineyard? How fast it had all crumbled! With what fortitude their parents had borne their sufferings! Yet she did not believe those short years at Ipswich were unhappy for them, they were free of care at least!

"You made them comfortable."

"Do not forget Annie, Libby! Oh! I miss her so, I long to see her and talk with her. Was she happy with Wickham, do you think? How I wish I could have done more for Carrie. Do you believe me, Libby?"

"Ssh, you are troubling yourself about nothing, I am sure no-one could have done more."

"Do you think so, Libby?"

"No sister could be kinder."

"You are so good to me, but it is not true, I know it. So often I reproach myself for failing people . . ."

Libby took her sister's hand and stroked it. "Oh, Emmie . . . !"

"And then the dear Leslies. Do you think if I had cared better for George . . . ?"

"You must not think like that, Emmie – "

"I have been so blessed, Libby, after George, to find Frederik! Am I not blessed?"

"Of course, Emmie dear."

"What have I done to deserve such good fortune? To be surrounded all my life by those I love, and to return so little! Libby, if wishes were enough, then I would wish to Pat and Kate their lives again, it has been so hard for them and I do not know if we always made it easier. George used to get so cross, it upset me and I blamed him. Then when he became ill I saw that I was wrong, and yet I often wished that Pat could share more in our success at Canning Downs, it must have been a torture to him to see George doing so well while everything fell to ruins for him – ”

“Emmie, that is not how it was – ”

“I feel so peculiar, I cannot tell if I am hot or cold, Libby, and there is such a pain in my belly!”

“Have faith and it will pass – ”

“I had faith all those years ago at Canning Downs, but it was not enough! I was so afraid, Libby, you cannot imagine, I hope you cannot! Though married, I was still not much more than a child, all I knew was the baby wanted to come and it would not! There was no-one with me but an Aboriginal girl and oh! Libby! I was so afraid!”

“Your faith was enough, you survived – ”

“But not the baby, not George’s baby! I wanted it so!”

“Do not torment yourself, Emmie!”

“But I am not afraid for myself now, Libby, if you stay with me I will not be afraid!”

“I will stay with you.”

“It is not right, I have known it from the start, in the ship, something was wrong. I will lose it, but it is God’s creature too!”

“And if you lose it then that too is God’s will.”

“You are a comfort, Libby, God bless you!”

In the morning Emmie’s temperature dropped, and she miscarried.

*

At the end of December, Frederik wrote to his mother that Emmie had now recovered from a severe illness. He did not specify its nature, but he supposed that it would be guessed from his remark that she had been in bed for several weeks under doctor’s instructions. Willy had also been suffering from dysentery, Frederik wrote, and his own cough had returned with a severity that made him a nuisance to his family. They had engaged and lost three maids, each of whom demanded twelve shillings per week – the wages for servants were exorbitant – and Norah too had been unwell. The season had been one of constant trials for them, but the Lord had given them the strength to endure. Now, following the respite of two agreeable weeks spent with cousins of Emmie's at Camden, it was to be hoped that they would be able to consider the affairs that had brought them to Australia. Until recently, he had not had the opportunity to discover much more about the country than he might have learned during an evening with Fairholme or another well-informed man in Europe.

From the Parramatta steamer, Emmie had pointed out Vineyard, now renamed Subiaco.

Frederik took her hand on the gunwale. He saw a large house with a portico and a broad veranda. A covered balcony ran the length of the first floor, behind which could be seen shuttered windows. A lawn sloped down to the river, with overgrown shrubberies separating it from vineyards on either side. Flowerbeds reached round to higher ground at the back. In the middle of the lawn, bisecting the view of the façade, grew a tall Norfolk pine. He wondered if the grandeur of the place made the sight of it more painful, or only more conducive to nostalgia.

But Emmie was fighting hard against sentiment. "It's a shame the name has been changed," she said, "because the site is where vines were first planted in Australia. They were introduced from South Africa by a Captain Waterhouse. He built a cottage here, which my father bought."

She had not set foot inside the house since the day of her marriage to George.

Frederik was taken on a tour of the Camden Park estate by Bessie's uncle, Sir William, an elderly but vigorous man with long legs, a pipe and an open sky-blue waistcoat. His knowledge and love of the place were evident both in the good order and in his eagerness to show it off to Frederik. As they rode, he pointed out vast areas of vines, wheat, maize, and grazing land extending to the bleary horizons. Much of the land was nowadays rented out, he explained. Easier to manage that way and often more profitable. It was not realistic to expect in other areas the returns they achieved on the main dairy farm (which they managed themselves) – £1,200 per annum – for the climate was erratic. Although the Camden wine was well flavoured, like Chablis, Frederik was told that the soil was nowhere nourishing enough to support red wines. Over the ensuing days, he saw this for himself as he visited some of the surrounding estates with Sir William. The further they went into the country's interior, the more visible were the effects of prolonged droughts: every blade of grass burnt up; only the miserable remnants of bastard rubber trees with long white trunks and withered grey foliage. Even so, he drank a home-grown wine on one of the estates that tasted like a good Mosel.

In the end it was not the vines at Camden that impressed Frederik so much as the violets, which spread away from one side of the house like the scatterings of a whimsical giant. When they arrived, Kiki ran shouting into them and threw himself down, as if the only appropriate response was to roll among them. Emmie called to him, scolding, but Sir William stopped her. "They will recover . . . And – " With his face lifted towards the patch where Kiki tumbled, he touched his nose and smiled – "they need a small child to roll in them to achieve their full glory."

As Sir William spoke, the smell of the tiny crushed flowers pervaded the air. Frederik and Emmie filled their lungs and held their breath, suspended, as if the sweet scent would vanish if they let it go. Frederik felt that he would remember Kiki among the violets if he lived to be a hundred. Then he wondered, if he lived but a short while, whether Kiki would remember his father watching him.

For the first time since her arrival in Australia, Emmie felt rested. She did not look forward to returning to Edgecliff, but she was determined to make the best of it for the term of their lease. Now that she was fit again, there were a great many people to see and acquaintances to be renewed; there was no reason to be confined to the house. Meanwhile it was high time that Frederik got out of Sydney: closing off their options at Gigoomgan had opened others for them which needed investigating. Besides, inactivity did not suit him and his health might benefit from a change of climate.

On the second day of the New Year, Frederik left for Hobart Town in Tasmania, whence he would travel to Launceston. A half day's travel would then take him to a farm belonging to Emmie's brother, Charlie.

On the way, the steamer put in for a few hours at Eden in Twofold Bay, to pick up some bulls. The bay reminded him of San Remo. Following a tip-off from a sailor, he persuaded two other passengers to join him looking for oysters. They took off their boots and socks and rolled up their trousers, and between them gathered six dozen, with which they made a good lunch with some bread and ale they had brought from Eden. One of his companions, named Fairfax, was on his way to study the last of the pure-breed Tasmanian Aborigines at the governor's invitation. He had with him a case of measuring instruments and papers, including phrenological charts. It seemed to Frederik to be an enterprise rooted in delusion.

During the course of his visit, he recalled Fairfax's project many times. Not because he encountered Fairfax again or anybody interested in his activities, but because it came to represent the uneasiness of the place to him. Signs of progress were all about, just as they were on the mainland: towns which had sprung from nothing in a few years; law and order; the cultivation of the land and busy markets. But while the progress on the mainland was sure, here it was shadowed by the possibility of instant corruption. Wherever he looked, he saw neglect – buildings with loose boards, fences with broken rails, skeletal mules, land that had been won from the bush and then abandoned. He wondered if the fault lay in his own perception, for he could not doubt that the place was thriving, nor be certain that the decay was more observable than in other places. It was more a sense of latent, brutal indifference, as if the inhabitants were so affected by living on the world's brink that they were no longer sure whether they were taming the wilderness or losing themselves to it. Even Charlie seemed resigned to the erosion of his world in a way that seemed both mysterious and unalterable to him, and which Frederik found surprising in a brother of Emmie's. He told Frederik of his visit to Scotland in 1835 and his return home with the Leslie brothers as if it were something that had happened to someone else. His wife had died young and there had been some trouble with his family, whose details Frederik did not know. Frederik suspected it was this – together with flight from his father's bankruptcy – which had brought him to

Tasmania, for he proposed no advantages to the place: on the contrary, he declared it to be the rump of the world, as the authorities had intended it to be when they seeded it with prisons. "No place for a fellow with ambition. Though it suits me well enough," he added.

Letters from Europe were awaiting Frederik when he got back to Sydney, in which he learned of his brother's marriage to their niece, Coco. Emmie expected him to be dismayed by the news, but he was not. It was not so very unusual, he said: first cousins often married one another – her sister Libby, for example – so why should Christian not marry Coco? It was a good match from both points of view. Coco had no money and therefore had done better than might otherwise have been expected, while Christian had acquired a wife on whom he could rely. At least they had mutual respect and understanding, which amounted to a better basis for marriage than many people had. He was pleased for them both, and had no doubt that his mother and sisters would feel likewise. What did worry him was the news that Alma, whom Emmie knew to be his favourite niece, had given birth to her first child in Rome. Emmie observed that he himself had been born near Rome, and he retorted that Rome's unhealthy air had nearly killed his mother afterwards.

The malignant influence that places could have on health was of great concern to Frederik. He had understood from Emmie's letters to him in Tasmania that Kiki and Willy had been unwell, but, not wishing to alarm him when he was unable to do anything, Emmie had kept the truth of the matter from him. Now he found that Kiki was as pale and sickly as he had been in Thun, while Willy was emaciated from dysentery: seeing him in his bath, Frederik was shocked by the prominence of his ribs, and his shoulder blades sharp beneath the skin. Emmie had concealed that she too was suffering from dysentery.

Without further ado, Frederik sought out Mick O'Shea at his hotel in Regent Street. Never mind if there were still some weeks left to run on the lease, it was imperative to move away. They would look for something more permanent from the base of a reliable hotel.

O'Shea was gratified to be asked. He pondered the matter, then conferred with his wife. Frederik heard them discussing it in Gaelic in his office, while he paced the lobby, hat in hand. When O'Shea emerged, he said his wife had come up with the very thing he himself had in mind, namely Peytons Hotel in Parramatta. He would send a boy there with Frederik at once, if it was convenient, and he apologised for not having the leisure to accompany Frederik himself.

Peytons Hotel was situated in its own garden within the town of Parramatta, neither cramped up against neighbours nor exposed to unwelcome winds. A genial hotelier, who turned out to be Mr Peyton, greeted Frederik. He gave a brisk nod of approval when he and the boy announced that they came on O'Shea's advice. He showed them to rooms on the first floor which were clean and airy, without the stench of drains which so intruded on them at Edgecliff House. Frederik took the rooms at once, regretting only that it would not be possible to get back to Edgecliff, pack up the household and return in the same day.

They installed themselves the following afternoon, and the effect on Willy was miraculous. Within twenty-four hours his dysentery had cleared up, and within a week he had almost regained his weight. Emmie's recovery was almost as swift. On Sunday they went to church at St John's to give thanks. Emmie had worshipped there as a girl with her family. As he prayed, Frederik found himself weeping, though he did not know whether it was from relief at his wife and baby's recovery or from the sudden glimpse of a chasm, magically spanned by Emmie's presence now. He thought of the bevy of pretty girls in their Sunday frocks and wondered if the shade of the young Emmie would recognise herself in the woman who now knelt beside him. The same notion occurred to Emmie, and bound to it was the further question of what she would then have made of Frederik.

Three weeks later they moved all the way back to Double Bay. Despairing of finding a house in Parramatta, they took the one that Libby's family were just vacating as they moved into a splendid house which they had bought on the shore nearby. It needed furnishing, and finding nowhere to lease all that was necessary they had to buy everything and risk the loss on the eventual sale. Emmie wrote to Bessie that she had been going in and out of Sydney every day in connection with the house. This meant leaving the baby for hours each day, which she did not like to do, but it was better than dragging the poor boy about. She felt unfit for such exertions, she said, though she did not complain; recovery from her illness had been so slow. Nor was Frederik any the better for his trip to Tasmania. It had been unseasonably wet there. When they were established in Sydney, he intended going to visit Libby and her husband at Goonoo Goonoo, their home near Newcastle. This would surely benefit him. Then she might spare a few days to find some rest with Bessie. Her present was full of care, "but of careful happiness."

*

The visit to the Kings in Newcastle had been proposed by Libby when she was nursing Emmie. If they were thinking of settling then they would want to look at the Hunter Valley, she insisted: she and her husband would welcome them at any time. Frederik did not need to be told that Philip King, as President of the Peel River Company, was well placed to give advice. Nor did he need any persuasion to take up the invitation, for of all Emmie's contacts and relatives in Australia, King was the one Frederik most wished to meet. He too had been to sea as a boy, and though he had never gone back after the *Beagle* put in to Sydney in 1836, Frederik believed that the ten years of his unusual apprenticeship would have shaped the man. Although Emmie had now been in Sydney five months, she still felt as if she had done nothing since her arrival and she did not wish to leave just when at last she was settled, so she did not accompany him. Frederik would be able to travel and look at the country much better on his own. She trusted his judgement and knew that he would make no decision that affected her without consulting her.

Philip King was a tall, massively bearded man with a forehead like a rampart and the disposition of a fourteen-year-old midshipman. He entertained Frederik with a trail of stories, as if being guide to the territory must run in parallel to being guide to the past. Although so different in temperament, as former navy boys they understood one another well enough for King to open up his world of *Beagle* memories with a readiness that surprised Libby. Frederik asked him about schooling, and King answered with a snort of laughter that his father had taught him Latin with an end of two-inch rope as they sailed around the Straits of Magellan. He had taught him to skin birds, too, which had proved useful later on with Darwin. Indeed Darwin had taken him ashore for several months at a place called Botofogo, where he kept house and looked after the specimens.

"And were the specimens sent back, or kept aboard?" Frederik asked.

"Sent back whenever we could, I used to help pack them. But the ship was like a tinker's yard with bones and stones all over. It made Wickham furious, he threatened to throw them all overboard, and the crew thought Mr Darwin was mad as a monkey. Now he says we're all descended from monkeys, and they tell us he's not mad at all, the mad one is FitzRoy, who killed himself."

"We were in Rome when that happened, poor man," Frederik said. "It was just after I had met Emmie. It made a great impression on her."

"It does. A man taking his own life, I mean," he added. "I remember Captain Stokes. Before FitzRoy, he was captain of the *Beagle*, which was the sister ship to the *Adventure* on the first voyage. He brought his vessel alongside the *Adventure* after a spell when we were separate, but his mind was impaired, poor fellow, and he shot himself. We buried him on shore where we had a garden of mustard and cress."

It struck Frederik that King was not a man given to understanding desperation, for which he should perhaps be envied.

King arranged a tour of the Hunter Valley which committed Frederik to days spent riding between vast pastures in the company of men whose conversation was limited to livestock, weather and feats of endurance. Among them he felt like an architect at sea, without the least hope of diversion or apt employment, while their necessary stamina reminded him time and again that he himself was not fit. It made him wonder about George and Pat. To his shame, he had to ask for breaks many times, and at night he woke up dripping with sweat. On some days he was accompanied by King or one of his sons, who were in their early twenties. He was first introduced to them as a man who had met the Tsar of Russia. Frederik supposed King was painting him as an exotic to make him feel welcome, but he was relieved and curious to note that the remark didn't cause a ripple of interest in them beyond a polite nod, for form's sake. Frederik denied it, but it made no difference to them.

Early one evening, Frederik was sitting with King on the veranda at Goonoo Goonoo, smoking, while King talked about how the land had been taken up by the squatters. Frederik felt the familiar grasp of fever, like an undergarment that he put on with his evening clothes. Exhausted after a day's riding, overwhelmed by the remoteness of the recent past in this land, he was not really listening. What had been virgin territory only a generation ago was now settled and peopled, and the pioneers had slipped with a blink into mythology as if time itself were sucked down a chute. As distance on land was tamed, distances in time became unrecognisable. Location in space was achieved at the expense of location in history, it seemed. In such a measureless place, a man must come adrift in one way or another.

"You know of course that the greatest of them all was Pat Leslie," King said.

"I have heard it said so," Frederik answered. "But I do not know exactly what was his achievement, only anecdotes."

King pushed back from the rail and kicked his cigar end into a bed of oleanders beneath. "Follow me."

In his study, he dropped to one knee in front of his map chest. He pulled out a drawer, then quickly closed it and pulled out another. He lifted some sheets and hesitated; was about to close the drawer when his eye lit upon what he was seeking and he extracted a wad of tracing paper. Summoning Frederik with a swing of his head, he unfolded a brittle chart.

Frederik bent to look. A trail wound up the paper between spidery rivers and the whiskery arcs of contours to an area near the top where he saw, in neat script, "Canning Downs".

"Take it! Take it!" cried King as Frederik studied it. "Give it to

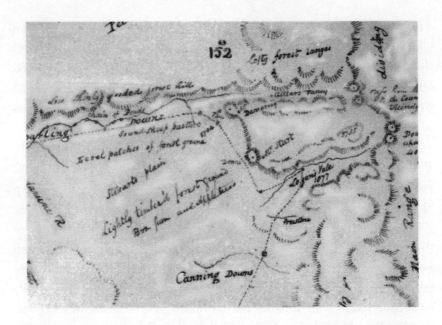

Emmie, I should like her to have it! It has more business with her than with me.

"I was at Vineyard one evening in 1839," King continued, "with Pat and Allan Cunningham. Cunningham was the botanist when my father was charting the Australian coasts. Afterwards, he made several journeys in the interior. He discovered the Darling Downs, but it was impossible to take advantage of this because Governor Darling was afraid that convicts at Moreton Bay might get ideas about a land of plenty beyond the mountains and bolt. When Pat and his brothers were looking for somewhere to stake a claim some years later, they were leasing my father's station, Dunheved, near Penrith. By then there were rumours that Moreton Bay was to be opened up and so Cunningham put his discoveries at Pat's disposal. They asked me to make a copy of the map for him – this is it. I tell you, Captain Ziege, it was an exciting moment! We had long sensed that Pat would do something splendid, and suddenly it was at hand! We had the feel of conspirators on the eve of a great event. Pat went, and we heard nothing of him for two months. Then he came back from the Bush trumpeting news of a fifty-mile run he had staked on pastures along a river – that was the Condamine. He swore it was the best pasture in Australia. A principality it was! Walter went up at once with the sheep, and George soon followed with the cattle. Pat married Kate and was to join them with the horses . . . After that, of course, everyone flocked there."

"And that was Canning Downs."

King grinned, revealing wet gums. Frederik turned back to the table and ran the pad of his thumb across the Downs area. When King had drawn it, Emmie must have been in the same house. Frederik thought of Pat in Malvern, hearty and seemingly carefree, yet with all this experience. And he thought of his own course snaking through Siberia. But that wilderness had paths across it. Travelling between Yakutsk and the coast was best done in winter, when the snow was hard and the sleighs ran free. In summer, countless swamps had to be crossed and bears preyed on travellers. In Ajan, he saw a native with atrocious scars from a bear's mauling, and tales of killings were numerous. But all this was known, and the climate was at least dependable, whereas here the floods and droughts were visitations of chaos on an unbounded land.

When Frederik returned a week later from a trip further up the Valley, King remarked that Colleroi was in that direction, on the Krui.

"Colleroi?"

"The station Pat looked after for his uncle, Walter Davidson, when he first came out here in the thirties."

"Ah," said Frederik. His eyebrows lifted and he smiled. "The Feud."

"Yes. When Pat first came out here – "

Libby groaned. She was sitting in a capacious armchair by the fire. "Philip, if you're going to go through that, give me some brandy!"

"Please," said Frederik, "I would not wish – "

But King was already pouring brandy from a decanter on the sideboard into three glasses.

"No," said Libby with a laugh. "If you don't know about that, you ought to hear."

"I have of course often heard it mentioned, and even had it explained to me after a fashion," Frederik said, hoping that he would not be thought disloyal to Emmie, "but I should like to hear it from you."

King presented Libby with a glass on a tray while Frederik lit a fresh cigarette.

Standing sidelong to the mantelpiece, King swirled the liquid in his glass, watching it shimmer between amber and gold in the light of the flames. Then he took a sip. "When Pat first came out here," he said, "the understanding was that he would knock some shape into a property bought by his uncle Davidson as a speculation when he was here in the first years of the century. The property had been shamefully neglected by its manager, but that was typical of such places belonging to fellows on the other side of the world. Davidson was right to expect more of a return from it.

"It was natural that Pat, who was Davidson's nephew, should be taken in on his arrival in Australia by Hannibal Macarthur, Emmie's father. Hannibal and Davidson had come to Australia together in the first place, and had been involved with Hannibal's uncle, John, in some trading scheme with Fiji and Canton. Hannibal had since done very well as a pastoralist and built a magnificent house, Vineyard, where Pat was very welcome. I think each of the girls in turn had a fancy to marry him – " Here King paused, smiling at Libby. "Did you draw straws? Anyway, Davidson could assume that Hannibal would keep an eye on things. I imagine it was a pleasant responsibility because Pat was very able – a superb horseman in a country where that counts for something – and always good company. After he had learned a few of the ropes with Hannibal, he went up to Colleroi and took the place in hand himself. Looking after the flocks and improving the property, draining and fencing and putting up buildings – there wasn't so much as a hut when he first went there – never mind labour and natives and all that. He had trouble from bushrangers too, escaped convicts. I remember great excitement after he got some guns sent from Scotland, his father couldn't imagine what he wanted them for, wanted Hannibal's approval. Pat insisted that if he had them then he would not need to use them, just so long as it was known he had them. And he was right about that, more than once he had to see people off, if I'm not mistaken he came in once to find his overseer tied up and a couple of desperadoes pinching his effects, but Pat saw them off. Then there were days and nights when there was scab-scare and he had to guard his boundaries, to keep other people from driving their diseased stock anywhere near his. If scab gets a hold, you're watching gold turn to dirt. That was something the Leslies were always very successful at: keeping their stock sound. Hard work, but Pat did it with style because he enjoyed it. Take Ernest Dalrymple, who came out with George and Walter, he was a good sort, God rest his soul, but he could never have managed what Pat did. Nor Walter, though he was all right to start with. It takes stamina, and Pat had it. Where was I? Yes, then after a few weeks or months up at Colleroi he would come down to Vineyard, where all of a sudden everyone had an excuse to visit – "

"Nobody bothered with excuses after a while," Libby said. "The word went round, 'Pat's down,' and suddenly we had visitors."

"He would spend an evening or two closeted with Hannibal, telling him what was going on. The way these places operated, there was always a cash hole, there was bound to be. That's still the way. You have your money all tied up in stock, which you won't get back till after shearing next year. And if you want to build, or get more stock, and there's wages too, then you have to borrow. So Pat would borrow on Davidson's behalf, taking out a bond which would be met by Davidson in London. That was normal, it was expected. Hannibal knew that, and he must have written to Davidson from time to time letting him know how things stood. They must have been in touch. And then came the thunderbolt – it was about the time George and Walter came out to join Pat. The idea had always been that, if things went well, then, when Pat was settled, his brothers would come out and they would start out together on their own run . . ."

"It was right after he got engaged to Kate," Libby said.

"Of course it was. What a shock it was for her. The thing was, you see, Davidson had refused to honour a bond for *four thousand pounds!*"

The affair still perplexed King. No doubt Pat was at fault for not keeping his accounts properly, but even so: why was Davidson so uncompromising? Such behaviour in a family was unthinkable. "At first they all assumed it was a misunderstanding," he went on, "which would quickly be resolved; that Uncle Davidson wished to frighten Pat into keeping his books more carefully. But Davidson was implacable. He went on believing that Pat had robbed him, had been running his own stock at his – Davidson's – expense, and no assurances of Pat's probity from Hannibal or anyone else would change his mind. He meant to ruin Pat, and he did it. It took Pat more than twenty years to get free.

"It put a chasm between the families, of course, and people lined up on one side or the other, as people do."

"Imagine how Pat's poor mother must have felt, Davidson's sister!" Libby said.

"And not just between Davidson and the Leslies," King said. "Between the two Macarthur families as well, because Edward Macarthur was in London and he believed what Davidson said, so at Camden they did so too. It was as if they all knew something about what Pat had been up to which they would not tell the rest of us."

"But there was nothing," Libby said.

"Of course not, my dear, I said 'as if' . . ."

"But it is wretched to hear Pat being doubted, even now!"

"At Vineyard," he said ponderously, teasing her, "they remained loyal."

"Yes, we did. The only good thing to come of it all, and it has been a blessing on all our lives, was the way it drew us close to the Leslies."

Frederik inclined his head, suppressing the Amen which he felt would suit Libby's tone. "I liked Pat," he said, as if Libby's implied eulogy might have put him off.

"It is said that the death of Davidson's first wife affected him very much," King said. "But it is no excuse for what he did to Pat."

"And him making all that money in China, feeding opium to those Chinese," Libby said.

"You don't know that," King admonished her.

"What else was he doing in Canton all those years?"

"He was a trader – "

"Huh!"

" – and now he is a banker."

"A rich one!"

King believed Libby was right, but it made him uncomfortable when she was so forthright. They did not know Frederik's views, after all, and he would not offer them now if they differed.

"Your husband has given me a map he copied for Pat, to give to Emmie," Frederik said to Libby.

Libby sighed. "That map opened the way to so much. It all seems so long ago," she said. "Now only Jack is there on the Downs, at Glenelg."

"And I suppose the country marked on the map is scarcely recognisable," said Frederik.

"It will be nice for Emmie to have it," said Libby with a smile.

*

So Frederik returned to Sydney after two weeks with a map to an obsolete promised land, and with the conviction that the Hunter Valley held no future for his own family. He was thankful to be back because Emmie had written to him that Kiki had been seized with "the worst form of Inflammatory Croup". He was better, she added, thank God, but such a cough remained that she had to watch him day and night. She had been dining out at Government House when it happened; had left him radiantly well at 6.30, but returned at 10.30 to find him gasping for life. Not a moment was lost in applying remedies, but she could neither move nor leave him. Her brother Henry had been with them at the time, in bed with influenza; unlike Bessie, she had no mother to act head nurse. It was expected that Henry would recommence his duties soon at Kings School but, in addition, the cook had left because Emmie told her she must sometimes put on a clean gown. She would try Libby's old Chinaman.

Emmie believed that she was keen for Frederik to find prospects for them on the Hunter, but, when he told her there were none, she could not mistake her feeling for anything but relief. She was concerned, however, to hear him coughing as he told her about his trip, and he continued to cough over the ensuing days. It was trying enough just listening to Kiki. The doctor said that it was a result not of overexertion but of climate, and remarked in passing that the location of their house, exposed as it was to the chill sea breeze, was not ideal. Emmie told him that they had only lately moved – for the sake of the improved air – and were not about to do so again, whereupon he murmured that a short holiday, say in Brisbane, might prove beneficial. Despite having just returned from such a trip – albeit to the Hunter Valley, where the weather was damp – the doctor's hint made the Zieges focus on a journey which they had preferred to ignore since their arrival in Australia.

Nothing could have been done to make the cattle that had vanished in Mant's care reappear, nor was anything to be gained by visiting Gigoomgan: the partnership was terminated in a Sydney solicitor's office. But other assets still remained from George's legacy, requiring decisions which were bound up with the more general question of where they would make their future. For if they were to leave Australia then it could only be for ever, in which case the experience of Gigoomgan demonstrated that they should liquidate their assets first. Although eager to go to Queensland himself, Frederik had put off all thought of it to spare Emmie's feelings. The doctor's advice was convenient because it neutralised the matter.

To his surprise, Emmie said, "If you do not mind going alone, I should prefer it. I would be a burden to you. I shall be much more comfortable here, with the children."

So in July, Frederik left his family for a third time, and on this occasion he found his heart was lighter. Because of the associations and the business matters, the trip was more complicated, but he sensed that he was now approaching the heart of something. Afterwards, things would be different. He would be with Emmie and his boys and the future would be clearer.

On arrival in Brisbane, Frederik was met from the steamer by Hugh Dalrymple, Ernest's brother, who escorted him to a club where he was to stay. Dalrymple was a stocky man with a head like a pumpkin, who made breathless enquiries after Emmie but none at all concerning

Frederik's journey. His speech was hurried, as if there could not be enough time to say all that needed to be said.

At eight o'clock the next morning, Dalrymple called for Frederik and took him out to Kangaroo Point for breakfast. They sat beneath an awning, facing the glinting water. The sun was already hot.

"What a beautiful spot!" said Frederik. "How kind you are to take such trouble!"

"Not at all, not at all! Besides, I wanted to meet you!" Dalrymple replied, fixing his restless eye on Frederik, a momentary challenge.

On first hearing of Emmie's remarriage, Dalrymple had been disappointed. His own proposal to her had been refused, so he was not disposed to favour the blighter who had snared her in Rome. When she wrote telling him that this new husband was coming to Brisbane, inquisitiveness and – in spite of himself – constancy to Emmie impelled him to offer his services. Meeting Frederik, he found that his latent jealousy was matched by an involuntary extension of his feelings for Emmie to the man whom she loved. Dalrymple had noted Frederik's sallow complexion and took it to be a result of travel. He had imagined a more solid-looking man. Seeing Frederik's pallor now, he remembered hearing that his health was delicate and wondered if his colour was symptomatic. The thought made him uneasy, as if he had caught himself wishing harm upon Frederik.

"What brings you to Brisbane?" Dalrymple asked, tucking a napkin into his collar while inspecting a plate of steak that had been put before him.

Frederik hoped his appetite would perk up. He ought to eat, but the meat did not tempt him. "It would reveal a great want of curiosity on my part if I had no desire to come here," he replied.

"Visiting Emmie's old haunts? Everywhere is much changed. In her letter she mentioned that you have business to attend to."

"George left some plots of land up here."

"Which you are going to sell?"

"We have not decided."

"I can see why George didn't want to sell them, but I don't see why you should want to keep them."

"Oh?" Frederik cut a sliver of meat and ate. It was tender as peach.

Dalrymple laid down his knife and fork. "George had an attachment to the place. You don't. You have to sweat blood in this land to feel attached to it," he said with the assurance of a practical man repeating an accepted truth. "It's different for Emmie."

"You mean she belongs?"

"If you like."

Frederik chuckled. He knew that if Emmie felt she still belonged here then she would not have married a Danish naval officer. "I'm not so sure you're right about that," he said, looking Dalrymple in the eye. Dalrymple's complacency made Frederik recognise with sudden clarity that her reason for not accompanying him now was not the inconvenience of travelling but profound reluctance to return to the Downs. For all her undoubted attachment, she felt herself to be an outsider now.

Dalrymple shrugged.

"And do you belong here?" Frederik said.

"It is where I have made my name!"

"And left it, I believe," Frederik answered, referring to the district named after Dalrymple.

"Well, there you are!"

Frederik was not sure the matter was so simple, but he did not feel he knew Dalrymple well enough to pursue it. By the same line of reasoning, he might come to feel a similar connection with the coasts of Greenland: but even if whole tracts of that desolate place were named after him, it would for ever be alien.

Dalrymple uttered a conclusive grunt and busied himself with another piece of meat. He would focus on things which interested him, but he was otherwise impatient.

It being Sunday, they drove to church after breakfast, their route passing through a succession of building sites which Dalrymple pointed at with glee. Afterwards they were joined by Bob Master, who had moved back to Brisbane after Lucy's death. It was more than three years since Frederik had seen him last – at his father's house in Bournemouth – and, when he took off his hat, Frederik was shocked to see that he was almost completely bald.

In the afternoon they went to Newstead House.

Built by Pat with a £300 loan from his father, Newstead had been bought by Wickham when he retired from the Navy and married Annie. It was here that Annie had died; here that Emmie came with George to collect Carrie. Now it belonged to people called Harris. Tall, with a perfect, heart-shaped face and humorous black eyes, Mrs Harris reminded Frederik of a ball in Irkutsk where one of Mouravieff's staff kept bawling at women, "Quelle superbe créature!"

The house was much enlarged since Pat's time, with twelve rooms on one floor. The land sloping down to the river, which Emmie had described as snake-infested scrub, was now a tropical garden in which pink and grey galahs turned and swooped, chattering to one another like a party of schoolchildren. A flock of white cockatoos watched them from a huge fig tree. The view must have changed, for the town was no more than a convict settlement when Pat arrived. But it was still magnificent, commanding a loop in the river where a town now spread. Pat had chosen well, but it made Frederik feel sad to stand there.

In the morning, Frederik walked out with Bob Master to look over the Enoggera land. He wore a cream suit and carried a stick, which from time to time he screwed against the ground with unnecessary force, as if testing to find out how it would feel to lean more heavily on it. Their destination was an allotment of twelve acres, bounded on one side by the river and on the other three by land belonging to a man named Cribb. The soil was poor, supporting nothing but mean-looking scrub, and Frederik judged it to be worth very little. Later he met Cribb in town who told him he would pay £50 for it, over and above expenses for transfer, but Frederik showed no desire to sell. Cribb recognised that it would represent a deterioration to his land if Emmie sold hers to a third party who intended living there, but, according to him, such a buyer was unlikely to be found.

"Hardly worth selling a bit of land which costs nothing to keep," Frederik said.

As they walked away, Master said, "It may be worth ten times the sum offered at a later date, or more if Brisbane takes a spurt ahead."

Frederik shrugged. He might not sell to Cribb, but he did not believe that this remote and dusty place could ever be of use to his family.

Dalrymple was supposed to meet him in the evening and take him to a concert, but he never appeared and Frederik spent the evening writing to his brother and to Emmie. *Kiss the boys for me. I wish I could hug you all three.*

The Bulimba land, which he visited the next day on horseback with Master, was more interesting. It consisted of ninety-five acres of good soil, clear of large trees, with a road close up to the southern boundary. An elevation ran across, parallel to the river which formed the northern boundary, about sixty feet above the water's surface. Visible at low water, along almost the whole length of the property, was a sandbank. It spread halfway across the river, which was very wide at this point. Frederik could not help thinking what such a piece of land with its beautiful view and surroundings would be worth in England or Denmark, or on the Lake of Geneva. Here it cost £20 to clear an acre of timber: there an acre of timber could be sold for £20. Here the sandbank prevented boats from approaching and thus was a drawback: there the bank would be redeemed by means of a dam, thus creating more than a hundred acres of land. Looked at from another point of view, here he would be lucky to get five shillings per acre, while there it would be worth at least £5,000. At Cannes, building twenty good houses upon it would generate a yearly income of £5,000.

Later, in the Club with Dalrymple and Master, he told them his thoughts. Dalrymple laughed. "But it shares with land the world over the property of being fixed!"

"Yes," said Frederik. "And it eats no grass."

Over the next few days he visited various agents and was informed that £110 might be got for the Enoggera land and £3 per acre for Bulimba at auction. These sums did not amount to a fortune, but the interest on the proceeds of a successful sale would be more secure than the land's value, while the capital investment would be easier to administer than these distant plots. In the light of his own uncertain health, security for the future was desirable. So he wrote to Emmie advising her to write to her trustees' attorney, authorising the auction.

It would not incur expenses, and if they failed to sell at the suggested values then they would at the least have tested the market.

The next day he was off to Ipswich. *Were it not for the tender associations with you that the coming days must yield, I would feel very disgusted at the idea of increasing my distance from you and the dear boys.*

After a night of fitful sleep in a bug-ridden bed, Frederik walked out to the cemetery. The grave where Emmie's mother lay was easily found because of the wooden paling surrounding it, from which a few brilliant red-breasted rosellas flew up at his approach. To the sandstone monument was fixed a marble panel inscribed with her name and "Departed for a better life 1st September 1852 – 59 years of age". A cypress grew at the head, its roots pressing up and causing the monument to lean a little. Another cypress grew at the foot. He considered taking a sprig for Emmie but thought better of it. The process of its fading, despite every care, could only cause sorrow, while the respect which he wished to express seemed better served by leaving the mourning trees untouched. His mother-in-laws's burial in this far-off place was the counterpart to the impression he had from Emmie, that she seemed set apart in life – more forbearing, kinder, more spiritually awakened than others. Having heard fond children describe dead mothers who were monsters with these attributes, Frederik remained sceptical. He wished he could have met her, if only so that she could see the man her daughter married. It was the natural order of things – but how heart-rending for a parent not to see what became of their children! To bring them into the world and then be forced to abandon them –

"Spare us, Lord, for one another," Frederik murmured, before turning away.

He was taken to the cottage where Emmie's parents had lived by a Mr Smith, the Crown Land Agent. He had called at the man's office to ask the way, not intending anyone to accompany him, but as soon as he mentioned the names Leslie and Macarthur, Smith pricked up his ears like an old cavalry horse on hearing the trumpet. Off he went with such a flourish about old times at Canning Downs, Goomburra,

Sydney and so on, that, before Frederik was able to make him draw breath, he had been ushered outside and shown to a horse. Smith would no more let him go alone than, as a young man, he would have given up an afternoon at the races. It took hours to get there, for it seemed that Smith had urgent business to attend to at every other house on the way, though what that business was besides introducing the occupants to "Captain Ziege, Emmeline Leslie's new husband", was not clear. At each stop the same questions had to be answered – no, they had not come back to live, he was just visiting, having a look around; Mrs Ziege, alas, was not well enough to make the journey from Sydney, nothing to worry about, no, two fine boys – broad smiles, bless them! – and yes, he would certainly convey their best wishes. The horse Frederik was riding, Smith explained, had been bred by David Fairholme twenty years ago, he was sorry it was not Sandy, Emmie's brother Arthur's old horse, who was vegetating somewhere on the ranges. When he and Arthur had ridden all the way from Sydney to the Downs together, Arthur was on Sandy. The journey took fifteen days. Later he bought Sandy from him – he had thought it a privilege to own that horse – although Pat was the real horseman among them. Poor Pat, such a shame things never really came right for him. All those who lived on the Downs, and many of them had made it rich – take Mr Hodgson, for instance – they all owed Pat a debt. It was he who staked the claim for Canning Downs, though it belonged to George and Walter, anything of Pat's being subject to seizure by the Courts. Even his horses were in Kate's name! It was agreed that he would act as agent for his brothers in Brisbane, working from Newstead, but that wasn't the life for him and in 1846 he got a foothold on the Downs again, running cattle on Canning Downs. Then he bought Goomburra with George's help. The property had belonged to Ernest Dalrymple, and if there was any truth in the rumour that Pat had gone sour on a debt to Ernest before his death then he, Elias Smith, would eat his hat because if anyone was a man of honour then that man was Pat Leslie. Many a night he had camped out with the Leslies, a man couldn't wish for a better companion; he had been in the New South Wales Parliament with George so he knew what he was talking about.

Observing the shredded brim of Smith's hat, Frederik wondered if he wasn't the first person to suspect him of telling a few crammers.

When they got to Woodend, Frederik found that the whole place had been rebuilt. Not a trace remained of its former occupants, but it still seemed a necessary part of his pilgrimage, the more so since Emmie was not with him: as if coming here were a way of grafting himself on to the memories she had of these places and becoming closer to her. The unquenchable stream of talk from Smith was wearisome but, like a penance before absolution, appropriate.

*

The day was fine as the train wound its way up and down the Dividing Range. A succession of gorgeous views was disclosed, and Frederik's heart swelled as he thought of Emmie coming here for the first time in a cart, dragged over the rough passes by bullocks. At last the Downs lay before him, fertile into the distance, as if the train had descended to the Garden of Eden, and he thought of the impression it must have made on the first squatters, Pat galloping off forty miles up and down the Condamine, whooping, giddy at the extent of the Paradise, *his* Paradise. Who would not feel that they had found what they were looking for, whatever it was, when they came this way?

In Warwick the talk was all of poor Deuchar, a pastoralist whose accountant, a Mr Armstead, had levanted with a large sum of money, leaving all the accounts in a mess. Now Deuchar was ruined and the place was in a flutter with bills unpaid, men laid off, stock going cheap, to say nothing of the rich gossip to be harvested from the scandal. Frederik duly reported it to Emmie, together with directions on what to say to her attorney following his inspection. For besides those in Brisbane, there were two plots in Warwick which had not been in George's sale of Canning Downs. Frederik suspected that George had kept them out of reluctance to make a complete break with the land on which he had lavished his strength. Perhaps this was what Dalrymple had been hinting at. The twelve acres known as Murray's Farm ought to be sold at not less than £10 per acre, he advised, and the Boiling Down Land – now the province of crows – at £5 per acre. But the land due to be cut off by the railway should not be included in the sale of the latter because compensation of £80 was to be expected, so it was just a question of thirty-three acres. Meanwhile, he had given instructions for the payment of ten shillings arrears in rates.

Towards sunset the following day, Frederik drove up to Canning Downs, the bush home George Leslie had built for his new wife. Built of vertical white-painted timber slabs, the house was a single oblong storey with a shingle roof; crested pigeons stood in a line along the ridge. Tubs were set at intervals on the broad veranda, where pink roses climbed over the eaves. Stables and sheds could be seen behind; in front, spreading to one side, was a fine garden planted with shrubs and fruit trees. The place was the image of a pastoral idyll.

In the end, Emmie had spent less than five years here.

As he approached, Frederik found himself praying that God would protect his wife and their little boys, together with those whom he had loved from earliest childhood.

The station was now owned by Walter Davidson's son, Gilbert. He was a ramshackle man with bronze-coloured hair, nervous eyes and whisky on his breath. He greeted Frederik with a clap on his upper arm. Then he insisted that Frederik drink some of his fresh lime cordial at once, which he did, with gratitude. It was served on the veranda by an Aboriginal girl who Davidson said was the daughter of a native girl trained by Emmie. Gnarled, splayed bare feet could be seen beneath her starched apron, and though neither her obedience nor her competence could be faulted, a strange habit of swivelling her eyes upwards made her seem detached, as if the apron and her domestic duties did not impinge on the currents of her life. As Frederik was drinking – while the tray was held in readiness for his glass – Davidson took him on a tour of the garden, explaining that its plan was the one laid out by Emmie.

Afterwards, Frederik sat down in what he gathered had been George's office and wrote to Emmie. He felt cramped and breathless, acutely conscious that the room, the house and the entire station were created by George and Emmie. He felt like an intruder in their domain, even though his presence was sanctioned by her and she would wish to hear his impressions. Knowing where to begin was difficult. He fancied he could see her walking about, he wrote, planting the different shrubs and trees which now had grown up. From the window he could see magnolias and honeysuckle; beyond, an orchard of orange and lemon trees, also quinces, that seemed to be flourishing, and there were numerous other plants that he could not identify. Galahs flapped about over the lawn, and some red parrots were squawking in a gum tree that was overrun by a vine. It would please her to know that her garden was cared for, he thought.

Frederik had with him a half sovereign from Emmie which she wished him to give to Keong. While in Warwick, Frederik had called at Keong's home and left word that he would be at Canning Downs, so it was no surprise when the Chinaman arrived the following day. Keong had kept house for Emmie and George during their year in Sydney and then gone to Pat and Kate at Goomburra. For the last few years he had been going back and forth between Warwick and the diggings, trading with the diggers. He looked well, and so young that Frederik asked him with surprise how old he was. This Keong could not recollect, but he did know that he had been baptised in 1857 at the age of twenty-four. He was very grateful for Emmie's present and said that he would not spend the half sovereign but keep it in his purse for good luck. He then produced from a pocket a little pouch stitched from kangaroo-hide, which he begged Frederik to take for Emmie and the children.

"Open, open!" he repeated. "Please!"

Inside was a nugget of gold, the size of a kidney bean.

"Are they yours?" Frederik asked, indicating the teeth marks that could be seen all over it.

"Mine, mine! Yes, mine!" Keong answered, in a frenzy of smiles. "Top-quality gold!"

Frederik thanked Keong with due warmth before replacing the nugget in its pouch.

In the afternoon, Davidson declared that he would show Frederik

about the place. He called for his groom, Jack, to saddle the horses, forgetting that they were out in some paddock. It was two hours before they were caught, by which time Frederik was tired of Davidson's company. The man was smug and ignorant and seemed to have come to this place only because the Leslies had been here, as if he had not the wit to think of anything he might do of his own initiative. It was a relief when at last the horses were saddled and they rode out to a new scouring shed, which Davidson wished to show off. Inside was a steam engine to raise water from the Condamine, he remarked, as if it were the existence of the thing that he expected Frederik to admire rather than its efficacy.

They went off then through the bush, following the edge of a vast pasture bordered by the river on the far side, where pelicans could be seen surging into the air. Numberless sheep straggled over the dun ground to the horizon. Presently, Davidson cut through a patch of scrubby trees, twisting and turning among fallen branches until they emerged at the edge of another endless sweep of pasture, the afternoon sun illuminating it in a bluish haze. It occurred to Frederik that Davidson had no direction in mind at all, and the thought made him suddenly aware of his own fatigue. Davidson was silent and Frederik did not feel inclined to question him. His neck felt hot and he pulled at his collar, telling himself that he must take care not to fall asleep on his horse. The aimlessness irritated him at first, but then it made him want to laugh, for did it not apply also to himself? What was he doing in this far-off place, riding through the bush in the company of a man whom he neither liked nor trusted? The habit of enquiry had brought him this far, but he felt so detached that trying to recall why he had come only confused him. The thought of Emmie swam into his mind, bustling and talkative, but the idea of her inhabiting this land was unreal. He imagined her turning to him with a complicit smile as Kiki earnestly told them a story; bending from the waist with a swish of skirts to pick up Willy – and he longed to get back to them.

Davidson had cut through the scrub and was out of sight. Suddenly his voice could be heard, uttering angry curses at the track, his horse and the trees. Fearing that something had trapped Davidson, or attacked him, Frederik dug his heels hard into his horse's flanks. He heard "Jack! Where the devil have you got to?" but when he caught up he found nothing more alarming than the sight of Davidson lashing feebly with his switch at a branch that had whipped against his cheek and scratched him.

"Are you all right?" Frederik said.

"Where's my vagrant groom?"

Frederik turned to see Jack riding up behind him.

"Come up here and help me, strumpet's whelp!" Davidson growled.

The lack of expression in Jack's eyes made it plain that he was accustomed to this abuse. "Stopped off to tup a sheep, did you?" Davidson persisted. There was no shame in his eyes, only bitterness.

It turned out that Davidson had got so distracted trying to pick his way among trees and fallen timber that he had lost his way. It was after four in the afternoon and they were riding with the sun in their faces, a course which Frederik pointed out must take them away from the head station. Jack nodded. It seemed no surprise to him that Davidson had not thought to steer by the sun. So they rode for half an hour in the opposite direction, through several fences, to a wide open spot above a lagoon, from which a path led to the house.

At the water's edge stood a solitary crane, which rose into the air with a languid flap of grey wings at their approach and flew off towards the distant hills. Jack, who was riding abreast of Frederik, drew his attention to it with a laconic nod.

"Your wife, Missus Leslie as was, she used to keep a tame one of them. It was killed by a stone thrown by one of Lord Ashley's boys."

"Were you here then?" Frederik asked.

"Been here twenty year."

"And – Lord Ashley's boys . . . ?"

"Poor boys. We come out on a scheme of Lord Ashley's."

Frederik digested this and then asked, "And the stone . . . ?"

Jack nodded.

Frederik wondered why Jack had told him this. Was it intended as some kind of belated apology for him to take back to Emmie, or was he just uttering whatever came into his head? The man's face remained imperturbable, so that Frederik had no way of knowing whether he regretted the action or was proud of it; whether he was well disposed to Emmie's memory, or hostile. Or perhaps Emmie existed for him only as the keeper of a bird that he had casually killed. The indifference repelled Frederik. He felt a chill at the back of his neck like a clammy hand.

"Very upset she was," Jack added, as if this puzzled him still.

Frederik shuddered, then pulled his elbows tight against his stomach. In his waistcoat pocket he felt Keong's pouch. Its solidity was comforting. He was glad to have something to take to Emmie from this wilderness.

Egypt, January–April 1870

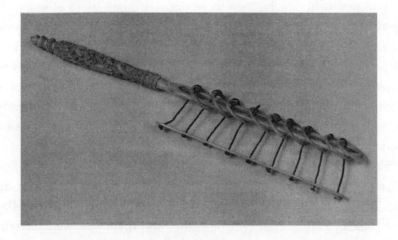

T HE exact origin of this puzzle is uncertain. It may have been brought from Canton by Walter Leslie in 1847, with other ivory trinkets and the camphorwood chest, as a wedding present for George and Emmie, or it may have been a gift from either of his Canton brothers, William or Tom. Perhaps it was among the shower of bounty sent from Canton by Walter Davidson in 1814 aboard the *Morning Star* to the Macarthurs in Australia. It might even have been bought by Frederik – from Russian officers in De Castris Bay in 1858, for example. But it is likely to have been among the "effects" that the tenant of Emmie's house in Rutland Gate, London, agreed to store when, in February 1870, he bought the house that he had been renting from her for the previous few years.

Emmie was in Cairo when she signed the contract for the sale, but the process was initiated from Australia. It seems a most surprising turn of events. She and Frederik had decided to sell up her Australian assets, abandoning hopes of making their home there. Never less than an emotional correspondent, Emmie wrote to Bessie just before leaving that they could not live in Sydney because of the *influence of sea breeze, but if we can't live here (& that's quite plain to us all) we don't feel disposed to go to stay in the interior without one interest, occupation, or amusement, beyond our children – that is the truth.* Amid worry over Kiki's recurrent croup and Frederik's health, which she was beginning to realise was a hostage to anxiety as much as to climate, the house was packed up and the furniture sold. Departure was harder for Emmie this time than all those years ago because there was a finality to it which had not made itself felt before, when she had expected to return. She drew strength from the hope of a settled existence in Europe, an end to the draining cycle of packing and unpacking. Yet at the same time she agreed to the sale of a good, spacious house in Rutland Gate.

Since Emmie was not pregnant and Frederik did not suffer from migraines, the return journey was more pleasant than the passage out. They travelled on the steamer SS *Madras* to Ceylon, where they met Duncan Ferguson at Port de Galle, and thence to Suez, arriving on New Year's Eve. At eleven o'clock the next morning, after a rail journey of three hours, they came to Ismailia, where they checked into an hotel which had changed ownership that day. The previous owner had taken everything with him so that there wasn't a stick of furniture in the house, not even a bed, but a good lunch was soon ready and their hostess proceeded to have someone prepare rooms for them as if nothing was out of the ordinary. During the day more travellers arrived. At seven in the evening they were sixteen round the dinner table. It was astonishing, Frederik remarked to the company, what their hostess had accomplished in so short a time. Asked what their travel plans were, he replied that they were not decided but that he, at least, was keen to have a look at the Canal and investigate what Ismailia had to offer in the way of comforts and climate. He was quick to respond and ready to laugh: everybody found him charming.

Emmie was pleased to see him on good form, but she was nervous. It was a relief to her too that their long ocean passages were behind them – she had suffered from seasickness, as usual – but still, there was no reason for stopping in this place longer than necessary. Frederik's appreciation of their hostess's efforts was kind but disproportionate, blinding him to the fact that the hotel's facilities remained rudimentary. From his heightened animation, which others might have attributed to alcohol, she could see that his temperature was up. In the morning he would be calm, and see things in their true light. But they were kept awake half the night by Kiki, who was gripped by a new bout of fever. They ate breakfast alone while Norah took the children. Tired, and demoralised both by the prospect of staying there and of packing up and going on, Emmie said – lightly, she thought – that the place was not suitable for a sick child.

"Why can't we just stop? Stop, for once?" Frederik said.

"My dear Frederik, you know nothing would please me more – !"

"Well then."

"But here? You cannot mean that? Whatever for?"

"You have not even looked around."

Coming from the railway station, she had seen that the place was still the dreary little town on the edge of the desert that it had been when she passed through with George in 1853, in spite of the upheaval because of the new Canal. "Nor have you, for the matter of that," she said.

"What do you propose then, now that we are back? We should look at every option."

"Back? We are not back! We are in Africa!" cried Emmie, bursting into tears. She knew that he wanted to settle somewhere as much as she – at least, she believed he did – which made it even more pointless to stop in a place where there could be no question of them staying. "It is impossible when you are so obtuse!"

"Then I shall spare you further suffering for the moment. I have a call to make upon de Lesseps, if you will excuse me," he announced, folding up his napkin and placing it on the table.

With her fingers pressed against her mouth, Emmie struggled to swallow the tears she knew he disliked. Avoiding his eyes, she nodded.

Frederik stood up and left the room.

Emmie leaned back in her chair and stifled a sob. He had mentioned the de Lesseps connection before, but in the flurry of arrival she had forgotten. Now she felt ashamed of herself. Of course his attitude to this place would be different from hers. She ought to have controlled herself instead of undermining what would be a pleasure for him, and one of which she approved. No wonder he was cross! But the constant worry of his illness – and the distress, if she allowed herself to dwell on it – made it easy to lose sight of such things. He never complained, for which she was grateful, but she was aware that his cough and nightsweats were fixtures now, not occasional visitors. They might slacken their hold according to climate or anxiety, but they never disappeared.

The day already looked as if it would be hot. Emmie wondered how Kiki's delicate constitution would cope. Willy seemed more robust than Kiki ever had; she had less fear for him. On board ship, Willy had taken to feeling the edge of her silk petticoat, which he had discovered to have the same texture as the piece of cloth he always had in bed with him. Frederik was cross whenever he saw the boy with his hand under her skirt. He told her that she should not encourage him, but the thought of Willy's neediness made her smile now as she went to find him.

After three months cooped up on board with nothing to do except make conversation, read novels from the ship's library, or play cards, the prospect of being outside, on his own, was sweet for Frederik. All his life he had treasured the first moments of solitude on shore after a voyage. Now the bad night had dashed his morning walk from him, a disappointment to which he had perhaps overreacted, but he still did not feel inclined to reflect upon his unfairness to Emmie. In the street he paused, filling his lungs with the dry, warm air. He wanted to walk, but the instant appearance of a boy, shrieking "baksheesh!", discouraged him. On foot, his route would be dogged by every kind of urchin and he did not feel up to running this gauntlet at present.

A nearby driver chased the boy away with a flick of his switch, and Frederik accepted the invitation to step into the waiting carriage.

The desire to call on Ferdinand de Lesseps had been growing in Frederik since deciding to leave Australia, where the Canal was a subject of intense interest because of the reduction promised on voyage times, and in Ceylon everyone had been talking about the grandeur of its opening by the Empress Eugénie. Evidently it was a great success and all the world was speaking about it. Frederik was not sorry to have missed the celebrations, but talk of them had reminded him that it was as French Consul in Tunis that the Canal's creator first became acquainted with North Africa. Not that Frederik remembered him, because de Lesseps arrived in 1828 and Frederik was not much older than Kiki when he returned to Denmark: but there could be no doubt that de Lesseps would remember his father, whose knowledge and enthusiasm for France were a consolation in his lonely posting. And if he did not recall the Danish Consul's young family individually then it would not be because he had forgotten their existence. It was pleasant to think about Tunis, Frederik found. Although he recalled very little, the air and the views here were suggestive: the driver's fez bobbing in front of him, the white walls bounding courtyards of flat-roofed houses; the domes of mosques and baths; the flashes of colourful costumes against the whitewash and the baked earth. He thought he remembered standing on a roof, leaning between what must have been low crenellations, and being suddenly dragged backwards – whether by his mother or a maid, or even Hannina, he did not know. It must have been the roof of the Consulate. In front (or was it behind?) lay a stretch of open ground, beyond which were low, stony hills dotted with houses. And was there a little castle on top of one of the hills?

Moments after Frederik left his card, de Lesseps himself strode into the hall where Frederik was waiting, and embraced him. He had abundant white hair, lively brown eyes and strong white teeth. It seemed to Frederik that goodness shone from his face, though Emmie told him later that it was the gleam of success. Apologising for disturbing him, Frederik explained that he could not come through Ismailia and *not* visit his father's former colleague, knowing (as how could he not? the whole world knew it!) that he was there.

With a self-deprecating roar, de Lesseps shook his head and declared that he would have been affronted had he learned of Frederik passing through without calling on him.

"And I would have discovered!" he added with confidence. "How long are you here?"

"I've just come up from Suez, on the way back from Australia with my wife and two little boys."

"Australia? What on earth have you been doing there?"

Frederik laughed. An ancient marble head on a pedestal in an alcove reminded him of the relics his father used to gather. He wondered if his mother still possessed any, or if they had all been given to his Prince. "It's a long story, and I expect you are busy."

"Well, now you mention it, I am. But come along to dinner with your wife — what's her name?"

"Emmeline."

"Emmeline," de Lesseps repeated. "Well, bring her along at seven o'clock, we shall be quite a party. My son is here with his wife, and some Greek colonel or other is joining us."

Then he placed his coach-and-four at Frederik's disposal for the rest of the day.

Frederik chuckled to himself as he returned to the hotel in the luxurious coach. Emmie would enjoy visiting the local sights in such style. They would give a fine report of their activities to de Lesseps, satisfying him that they had made good use of his hospitality. He was in a better humour than he had been in earlier. He would apologise to Emmie.

But Emmie was in no mood to appreciate the coach, which only placed fresh demands on her. Not only was Kiki still running a fever, but both the boys had diarrhoea. They would have to stay indoors. If Emmie went anywhere, it must be to find suitable food, which she could prepare for them on her spirit lamp. "I'm sorry not to be more enthusiastic about this evening. It is most kind of Monsieur de Lesseps to invite us and I'm sure I shall enjoy it. But now I want to look after my children, and perhaps they will let me get some rest, for I am worn to the marrow of my bones."

Frederik's spirits sank again. Emmie would not try to dissuade him from going out alone, but he had been looking forward to her company. It would not be the same without her, and her pained expression would sour whatever pleasure might be had. So he sent the coach back to de Lesseps with a note of thanks, saying that he had come back to a domestic situation which prevented their using it, but he trusted all would be settled by the evening. It was the right thing to do, he was sure of that: but the sense of wasted opportunity lingered for the rest of the day, with an aftertaste of betrayal that disgusted him, although he could no more eradicate it than he could justify it. The children were said to be ill, but they were wild all afternoon – and who could blame them, confined as they were? All he had to offer was his irritation, which made them cry, and then it was infuriating to see Willy tug at Emmie's petticoats, whimpering. He wanted him to be tougher than Kiki.

Besides some discussion of the Canal and the inaugural festivities, conversation at dinner turned about de Lesseps's memories of Tunis and of Frederik's father. This was intriguing for Emmie because she had never spoken to anybody outside Frederik's family who had met his father. De Lesseps described him as "clever and meticulous, the most diligent man I ever met," but a note of reservation remained in his otherwise ebullient tone. Emmie was confirmed in her belief that Frederik's father had the habit of making others feel incompetent and that he resented the luck of those more successful than himself.

Frederik did not know that his father had done a chart of the harbour at Alexandria. "He did it in 1817, or thereabouts. A remarkable piece of work, considering," said de Lesseps. "I remember him showing it to me."

"I'm sure he was pleased by your interest."

"I wish it had been Port Said," de Lesseps added.

Afterwards, on the way back to their hotel, Frederik said that de Lesseps's wife looked like an actress playing Princess Metternich, whom he saw in Paris five years ago.

"Five years ago? With me?"

"Just before we met. En route to the south."

"It seems so long ago," said Emmie.

"Another life," he replied.

Although she was tired, the agreeable evening had diverted Emmie from her worries – which did not, in any case, include wistfulness for the time before she met Frederik. But she detected in his remark, or in his glance away from her as he spoke, an unsettling flash of nostalgia.

That night, Kiki slept badly again. His temperature was lower by morning, but though Emmie still felt obliged to stay in, she encouraged Frederik to go on an excursion alone. There was peace of mind in knowing that he had something of what he wanted.

Frederik immediately bought a ticket for the Egyptian Post Steamer along the Suez Canal to Port Said, where he arrived at three in the afternoon. After an hour or two knocking about the harbour and piers, he returned. When Emmie asked him what the Canal was like, he replied that it would only ever be useful for irrigation, being unsuitable for ships of more than eighteen feet in draught except in the very deepest channels. Since pilots of requisite skill were presumably in short supply, he hoped that de Lesseps was prepared for accidents.

Frederik lit a cigarette. "I wish you and the children had accompanied me," he said.

He had imagined that their return from Australia would make things clearer, but circumstances in Ismailia seemed to conspire against him. Three months ago Kiki was a good and obedient boy, but now he cried and stamped his feet when he didn't get his way. He kicked, punched and bit his little brother, was continuously naughty to Norah, sometimes also to his mother. A few times he had even tried how far he could go with his father. "The child has worms," Frederik insisted one day, but the doctor recommended by de Lesseps could find no trace of them. Of course the journey had irritated Kiki's temperament, but he was already starting to show ill will before they left Sydney. Frederik had hoped that their arrival would benefit him. He had looked forward to taking him out in the streets, showing him the boats on the

Canal. The climate was good and the cost of living in Ismailia was half that in Cairo – why should they not be happy there? His own infancy in Tunis had been happy, hadn't it? Why should the children not be healthy and happy here? Willy was well, after all, and so was Emmie, despite the worry, the work, and the sleepless nights which the children had been giving her. The hotel was not cosy, but the food was good and their hostess was a nice lady who did her best. Yet it was not working: Kiki was unwell; he himself was disappointed and frustrated. Emmie could not be expected to endure the situation for long. Twice in the following week he found himself eating alone with the de Lessepses *en famille* because Emmie did not want to leave Kiki, whose cough worsened once more. While he did not believe that her absence was rude, he was afraid of it appearing so. He was concerned too that he might seem negligent, when in fact he was wracked with anxiety which was made more acute because there was nothing he could do to help – nothing, it seemed, except agree to move on, and his faith in this as a solution was meagre.

Frederik knew that Emmie would prefer to proceed at once to Malta and then to Europe, but he was reluctant to abandon Egypt so soon. In February, he agreed to go to Cairo, which seemed a reasonable compromise. By choosing to stay at Shepheards Hotel they felt that at least they must gain the best available. However, instead of improving anything, the move at once threw the difficulties of their situation into starker relief. The nights were cold and the days were hot. Kiki's rattling cough was as fierce as ever; Willy was cutting two new teeth; both boys had constant diarrhoea, though Emmie and Frederik monitored the boys' food with care and forced them to swallow quantities of medicine. Emmie was pleased that Frederik took an interest, but the way in which he did so annoyed her. He had fixed ideas about what the children ought or ought not to be able to eat, based, it seemed, on what he supposed himself to have eaten at their age in Tunis. She pointed out that what he ate in Tunis forty years ago might not be relevant to what was appropriate now in Cairo, which irritated him though he knew it to be true; and moreover, she said, how could he possibly remember? Eggs, he said, he was sure that he had eaten things with eggs. But the one thing beyond dispute in Cairo was that small children should not eat the eggs or drink the milk.

The mats in the hotel were infested with fleas and the streets were so filthy that Emmie would not let the children go out on foot. Carriages were expensive and anyway their progress was plagued with beggars who were encouraged by Willy's piping squeals, "Me got no baksheesh for that little girl!" There was some consolation in that for Emmie, because Frederik was delighted by Willy's combative spirit and laughed. Even though his laughter degenerated into a fit of coughing, it was cheering to see pleasure in his face.

Aware of his anxiety and the frustration he experienced by staying indoors – it affected them all – Emmie urged Frederik to go out by himself. She had been to the Pyramids and "all those other places" years ago, she said; she did not need to go again, but would enjoy talking in the evenings about what he had seen. And so he went, but he took nothing in. Faced with the splendour of ancient Egypt, his mind visited his own past at random: being welcomed at Arsenieff's family home in Moscow after their journey together from Irkutsk, and his pleasure there at taking a hot bath; acting in plays in Kronstadt; a weird nocturnal fog in Paris in 1849; the gasping, sweating face of his sister Ida as she died on the ship taking them to the West Indies; the forbidding coast of Sakhalin; the fresh faces of cadets at the Frederiksborg ceremony, his own among them; the Yakuts' fishy reek; being taken by de Torné to see his family after the ship put in at Piraeus and finding Christian with his leg in splints . . . From time to time, like a fly returning to the same invisible speck, his mind alighted on the need to give the children a home, but the obstacles seemed insurmountable. Had he not tried to find one? London was out of the question because of the damp climate. Was it to be an arbitrary decision in the end, then? In which case, why not Egypt? Yet here he was in Egypt, thinking of anywhere but where he was.

Finding Frederik reticent about his days, Emmie told him instead about the children. "The boys are always playing at riding camels or donkeys now," she began one evening.

Frederik was writing to his brother, who had misconstrued Frederik's instructions about his *poste restante* address, so that a letter had gone astray. Frederik knew that he should not be cross, but the right tone would not come to him. He was glad to be interrupted. "I suppose they watch them from the windows?" he said.

"Yes. Kiki rides Willy with his legs dangling down, which sometimes upsets him and he cries, 'Kiki not hold so hard!' – 'Don't cry Willy, swallow it down!' Kiki replies. 'You know that's what Father says – Swallow it down!'"

This tale made Frederik laugh but – poor things! They did not know! Lambs for the slaughter! – at the same time he wanted to weep for his children. "The young man preaches better than he practises," he said when he had recovered his breath, "for he does *not* swallow it down!"

Seeing Frederik so moved, and trying not to show it, disconcerted Emmie. She did not understand why her harmless report should have such an effect, but, seeing that he seemed to appreciate it, she continued: "Today some ladies came out suddenly into the corridor and saw Willy with my bonnet on his head, the one with the little wreath of blue convolvulus. He had taken Kiki's arm and they were walking up and down as Captain and Mrs Ziege. They looked charming, of course, and the ladies rushed upon them and kissed them. Kiki took off his hat and then they turned to Willy, 'What a lovely little girl!' 'Pardon me, he is a boy,' said I, coming upon them all – 'What a pity, with those superb eyes!' came the reply . . . And all the while, Kiki and Willy stood smiling and blushing under their assumed characters. They thoroughly act their play and imagine every sort of thing . . ."

There was a knock on the door and Emmie stopped talking. She could see that Frederik was disappointed by the interruption, but he went to open the door. She saw his face in profile, baffled for a moment by whoever it was and frowning with displeasure. Then she heard a woman give her name, prompting a shout of surprise from him, before he stepped back into the room with a sweeping gesture of welcome.

A tiny, stately woman approached Emmie. She had vibrant jet eyes and a wide, buck-toothed smile. Wild black hair hung in collapse about her shoulders. Her clothes were dishevelled, as if she had come straight from a journey. Behind her was a European man wearing a fez, her companion.

"My dear, this is Madame Jerichau. My wife, Emmie," Frederik said as Emmie stood up to greet her.

"We have just this moment arrived from Alexandria, and saw your names on the list at the door, I couldn't help but come and make myself known at once!"

Madame Jerichau was a Russian who for many years had made a living in Copenhagen as a portrait painter. She knew all Frederik's family and their circle. Just now she had come from Greece, where she had been painting King George and his family. She had arrived in Cairo with the intention of painting the Khedive, his wives and children and any pashas she could accommodate in her schedule. She would remain three weeks before returning to Copenhagen. It was this information which seemed to excite Frederik most of all, and during the following days he kept thinking of things to give her for his family. He insisted that Emmie write down her descriptions of the children at play so that she could take these. Emmie objected that they could perfectly well send them by post rather than burden Madame Jerichau, but it seemed the old painter was only too happy to be involved. It would be a fine excuse to visit old Madame Ziege, she said, which Emmie interpreted as an opportunity to tout for business.

"And what about you?" Madame Jerichau asked Kiki, for she was in the Zieges' sitting room again. "Do you like your Grandmama?"

Kiki was shy and made no reply, but afterwards he was curious. "Will she tell Grandmama she has seen us?" he asked.

"Yes, when she goes back to Denmark," Emmie replied.

"Was my Grandmama very fond of me? When I was a tiny baby, did she kiss me very often?"

"Yes, she did."

"Is she a nice old woman?"

"She is very nice and has pretty grey hair."

"When I was a tiny wee baby, did she kiss me all night?"

"No," said Emmie, laughing. "Why should Grandmama sleep with you?"

"If she put on her old boots, I suppose she would not have wakened me," said Kiki gravely.

Frederik was not in the room when this exchange took place, and Emmie wondered whether to tell him about it. She knew that he would love to hear it, and might even be able to explain the conclusion, but she feared that it would also make him sad. The arrival of Madame Jerichau had delighted him, but such pleasurable interludes were fitful and always seemed to be followed by a lapse into the listless irritability that marked his behaviour since their arrival in Egypt. It was very hard to gauge whether a bad mood was the result of his natural temperament or of feeling unwell, but she had no doubt that his health affected his mood more than he acknowledged.

A week after Emmie signed the papers for the sale of her house in Rutland Gate, they went to Alexandria, from where they took ship for Malta. She wrote to the new owner that she would send for the effects, which he was kind enough to keep in store, as soon as they were settled.

France, April–May 1870

AS Emmie came ashore at Marseille in mid-April, she thought of Willy's eager nodding and breathless little yelps when he was excited; she felt as if her own arms and legs might start punching back and forth like pistons, just as Kiki's used to do. Excitement had prevented her from sleeping the night before, and, as she stepped onto the quay, the tiredness which she had not allowed herself to feel until now made her want to sink to the ground in the billow of her long grey skirt.

It was the same quay that she had come to five years before on her return from Italy with Frederik's family. The coincidence struck her as auspicious and sustained her for the journey to Cannes, where they booked a clean, high-ceilinged suite at the Hôtel du Nord, with a view over the garden.

"So here we are again," said Emmie, after lunch on the day following their arrival. Wearing a high-collared white dress, she was sitting with Frederik in the garden, on wicker chairs in the shade of an umbrella pine. Norah had taken the children off for a sleep.

"There's nothing like going to the other side of the world for making you appreciate the place you started from," said Frederik. He wore a dark jacket because the lapels on both his white suits were stained with blood from coughing on the way from Malta. He hoped that the hotel would be able to clean them.

Emmie reached for his hand. "We start and end with one another. And what could be better than that?"

"God bless you," said Frederik, and raised her fingers to his lips. "Amen!"

Emmie closed her eyes, shutting out any sensations that might spoil the purity of the moment. She smiled. The warm air and the unfamiliar sense of peace enfolded her like a soft embrace, making her feel sleepy: and there was no need to resist.

They had come from Alexandria during the worst gale Frederik had ever experienced in the Mediterranean, and their passage was not improved by Willy's howling because of two teeth that were coming through. Although they arrived in Malta without mishap, Emmie's stay there was overshadowed by the journey's forthcoming final stage, not so much for its discomfort as for Frederik's agitation. It seemed strange to her that a man who had spent most of his life at sea should be such a difficult travelling companion. Although he had no specific worry that he wished, or was able, to communicate, his lips would set in a rigid line days before departure, and the blood would wane from his face. On board, he fussed about Emmie and the children, as if fussing alone would quell the sea and nullify its influence on her stomach. He drew attention to the inconveniences, making them harder to endure – which was all, in the end, that could be done. She ought to be pleased by his concern, but she associated it with his feeling unwell, and this added to her burden.

There were dinners during their month in Malta and even a ball, a regular event hosted by the Governor for the garrison and those *en route* to or from India or the East Indies. It was the sort of gathering where you expected every moment to run into someone you knew: but there was nobody. Emmie had exchanged letters with Coco in Vienna about toilettes and corsages, but since she had sent her ballgowns ahead to Cannes, Coco's suggestions were useless. The only profit was in the pleasure it gave to Frederik, who liked the idea of her corresponding about such matters with Coco. And though Emmie was pleased to hear that Coco was feeling well, her remarks about her condition – she felt marvellous; could not understand the tumult some women made about it – were insensitive.

Because of an outbreak of cholera in Italy which forced many residents to seek temporary shelter in Malta, finding rooms had been difficult. For lack of any choice, Emmie and Norah and the children occupied two windowless rooms in an hotel while Frederik stayed at the club. Search as he might over the ensuing days, he could find no better accommodation and they lived in those airless rooms for the duration of their stay.

Near the hotel there was a grassy bank covered in daisies where Emmie used to sit with the children. Frederik found them there one morning after breakfast making daisy chains. As he approached, Emmie looked up, but she did not recognise the thin figure leaning on the stick in the distance. She concentrated on the business of threading the stems together, while trying not to let the children pull the flowers away before she had finished. The sky was azure. Frederik could hear Emmie's laughter in the still air. The boys squealed with excitement and he heard her light admonition, "Not so rough, boys! Gently!"

Kiki was wearing a garland. Seeing his family in this setting, Frederik was reminded of the violet fields at Camden. He knew the image ought to please him, but he felt heavy-limbed and intrusive on their contentment. Emmie had hoped that he would find acquaintances at the club to entertain him, a cohort of hearty officers and clever gentlemen with whom he could swap yarns and discuss the political situation in Europe – or whatever she imagined . . . But he felt not the least temptation to seek out such people, no longer feeling that he belonged to their world. Neither they nor their future interested him, nor did he suppose that they would care about him.

"Papa!" cried Willy, smacking his father's knees with one chubby hand, then scuttling back to Emmie's side.

"Good morning, my dear," said Frederik to Emmie. "Are you making fairy princesses of my sons?"

Emmie laughed. "Are they not pretty?" she said, extending a slender hand to each of the little blond heads, as if they were angels she had just conjured from the air.

"You are making fun of them."

Emmie was hurt. "Indeed I am not!" she answered. A glance at Norah, who had turned away in embarrassment, reproached him.

Willy was sitting between his parents. His left hand slipped beneath

Emmie's outspread dress and tugged at her petticoat. Frederik pulled his son's hand roughly away.

"I wish you would not wear that petticoat," he muttered. "It only encourages him."

Sitting in the hotel garden now, Frederik thought of this incident and felt ashamed of himself. "I am sorry, my dear, if I sometimes behave rudely," he said, uncertain if Emmie was awake.

Emmie said nothing. With her eyes still shut, she withdrew her fingers from his clasp and curled them round his hand.

Frederik recalled how two nights before, as they were passing through the Straits of Bonifacio, word had gone round that Garibaldi's house could be seen. Emmie went up on deck to look. When she returned, Kiki said, "Do you see the land quite near, Mother?" – "Yes, Kiki." – "Oh then! If Fa'er would get a boat he could go ashore and look for a house for us, and then we could get out of this horrid ship tonight!" And it *was* a wretched, dirty ship, and if only it were all as easy as Kiki imagined! Surely, Frederik thought, he had not been so inept in the past? On the contrary, as an officer he had a reputation for competence. Yet his own son noted his failure to provide what all but indigents managed – a home; and it appeared that he was cruel to his wife. The cruelty was borne not of malice, however, but of growing despair, as if the return to Europe were a fresh confrontation with the uncertainty of his own future. Reaching the Mediterranean once more, he could not fail to be aware that his health had deteriorated since he was here last. He had only to look in the mirror and see his sallow face. He did not know how conscious Emmie was of this, nor did he believe it would help if he drew it to her attention, but the possibility of his own death had burgeoned within him and was now sordidly real. It brought upon him a terrifying lassitude, as if nothing that he now did could matter, and the simultaneous, opposing sense that he must exert himself at once to take control over his sons' futures.

In the weeks that followed, it seemed at last to Emmie that a settled existence was within their grasp. The days were warm and lovely, the garden full of lily of the valley. Willy's opinion that he could drink tea from the tulips amused the other guests. When the greensward was cut, the children tumbled over and over, covering each other in the sweet, fresh grass. As her old friend Dr Wright predicted, the steady climate and a wholesome diet restored the children to health; their nights were undisturbed. It seemed obvious that they should look for a house here again. Anywhere that suited Frederik in winter would probably be too hot for the children in summer, but if they were careful then they could remove somewhere cooler for three months. This year, there could be no question of it being anywhere other than Denmark.

To Emmie's wry delight, Frederik found a house which none of the agents knew anything about because it had not yet been furnished for letting. About six minutes from the market and ten from the railway station, it had a view to the back of Cannes but none to the front because of a slight rise in the ground which would shelter them from the Mistral. Although the exterior was very ugly, the interior had plenty of fine, airy rooms, all newly papered and painted. The owner agreed to let Emmie choose carpets and furniture, and to make some changes to the nursery accommodation. The rent was a little higher than they had intended to pay, but Frederik and Emmie were so pleased that they did not rue any of it. It would be far cheaper, at any rate, than living in a sanatorium for several months of the year. Emmie imagined Frederik watering the small garden with a hosepipe. When Lady Woolfield showed them two fine pullets that were reared from chicks hatched in Frederik's care at the Villa Louisette, she started to plan a *poulailler*.

She also sent for her belongings.

They were to arrive from London as soon as possible after the 23rd September, the date set for their return from Denmark and the start of the lease on the house. Not since George died had she lived in a home where she was able, or cared, to have them around her. Now she anticipated unpacking them with relish. Since Frederik had been to Australia with her, he would appreciate them. Mr Martens's pretty watercolours and the little sketch of Canning Downs by Thomas Huxley were all views known to Frederik since his trip to Queensland. There was her camphorwood desk, her books, her chaise longue, her porcelain, her silver, her Chinese puzzle, all the bits and pieces gathered over the years which were like so many talismans to the parts of herself which events had exiled to the past. Between them they added up to something like a portrait of the composite being that she had become, random sections through a prism. Emmie even arranged for her piano to be brought out. It would be a tremendous asset if any of the Ferguson girls visited; or Alma and Carl with their baby, or Coco and Christian with theirs. It would be a home, she insisted, where their families and friends would be welcome.

And if, in her passionate planning, she never stopped to wonder for how many seasons Frederik would enjoy their new domestic felicity, it was because she knew the answer could make no difference now. Frederik understood this, and her happiness ought to have encouraged him to believe that he might live on. But as he saw her attach herself to the idea of their shared future in this place, his own death loomed over it. He could not believe that he deserved this future, or belonged in it. He recognised that he had been granted this taste of another, blessed life as a reprieve: it was not his and could not last. The closer it came, the more improbable it seemed and the more certain it was that he must die soon. Early in his marriage, he had thought that he would wake to find himself alone in a ship's bunk, or still stranded like a soul in purgatory in his Greenland winter quarters. Now, though his Bible would say – and Emmie too, if he asked her – that he would wake to Eternal Life if he made his peace with Jesus, he sometimes feared that he might simply not wake up at all.

Denmark, Summer 1870

AS she did every year, Frederik's mother had rented a house in Vedbek for the summer, a few miles along the coast from Copenhagen. There was a garden where the children could play, sheltered from the north wind by lines of splendid beech trees going down to the shore. From a human point of view, it was a peaceful place. Its drama lay in the titanic conflicts between light and dark that ebbed and surged between earth and sky. In the evening sun the clouds' swollen bellies would be washed with orange over the cornfields. Over the sea, the clouds were swift banks of slate advancing to the land until a shaft of light pierced them, when the sea's sudden, iridescent blue would burst into the reflection. As the louring firmament dispersed, the landscape would be shot with a million shadows, sharp wedges tucked behind each illuminate thing, dandelion stalk and tree, open door and running child. The skies were low and immense, the clouds like gloved fists which might withdraw to allow a day of luminous sunshine, only to gather again on the horizon, as if brooding upon which colours to unfurl across the heavens.

It was not only Emmie's mother-in-law and Hannina who were spending their summer at Vedbek. Christian and Coco were there too, on leave from Vienna for at least a month while she had her baby, despite concerns regarding the accession of Leopold of Hohenzollern-Sigmaringen, a cousin of Wilhelm of Prussia, to the Spanish throne. Clara and her husband Louis Rothe had at last sold up in the West Indies and were home for good: they had taken a house nearby, where their sons Carl and Willi also stayed as often as their duties and studies in town permitted. Alma and Bloch and their son were regular visitors to both houses. The family had not achieved such a gathering for many years.

But it was not only family who welcomed them. It seemed to Emmie that the whole of Copenhagen was lining up to greet Frederik and get a look at her, beginning with the King. She was formally presented to him at a dinner within a week of arrival, to which they were most particularly invited.

She found this rather gratifying. She supposed that Frederik's long sojourn abroad, and the exoticism (from the Danish perspective) of her own background, endowed them both with glamour in Danish eyes. In this, she was mistaken. With one princess married to the Prince of Wales and another to the Tsarevich, the Danes had no further need, beyond the dictates of good manners, to be impressed by the activities of compatriots who chose to go abroad. However, the King wanted the benefit of Frederik's services, and this was enough to guarantee that his company was sought.

Fru Ziege was determined that Frederik and his family should enjoy their long-overdue visit; that they should remember it with happiness, and come again. Accordingly, everything was organised for their comfort. It was a summer of tea and cakes upon the lawn (an English practice, Hannina admitted, but a surprisingly civilised one; it had become fashionable in Denmark because Princess Alix insisted on it when she visited). Kiki and Willy were doted on. Adults vied with one another to toss balls for them, build sandcastles, set up rows of lead soldiers. Hannina took them for rides around the lanes in the dogcart. Above all, for Emmie, there was rest: afternoon sleeps founded on the certainty that the boys would be safe and happy; evenings at the theatre and nights in town, which could be followed by late rising in the morning. Frederik's feelings might be more complicated, but he could not fail to find some satisfaction in being made much of, nor be insensible to the pleasure his visit gave to his family.

They took a box one evening at the Royal Theatre for a performance of Rossini's *La Donna del Lago*. Emmie sat between her husband and mother-in-law, basking in the plump pleasures and spectacle which she had been without for so long – the rich music, the velvets and gilt, the twinkling chandeliers of the grand interior, the gentlemen with their white waistcoats and opera hats. In the stalls below, jewels glinted on the shoulders and in the hair of the ladies. Emmie loved the sense of occasion generated by the opera. She was reminded now of being with the Zieges in Rome: apart from the addition of the Rothes and Christian, whose absence was felt by their family then, the party was the same. Alma and Bloch occupied the chairs beyond Frederik, and behind them were Coco and Christian, Hannina, Clara, and Louis Rothe. Frederik pointed out the aged, ungainly Hans Christian Andersen in his customary box, sitting with the Melchiors – it was said that he never missed a production if he was in Copenhagen, and often went to the same one many times. Through her opera glass Emmie could see what appeared to be a lady's shawl around his shoulders.

The position of the Royal Box was such that Emmie could not help noticing the discreet hubbub there from the middle of the first act. While a messenger came and went, a succession of gentlemen who must have been summoned came to speak with the King. So intent was Emmie on trying to make out what was happening, without staring through her glass, that she missed the movement behind her own chair and was startled to see Christian appear beside him. Seated in the chair indicated, Christian listened while the King told him something. Then he stroked his beard before answering – hesitantly, it seemed to Emmie – the question put to him by the Crown Prince.

When Christian slipped back into his chair between Coco and Rothe without a word, it was tantalising for Emmie not to know what had been discussed, but Fru Ziege was concentrating on the stage and Emmie knew better than to ask questions. She saw Bloch whisper to Alma and turn in his seat, but everyone else behaved as if they were unaware of anything besides the drama on the stage. Not until the curtain had come down on the first act and the applause subsided; not until a waiter had brought and poured champagne for them and passed around the glasses on a silver tray, and everyone had made themselves comfortable, did Christian clear his throat and remark, to nobody in particular: "It seems France has declared war on Prussia."

Rothe uttered a satisfied chortle, which made his thick shoulders shake. Then he raised his glass in salute and said that it was high time the Prussians were taught a lesson. Clara and Hannina smiled, as if he had told a joke; they appeared comforted. Rothe had been out of Europe for the best part of twenty years.

Emmie looked at Frederik. His face was white as whey, but he was sweating. He was looking out over the audience in the stalls with trance-like intensity, as if he had been stunned and was looking at some rude horror inside his own head. He could see that the news had spread. The men bristled with grand gestures while the women twittered and smiled in unctuous collusion. Was it possible that they all shared Rothe's foolish view? Even if Rothe were right, it did not seem something to rejoice in.

Emmie touched his knee. She wanted to speak to him, but she did not know what to say. She smiled at him. It made him want to weep, and he looked round at the others in the box.

"Is it all because of this telegram?" Fru Ziege asked, turning her head. Mention of war always made her think of fleeing from Copenhagen when she was a girl, amid the conflagrations and the screams of the mutilated. The horror she had felt at the destruction, and the astonishment that anyone should wish to perpetrate it, had never left her. She was inclined to think that she had not the mental capacity to understand war.

"It is Bismarck's doing," Christian stated. "The man is a warmonger."

"But won't the French trounce them, Uncle?" Alma asked.

"That is what everyone believes," he told her, with a nod towards the stalls, "but it will not be so easy."

Frederik caught his brother's eye, then looked away. He was surprised by his opinion although it matched his own, but he did not wish to be drawn into the conversation. He suspected his brother of being secretly thrilled by the news. The tongues of all the diplomats in Europe would be wagging, analysing Benedetti's words and actions, making predictions and recommendations. Careers would be made or ruined from the carnage of battlefields, and the idea sickened him.

Frederik felt disgusted with himself. What did it matter if Christian stood to gain? It did not alter the fact that the Prussians should be resisted. And if Christian's mistrust of the Prussians were not so profound as his own, why should he be blamed? He had suffered at their hands, which Frederik had not – despite a career in the navy, he had never seen combat – and he was certainly better informed: ought he not to admire the fluidity of his brother's views? He saw how different would be the world which his sons occupied as adults from that in which he himself had grown up. Were he to live, he would be an irrelevance. Only those like Christian, who found their identity reflected in the eyes of others, rather than in their history, would make the transition. And Emmie? He foresaw her long widowhood, where, as she advanced into old age, her past contrasted ever more improbably with the present, and grew more wonderful.

As the curtain went up and the opera continued, a great wave of sadness rolled through Frederik's chest and down to the tips of his toes. The news, he realised, must threaten their plans for returning to France. He wondered why the French let themselves be inveigled into it. Were they so complacent that they believed they would win without a fight? Did they need to risk the catastrophe of losing? The thought of beloved France being overrun by the same soldiers who had murdered the Danes in Holstein was appalling to Frederik. His family would be in a conquered country, prey to the whims and savagery of the Prussians, and he himself would be powerless to protect them. His boys would be taken for Prussian soldiers and Emmie – who knew what would happen to her? He did not follow what was happening on stage: throughout the second act, the actors were no more than a meaningless, weird gallery of strutting, squawking players. In his mind's eye he saw cannon and soldiers; bloody, dismembered men writhing in mud, being clubbed by rifle butts or stuck with bayonets by grinning Prussian youths. The bellowing of armies filled his ears, the shrieking of horses, the screams of women dragged from homes and carts, of children dropped and grabbed and swung by terrified mothers, torn away by monstrous invaders; fires raging through houses and fields, the possessions of families ripped and tipped, their histories shattered. Without taking his eyes from the stage, he reached out for Emmie's hand. She felt the stickiness of his touch and looked up to see that his face was like wax. Sweat ran into the white collar which had sagged against his neck; his eyes glittered.

Gaining his attention, Emmie tried to ask if he was too hot, but he just smiled and nodded, as if she were asking him whether he was enjoying himself. She touched her throat, indicating that he should loosen his collar. Only then did he realise that she was concerned for him. But though he felt strange and feverish, his anxiety was of a different kind and he shook his head. Beyond him, Emmie saw that Alma too was watching him. Alma raised an eyebrow, asking Emmie if he was all right. Emmie mouthed "hot". This distressed him, for he wanted Alma and Emmie to enjoy the opera, not worry about him.

With deliberate purpose, he concentrated on the stage. He had not been listening, but he had the impression that the sequence of splendid tunes in the first act had lapsed in the second to a muddle of hectic runs, which the overworked tenor could not manage. Now three firm, martial chords arrested him, and the music coalesced with a vertiginous rush to the sublime. It was like stumbling up to a blind horizon and meeting the landscape of Paradise beyond. The soprano – he did not know whose character she was supposed to be playing – was standing in the middle of the stage. Sparkling cascades of notes poured from her, soaring leaps of melody of such transfixing beauty and skill that he wanted, all of a sudden, to laugh; as if actors who had been shadows cast upon a wall were adjusted before his eyes into robust figures in bright sunshine.

Nothing had prepared him. It was a moment of holy intensity, like stepping through a rent curtain to enter a tent in the middle of a wasteland, and being confronted by the essence of perfection. A succession of long descending notes brought the passage to an end, and the singer was answered by a blast of trumpets. The image of warring armies rose again, terrorising him with the thought that they would somehow take over and put the glimpsed marvel to flight, but in a moment the singer resumed, chasing the trumpets away, reducing them to an echo. She paused, as if to look about and consider her effect, before her voice skipped with glee and dipped like a snipe before running off in glorious swoops and turns that induced in Frederik a wild exhilaration, as if she were crying to the heavens themselves that she could do it, that this miracle could be achieved, that it was achieved, and here it was! The opera's name came to Frederik's mind, and he thought of Alma and the moment by the lake at the Pallavicini Gardens. He thought that the sounds he was hearing were the sounds that a person's spirit should make if they died a good death, a death which honoured all that was and could be achieved in life, a celebration of the miraculous instead of a lament that the miracle was over; thanks for what was given instead of distress at what was taken away. He felt as if he had been winded by the music, so immediate and engulfing was its effect, or as if it had reached into him and pulled him inside out. And though his rapture seemed to oppose his thoughts, he did not feel that it negated them, as if they were two facets of the same raw stuff.

As the aria concluded and the auditorium burst into applause, Frederik realised that it was also the end of the opera. It was like a death, yet his heart was full of happiness even as he wept, of passionate gratitude for the privilege of having witnessed, or suffered, this phenomenon. He was aware of Emmie and Alma watching him, but he did not mind that they saw him weep because it seemed to him, in a way, that he was weeping for love of them, and that they would understand this. And when his arms grew tired from clapping, he took one of their hands in each of his and sank back into his seat, exhausted.

*

After hearing so much in letters from Emmie during the last two years about her family's health, Frederik's family were ready to receive them as virtual invalids. Finding that the children were blooming with health surprised them, and Emmie's evident pleasure at being in Denmark was disarming. The nervousness that had appeared from her reports was nowhere to be found: on the contrary, she seemed self-possessed and capable. And though Frederik was thin, and he coughed, he was still just as they had always known him: humorous and kind, firm and intelligent. They assumed that Emmie had exaggerated, and he was quite safe.

Whatever the aesthetic content of Frederik's experience in the theatre, its physical aspect was what concerned the Zieges. They were not used to seeing gentlemen weep in public. Frederik should have governed himself. When Emmie had informed them that he often ran a fever in the evening, his mother and sisters were puzzled. It had not registered with them that he might show any symptoms of illness. But as he stood outside the theatre, pale and stiff, they recognised that something was wrong. It could only be assumed that, after all, he was not well. Emmie supported him at one elbow: she appeared calm, for she was familiar with his condition, but she asserted herself in the manner of someone taking control of a crisis, stating that they must go at once to Fru Ziege's apartment across Kongens Nytorv, where Frederik must spend the night. On his other side stood Alma, who was on the brink of tears. There was a sense of detached but palpable excitement to Frederik's face as he turned it to the breeze.

On the mantelpiece in the dining room of Fru Ziege's apartment stood a clock. It was an imposing, heavy object made of bronze, shaped and stepped like a pedestal for a figure sitting on an anchor. Emmie had admired it when she first saw it during the week of her arrival, not because she liked it – she did not; it was ugly – but because its imposing presence invited attention, and commenting on it was an easy way of making conversation with Frederik's mother.

The clock was a gift to Frederik's father from his friends and supporters in Greece to mark his recall to Denmark in 1835. He had occupied the position of Consul for only eighteen months, working in conditions of extreme difficulty. The quarters that he and his family were obliged to occupy in the capital at Nauplion were barely habitable, and the country was infested with bandits. Conscious of his own limited funds, Ziege applied himself to the study of antiquities with characteristic zeal, keeping the Crown Prince informed of all his endeavours – his attempts to acquire items for the Royal Collection; his travels through Sparta and the Peloponnese; his opinions concerning the desirability of acquiring land in Athens; his hopes for the future, and the difficulty of looking after his own family in such uncivilised circumstances. Whether overwhelmed by his epistolary mania or for independent reasons, Denmark decided that they no longer required a representative in the new Greece and Tuxen Ziege came home – briefly, before trying his luck again in North Africa. But his disappointment at leaving was  soothed, at least in part, by the generous gift of the clock. It was imagined that the figure of the hero (adorned with a Phrygian cap), offering himself to his country, would remind Ziege of the heady months he had spent helping to forge the future of resurgent Greece on the anvil of hardship. In fact it taunted him with his failure to bring home enough of the booty of Antiquity to gild his own and his family's future. Worse, it smacked of the silly philhellenism fashionable among the English.

After her husband's death, the clock also reminded Fru Ziege of her time in Greece – a period of protracted torture in a roasting, stinking nest of cut-throats, where discomfort reinvented itself each day. Constant, wearisome ingenuity was needed to obtain clean food and water. In such disorder, keeping the children safe and clean required the utmost vigilance. After ten years of relative comfort in the Ottoman province of Tunis, where she had enjoyed the exoticism and the oriental way of life, the barbarity of Greece was a poor reward. She regarded the European fashion of glamorising the new Greeks with contempt. Yet she was proud of her husband, and loyal. Disposing of the clock was unthinkable and it was too large to be inconspicuous. The only option acceptable to her own sense of honour was to allow it the prominence for which it was designed.

It had been sitting on this mantelpiece for thirty years.

When Emmie admired the clumsy object, a delicious, uplifting notion came to Fru Ziege. She did not imagine that Emmie liked the clock, although she understood why she had said she did and thought no worse of her for the falsehood. But if she was keeping the clock in trust for her eldest son, along with so many other things, then he ought by rights to take possession of it as soon as he was settled. The thought of not being bullied by it each day rippled in Fru Ziege like a sensual afterglow, so that she smiled, and was forced into a cumbersome fib to justify the smile: "It reminds me of happy days in Greece, when Frederik was little."

"But I thought Frederik was on a ship when you were in Greece?" Emmie said.

"Yes, but you understand me – when the children were small."

"Anyway, one forgets."

"Some things, one never forgets!" said Fru Ziege with feeling.

"When we were in Egypt, and the boys were ill, Frederik kept saying that they ought to be able to eat certain things because at their age he had eaten them in Tunis. I said, How could he remember?"

Fru Ziege laughed. "Quite right! And it was because he was *ill* that I came back to Denmark early with the children, leaving my husband on his own for two years."

The subject changed, but Fru Ziege did not forget her exchange with Emmie about the clock. Hannina, who had not overheard her mother's untruth and therefore could not expose it, inadvertently compounded it by references during the following days to her father's time in Greece. It was natural that his name should come up when they went together to see the Royal Collections, and when somebody pointed out some vases which had been acquired for the Collection by Kammerherr Ziege from Christian Hansen, Hannina remarked that Hansen had been among the contributors for the clock presented to her father; she had half an idea that one of the brothers had designed it.

When they came to the apartment after Frederik's dizziness at the opera, they brought him first to the drawing room, where he sat and was given brandy. Although his family were alarmed, they were disorientated by the sense of euphoria that still radiated from him as he looked around. Elation was so misplaced as to be ridiculous, yet it hovered about like a swallow in winter, embarrassing them. They wanted to do something, but there was nothing to be done. Meanwhile, Frederik's bright, piercing eyes made them nervous.

"Am I the only one drinking?" Frederik asked. "Will no-one join me? Christian?"

"Why not? Perhaps I will, after all," Christian said, taking a glass from the cabinet and picking up the brandy decanter. He felt uneasy and conscious of his own limitations. He was displeased with Coco because she was cross with Frederik, as if she resented the attention being paid to him.

Frederik clinked glasses with his brother.

The ring flowed into the sound of the clock striking the hour, as if it had triggered it. The chime was a clear, metallic TING, repeated eleven times.

"I have been meaning to say that I want you to have that clock, Emmie, if you would like it," Fru Ziege said.

Emmie was wondering how to get Frederik to bed and make the others go, as soon as possible. Her mother-in-law's offer was a distraction, but she felt it must be a compliment which should be responded to with grace. "Oh, Mama! How kind of you! It is so splendid! But can you spare it?"

"Spare it? Why, I shall be pleased to have the space!"

"But its associations – "

Fru Ziege jerked her head in dismissal, as if to signal her readiness to surrender her own pleasure in the clock's associations for Emmie and Frederik's sakes.

Although Emmie was pleased to be offered the clock, its presentation was so sudden and awkwardly timed that she turned to Frederik for help in giving a suitable response to his mother. She did not want to offend anyone, and she did not know how the rest of his family would feel. And when she saw the dismay on Frederik's face, she realised that she was mistaken in assuming that he would be pleased too.

His eyes seemed to strain in their sockets as he stared at Emmie and his mother. The brandy glass was frozen halfway to his lips. It quivered, as if the liquid itself were outraged at the notion of Frederik being offered the clock. Frederik had never liked it, but only now did he understand why he hated it. The ridiculous Phrygian cap harked back to a past that never was: neither in Antiquity nor in the Greece of forty years ago was that Arcadia to be found. The clock represented only a kind of nostalgia that propagated lies. Thoughts of the Greek War of Independence reminded him of the situation at home and in Europe, as it had been revealed to them this evening; inspired in him not sentimental admiration for heroism, but revulsion. Welcoming this clock, he felt, would amount to an act of complicity with those who were foolish enough to relish this Franco-Prussian war. It was repulsive.

Yet he understood why Emmie might be pleased, and that it was up to him now to say something. "Do you really suppose we shall have room for it?" he said. "The figure has always made me think more of *sans-culottes* than heroic Hellenes."

Hannina, who had heard in her mother's offer an alarming threat to the order of her world, now said, "Will it be safe on the journey?"

"Of course, Hannina dear," her mother replied. "You do always worry so – "

"But she is right!" Emmie declared, seeing a way out of accepting the gift now.

Clara, who always made it her business to take up the wrong side in an argument, disagreed. "No, she isn't. It's just a question of packing it properly."

"After all, it came from Greece without mishap," Fru Ziege said.

"But does he actually want it? Look at the poor fellow!" cried Rothe.

"Of course he does," Hannina insisted, as if only a rogue would not want their esteemed father's clock.

"Do you, Frederik?" Fru Ziege asked, fascinated by the thought that her son might not want it.

"Oh Mama, don't go on at him so," said Hannina. "And it was Emmie that you offered it to. The question is whether *she* would like it. Perhaps she was only saying that she would to be polite!"

"Oh!" cried Frederik. "Stop it!"

Slowly, with great care, he set his glass on the table beside him. He felt so tired that it seemed he could feel gravity like ropes pulling on his limbs, and he covered his face with his hands.

Carl Bloch was at the piano, doodling a few notes. Now, in the silence, he picked out a scrap of the theme from the last aria of the opera.

Alma was standing at his shoulder. "*Tanti affetti,*" she sang, "*in tal memento,*" and proceeded softly to the next sequence of rising notes. But as she reached the top she caught sight of Frederik's devastated face and burst abruptly into tears, for she understood that her uncle would never meet the new child growing inside her. And instead of making him happy in the time that remained to him, his family were pulling him apart with squabbles!

Frederik rose. He made his way over to Alma, finding furtive support from a high-backed chair, the lip of a console table, the piano. Taking her gloved arm, he let her escort him to the staircase as he made his way to bed.

"God bless you, Alma dear," he said.

*

As they waited to see what would happen in the new war, Frederik ached to get away from Denmark. It seemed fantastic to him that, after all his longing to see his family and be in their familiar surroundings, and in spite of his passionate desire for his sons and Emmie to come here, he should wish to leave so soon. He thought of previous returns – from Siberia, from Kronstadt, from Greenland – when he had entered with enthusiasm into the goings-on at Court, and the rounds of dinners and theatre and gossip that constituted social life in Copenhagen. This time, all these things were irrelevant. The demands and habits of

Danish society might be diverting to Emmie and the boys, but the more they adopted them as their own, the harder it would be for them to integrate themselves elsewhere. He was conscious of them as foreigners, and therefore conscious of himself as not quite belonging. The fact that he did not speak Danish with his sons was noted and frowned upon, and he was obliged to admit to himself that a distance must exist. But most of all, as the war confounded their plans, the more he wanted to leave.

Frederik knew that the logic of this was uncertain. Since it was France who was at war rather than Denmark, it was reasonable to suppose that he would be safer with his family in Denmark than in France. But he disliked being so far from Cannes, which he was teaching himself to think of as home. He believed that Denmark was a trap, that France could always be escaped from. Unfit to fight himself, he dreaded his sons and Emmie being locked into Denmark by the consequences of the conflict.

On 1st September, however, he found that he was locked out of France. The German victory at Sedan was complete, and now their armies threatened Paris. Travelling through France to the south was out of the question, and it was pointless struggling to get there by boat when there was no guarantee that they would be able to stay for any length of time. It would endanger his health, however, to spend the winter in Denmark. The doctor told Emmie, who reported it to Fru Ziege, that it would be an act of "extreme irresponsibility" to stay there, when there was an alternative.

The alternative was sailing to England, which they did at the end of the month. England was closer to Cannes than Copenhagen; and St Leonards-on-Sea, with which Emmie was already familiar from earlier days, was a comfortable resort whose climate would be better suited to Frederik's condition than Copenhagen's.

No more was said about the clock, but it caught up in the end.

St Leonards-on-Sea, 1870–71

ONE day in Copenhagen when they were all in town for a lunch party, Frederik used the excuse of fatigue to escape from a shopping expedition with the ladies afterwards. Instead of resting, when he returned to his mother's apartment he went straight to the caretaker and asked him to open up the storeroom in the basement. He trusted that the man would not dare refuse him access.

He found his old tin ship's box after a few minutes. Unlocking it, he saw with amazement that his hand was shaking like a faint-hearted thief's. These were his possessions, yet his body betrayed him with its childish reaction. Exhausted out of all proportion, he lay down on a sofa and slept until Emmie woke him two hours later.

It was only when Frederik was in England, installed like an invalid in an upstairs room of a house that didn't quite overlook the sea, that he began to question why he had been so secretive. He was in a comfortable armchair before a fire that Emmie was stoking, around him the paraphernalia of illness: a rug over his knees, his bed with too many pillows, extra blankets, bottles of medicine on the table against the wall, a vase of hothouse flowers in the alcove beside his writing things; and books – most notable of which, on his bedside table, were his Danish Bible and Prayer Book.

In Denmark, they had spoken as if they would only stay in England until the situation in France improved enough for them to go on to Cannes, but the deterioration in Frederik's health meant that they no longer discussed the war as if it affected them. They read about the Siege of Paris and wondered how Oscar was managing, but it was a remote affair and the house in Cannes an irrelevance. Wrapping up and walking along the seafront to the Royal Victoria for tea was as much as he could manage. It was now February, and he knew that he had come to this place to die.

In his hand was the packet. The need to retrieve it had come upon him with the urgency of a physical craving, which seemed in some way shameful; better not discussed, in case he had to explain it, which he doubted he could do. He did not know if the reason was complicated or simple, but it shocked him: he wanted the contents preserved for his boys.

Ever since learning that he suffered from consumption, Frederik had known that his life might be cut short, but he had never wittingly behaved as if he were about to die. He hoped that he would have faith in his Redeemer to accept his end with humility. Meanwhile bouts of ill health had been followed by recovery and there was no reason not to hope that this pattern would continue. Undue morbidity on his part would have been a betrayal of both his desire and his duty to live, for Emmie and the boys. In Copenhagen, however, he had acted as one who knew that he would never return. Some unrecognised part of him heard the shuffle of death's approach and saw that this would be the last opportunity to secure his packet. Now that open recognition had come, forced into the light by the jabs of physical debility, it made him smile. Had his family known what he was doing, how horrified they would have been! His sisters would have reproached him for seeming to give up, while suffocating him at the same time with pious, tearful expressions of hope in the hereafter. Soon afterwards would have come the mystified questions as to why he wanted to single out these peculiar pictures. What about all his other things? His sextant and compass, citations and medals, letters . . . And what about family things? Didn't he want his children to have those too? These pictures given to him by the melancholy Doctor Rink – how would he have explained why he wanted them, above all, with such passion? No map to buried treasure was concealed among them. Even as pictures they were poor.

The hardest thing about dying was knowing that the boys would not stay as they were, but would develop. To a lesser degree, the same applied to Emmie, and to his family. How easy death would seem if the only pleasures at stake were selfish ones! The difficulty of facing it was shown up by his stealth in Copenhagen. Not to know what Kiki and Willy would be like when they were older was bitter. That his death would mark them was sure, for even if they had no memory of him as they grew up – and Willy would surely not have – the fact of their fatherlessness would have its impact. For Emmie, it would be more acute. She would be a widow, again, wearing a widow's clothes, bearing responsibility for the children. She might marry again – though Frederik doubted this, not least because she would be preoccupied with the boys. He found George Leslie appearing in his thoughts more often: what future had he imagined for Emmie, and how – if he could look down from wherever he was – would he regard Frederik? Would he blame him for visiting this grief on her a second time?

There was a parallel track to the one where he pondered the future of his family. It ran backwards, through shadows. It concerned his own past and seemed an improper subject for contemplation because it was selfish. He tried to explain it now to Emmie as she desisted prodding the fire and came to sit on the chair beside him. She wore a simply cut, deep blue dress that Frederik liked because he said it sharpened the blue of her eyes. Her hair, as ever, was drawn back flat over her ears and pinned in a knot at her nape. She was quick and precise in her movements because she was eager to see whatever it was that Frederik wanted to show her. It was most unusual for him to volunteer something from his past for her inspection, and she knew it concerned his past because he had told her, with an amusing slyness, that he had brought it from Denmark.

When she saw what he had written on the envelope, she was not offended. Although she found the idea of Frederik's end terrible, she believed it was her Christian duty as his wife to help him accept God's inscrutable will. She thought it right to talk about the religious implications, and from there it was only a short step to discussing what it would mean for herself and the boys. It must be easier for her than for Frederik, she thought: not because she had been through this before – for while awareness of the impending grief might soften the blow when it came, it made it more frightening beforehand – but because it comforted her to have Frederik imagine her future with the boys. Whatever thoughts he offered now would help her to live, would become a part of her and influence her: they would be a way of sharing her future with him, and of sustaining some image of him for Kiki and Willy. At first they would have the memory of his face and movements, and of the tendencies of his mind, which would very likely direct them in their sorrow much more powerfully than she or Norah ever could. But these impressions would fade as they grew, and Emmie was anxious that they should understand more of their father than the dry facts of his life. Yet she herself knew so very little! Only anecdotes: shooting in Siberia (was it bears? birds?); the fishy smell of the natives; travelling in a sledge; saving a Russian sailor's life; amateur dramatics with Russian officers and whoever that little prince was . . . Of the texture of his life then, or at any period, she had no sense. There were years he had spent in the Danish Navy that he had never spoken about. She had once asked, and he replied that they were dull – and they were lost. And if this was the case with her then it would be much more acute for the boys. No doubt she would try their patience in years to come with stories of her own past, but half-remembered, second-hand anecdotes about their father's past – before she even met him – would be remote to the point of meaninglessness.

When she saw the envelope marked "To be kept for my boys", Emmie's eyes filled at once with tears as she understood what Frederik meant by the phrase, and the trust implied by his sharing it with her now.

"Greenland," Frederik said, handing it to Emmie. "I should like them to see these, later on."

Emmie took from the envelope a sheaf of pictures. A few had already faded, but the definition in some remained clear; others had been tinted afterwards with watercolour. She saw Greenlanders with obdurate, slab-like faces squinting at the camera and short, broad bodies bundled up in layers of embroidered skins. And she saw in different seasons, from different angles, a huddle of wooden houses – one most evidently a church – perched at the foot of an immense, barren hill. In three of these, only the church's stumpy tower and the vertical lines of the higher parts of the buildings could be made out from the thick canopy of snow all about.

"Perhaps it is a foolish whim, but I know you will indulge me," Frederik said.

"If you took the trouble to bring them from Denmark, it cannot be a mere whim," Emmie replied, as she examined one. It seemed to be a photograph of many faces assembled from other pictures. In their closed expressions, they reminded her of Australian Aborigines.

"You want them to see something of what you have seen."

"Something like that."

Of course it was impossible that they should ever have a true idea of his experiences in Greenland. Even had he lived, it would have been so. But looking at the desolate landscapes of the pictures, in the knowledge that he had spent months trapped there, they might gain an inkling of how it had felt to him – the loneliness, the homesickness – and they might infer, from the contrast, something of what their mother and they themselves meant to him. In these murky images, these narrowed eyes, they might find some reflection of him as a perceiving eye, obscure proof of his independent existence. But there remained something more, he realised, something which fascinated him about the pictures although he had never noticed it when he was actually in Greenland, which made him want his sons to see them even if he could not guide their interpretation.

"It is their remoteness too," he said; and after a sharp intake of breath, he continued: "The people look as if they do not belong in the pictures, which of course they do not, because they don't understand what is being done. And the reverse: because they are in the pictures, it is as if they do not belong in their own land, as if they have been stolen away."

"I'm not sure I understand you," Emmie said.

"I'm not sure I understand myself! It does not matter, they will make of them what they will."

"But it does matter, Frederik my dear, it clearly matters very much to you!"

"Well perhaps it does, but I'm not sure that I could explain it. I do not want them to be lumbered with my thoughts, anyway, when – if – they see them, but to see them with their own eyes, and make of them what they will."

Emmie was puzzled, but she did not press him. "Well, it is strange to think of you there, and little more than a year before we met! How odd it must have seemed!"

"Greenland?"

"No, Genoa, Rome, Naples . . . me!" And handing back the envelope of photographs, she went over to the window and stared at the sapphire sky. In the autumn, Frederik had been many times to the new Turkish baths on West Hill. He stopped going when the weather turned windy, but she wondered if the succession of fine days that they had been enjoying might not encourage him to go there again. She could tell that the air outside was still because the smoke from the chimney-pots ascended straight to the sky like so many taut ropes.

"It did!" he said. "You did seem strange! And that was part of it . . . Do you not think that it was the differences that drew us to each other?"

Emmie had always assumed that they were attracted because they thought similarly about things. She did not think this was wrong, but she saw that Frederik's suggestion could also be true. Just as she had taken him away from Greenland and Danish society – as far off as Australia! – so he had taken her away from George and Australia, to Denmark. She had learned less of his past than he had of hers, but there was a symmetry in their experience. "Yes, maybe. But you have always been more than an escape to me," she said.

He raised his arm towards her so that she came up to his side, and he kissed her wrists.

"It is a fine day," he said. "Are the children in the Square? I think I shall go out."

Later, lying alone on his bed, Frederik smiled as he saw how he and Emmie had become defined in each other's eyes by the very past they were trying to escape. Yet even this was not fair, for – as Emmie pointed out – there was more to each of them than the sum of their pasts. The idea that either had escaped their past was nonsense too, however removed their lives had become from what went before: neither of them *wished* to escape their past. He did not know whether he was exiled *from* his past, or exiled *to* it, but it seemed certain that he was bound to its tatters in some critical way, as Emmie was to hers. Exiled to life or exiled to death, it made no difference to anyone except parsons: everyone was an immigrant to the present, even the Greenlanders.

The winds that tore along the esplanade throughout the winter seemed to abate in March, and Frederik could feel some warmth against his cheek when he ventured out. From time to time a gust would slice through his overcoat as he sat in a chair on the beach, chilling him to the marrow, or threaten to send him tumbling along the road, end over end, no more able to resist than a leaf or a stick. For a moment, Emmie dared to think that he might recover somewhat, but her hope was washed away by a new haemorrhage. The doctor told her that it would not be long now.

For the children's sakes, Frederik yearned to be out of doors. Inside, he could do nothing with them and they were uncomfortable with him. He had not the strength to play games – he could no longer even blow his old whistle properly – and he could not manage them if they were rowdy. But he could watch them for hours outside without unnerving them or needing to respond in any way, besides a smile and an occasional word. Emmie bought a Bath chair so that she could wheel him, as walking became too difficult. On the beach, in the garden, in Warrior Square; on good days in the public gardens, he watched them at play with Emmie and Norah with balls and hoops, toy soldiers and horses, spades and sticks and rugs. In his pocket, he played with his piece of carved amber, turning it over and over between his bony fingers like the stones of a rosary. Most of all, he liked just to see them run about, laughing and chattering. At three years old, Willy was not as articulate as Kiki had been at that age, but he was sturdier and more methodical. He could drive his brother to fury with a word, or a careful blow, or assent withheld – always accompanied by a steady glare that left no doubt of his intentions. Each time, Kiki would flail at his goading, unable to restrain himself though he knew that this was the result Willy had been hoping to provoke. But their quarrels were few and brief. Frederik was pleased to see that in general they got along very well together. For the moment, Willy accepted Kiki's instructions with docility. And the presence of their sick father was reassuring, not a distraction.

Watching the children also calmed Frederik. If it made him sentimental, he judged that to be preferable to the sweats of anxiety that his feverish mind produced as it snuffled among the futile hauntings of his life during the hours of solitude. Since examining the pictures, he found that it was Greenland above all which preoccupied him.

From his superiors' perspective, the expedition was a success because he completed the surveys. But he had always thought of it as a disaster, a year of unmitigated torment. The long, stormy passage aboard the filthy *Tjalfe* was an inauspicious start, which was made worse on arrival by finding that the country was still covered with snow from an exceptional winter. Proceeding south to Ivigtoot and Kajartelik, he had worked around the bays in a boat ill suited to the difficult work among icebergs. Southerly storms, snow and biting northerly winds with eight degrees of frost were their companions. Putting up a frozen tent to boil water or catch some rest was itself a challenge, and clear nights on which to take readings were so rare that their stay had to be extended. By the time the work was accomplished to Frederik's satisfaction, it was plain that no more ships would be able to get in or out of Ivigtoot that season.

At Godthaab, a little brig called the *Lucinde* was anchored in the harbour. She was due to sail, and Frederik ordered Bluhme to return home in her, since he would not need him for the remaining work around Godthaab. A supply ship was expected in a few days, which would pick up Frederik and his two assistants, Nielsen and Thomsen, when they were finished. However, the *Lucinde* returned after four days, having found that the Davis Strait was already blocked with ice. From then, it was certain that they would all remain in Godthaab for the winter.

Throughout the season he was cramped among people with whom he had no sympathy. At seven in the morning he pulled on his clothes and fastened his kamiks before filling his stove and eating some ship's biscuit. Then he went outside to meet Lieutenant Moberg of the *Lucinde*, who would be walking up and down in the snow. "Good morning, Lieutenant Moberg! How many degrees of cold have we today?" – "Good morning, Captain. Sixteen degrees by Mr Svanberg's thermometer, seventeen and a half by the Inspector's." – "Not more? Yesterday we had twenty-two." – "Quite right, Captain, but God is good!"

After some desultory work on his maps, he would go skiing, returning at midday with his beard white from frost and icicles around his mouth. Having thawed, he changed his clothes and then sat down with his colleagues and Lieutenant Moberg for lunch at the table of the Colonial Administrator, with whom they were quartered. A visiting missionary might join them, or Doctor Rink and his wife. The talk would be very slow. Everyone knew one another so well that they knew in advance what each would say as soon as the first word was uttered. If someone attempted something serious, it would soon be given up with a self-conscious laugh, while the rest of the party smiled or just sat glumly chewing their food. Only Moberg, with his dry manner, sometimes introduced some humour. Grace was said after the meal. In the afternoons, Frederik read, or tramped through the snow. For some weeks he tried to learn the native language from a Herr Kleinschmidt, but he found it harder than Russian.

Sooner or later during the day, however, it was impossible not to take some notice of the Greenlanders themselves – exhausted, ruined and wretched beyond any people that Frederik had encountered. In Kajartelik, they had been healthy and vigorous, but it seemed that the closer their association with Europeans, especially the Company that ought to have protected their interests, the worse was their condition. In Godthaab they lived in abject squalor. Apart from a few odd jobs, none of them worked, they owned nothing and were no longer capable of catching any animals to make clothes or kayaks. In one hut lived a loose family group of about twenty, where the mud oozed over their feet and the lamps were useless for lack of whale blubber. In temperatures of fifteen degrees below freezing, they walked through the snow with strips of old sole skin bound with twine around their feet. Their rags went unchanged, they ate seaweed with a little flour stirred into water, raw fish and occasional raw birds. Frederik and his colleagues were not busy enough to find distraction from the horror, but he had no authority to do anything. He was an employee of the Naval Ministry, not the Greenland Company: he could not tell the Administrator how to run what amounted to his fiefdom, any more than he could insist on the doctor tending to the Greenlanders' malnourished, diseased babies. It was not his business. Any gifts of skins or food that he or his team made were swiftly traded with other Europeans for aquavit or coffee from the Company's stores.

In the evenings, at seven o'clock, Frederik had to sit down again to supper with the same group of people. The Administrator would complain about the laziness of the natives, or brag about his conquests among their women. The doctor might share with them his concern about his daughters passing near the Greenlanders' huts – did not Captain Ziege think their settlement an affront to civilised people? And the missionaries grumbled that the threat of fines for natives who failed to attend morning and evening prayer was pointless because they had no money – which left punishment of their persons the only option. What could you do with such a people? Afterwards, rum and sugar were brought in and the hours before bed were stuffed with a fug of toddies and tobacco, or cards. Then the cold, miserable room where, eyed by the eagle, he wrapped himself in his blankets, and always thought the same thoughts: what could he do?

It had seemed at the time that he could do nothing. The state of the Greenlanders truly was not his business, and any attempt to inter-fere would have threatened a relationship on which he and his team depended. Bluhme, Nielsen and Thomsen were as shocked as Frederik by what they saw, but it was clear to him that their own conditions would be made worse if he confronted the local authority. For the Administrator's obligations towards Frederik's expedition were modest, and he might reduce their supplies of fuel and food with impunity if Frederik was reckoned to have been a nuisance. If Bluhme, Nielsen and Thomsen spent the winter hungry and shivering in tents, they might have second thoughts about their desire for action. In any case, Frederik believed that it would be irresponsible of him to put them at risk. Furthermore, there was no good reason to suppose that inter-ference would improve the lot of the Greenlanders. It made better sense to bide their time and make an official representation to the Greenland Company once they were returned to Copenhagen.

It was the isolation he had experienced in Greenland which kept returning to Frederik as he sat and waited in St Leonards-on-Sea; the agonising isolation and the pricking of conscience, for he still did not know if he had done the right thing. Had he done nothing because it was easier? Though, God knew, it was not easy. Or should he have made an effort at the time – inadequate, probably detrimental, but at least *an effort* – to do something for the abused Greenlanders? Though, God knew – didn't he? – that doing nothing was an effort.

Everything seemed uncertain in retrospect, its meaning shifting to and fro with wild, mocking swings. What if he had allowed that merry wife in Irkutsk to lead him to her bedroom? If he had not rushed back to Moscow but loitered, as he could have? What if he had accepted Mouravieff's offer and gone as a courier to Peking? What if he had married one of those Russian girls who formed part of the Grand Duke's entourage? What if? What if . . . ? Was it no more than a sequence of accidents that had brought him here, or had disposition played a part? By marrying Coco, Christian ensured that his life would remain circumscribed by what he knew, whereas Frederik, in marrying Emmie, seemed to have pledged himself to a permanent state of rough transit. And how strange that these short years of illness at the end of his life, unconnected to all that had gone before, should be the ones, in the end, that mattered! Even the simplest things were turning out to have been something else. Now, as he saw his two tow-headed children, muffled in coats in the spring sunshine, run out to the garden where he sat like an old dotard in the shade of a tall elm, he felt not the unalloyed joy he wanted to feel, but irritation that his thoughts were about to be interrupted. But a person without regrets, he thought, would have to be a person without imagination. It was a question of reconciling yourself to your regrets –

"Father! Father!" they cried together. "Aunt Hannina is here!"

Norah pounded behind them in her stout shoes. "Boys! Not too rough, now!"

As their tender bodies pressed against his bony knees, and their warm little hands clutched at his grey, papery fingers, Frederik felt in the furthest, most confused recesses of his soul the sadness of it all.

"You will not leave them, will you, Norah?" he said.

"Sir, as if I would!"

Above the children's heads, he met Norah's hurt expression and his eyes held hers, so that they softened.

"I am grateful, Norah."

His gaze shifted back to the children. "Now, boys, show me that you are good for dear Norah. I want you each to take one of her hands and go back inside with her. Tell your Aunt Hannina that she must come and talk with me before she plays with you."

As they went off, boys in white sailor-suits on each side of their white-clad nanny, his mind jumped to Shanghai and the noise on board the junks in the harbour at sundown, with gongs and bamboo pipes being hit to frighten the evil spirits which would otherwise steal the sun from the sky. Ashore he saw two letters on red paper with gold script in large, elaborate envelopes, which were meant to be sent by the Chinese to their dead friends. They were dispatched by burning in a holy fire. He recalled a funeral procession with people on foot and horseback, in a particular order, the women at the rear. They carried wooden shrines, and there were lots of flags with inscriptions. Both men and women were dressed in white, the colour of mourning.

*

Emmie had discussed Frederik's end with Hannina when they were still in Denmark, and it was agreed that she would alert her sister-in-law if it seemed near. When the time came in May, she consulted Frederik, who said that he would like to have one of his own family with him if Emmie did not mind. He knew they would want this, and it was his own wish. It suited Emmie too, for Frederik's nights were now so broken that she often had to sit up with him for hours at a stretch.

Hannina arrived with a large trunk that only just fit through the front door, two matching hat boxes, and plenty of advice, some of which was good. As soon as she saw Frederik and the arrangement of the house, she declared that he ought to be moved at once into the large front room on the ground floor. Since he could not get upstairs without help now, it would be better for them all. Her frankness disguised extreme dismay at her brother's condition. When she had last seen him, he had lost weight and he coughed frequently, but his appearance was not much different from normal. Now he was frail like an old man. All colour was gone from him and his bright eyes protruded. She wrote home at once to her mother that Frederik was on the brink of death and, with Emmie's nervous approval, she also wrote to Christian telling him that he should come at once.

In the terrible days that followed, Hannina applied herself with tact and energy to easing the burdens of those around her. She sat up with Frederik at night when Emmie could stay awake no more, and during the days she took the children out to play with Norah. They went for carriage rides together along the coast, and she always treated them to sweets and small gifts on the way. It was warm enough to bathe in the sea now, and she played in the shallows with them. The merrier they were, the more she lavished affection on them and the more she thought her heart would break.

It was fortunate that Hannina was so ready to take the children out, for when Frederik moved downstairs it became much harder for them in the house. Their noise upset him. He found it more and more painful to have them with him, but at the same time he became suspicious of Hannina when she took them out. He wanted Emmie to be with him, and he wanted her to be with the children too: yet he could not bear the children to be with him. Emmie asked him what she should do, but he only advised that she must be careful.

"Careful?"

"Don't you see?" he uttered in his feeble rasp. "Once they get their hands on the children . . ."

"Frederik, my dear, whatever do you mean? Once *who* get their hands . . . ?"

"My family! They will try to get you to take the children back . . . !"

"Back? To Denmark?"

Frederik nodded and closed his eyes. Trying to explain these things wore him out, but it seemed of the utmost importance to make Emmie understand. When Christian was summoned, it had become clear to him: as soon as he was dead, they would persuade Emmie, in her grief, to give them some authority over the children – out of love, he had no doubt, and all the very best intentions – but then, before she knew it, his boys would be Prussian soldiers.

It was a notion he could not endure.

When Hannina wheeled him along the marina in his Bath chair, holding her parasol aloft in her left hand (was he so light? he wondered), he felt that she was trying to lull him into indifference, or blindness to her intentions. If she spoke to him of the family or Denmark, he cut her off. Only when she read to him from his Bible or Prayer Book did he find her presence acceptable. Yet it seemed to Emmie that he did not want his sister to go away either, for he did not want to inflict such an injury on her and on their family.

Once, when Emmie had thought he was asleep, he stirred himself and asked her to fetch some writing paper. He wanted to dictate a letter.

"And fetch Hannina. I want her to hear it."

Frederik knew that Hannina was resting: the children had been taken to the pier. But Emmie roused Hannina, as he had instructed, and told her that Frederik had asked for her.

"Dear Mr Burton," Frederik began, when the two women were seated by his bed.

Emmie felt a swoop of misgiving. Turning to Hannina, she explained with a note of apology, "Mr Burton is the solicitor."

"Dear Mr Burton. I wish to ensure that, in the event of my death, no interference is possible between my wife and the children . . ." Frederik paused to get his breath. The scratch of Emmie's pen had ceased before he continued: ". . . and if my present will is not sufficient to establish this, considering the present state of Danish law . . . I wish every possible means used to guard against Danish interference. Yours sincerely . . ."

Frederik coughed into the silence as Emmie finished writing down his words.

"And now, if you would pass it to me," he said, dabbing at his mouth, "I will sign it."

As Emmie passed the letter and the pen to him, she was crying silently.

Frederik added his shaky signature to the document. He was aware that it might have little power in law, but he wanted Hannina to witness the complete authority he entrusted to Emmie. It would be something for Emmie to use in future, were it necessary.

It was grotesque for Hannina to see her brother working himself into such mistrust of his family, and she did not understand why it was happening. Nobody had any intention of prising the children from Emmie – why would they? Excitable behaviour was a feature of his illness, she reminded herself, and she must not blame him. Hoping to reassure Emmie that she did not hold her responsible either, she took her hand and squeezed it. Then she left the room.

Christian arrived ten days later, but by then the effort of speaking exhausted Frederik within a minute or two and there was nothing for Christian to do except watch, and wait. He had bought a special respiratory device in Vienna which he could see was useless now, but he translated the instructions with painstaking precision all the same and said that he wished there was something more he could do.

"And you think I do not?" Emmie retorted.

Having to be pleasant to Christian did not make Emmie's circumstances any easier, but she knew how necessary good relations with him would be in years to come and she apologised. "I'm sorry, Christian. Of course it is difficult for you, too. Frederik appreciates your coming very much."

A hundred times, Christian walked along the esplanade to the Royal Victoria, where he was staying, and back again. On one side lay the unforgiving sea; on the other, the respectable watering-hole of St Leonards – half a mile of white stucco patrolled by retired colonials, governesses and children. Not Bath, but South Kensington parked by the sea: not the kind of place in which he would ever have expected to find his brother.

Each time he passed the Post Office, he thought of the telegram he would have to send.

While Emmie sat beside Frederik late one evening, he asked her if she forgave him. She answered that forgiveness was not hers to confer or refuse, but that if it were, then how could he doubt? For he was all in all to her. Then she asked if there was something on his mind.

His lips pulled back in a travesty of a smile, revealing his sore gums. "My mind? Or my conscience?"

He wanted her to know, but he could not tell her. He lacked the strength.

But Emmie felt she had her answer. She was composed and attentive. "Would you like to pray?" she asked.

An oil lamp glowed on the table beside her. She made to turn up the wick, but he signalled her to wait. He was enjoying the subdued light in the room, the mingling of shadows as the lamp's light merged with that of the flickering fire. He wanted to hold the moment, to tell Emmie that he did not know why he had been selected to die, but God's ways were unknowable and he had faith in His mercy. No more did he know why God had blessed him by bringing her to him as his wife, for he knew he did not deserve her. That it was a blessing, he never had the least doubt. He wished to thank her, to tell her of his love so that she could carry it into the future, be inhabited and fortified by it. Her faith too was strong, and he loved her for it; he believed they would meet again, by the grace of God . . . He hardly knew if he uttered these words, for his breath seemed light and faraway

"Bless you."

On hearing himself, Frederik realised that he might not have spoken his thoughts, but he saw in Emmie's eyes a gentleness that passed for understanding, and he was calm.

Emmie knew what was required of her. Soon her sorrow would be complete, and then the flood would find its channels: but now, though already beyond measure, it must be withheld.

"I shall read from Psalm 107," she said, then paused to govern the tremor in her voice. She thought of George, how he had died peacefully, in the knowledge of God, and how this had been a comfort to her, and she thought of her mother and her father; of her dead sisters, Annie and Lucy. Then she thought of Kate and Pat, starting out again in New Zealand, and she wondered whether they would ever meet her children.

It was a passage they both knew well and had often read to one another, but it seemed to renew itself as Emmie recited:

> "They that go down to the sea in ships: and
>   occupy their business in great waters;
> These men see the works of the Lord: and His
>   wonders at the deep.
> For at His word the stormy wind ariseth: which
>   lifteth up the waves thereof.
> They are carried up to the heaven, and down
>   again to the deep: their soul melteth away
>   because of the trouble.
> They reel to and fro, and stagger like a drunken
>   man: and are at their wits' end.
> So when they cry unto the Lord in their trouble:
>   He delivereth them out of their distress.
> For He maketh the storm to cease: so that the
>   waves thereof are still.
> Then are they glad, because they are at rest: and
>   so He bringeth them unto the haven where
>   they would be."

When Christian came up to the house in the morning, he found that his brother was dead.

Epilogue

AFTER Frederik's death, Emmie went to stay with the Fergusons at Inchmarlo, in Aberdeenshire. She had stayed with them after George died, and on a number of visits in the years before she met Frederik. Mary Anne Ferguson had more than the usual resources of sympathy. She was gentle, calm and patient, and she was interested in people she liked: and though they only met him twice, the Fergusons had liked Frederik. Knowing this, Emmie was able to rest and care for her boys without having to trouble herself about the day-to-day business of life.

Each day, Emmie wrote a long letter to Frederik's mother. She said it comforted her to do so, to think about Frederik, which she did all the time. She told her what she had eaten and whether she had slept well. If she detected the symptoms of a cold in herself or the boys, she explained what remedies she was applying. She described how soothing was the view from her window, how sheep grazed on the birch-fringed slope down to the reposeful River Dee. On the far bank stood a turreted house embowered by ancient trees; heather bloomed purple on the hills behind. She said how she longed to come to Denmark next summer, and how she blessed God in His goodness and mercy for having granted to her the years, however short, with Frederik. For his epitaph, she proposed using a few words from Psalm 107, "He bringeth them to their haven"; for his headstone, Aberdeen granite. She took pleasure in recording the activities of the boys. They were great favourites, she said, even when they imitated the Scottish accents they heard around them, and their manners were so good. Kiki would glance at her whenever he heard his father mentioned, as if anxious of the effect on his mother, while Willy would not now accept the name Willy but insisted on being called by his second name, Frederick. Once, when they were looking at Frederik's picture and Emmie said how they must not forget his dear face and his sweet soft eyes, Kiki responded, "We will remember it all, and his beautiful teeth – they were magnificent!" – "And do you recollect how he patted your heads and said God bless you?" – "Dear kind hands they were!" Willy said. Emmie observed that they seldom mentioned their father in front of anyone but her.

There were surprises that made Emmie realise, as she had not when he was alive, how little she knew about Frederik. Looking at the Greenland collage, she found a European face that she had not seen before. It was almost as if it had materialised since his death. She wished she knew who it was. The Thomsen legacy in his will was another mystery: why, she wondered, of all his colleagues and acquaintances, had he left something to one of his Greenland assistants? She supposed she would be confronted with questions like these for the rest of her life.

With Christian's help, most of Frederik's clothes had been divided up and given away, but Emmie kept his naval uniform in its entirety despite never having seen him wear it. His remaining effects had little meaning for her beyond the all-important fact that they were his, and she guarded them like rubies and topaz, in locked drawers.

Late in her life, perhaps thirty years after Frederik's death, Emmie made a detailed inventory of the possessions which she intended passing on to her sons, a sort of appendix to her will. In a section entitled "Sundries Worth Keeping", she mentions a dessert set consisting of "16 plates, 3 shell dishes, 4 standard ditto modern, 2 square ditto, 2 oval ditto, 2 dishes gilt handles modern". She adds, "This dessert set was given to my grandmother Mrs King (wife of Cap. King RN Governor of Australia) by the Commodore? who was sent in search of the expedition of Capitaine La Pérouse. It was much broken by the Customs search in 1854 when it arrived in England in my possession. I employed Copeland to make high dishes & long ditto to replace some plates. French china, name unknown."

It can be assumed, I think, that the set was given not by Baudin but by de Freycinet, commander of the subsequent French expedition to Australia, on behalf of Baudin, in thanks for Governor King's assistance in 1802. By then (1818), King was dead and his widow was living in England. De Freycinet sought out King's daughter-in-law where she was living near Parramatta, cheek-by-jowl with Emmie's parents. She was married to King's son, Phillip Parker King, who was already well ahead of de Freycinet in their simultaneous commissions to chart the Australian coast.

In 1847, the Bank of Australia crashed and Hannibal, who had given a personal guarantee, went bankrupt. His house, Vineyard, and most of his possessions went under the hammer. A few things were bought back for Hannibal and Maria by their sons-in-law, George Leslie and Hugh Gordon, who by then had some spare cash. Certain household goods, such as linen and crockery, were exempt because deemed by law to belong to the wife. Many of these can be identified in Emmie's inventory of 1900, and can be located a hundred years later.

What happened to the dessert set?

In a cupboard full of bits and pieces can be found two from a set of Japanese saucers brought by George FitzRoy from Lord Elgin's mission to Japan in 1856; a Cantonese plate given by William Leslie (fatally cracked a generation ago); the remaining Vineyard plates, with monogram, grapes and vine leaves, from the set commissioned by Walter Davidson in Canton in 1812; and many more. But there is no trace of Baudin's dessert set, and Malletts in Davies Street inform me, with regret, that the single piece I had hopes for is at least forty years too late.

One of my aunts alleged that while moving house once during the First War (it was a frequent occurrence: their father – "Willy" – was a serving regular soldier), there was a great smashing of crockery as a tea chest was unpacked. Someone had pulled out an eiderdown, not realising that it was being used to protect fragile objects. She does not know what the broken objects were. They may have been Baudin's dessert set, or they may not. In any case, there is no trace of it now; it amounts to no more than an entry in Emmie's inventory – and whatever story you care to spin from that.

Although formed by her Australian past, and attached to the memory of it, Emmie was an immigrant; loose, but never quite separate from her origins; in want of a haven. She lived in St Leonards-on-Sea and later in Cheltenham, a Victorian widow with a sharp eye for her sons' best interests. These children were cherished not only by their mother but also by their Danish grandmother and their Aunt Hannina. A portrait of them was painted when they visited Denmark in the year after their father's death. On their slight shoulders was thought to rest a burden of continuity without which everything would lose its meaning.

The Danish family died out, and when Emmie died in 1911 she still had no grandchildren. Her older son was a roué. There is a letter from his Uncle Christian to Emmie lamenting that he had seen his nephew talking to the Prince of Wales with his hands in his pockets, but some of his habits proved more fatal and he died, drunk and child-less, three years after his mother. The younger son, already older than his father ever had been, inherited quantities of papers and an assort-ment of objects salvaged from Vineyard and Canning Downs, together with those things Emmie had preserved of his father's.

The year after her death, this son married a granddaughter of William Leslie. He had four children, but he was already elderly and beyond passing on much information by the time they were old enough to appreciate whatever he knew. Perhaps (like many second-generation immigrants) he had little interest in the details of his parents' origins. By the 1920s they must have seemed too distant to be of any relevance.

Unknown to him, he had many grandchildren, of whom I am one.

I was taught how to do the Chinese puzzle when I was about ten by my Aunt Alma. It looks complicated if you don't know how to do it, but it's just a knack; you can do it while chatting, like knitting. Alma was taught by her Aunt Agatha, an amateur artist who did some fine charcoal sketches of peonies and a great many gloomy landscapes of the Isle of Skye. Presumably Agatha was taught by Emmie, for Emmie remained on excellent terms with the Leslie family, and she had a long widowhood with plenty of time for puzzles. I do not know how – or if – Emmie herself learned how to do the puzzle. Maybe she was even taught by Keong.

The puzzle's frame is snapped at a critical point, where the tines of what is otherwise a two-pronged fork curve round to meet at the end. It has been so at least within living memory. For all I know, Emmie broke it herself as a little girl. Attempts have been made to glue it from time to time but the ends never stuck, as if the thing itself regarded such efforts as unnecessary or futile. For the ivory is strong enough to allow the contraption of rings and rods to be threaded back and forth *as if* it were still intact, and you know that at any time you could slip the whole lot in or out through the break. It is not so much the puzzle itself which is broken, for you can still do it on its own terms if you want to. It is rather that its formal integrity has been lost: strictly speaking, you are no longer solving a puzzle, but rather *performing* the solution of a puzzle.

Tuxen Ziege's clock, bought in Paris in 1839, is now in my possession. Its winding key has not been lost. It is attached by a fraying red cord with a brass clip at each end to the clock's base. The cord, my father told me, was used by his father to clip his top hat (by a loop beneath the brim) to a hook on the collar of his hunting jacket, so that if the hat were knocked off by the branch of a tree, or as he jumped a gate, he would not have to dismount to retrieve it. I never knew my grandfather: he would have been ninety-six when I was born. But the cord – auspicious, perhaps, in its levity – connects me to an image of him. At the same time, it connects me, his grandson, as I wind the clock, to his grandfather, Tuxen. My father remembered that, when he was little, this clock used to sit on his father's desk. Each morning, after breakfast, his father went into his study to wind it, keeping in motion a mechanism that helped to regulate his life. I would very much like to know what he knew of its history. For while it seems certain that the clock belonged to his father – to Frederik – if I am honest (and what is the point of an epilogue if not to tie up a few loose ends?), I do not know that it was bought by Tuxen in Paris in 1839. But it was bought by somebody, somewhere. And while the object survives with a plausible story there is a connection, however frayed, with lives and events in which we may learn to recognise ourselves.

Acknowledgements

I WOULD like to thank the following for their help with *The Bequest*:

My parents, for sharing their own researches and ideas with me;
Kjell Hauge and Charlotte Holmes, who translated reams of ancient
   Danish letters;
Nell, my wife, for many things – not least, drawing the cufflinks;
Richard Sainsbury, who took the photographs;
Christopher MacLehose for his editorial work.

And for their help at various stages I am most grateful to: Alan
Atkinson, Paul Baggaley, Harry Barnes, Andrea Belloli, Andrew &
Pam Bickley, Arabella Boxer, James Broadbent, Gérard Brunin, Marie-
Christine Brunin-Willis, Paul Brunton, David Crane, Daniel Creamer,
Marion Diamond, Patrick Dillon, Christian de Falbe, Polly de Falbe,
Ida Haugsted, Victor Kanellopoulos, John Lund, David Miller, Graeme
Powell, Françoise Simon, Colin Thubron, Karen Wadman and my other
colleagues at John Sandoe's, Thomas Woodham-Smith.

Author's Note

THROUGHOUT *The Bequest* I have quoted and adapted passages from unpublished sources, and also from the memoirs of Emmeline Macarthur as they appear in my mother's book, *My Dear Miss Macarthur.*

Unpublished sources

de Falbe Family Papers
Macarthur Papers at the Mitchell Library, Sydney
Leslie Letters at the John Oxley Library, Brisbane
Journal of G. F. Leslie at the Mitchell Library, Sydney
The Letters of the Leslie Brothers in Australia 1834–54
    (Ken Waller) – thesis, University of Queensland, 1956

Published sources

Atkinson, Alan *Europeans in Australia* (Oxford, 1997)
Bassett, M. *The Governor's Lady* (London, 1940)
Bedford, Ruth *Think of Stephen* (Sydney, 1954)
Blainey, Geoffrey *The Tyranny of Distance* (Melbourne, 1966)
Bluhme, Emil *Fra et Ophold I Grønland 1863–64* (Copenhagen, 1865)
Brewer, David *The Flame of Freedom: The Greek War of Independence 1821–33* (London, 2001)
Cameron, Roderick *The Golden Riviera* (London, 1975)
Crane, David *Lord Byron's Jackal* (London, 1998)
Crossman, Carl L. *Decorative Arts of the China Trade* (Woodbridge, 1991)

Davis, Nathan *Carthage and her Remains* (London, 1861)

de Falbe, Jane *My Dear Miss Macarthur* (Sydney, 1988)

Dormandy, Thomas *The White Death – A History of Tuberculosis* (London, 1999)

Edric, Robert *Elysium* (London, 1995)

Eldershaw, M. Barnard *A House is Built* (Victoria, 1972)

Erngaard, Erik *Greenland Then and Now* (Copenhagen, 1972)

Falbe, C. T. *Recherches sur L'Emplacement de Carthage* (Paris, 1833)

Falbe, C. T. and Temple, Sir Grenville *Excursions dans L'Afrique Septentrionale* (Paris, 1838)

Fidlon, Paul G. et al. (eds.) *Journal of Philip Gidley King* (Sydney, 1980)

French, Maurice *A History of the Darling Downs Frontier* (Toowoomba, 1989)

Hainsworth, D. R. *The Sydney Traders* (Melbourne, 1972)

Hall, Coryne *Little Mother of Russia* (London, 1999)

Haugsted, Ida *Dream & Reality – Danish Antiquaries, Architects and Artists in Greece* (London, 1996)

Haugsted, Ida "Christian Tuxen Falbe and the Pioneer Daguerreotypists in Denmark", *History of Photography*, vol. 14, no. 2, April–June 1990

Haugsted, Ida "Second Lieutenant Christian Giede – A Danish Numismatist in Athens", *Nordic Numismatic Journal*, 1989–90

Hordern, Marsden *King of the Australian Coast: The Work of Phillip Parker King in the Mermaid and Bathurst 1817–1822* (Melbourne, 1997)

Howarth, Patrick *When the Riviera Was Ours* (London, 1977)

Hughes, Robert *The Fatal Shore* (London, 1988)

Johnson, Virginia W. *Genoa the Superb* (Boston, 1892)

Keynes, R. D. (ed.) *The Beagle Record* (Cambridge, 1979)

Lund, John "Archaeology and Imperialism in the 19th Century: The Case of C. T. Falbe, a Danish Agent and Antiquarian in French Service", in *Aspects de L'Archéologie Française au XIXème Siècle, Actes du Colloque International*, ed. P. Jacquet and R. Périchon (Montbrison, 2000), pp. 331–50.

Lund, John "The Archaeological Activities of Christian Tuxen Falbe in Carthage in 1838", *Cahiers des Études Anciennes*, vol. 18, 1986, pp. 8–24.

Lund, John "Royal Connoisseur and Consular Collector: The Part Played by C. T. Falbe in Collecting Antiquities from Tunisia, Greece and Paris for Christian VIII", in *Christian VIII and the National Museum*, ed. B. Bundgaard Rasmussen, J. Steen Jensen and J. Lund (Copenhagen, 2000), pp. 119–49

Lund, John and Sørensen, L. W. "Vejen til Segermes. C. T. Falbes rejse gennem Tunesien i 1838", *Nationalmuseets Arbejdsmarki*, 1988, pp. 9–23

McDonald, Roger *Mr Darwin's Shooter* (London, 1998)

McMinn, W. G. *Allan Cunningham – Botanist and Explorer* (Melbourne, 1970)

Murray's Handbook for Rome & its Environs (London, 1875)

Murray's Handbook for Northern Italy (London, 1877)

Newsome, David *The Victorian World Picture* (London, 1997)

O'Brian, Patrick *Joseph Banks* (London, 1987)

Quested, R. K. I. *The Expansion of Russia in East Asia 1857–60* (Kuala Lumpur, 1968)

Scavenius, Bente (ed.) *The Golden Age Revisited – Art & Culture in Denmark 1800–1850* (Copenhagen, 1996)

Sutherland, Christine *The Princess of Siberia* (London, 1984)

Tarling, Nicholas, *Anglo-Dutch Rivalry in the Malay World 1780–1824* (Queensland, 1962)

White, Patrick *Voss* (London, 1957)

Wilson, A. N. *God's Funeral* (London, 1999)

Wullschlager, Jackie *Hans Christian Andersen* (London, 2000)